T. Bennett Photography

NEVADA BARR

Award-winning Nevada Barr is the author of eight previous Anna Pigeon mysteries, including her most recent *New York Times* bestseller, *Blood Lure*. She lives in Mississippi, where she was formerly a ranger on the Natchez Trace Parkway.

Also by Nevada Barr

Track of the Cat
A Superior Death
Ill Wind
Firestorm
Endangered Species
Blind Descent

Bittersweet

NEVADA BARR

HARPER

NEW YORK • LONDON • TORONTO • SYDNEY

HARPER

This is a work of fiction. Names, characters, places, and incidents either are the product of the author's imagination or are used fictitiously. Any resemblance to actual events, locales, organizations, or persons, living or dead, is entirely coincidental and beyond the intent of either the author or the publisher.

BITTERSWEET. Copyright © 1984 by Nevada Barr. All rights reserved. Printed in the United States of America. No part of this book may be used or reproduced in any manner whatsoever without written permission except in the case of brief quotations embodied in critical articles and reviews. For information address HarperCollins Publishers Inc., 10 East 53rd Street, New York, NY 10022.

HarperCollins books may be purchased for educational, business, or sales promotional use. For information please write: Special Markets Department, HarperCollins Publishers Inc., 10 East 53rd Street, New York, NY 10022.

First Avon Books edition published 1999.

Reissued in Perennial 2001.

Designed by Kellan Peck

Library of Congress Cataloging-in-Publication Data is available.

ISBN 0-380-79950-2

09 10 FG/RRD 20 19 18 17 16 15 14 13

For Barns

A RAWBONED WOMAN NEARLY SIX FEET TALL PULLED ON THE BRASS handle; the door was wedged against the lintel and wouldn't close— the fog that had lain over Philadelphia since late September had swelled the wood. Kicking a duffel bag out of the way, she grasped the knob with both hands and yanked. With a screech the door slammed shut. "Try opening that, Mr. Neff, you little, little man." She turned the key and the bolt clicked home.

It was a brass key ornate with scrollwork; the initials AMG had been engraved on the lemon-shaped head. The woman ran her thumb over the worn letters. "Amanda Montgomery Grelznik," she said softly and hurled the key over the porch railing into the fog. She listened for it to hit, but the thick mist swallowed the sound.

"Imogene." An angular man, all in gray, stood at the gate watching her. His head was bare to the cold and his hands, knotted with arthritis, rested on the pickets of the fence like gnarled winter branches.

"Mr. Utterback!" She picked up her suitcases and came down the steps to meet him. "I didn't hear you. With the fog I feel both deaf and blind."

"I see thee are packed. I might have known thee'd be ready."

"I sent most of my things ahead. The new owners, the Neffs, can have what is left."

They looked back at the house in silence. It carried its age with dignity; the fine woodwork on the porch had been newly painted in summer and the yard was immaculate. "Mother and Father bought this house in 1842. I was born in that room nine months later to the day." Imogene pointed to the gabled window above the porch. "Come April, I would have lived here thirty-one years."

"I am sorry, Imogene."

"No need, Mr. Utterback." She laid her hand on his arm.

"I think thee might call me William."

She laughed. "My tongue would cleave to the roof of my mouth."

"Thou art the best teacher I have ever known," he said simply. "I shall miss thee."

Imogene's narrow lower lip trembled; she pressed her fingers against it and coughed.

"Well." He cleared his throat and looked away. He cleared it again. "Does thee have the letter?" She patted the leather duffel bag she had put on top of her suitcase. "Thee can read it. Joseph was a student of mine. I've told him of thy merit as a teacher and made no mention of the other."

"Thank you."

"Go on teaching, that is thanks enough." He dug into the folds of his gray coat until his arm disappeared to the elbow, and pulled out a sheet of paper. "This came. I thought thee might like to read it. Isabelle Ann was a friend of thine."

"Isabelle Ann Close?" Imogene came to his side to look over his arm.

"It's Englewood now. She married a boy from Virginia and went west. This is all the way from Nevada Territory." He shook out the letter and held it away from him in the manner of farsighted people. "She writes there are no qualified teachers there, and she asks after thee." He handed Imogene the letter.

Imogene folded it up and put it into the pocket of her skirt. "I'll read it on the train." She looked at the little silver watch pinned to her coat. "I'd best be going."

"Did thee leave the key for Mr. and Mrs. Neff?"

"I threw it away. It was Mother's. There's another on a nail just inside the back-porch door."

"I wish he had offered a fair price, but he knew thee had to sell." He smiled. "Thee really threw it away?" She nodded. "I'll walk with thee to the train station."

Imogene took up her suitcases abruptly. "No, please. I appreciate the offer, Mr. Utterback, but I'd rather go the last by myself. I have so much to look at on the way, I'm afraid I shouldn't be very good company." She set the suitcases down again and extended her hand. "Thank you again. I'll write often."

He took the hand and pressed it warmly. "Good-bye, Imogene. Give my regards to Joseph." He preceded her out of the yard to hold the gate. "Thee are sure I cannot walk with thee?"

"Yes." Her voice broke and she turned away.

The street was empty; people were closeted in their homes, with curtains drawn against the cold and fires lit against the damp. Windows showed yellow in the October afternoon. Imogene walked quickly down a footpath that was separated from the rutted street by a line of trees. Their branches vanished above her into the fog. Her breath came in clouds and beaded on the soft down of her upper lip.

The front door of the house on the corner opened as Imogene was passing, and a middle-aged woman muffled in a fur-lined cape emerged with a ten-year-old boy in tow. The child saw Imogene and snatched his hand free. He ran across the yard to where she walked by the fence.

"Miss Grelznik!"

Imogene stopped and smiled at him. "Where are you and your mother off to, Barton? You are dressed fit for a king's coronation."

He smeared his hands down over his dark wool suit, endangering all the buttons in their path. "We're going to Uncle Herbert's for dinner."

"Barton Biggs!" Careful of her shoes, his mother picked her way over the frozen yard and clutched his arm. "Come away now." She never gave Imogene a glance.

"Ma, Miss Grelznik asked—"

"Never mind." She pulled at him until he let go of the fence and clumped along after her. He resisted, crying "Bye" over his shoulder, until she slapped his face.

Imogene watched them walk away. Her cheeks, already stung pink by the cold, deepened to scarlet and her hands shook when she picked up her bags. "Good-bye, Barton," she called to his retreating form. "Take care." Mother and son turned out of sight around the corner, and Imogene went on. A door slammed shut somewhere and she walked faster, keeping her eyes front.

A quarter of a mile brought her within sight of the train station—an imposing edifice with a cascade of shallow steps ending at a row of cabs parked in the street. A few of the drivers sat hunched on the seats, as dumb as their horses; the rest had crawled inside the cabs to await their fares in relative comfort. Imogene set her bags on the ground and rubbed her hands together. Her cotton gloves were the black of fall fashion, but too thin for warmth.

Several young men loitered at the top of the stairs. As Imogene threaded her way through the horse manure between the cabs, the eldest of the men—a slight fellow in his early thirties—pointed, calling the attention of the others to her, and said something. Imogene looked up when they laughed. He stepped out from the group and stood in front of her. "Just seeing you caught your train." Imogene started to walk around him. He sidestepped and stopped her again. "Mary Beth ain't here to see you off. I seen to that." Imogene stepped to the right; he moved with her, blocking the way. Finally she looked at him, and though he stood on the step above her, they were eye-to-eye.

"As you said, Mr. Aiken, I have a train to catch. Be so good as to let me pass."

He pushed his face near hers. "You stay clear of her." His breath stank and Imogene stopped breathing.

"Don't you go writing her none of your talk, neither."

Imogene tightened her jaw until her lips and nostrils showed white against her windburned face. "Get out of my way." She spat the words at him and he stumbled back.

"Darrel, come on." His fellow loafers had grown uneasy.

Imogene pushed by him.

"Don't even think about Mary Beth," he yelled as the doors swung shut behind her.

Imogene bumped the big suitcase along the floor and dropped it in front of a wooden bench. She sat down stiffly with the smaller bag on her lap and rested her forehead against the back of her hands, listening to the somber tick of the station clock as its pendulum paced out the minutes. The clock had just struck four when the doors at the end of the station opened a crack and a man shouted through the narrow opening: "Now boarding, three-twenty-eight to Harrisburg. All aboard."

Imogene hauled herself to her feet and hefted the bags. As she stepped out onto the platform she handed the heavier of the two to a boy in a scarlet uniform. "The train is running late. I have a connection to make in Harrisburg for Calliope. Am I going to make it?"

The boy looked blank.

"Calliope, Pennsylvania."

"You're meaning Cally-ope?"

"Yes. Yes. I expect. Calliope." Imogene mispronounced the word carefully.

"Yes'm. Train's considered to be on time today." He thrust out his lower lip and nodded smartly as if it were his doing. She pressed a nickel into his hand and climbed the steps into the car.

The floor was slippery with tobacco juice and the air thick with the stink of the rancid animal fat used to grease the axles. Imogene pulled her skirts as high as she dared and trod carefully down the narrow aisle. At the far end an iron stove roared; its door was red-hot, and fire flickered behind the grille in its round belly. She settled herself into one of the hard wooden seats near a window in the middle of the car—far enough from the stove to be comfortable but near enough to keep warm—and set her duffel bag next to her to discourage company.

The peanut butcher, a grimy boy of indeterminate age and race, waded down the aisle hawking his wares. He tossed an apple and a dog-eared novel into her lap. The man across from her was already reading, so the boy expertly lobbed a pouch of tobacco between the newspaper and his chest. Imogene set the book and the apple on the edge of the seat, where the boy could get them on his return trip, and turned her face to the window. Outside, people were laughing and crying, taking leave of friends and family. She leaned her head on the cold glass and put her hands over her ears.

When the train lurched forward, Imogene opened her eyes and wiped a space clear on the pane with her handkerchief. A light rain had started to fall, mixing with the cinders that poured from the engine's stack. The fog had lifted, drawn up into the storm. Her breath began to steam up the window again. As she turned away, a spot of bright red caught her attention. A girl of about sixteen, bundled up against the damp in a worn red cloak, stood at the summit of a treeless knoll near the tracks. Her pinched, childish face peeked out of a film of brown hair blowing forward in the wind. The girl held her cloak around her with one hand and waved to the train with the other.

In desperate haste, Imogene wrenched at the window; it was stuck fast. She pulled her gloves off with her teeth and banged her fists against the frame. The window came open all at once. Imogene twisted in her seat to put her head out. The wind snatched off her hat and tore her hair loose from its pins. "Mary Beth!"

The clatter of the wheels drowned out her voice, and the girl went on waving to each car as it passed.

Imogene closed the window. She had skinned one of her knuckles, and she dabbed at it with a clean corner of her sooty handkerchief. "Little Mary Beth Aiken came to see me off," she laughed, and wiped the tears from her face.

2

A WILLOWY GIRL IN A THIN DRESS DARTED OUT OF THE HOUSE, ACROSS the yard, and through the open door of the cowshed. She dragged the shed door shut behind her and threw herself up onto the hay piled in an empty stall. The stall next to it was occupied by a brown and white milk cow. The cow rolled one dark eye toward the source of the disturbance and lowed softly.

"Moo your ownself, Myrtle." She poked her hand between the slats and stroked a ragged ear. Myrtle went back to her cud and musings.

The girl rolled onto her back and scooped handfuls of straw over her for warmth, piling it up until there was nothing of her showing but her face and straw-colored hair. The shed smelled of Myrtle and leather and apples. She ran her hands up her bodice until they rested over her small breasts. Then, with a shiver, she snatched them away and covered her face. She peeked at Myrtle, but the cow was chewing contentedly and hadn't been watching. Digging in the pocket of her housedress, the girl drew out of stub of charcoal wrapped carefully in brown paper. With sure, light strokes she sketched the cow's profile on the time-bleached wood of the stall. A few lines, and the soft curve of Myrtle's jaw and liquid eye emerged.

The shed door slammed open and shut. The girl ducked and lay still, hidden in the straw.

"Damn him to hell! Goddamn him!"

An ox yoke smashed into the wall above her head and fell into the straw.

"David?" She sat up quickly before he could lay his hands on anything else. Startled, he yelped.

"Sarah, you could scare a body to death, creeping around the way you do!"

"I wasn't creeping. I was hiding from you and Pa's bellowing."

David, scarcely twenty, stood six foot two, a wild red beard and a slightly receding hairline belying his age. "Damn!" he exploded again, slamming the flat of his hand against the beam that ran the length of the roof. The shed shook and Sarah shrank down into the hay. He spat then and wiped his mouth on his upraised arm. "I'm getting out."

"David?"

He looked over at his sister, half-buried in the straw, watching him from round, frightened eyes. The muscles of his jaw relaxed and he dropped his hand from the beam. "What, Sare?" he asked gently.

"Pa whup you, Davie?"

David laughed shortly. "I've been bigger than Pa since I was sixteen." He looked past her, his eyes darkening. "I'd like to see him try."

"What were you fighting about this time?"

"The mine—that bung hole!" He burst out. "If Pa thinks I'm breaking myself in that mine for the rest of my life so he can buy hay for a horse nobody rides, and then break my back for asking for a couple of dollars of my own pay—my own pay for Christ's sake, I wasn't asking him for nothing I didn't earn—he's got another think coming."

"Is that what set him off? You'll be twenty-one next September, and Mr. Gumpert'll have to give the money to you 'stead of Pa."

"Jamie Locke's pa told him me and Jamie were drinking last Saturday night."

"David!" Sarah sat bolt upright, her mouth agape. "That's not so, is it?"

"What the hell else is there to do in this black backwater of a town? A man would go crazy looking at the same rundown shacks, crawling in a hole in the ground every time the sun comes up, breathing everybody's stink." He paced the small space between the stalls and the door. "It's so."

"Don't all the time swear. You didn't used to swear."

"You're beginning to sound like Pa." Sarah bit her upper lip, sucking it in.

"I'm sorry, Sare, Pa's making me crazy. This town's making me crazy; I feel I could tear it down with my bare hands." He struck the side of the stall with his fist, and Myrtle kicked out at him.

"Stop, David. You're scaring Myrtle and me." Suddenly he roared and hurled himself into the straw. Squealing, Sarah rolled out of the way and scrambled for the floor. David caught her easily, tickling her until she begged him to stop and they lay side by side in the straw, panting. David picked up the heavy yoke with one hand and turned it above him; sunlight, broken into stripes by the shed wall, flickered across his hands.

"Jamie's brother, Matthew, went west after the war," he said. "He told Jamie after leaving this place you can't come back, least not for long. He says they're mining silver out of Nevada Territory till hell won't have it. He says a couple of boys like me and Jamie could make a fortune. They're always needing men that know mining. Matthew says they're even hiring Mexicans.

"There's hardly a piece of equipment in that mine I can't fix, and I can mine more coal than most. Coal!" He laughed. "Smothering and sweating for coal!" He threw the yoke at the peg where it customarily hung. He threw too hard and bouncing off the crossbeam, it crashed to the floor. David pushed up onto his elbow. "I can work my way to Virginia City on the railroad, Sare."

"David, don't tease." Sarah clung to his arm.

"Maybe I'm not."

Her eyes started to fill. "You got to stay with me, Davie. Gracie's little and hateful and Lizabeth's just a baby."

He gathered his sister to his shoulder, patting her back with his big hands. "Don't cry; there'd be Mam and Walter." She clutched at his shirt, crying harder. "Well, Mam anyway. Walter's just Pa all over again. Or maybe Sam Ebbitt. You got your friend Karen. You and Karen get on real good." David jounced her like a mother with a fussy baby. The tears poured down her cheeks. "Come on, Sare, don't cry anymore and I'll tell you something."

"You don't know nothing," she sobbed.

"I do too—Mam told me. Swear to God."

"Swear." He did. She sat up, cocking her head to one side like a bird. "Now tell me."

He started to climb down out of the straw. "Nah. I got to go." She pounced on him, pulling at his beard, and he fell back laughing. "Okay, okay. Let go and I'll tell you. There's a new schoolteacher coming."

"You're not joking me, David?"

"Mam said. You calling Mam a liar?"

"A schoolteacher! It's been forever."

"Six weeks."

"Almost forever," she amended. "What's he like, this one? Mr. Richardson was rumply and smelled."

"You speak mean of the dead, they come back and get you." He moaned and rolled his eyes.

"Don't. You're scaring me." She pulled the straw behind him down over his face. "Mam say what he was like?"

"It's not a he." He caught both of her hands and held them out of mischief.

"A lady? A lady teacher?" He let go as Sarah scooted to the end of the stall and jumped to the floor to shake out her skirts. "No fooling, David?" She picked at the straw stuck in her braids, managing to pull as much hair out of the ties as straw.

"No fooling," He slid to the floor and brushed off her back.

"You think Mam'd let me go over to Karen's? It's nowhere near suppertime. Karen'll know everything. Her pa, Mr. Cogswell, is on the school board." Sarah chattered as David followed her into the pale sunshine and pushed the shed door shut. A sharp wind, blowing out of the north, snatched it from his hands and banged it. Sarah pulled her top skirt over her arms and ran for the kitchen door.

The cold light showed the house to disadvantage; the wood was weathered gray and the screens were patched in half a dozen places. The house had been carefully husbanded over the years, effort taking the place of money, and was tidy and serviceable. A round face peeked at them through the kitchen curtains. Moments later the porch door opened and the doorway was filled by a short woman of considerable girth, with a wide, generous mouth and eyes warm with love and cooking.

"Where've you two been? Out without a wrap. Catch your death, I tell you. You stand there by the stove, Sare, until that color goes off your nose. Davie, close that pneumonia hole and stand here by your sister."

"Mam"—Sarah squeezed a word in as she was shepherded to

the big cook stove—"David said you said there was a lady teacher coming. Can I go to Karen's?"

"Is Pa back to the mine?" Mam pulled back the curtain and looked around the yard.

"Where else was Pa ever known to go?" David said. His mother shot him a reproving look.

"Then I suppose your going won't hurt," she said to her daughter. "But you be here when your pa comes home for his supper. Tell Mrs. Cogswell not to let you be a bother, and bundle up good—there's a storm blowing in."

Sarah ran through the kitchen and into the back room she shared with her sisters.

Mrs. Tolstonadge laid her hand on David's arm. "Go back to the mine, Davie. Your pa gets himself worked up, it doesn't mean anything. You're his oldest—he expects too much of you is all."

He looked down on his mother's worn, earnest face and the anger drained from his eyes. "I'll go, Ma. I'll walk Sare to the Cogswells' on my way."

"You're a good boy." She patted his arm. David slipped his heavy coat off a peg near the porch door and she helped him into it. "If you see Sam, ask after that horse your pa thinks so much of. He said it's off its feed."

"I thought Walter was seeing to that horse." His back stiffened under her hands and Mam patted him comfortingly.

"Your brother kind of takes after Sam. He doesn't think much of mollycoddling animals."

"Pa never lets anybody ride it. He hardly rides it himself. I don't know why he keeps it."

"Your pa always wanted a good horse, a breed—more'n just a cart horse. A man ain't like a woman, David; sometimes he needs to stand on a box to make himself feel taller."

David grunted, almost a snarl. "You and the girls don't have decent clothes for winter. Sarah's wearing that blue thing you made for her two summers back. And he's buying hay for a horse that's too good to use."

"I don't mind," Mam said patiently. "A man's got to have something. It don't cost so much. Sam lets Walter work off most of its keep."

"You never see Pa dragging Walter down into that goddamn mine."

"David!"

"I'm sorry, Mam."

"Your brother's learning farming. Your pa wanted it to be you," she reminded him, "but you fought with Sam till he went and sent you home."

Sarah bounded out of the back, pulling on her coat and buttoning it crooked. Mrs. Tolstonadge made a grab for her as she slipped out the door, but Sarah was too quick. "Honey, you've got Sunday buttoned to Monday!" she hollered. "You look like a ragamuffin." Sarah waved, and slipped her hand into her big brother's.

3

IMOGENE WALKED OUT ONTO THE WINDSWEPT PLATFORM AND, squinting against the blowing rain, listened for the crunch of wheels. The stationmaster poked his head out the door. "Miss? Joseph might be held up by this rain. I'm closing up here pretty soon; I'll see you to your people if you like."

Imogene smiled and thanked him curtly. "That won't be necessary." He held the door open and she stepped back in out of the wind. "I'd rather wait for Mr. Cogswell."

The stationmaster, a wiry man with tobacco stains on his fingers, smoothed his thinning hair back under his cap. "Ma'am, I'll be closing for the night at ten-thirty or thereabouts, and you can't stay here. Can't let you wait inside without my being here, and can't let you wait outside, neither; it's too blasted cold."

Imogene opened the door again and looked out. There was nothing but the lights from the houses on the far side of the tracks and the sound of the wind. The stationmaster waited for her answer. "I'm the new school teacher," she said finally. "I don't have any people here." She sat down on her suitcase. "I'm afraid the only place I can ask you to take me is the schoolhouse."

"Oh no, ma'am . . . nope. No." He scraped at his brow with a smudged thumb, unfettering the hairs he'd pressed back. "That wouldn't do."

Imogene smiled. "Is it that bad?"

"Yes, ma'am, it is," he answered gravely. Before he could go on, the door opened again and a man squeezed in, closing it quickly behind him to shut out the draft.

"Joseph! We'd about given you up for lost." The stationmaster sounded relieved.

Joseph Cogswell was of medium build, about forty, with sandy blond hair liberally mixed with gray.

"Good to see you, Jackson. Storm slowed me up." He turned to Imogene. He had a friendly, lived-in face. "You must be Miss Grelznik. How do you do?" He took his hat off. "We're pleased to have a teacher come out here. Especially one that Will Utterback thinks so highly of."

"Mr. Utterback is a generous man. Thank you," Imogene returned.

They took her suitcases and escorted her to Joseph's shay. He clucked softly and the horse jerked the carriage wheels free of the mud. The wind had dropped off and stars showed in patches as the storm blew to the south.

Imogene settled back against the seat and tucked the lap robe snug around her waist.

Calliope showed quaint and pretty in the night. The grime of coal dust and poverty was covered in darkness, and lamplight was warm in the windows. They drove toward the center of town. To the right stood the mansions of the mine owners: great imperious homes in the Victorian style, partially hidden by a thick screen of trees. The big homes gave way to smaller ones and then to the few shops that served the town. At the very end of the main street were two identical buildings, squat and dark, like sister boxcars stranded too far from the tracks.

Joseph pointed with his whip handle. "That's the school and the schoolmaster's house." He looked at Imogene's dismayed countenance. "Teachers here have been of a rougher cut before now. We get subscription fellows mostly, they stay about a year or so. This last one quit blacksmithing and was going to do teaching full time. Looked like he'd be staying a while, so we got together a school board and put him on salary, but he cut himself chopping wood and died of blood poisoning before he could collect his first pay."

They reached the twin buildings and, clucking to steady the horse, Mr. Cogswell hauled back on the reins. He climbed down and unstrapped Imogene's suitcases from the shallow baggage shelf on the back of the shay. "We'll get the rest of your things brought over from the station in the morning. They came in a week ago Sunday." As he handed her down from the carriage, Imogene looked at the blank, rickety visage of the schoolmaster's house, and her mouth thinned to a frown.

She followed him silently. There was no winter garden or any other vestige of foliage in front of the house. The packed earth sloped down in an unbroken line until it blended into the street. Foot traffic had worn a shallow trough from the front door to the gutter. On the right, the water pump stood in an eroded basin. Joseph opened the door and hoisted the suitcase over the raised sill.

"Just be a moment, miss. I'll get some light for you." After some minutes of rustling, the single flame of Mr. Cogswell's match was joined by the steadier light of a candle. Imogene lifted her skirts and stepped over the sill. "Wood floor—milled planks. All the walls are finished wood," Joseph said, and smiled reassuringly. He lit a lamp and held it high so she could see better.

The room boasted two windows, one on either side of the front door. In the opposite wall, at the other end of the rectangle, a low archway indicated a kitchen or pantry. A stone fireplace was set square in the middle of one long wall, and a doorway in the other. Imogene walked past him, holding her skirts off the unswept floor, and looked into the side room. She had to duck to see; the door was scarcely five feet high.

"That'll be the bedroom," Joseph said.

It was furnished with a narrow cot and a ladder-back chair with several of the rungs missing. Two rows of pegs on one side of the single window served as the closet. Imogene pulled back the edge of the mattress, and three flat, round insects scuttled for cover. She wiped her fingers on her handkerchief. "A kitchen?" she asked. He had followed her and she nearly bowled him over when she turned. Joseph led the way through an opening in the middle of the back wall. The kitchen ceiling was smoke-blackened and the floor scattered with litter. A square wooden table leaned against the wall. Imogene stayed in the doorless arch.

"Door's bigger," Mr. Cogswell said hopefully. "You don't have to stoop." Imogene cocked an eyebrow at him and he fell silent. Nervously he set the lamp down on the edge of the table, but it threatened to tip, so he moved it to the center. The mate to the broken chair in the bedroom leaned drunkenly against the wall, and one of the cupboard doors hung off its hinges. A puff of wind rattled the piece of cardboard the previous tenant had put in the window in lieu of glass. Joseph Cogswell eyed the broken glass and the mouse droppings in the sink and shifted uncomfortably under the tall woman's gaze. "It's a bit rough, as I said."

Imogene was silent.

"I apologize to you, Miss Grelznik, I should have checked it myself. I'll see to it everything's fixed up." He pulled the cardboard from the window and looked out. "Looks like there's no firewood, either. I'll be just a minute; the Beards'll let me borrow some until we can get a load cut for you. They're just down the way. Excuse me." He backed out of the kitchen with the air of a man escaping. Imogene straightened the chair, and, after looking at the dirt-encrusted seat, returned to the living room to perch on her suitcase and wait.

He came back in less than ten minutes, carrying an armload of wood. With him, similarly laden, was a stocky boy of fifteen with a wide, good-natured face. "This is Clay Beard, Miss Grelznik, Mrs. Beard's second boy." He indicated the hearth with a jerk of his chin. "Just set the wood down over there, Clay, and see if you can get a fire up."

Soon a fire was roaring in the grate, and Joseph had the kitchen stove going. Imogene moved closer to the blaze and held a foot out to the flames. Mr. Cogswell and Clay, having no work for their hands, stood awkwardly shoulder to shoulder as if awaiting further orders. "I'm awfully sorry, ma'am," Joseph began again, "I could go get some of the women up—"

"No need." She escorted them to the front door. "I shall be fine until morning. Thank you both for taking such trouble. I can make do for one night; I have a few things with me." Thanking them again, she shut the door behind them.

"Lord, Lord," she said quietly, peeling off her cloak and unpinning the little hat she had bought in Harrisburg to replace the one the wind had taken. There was a nail driven into the door frame, and she hung her things on it. Hands on her hips, she surveyed the room: a ragtag broom leaned in the corner. Imogene snatched it up like a weapon and attacked the months of accumulated filth.

When the floors were cleared down to the tobacco stains and splinters, she unearthed a dented tin pail from behind the stove, filled it from the pump, and set it on the stove to heat. While she waited for it to boil, she dragged the mattress from the cot and pushed it out the front door.

The town was dark and utterly still. She stood, watching the clouds scud away from the stars, until the water boiled and the clacking of the pail against the stove called her back inside. Using her skirt as a potholder, she carried the boiling water into the front room and sluiced the floor. "That should kill all but the hardiest denizens," she said. When the floor had dried, she wrapped herself in her traveling cloak, settled in front of the fire, and wrote. The wood had burned down to embers, and the candle Joseph Cogswell had stuck on the corner of the mantel was guttering out as Imogene finished the letter.

She threw it into the fire before the ink was dry.

4

SARAH CLAMBERED OUT OF THE CARRYALL, KEEPING AN EYE ON THE gaunt, brown, yellow-eyed dog tied on behind, and helped her mother down. Margaret Tolstonadge managed her bulk with surprising grace. "Thank you, Sam," she said as she pulled a heavy basket out after her. "Me and Sare appreciate the ride."

The church bells began to ring, and Sam grunted and blew his red nose on a cloth of the same color. "That's a half-hour warning, Margaret. You get on with your visits." With a barely audible "hmph," Margaret pushed the basket at her daughter. Sarah grabbed her side of the handle to help carry it and dropped a lopsided curtsy. "Thank you, Mr. Ebbitt," she said automatically.

Nine-year-old Gracie Tolstonadge sat close to Sam on the wide front seat. "That's jist half-hour warning, Sare," she parroted. Sam smiled down on the little moon face thrust out between the layers of wool.

"You got more sense than the rest of 'em together, don't you, Missy?"

Gracie beamed. "Can I drive, Mr. Ebbitt?" She smiled coyly up at him.

"Come on." He held his arm up and she ducked under it to stand between his knees. Sam eyed Sarah and her mother for a moment. "Mind your manners, Sarah, you're gettin' to be more'n a little girl. Don't dally in late." He called to the horses, and the wagon lurched forward.

Margaret Tolstonadge firmed her generous mouth into a tight circle. "That man!" she huffed as he rolled out of hearing. "Always bossing everybody." Sarah was pulling at her fitted coat, plucking it away from her chest. "Stop your fussing," Margaret said. "What's the matter with you?"

"He makes me embarrassed," Sarah mumbled.

"Oh, for heaven's sake." She tugged Sarah's jacket straight. "He's paying you a compliment. Noticing that you're becoming a young lady."

"I don't see why he goes and spoils Gracie the way he does. She's such a priss already."

"Little Miss Green-Eyes." Mam smiled knowingly and Sarah sniffed. Margaret tucked her daughter's fine hair back behind her ears. "Come on, let's meet your new schoolteacher."

Carrying the basket between them, they made their way carefully up the muddy path. At the door, Mrs. Tolstonadge took the basket and turned back the cover to give the contents a quick inventory. "Let's knock," she said and set the basket down to rap on the door.

"Mam, she's thrown her bed out!" Sarah exclaimed, pointing at the mattress crumpled near the corner of the cabin. The door opened and Imogene loomed large on the top step, filling the door-way. Sarah snatched her hand behind her and stepped back involuntarily.

Mrs. Tolstonadge sucked in her breath.

"You are my first callers. Won't you come in?" The school-teacher stepped aside and gestured graciously.

Margaret recovered herself. "I don't know why I'm surprised, I'm the one that's come on you unannounced. I'm Mrs. Emmanuel Tolstonadge. Margaret." She extended her plump hand. "And this is my oldest girl, Sarah Mary." She nudged Sarah. "Hon?" Sarah broke off staring and curtsied, rocking the basket dangerously. "And you," Mrs. Tolstonadge finished with an air of triumph, "are the new schoolmistress."

Imogene ushered them in. "I'd offer you tea or coffee, but my things haven't been brought from the station yet."

"We can't stay anyway," Margaret assured her. "We just wanted to bring you a little welcome gift and see if you'd join us for church."

"I'd like that. Excuse me a moment." Imogene went into the bedroom and shook out her traveling cloak.

"Mam, she's a giantess," Sarah whispered.

"You hush." Margaret looked around at the greasy walls and black ceiling. Leaning to her right, she peered into the kitchen. Imogene came back in a rumpled but presentable cloak, and Mam straightened up. "Miss Grelznik, this place is a mess. I'm ashamed of us. I'll get some of the women and we'll get it cleaned up for you. My sons will see to the repairs." Mam looked past her into the bedroom at the bare cot. "Where on earth did you sleep?"

Imogene pointed to the floor.

"Oh dear." Mrs. Tolstonadge clucked her tongue.

The church bells rang again. "We're late! Sarah, get your coat." She made a little dash at her daughter. "Oh. You have it on." Mrs. Tolstonadge fluttered her hands over her ample bosom. "Emmanuel is always telling me what a fool I am. Sometimes I think he's right."

Without a veil of darkness, the town lost much of its charm. The buildings that lined the main street had a sorry air of neglect and poverty. There were no sidewalks and unfenced dirt ran down to the rut that served as a rain gutter. The yards were devoid of any growth but trees. Trees bordered the street, the forest creeping to the very edge of the town, and where there weren't trees there were stumps. The generation before had fought back the forest and won. To the west of the town, behind the schoolhouse, a meadow swept up a long low hill to a crest of oaks, withered autumn leaves brown against the hard blue of the sky.

At the opposite end of the main street, as it turned south to the railroad station, stood the church, neatly painted, with a steeple bell. Two oversized wooden doors were set squarely in the front, with a high, rectangular window to either side.

The three women walked far to one side of the main street, where the morning traffic hadn't churned up the mud. Sarah skipped lightly ahead. The sun turned the strands of hair that escaped her hood to silver and gold. Margaret trudged over the uneven ground with difficulty, puffing huge clouds of steam in her exertion. Imogene kept beside her, ready at her elbow to steady her. Margaret smiled up at her as they gained the church steps. "You'll see—last night's storm took a lot of the leaves but in summer when they come out the houses all but disappear. It's a nice little town."

The service had already begun. Mam took Sarah's hand as they crept in and stood behind the last pew. The minister stopped the sermon to glare at them, and the congregation craned their necks around. Emmanuel Tolstonadge, a short spare man, with a head as round as an orange, sat with his son Walter on one side and the top of his youngest daughter's head just visible over the back of the pew on the other. Sam Ebbitt sat stolidly at the end, facing front, Gracie close beside him. David was not with them. Emmanuel frowned at his wife and daughter, pressing his mouth together like a seamstress holding pins, and his face grew red—the flush creeping up from his collar until his bald head was beet-colored. Neither Sarah nor Margaret would meet his eye. Imogene stepped out in front of them and walked up the aisle. She smiled at the minister, inclining her head slightly in apology, and nodded a greeting to Joseph Cogswell. Sarah fell in behind her and, like a duckling carried safely in the wake of its mother, glided into the pew beside her. Mam scooted in next to Sarah, still avoiding her husband's gaze.

A pale, thick woman seated next to Joseph Cogswell sniffed audibly, and a pretty girl with a full figure and the apple cheeks of a child waved at Sarah. Sarah waved back and mouthed, "Hello, Karen," soundlessly.

Three hours later the congregation broke for lunch. People spilled out, easing their cramped legs and backs, the children making it as far as the wide double doors before dropping their Sunday manners to run shouting into the open. The patches of mud drew the children like bees to pots of honey. Women unpacked baskets of food, and people stood around the tailgates of the wagons, eating and talking.

After lunch, people gathered around the Tolstonadge wagon to meet Imogene. Mr. Cogswell welcomed her again and Karen curtsied, dropping her skirts into the mire. Judith Cogswell stood stonily until her husband nudged her elbow, then she took a deep breath through her nose and acknowledged the introduction.

"Don't you mind Judith," Mam said as Mrs. Cogswell left several paces in front of her husband. "She doesn't have much use for her own sex."

"What are you two gossiping about?" Sam asked as he joined them. "Mrs. Beard and Mrs. Thomas have got some cocoa in the church kitchen to warm folks before afternoon service." He pulled out a turnip watch. "Better go now."

Mam introduced him to Imogene and he looked at her without apparent interest as he pocketed his watch. "Hope you can handle the bigger boys. I don't mind telling you I was against hiring a female. Still am. Some of those farmboys are just plain mean."

Imogene extended her hand but he didn't take it, so she tucked it back under her cloak. "I am bigger than most of your bigger boys, Mr. Ebbitt."

Mrs. Tolstonadge laid her hand on his sleeve. "Sam, where's David?"

"Seems he hasn't time for church."

"Did he and Emmanuel quarrel after we left? He tells you."

"David's no concern of mine, Margaret. I got shet of him seven years ago. I said he was trouble then and I say it now. I'll get nothing but a thick finger for stirring. Leave me out."

"Please, Sam, did they fight?" Margaret was whispering.

"They did."

A fat woman with unkempt hair and dirty nails called to them from the side door of the church. "Last call for hot cocoa!" The woman bustled herself out of sight and was replaced by a younger, thinner, dirtier version of herself.

"How do, Mrs. Tolstonadge," the girl said pleasantly.

"Hello, Valerie. This is your new teacher. Miss Grelznik, Valerie Thomas—her Ma's the midwife." Valerie exposed a smile marred with rotten front teeth, and bobbed, clutching at her skirt. "Tell your Ma there's two more for cocoa," Mam finished.

Imogene looked askance at the smeary mug Mrs. Thomas offered her, and watched the woman poke a grimy, black-nailed finger into the pot to test the temperature. The church bells were ringing them to afternoon service, and Imogene discreetly set her cup aside.

The faithful were lit home from the seven-hour service by a bright half moon. Silver-edged clouds scudded overhead, blown by a wind that never reached the ground. Sarah held her cloak tight over her chest, and Gracie crowded against her for warmth in the back of the open wagon. Beside her, Lizabeth slept on Mam's lap. She was no longer a baby and her legs sprawled long and cumbersome over her mother's knees.

Sam pulled the carryall to a stop in front of the house and Sarah jumped to the ground running for the porch. "Sarah!" Her father's voice stopped her. "Thank Sam for the ride." He winked at his wife. "You'd best start teaching this girl manners if she's to get herself a husband."

"Thank you, Mr. Ebbitt," Sarah said, and escaped indoors.

Walter was already in the small storage room off the porch, which he shared with David, the fruit their mother put up, and Emmanuel's good saddle. The saddle stand was empty. As he was lighting a stubby candle-end, Sarah pushed by him and perched at the foot of David's bunk. Walter set the candle on an overturned barrel. The ceiling was so low he had to stoop, and he was half a head shorter than his brother. "Your precious Davie ain't here," he said, and pulled his shirt off. "Pa's going to whup him good for missing church." Sarah snuggled down on David's cot, piling the quilt over her feet. "Sare, I want to get undressed, will you quit? Go wait in your own room." Sarah let her tongue stick out a quarter of an inch between her lips.

"Go on, or I'll tell Pa." She got up reluctantly and went to the door. Walter turned his back on her.

With a bend and a puff, she blew out his candle and ran.

Both Gracie and Lizbeth were sleeping. Mam had blown out the lamp. Sarah undressed in the dark, leaving her clothes in a heap on the floor. Moonlight shone through the window, projecting a black cross in a square of silver where the mullions threw their shadow on the floor. Sarah sat down on the bench under the window. Shivering in her thin cotton shift, she pressed her thighs together and held her arms close over her chest. Looking past the corner of the cowshed and out over the untilled land, she watched the edge of the woods and the knife-sharp shadow of the creek gully. Nothing moved. She sighed, an airy, sad sound. It was echoed from the bed as one of the little girls stirred in her sleep. Sarah left the window for the warmth of the bed shared by the three girls. She crawled in and jerked the covers sharply, winning a corner from Gracie.

Sarah was fast asleep when David finally came home. The moon had set, and he fumbled with the door latch in the dark, cursing under his breath. When it opened, he stumbled against the top step and fell to his knees on the porch floor.

"Where have you been?" Emmanuel, ghostlike in a long pale nightdress, stood in the kitchen door. David grabbed the jamb and hauled himself to his feet. His eyes were half closed. He rubbed them with the heel of his hand before he looked at his father again.

"It's near three in the morning; I asked you where you been?"

David swayed. "What's it to you? You've never given a damn."

Emmanuel sucked in his breath. His eyes widened slightly and his lips twitched. "You stink of spirits. On the Sabbath. You're drunk!"

"I'm drunk. If I wasn't drunk, I never'd've come home. Home!" He laughed and gestured wildly at the porch, the house, the barnyard. "A pigsty. We live in a pigsty. Mam working, no better'n an Irish nigger, and me dying in that goddamn mine."

Emmanuel backhanded him hard across the mouth. A thin black line of blood trickled from David's lip; he wiped his mouth and stared at the blood on his fingertips. Suddenly he let out a yell and, grabbing his father by his nightshirt, slammed him against the wall. David shoved his face at his father's until his beard brushed the older man's chin. David was breathing hard, his eyes opaque. Pinned against the wall like an insect, Emmanuel stared back, shaken and scared.

The curtain that separated the master bedroom from the rest of the house was drawn aside. "Davie? Davie, are you all right?" From where Mam stood, across the width of the kitchen, only her son was visible through the doorway—a dim profile on the dark porch.

David turned his face away from his father's. Margaret hovered anxiously in the bedroom doorway, the curtain crushed in one hand, the other clutching a grayish robe around her throat. "I'm all right, Mam, go back to bed." His voice was hoarse and thick with drink.

"You get some sleep now. It's awful late." She paused a moment more, then dropped the curtain.

"I will, Ma." David lowered his father gently to the floor and, turning, ran from the house. Emmanuel caught the door before it slammed behind him.

"You're dead!" he screamed after the running figure of his son. "Dead, and I'll see you buried in this house!" His voice shook, and his hand trembled so violently that the screen rattled in the door.

"Emmanuel, what's wrong?" Shrill with worry, Mam started through the kitchen. The two older girls peeked from behind their bedroom door.

"Go to bed, Margaret!"

"Manny?" Mam's voice quavered.

"Now!" He was scarcely in control of himself, and Margaret retreated behind the curtain. Dark-faced and speechless, he pointed a rigid finger at his daughters. They closed the door quickly and raced back to the bed, diving under the blankets and pulling them over their heads. They could hear their father crashing around the kitchen for a while and then the house was still. Sarah lay sleepless, listening to the deep, even breathing of her sisters.

Near dawn there was a scratching at the window, the sound Sarah had been waiting for. She slipped quietly out of bed and padded across the cold planks. David scratched again. She unhooked the latch and pushed the window open. It was hinged at the top and opened out like a trapdoor; two small chains tethered it to the sill to keep it from opening more than eight or ten inches. "You okay, Davie?" Sarah whispered. His face, drawn and bloodless, showed wan in the night and he smelled of vomit.

"I'm okay, Sare. Been getting rid of some bad drink is all." He reached up behind the glass and took hold of her hand. "Sare, I got to go. You understand that?"

She started to cry.

"Don't, please. Oh Jesus." He squeezed her hand. "Sare, listen to me. I can't be too long; it's pretty near daylight." She sucked in her upper lip, biting it, and fought down her tears. "That'a girl." David smiled at her through the glass. "Can you get me something to eat?" She nodded and tiptoed out of the room. She was back in seconds.

"Pa's asleep on the kitchen table." She thrust her hands out through the window and clung to her brother's arm. "Please don't go, David. Mam'll talk to him. Please say you won't go!" Tears coursed down her cheeks and she held on to him with all her strength.

David gently pried her fingers loose and patted her. "I got to, Sare. You tell Mam good-bye for me. And the little girls when they wake up." Sarah clutched at him, trying to catch his clothes and his hands, her forearms scraping splinters from the windowsill. David caught her wrists and held them still. "Good-bye. You'll see me again, Sarah. I promise. I promise."

Her hands clawed at the empty air; tears blinded her. Desperately she scrubbed her eyes on her sleeve and pressed her face to the glass.

David loped across the barnyard and disappeared into the inky shadow of the cowshed. A moment later he reappeared, leading his father's prize stallion. When he was out of earshot, he pulled himself into the saddle, waved once, and cantered out of sight into the trees.

Sarah crept back to the bed. Lizbeth pushed close to her. "I'm cold, Sare." Sarah put her arm around the little girl, tucking the covers snug.

"Me too, Lizbeth."

5

THOUGH THE TREE BRANCHES WERE BARE IN NOVEMBER, THE FOREST floor was still fired with color. The dirt wagon track between the Tolstonadge place and Sam Ebbitt's farm was bordered closely with trees and occasionally a field hacked out of the forest and put to the plow. The narrow track dipped and turned around outcroppings of rock and stands of trees that had proven too formidable for pick and ax. The road was littered with bright scraps of autumn; leaves, bitten red and gold, picked up the sunlight until each leaf seemed to glow of itself.

Sarah held her hands out from her sides as she walked, watching their shadows flicker over the ground. Gracie, skipping beside her, scuffed her feet through the fallen leaves.

"You're going to wear your shoes out before they're too little," Sarah said mildly. The air smelled of winter; she pulled her shawl closer around her shoulders and tied it. She laughed, spinning herself forward in great leaps. "Look, Gracie, I'm a gypsy dancer!" Gracie tied her shawl at her thick middle, following her sister's lead. They twirled until they couldn't stand up, then threw themselves onto the bank by the roadside.

"I wish there was more Saturdays. I hate school," Gracie said.

"You do not."

"I do so. You're the only one doesn't. You like it 'cause Miss Grelznik is all the time letting you draw your pictures."

"Only if I finish my work early. You could draw too, if you'd stop messing and finish."

"I don't mess."

Sarah rolled her eyes.

"You got a crush on the teacher," Grace said spitefully.

"I do not."

"Do so. I see you sneaking looks at her when you're supposed to be at your lesson. I've seen you sneaking peeks at her in church. That's a sin. You got a crush," Gracie chanted.

"You don't know what's what, maybe I'm making her likeness," Sarah retorted. "Ever think of that, Miss Smartypants?"

"Let me see it."

Sarah scrambled to her feet. "Leave it go, Gracie. It's getting late. You're stuck up with leaves. Come on, I'll dust you."

"Show me or I'll tell Mam you're making pictures in church. It's a sin."

Sarah grabbed her sister's pigtail. "I'll tell Mr. Ebbitt you like to look at his belly when he laughs."

"Sare! You wouldn't dare."

"Quits?"

"Badger face," Gracie muttered. "Quits."

"You ready to go?" Sarah pulled her to her feet and picked the leaves out of her hair.

"I don't mess."

"Okay." Sarah tugged a brown plait.

The road widened out, and a split-rail fence replaced the trees to the north. Beyond the fence lay a field, harvested and plowed under, looking rich with its jeweling of colored leaves. They climbed over the rails and struck out across the plowed ground toward the Ebbitt house and barn, a quarter-mile distant.

Gracie stumbled and caught her sister's skirt to steady herself. "Mr. Ebbitt don't like us walking through the field," she said peevishly as the clods broke under her small boots, turning her ankles and tripping her. "Mr. Ebbitt says we're to go around on the road like people, 'stead of traipsing through the field like rabbits."

Sarah raised her skirts a little and picked her way daintily over the uneven ground. "Road's the long way 'round, Gracie."

Gracie gave her sister a baleful stare.

Beyond the barn, Sam, his shirtsleeves rolled down and his collar buttoned to his throat, stood with his back to them. Lifting his powerful arms over his head, he squeezed the wooden legs of a post-hole digger together before plunging it into the ground.

"Hey, Mr. Ebbitt," Gracie called. She waved as he put his beard over his shoulder to see who was hailing him.

"Afternoon, Gracie, Sarah." He set the post-hole digger against the rails and mopped the sweat from his eyes with a grayish handkerchief. "How's your ma and pa?"

"They're fine, Mr. Ebbitt; we come to ask you to dinner before the hayride, is all." Sarah chewed on her underlip. She stopped when she realized he was noticing.

"Sarah," Gracie piped, "Mam said I could ask, and now you went and did it!"

"You ask me too, punkin, and I'll come sure. How's that?" Sam leaned down, putting his hands on his knees; his torso was big for a short man.

"Come on, Gracie, we'd better be getting back." Sarah squinted at the sun. "It must be after two."

"Whyn't we ride back with Mr. Ebbitt?" Gracie jumped onto the fence and sat on the top rail with her feet curled behind the lower one to steady herself.

"We ain't been asked. Besides, we'd best be helping Mam with dinner." Sarah took her sister's hand and tugged, but the little girl clung like a monkey.

Sam pulled his watch out of his pocket and flipped it over in his palm. "It's near three. You may as well stay put and I'll run you home when I go over. No sense walking all that way." Sarah started to protest, but Sam had turned back to his work. "I'll square it with your ma." Gracie shot Sarah a triumphant glance before bestowing all of her attention on Sam Ebbitt.

Sarah leaned against the fence, her face tilted back to catch the sun. The regular *chuff-chunk* of the post-hole digger biting into the earth was hypnotic and the day was still and dreamy. Sam worked on, lifting and plunging mechanically, a pile of dark earth growing beside the neat round hole. Gracie chattered, sometimes eliciting a grunt in return, but not seeming to mind when she didn't.

Bored, Sarah walked along the fenceline back toward the farm buildings. The doors of the barn stood open and a block of sun fell on the mountain of chopped hay stored against the winter. On the back wall, up under the rafters, were row on row of mud-and-straw bubbles the size of a man's two fists. The swallows had deserted them for the south but, protected from the rain, the nests stayed on. Sarah threw her arms back and, chin high, ran through the wide doors to fling herself into the hay.

There was a clanking as a length of chain was let out and Sam's dog careened around the corner of the house, teeth bared, growling. Sarah sat up abruptly and started to scratch her way up onto the piled hay. The chain ran out when the dog was still twenty yards from the barn, and jerked him off his feet. She leaned forward, elbows on knees, chin in hands, and watched the yellow-eyed dog strain against his collar.

"*Meow. Meeeow.*" She cupped her hands over her mouth to make the sound carry. The dog went into a frenzy of barking, hurling himself against his collar until the tendons in his neck stood out against his hide and his eyes bulged. Laughing, Sarah crawled farther up into the hay.

A rope hung from the center beam, a half-dozen mud nests having been destroyed to make room for its thick coils. Taking hold of the rope, she yanked on it. It held, and lifting her feet from the haystack, she clamped it tight between her legs and shinnied up. She reached the beam and grasped it with both hands, but still moved against the rope as though she were climbing, enjoying the warm, tingling sensation between her thighs.

"Sar-ee." The high voice ricocheted through the rafters. Sarah looked over her shoulder so abruptly that she nearly lost her grip on the beam, her face burning with embarrassment. Gracie stood in the retreating square of sunshine on the barn floor, peering up into the gloom, her little round fists planted importantly where her hips would one day be. "What're you doing up there?"

"How long have you been here, you little sneak?" Sarah snapped. She slid down the rope so fast that she burned her hands. "Why don't you just go away and leave me be? You're always creeping around."

"Am not!"

Sam stepped into the light beside the small defiant figure of sister Grace. "Here now. What's the row about?"

"Nothing, Mr. Ebbitt." Sarah blew gently on her hands.

"Sarah was climbing the rope and messing with the swallows' nests." Gracie pointed an accusing finger at the broken teeth of mud.

Sam turned his eyes on Sarah. "Don't you be climbing that

anymore. You could fall and hurt yourself. Come on down off of there. Wagon's hitched, it's time we were going." Sarah slid off the haystack and shook out her skirts. Sam eyed her ankles. "That dress's a mite shorter than's proper. How old're you, Sarah Mary?"

"Fifteen."

"Shorter than's proper. Get your mam to let it out."

Sarah looked at the ground, crouching a bit to make the skirt reach the top of her boots. "Hem's down," she murmured.

"Speak up now. I can't hear you."

"Hem is down!" she burst out.

Sam nodded slowly and worked his jaws. "Well," he said finally, "day's not getting any longer." He led the way to the wagon.

It was huge, with a bed seventeen feet long and hemmed in on three sides with one-by-twelve-inch planks; a team of six draft horses stood stolidly in the traces. Each year Sam donated it for the hayride. He had pitched a great mound of loose hay into the shallow box, piling it higher than the driver's seat. Wisps poked out between the planks and scattered over a heavy fur lap robe that took up half the seat. Gracie pulled herself onto the wagon and settled in the remaining space.

"Punkin, why don't you ride back there in the hay and let your sister ride up front with me?" Sam climbed up beside her and unwound the reins from the post, stringing the leads deftly through his thick fingers.

"I want to ride with you," Gracie pleaded. "Why can't Sare ride in the hay? She's all over straw already."

"Sarah's older'n you, that's why," Sam said. Gracie threw herself sullenly into the hay inches behind the wagon seat. "Don't lay there right on top of us, move on back and let us talk a bit." He jerked his thumb toward the far end of the wagon bed. Grace moved back another eighteen inches.

Sam handed the older girl up. Uncomfortable with the attention, Sarah sat hunched against the robe on the far side of the seat. He shook the reins and the wagon lumbered away from the farm, back down the track toward the Tolstonadges' and the town.

The sun was partway down the western sky, burning the edges of Sam's beard and throwing long shadows over the road. November's fragile warmth had gone and the smell of frost was in the air. "You can bundle that old robe around you if you're feeling cold," Sam said. "That's what it's there for." Sarah pulled the fur over her shoulders. "You been running off and on that farm of mine since before you can remember, ain't that right?" He waited for an answer.

"That's right, Mr. Ebbitt." She peeked warily at him from the corner of her eye.

He nodded shortly, satisfied. "You like that farm?" He waited for a reply.

"Sure, Mr. Ebbitt," she said at last, and hid deeper in the stiff robe. There was a flouncing in the straw behind them.

"I'm cold, too," came an interfering little voice. "A body might happen to think maybe other people get cold, too." Sarah looked back; Gracie glowered out from a mound of straw she'd heaped over herself, her pudgy face pursed and indignant.

"Come up here with me," Sarah said too quickly. "I'll make room in the robe." Gracie scrambled over the seatback and snuggled under her older sister's arm, pointedly ignoring Mr. Ebbitt.

Sam spat over the side of the wagon and turned his attention to the road.

The table was set and dinner was hot and good-smelling on the stove when Sam's haywagon rolled into the yard. Sarah and Grace raced for the house. The stove chuckled in the kitchen, flames flickering behind the door of the trash burner. They crowded close, holding their hands out.

"Careful. It's awful hot. I've had it going all day." Mam caught up a dishcloth, deftly wrapped it around her hand with a flick of her wrist, and opened the iron door of the warming shelf. There were plates of fresh doughnuts, brown and brushed with butter. She hooked two, one on each of two fingers, and held them out to her daughters. "The rest are for the doings, so eat 'em up quick before your pa and Sam see them."

"They'll smell 'em, Ma," Sarah said with her mouth full. "The house smells like Christmas."

"But they daren't ask." Mam winked. "Show there was something they didn't already know." The porch door banged and the girls shoved the doughnuts into their mouths. Keeping their backs turned, they munched surreptitiously.

It was still light out when they finished supper. Sarah scraped her chair back, poised on its edge for flight. "Can I be excused, Mam? There's enough light so I can finish with Myrtle."

"Are you making still another picture of that poor old cow?"

Mam patted her arm. "Well go ahead, but don't be forever about it. I won't be having the dishes left till morning."

"That was a fine meal, Margaret." Sam nodded a benediction in her direction. "Emmanuel, I need to have a word with you; let's walk off some of that stew."

Mam snorted. "You two can talk here, nobody'd pay you any mind." As they left the house, Margaret harrumphed to herself.

Out in the cowshed, Sarah sat on the three-legged milking stool, her head bent over a scrap of paper. Holding her braids out of the way with one hand, she sketched with the tip of a burned stick. "Just a minute more, Myrtle, then you can move." Myrtle lowed softly, her jaw grinding. Sarah nudged the door open for light. The first star of evening was caught in the crack of daylight, burning close and clear in the autumn air.

Boots sounded and there was a thump as someone leaned against the shed. Sarah held her breath and listened. Sam Ebbitt began to speak and she bent to her task again.

"I'll come right to it, Emmanuel. Didn't want to say anything in front of the missus, this being your affair." Sarah's ears pricked up. "Mrs. Beard give this to me when she saw me heading out of town yesterday," Sam went on. "Said she didn't see as how it had come to her, being's it was for Margaret, but as I was coming this way anyhow, could I leave it by. Your boy, David, did my seed orders and I know his writing. I figured you best see it first."

"Burn it." Emmanuel's voice was hard and clipped. Sarah started to her feet. The drawing slipped from her lap and she slammed it into her knees. "Shh," she hushed herself. Her father's footfalls grew faint. She tiptoed to the door, putting her eye to the crack. Sam faced the evening star. Shoving his blunt thumb under the flap of the letter, he tore it open. Holding the pages to the last light, he read them, then took a tin of matches from his shirt pocket. Sarah ran from the shed. She stopped abruptly when Sam looked up.

"You know I can't show it to you. You heard your pa." Sarah said nothing. Sam took a match and struck it against the sole of his boot. The breeze had died with the sun, and the flame burned steadily. He looked past the match at Sarah, her eyes pleading, catching the reflected fire, her lips parted. She scarcely seemed to breathe. Sam lit the corner of the paper and she cried out as though he had put the match to her skin. "Your brother's okay," he said.

"I don't suppose there's any harm in telling you that." The paper flamed and he dropped it to the ground. Sarah took his rough hand between hers, pressing it to her cheek.

"Thank you, Mr. Ebbitt."

Sam looked at the small pale head bent over his fingers. He raised his free hand toward her hair; it faltered and froze midway. "Now, now," he said gruffly, "quit your crying, it's time we were going."

Sarah smiled up at him and squeezed his hand before releasing it.

The hay was alive with young people when the wagon pulled away from the church. A harvest moon, full and fertile, hung on the horizon. Frost covered the ground with translucent silver, and the sound of the horses' shod hooves striking the frozen earth echoed through the babble and laughter. Sarah and Karen were snuggled down in the straw near the rear of the wagon bed. Sarah waved to Mrs. Beard and Mam Tolstonadge. The women called their farewells from the steps of the church. Behind them, the windows were ablaze with light, and strains of accordion music sounded, muted, from within. "You girls stay warm," Mam hollered. Sarah waved again.

Karen didn't. "Your ma thinks we're babies."

At the end of the main street, where the road started down toward the railroad tracks, Sam turned the wagon into a wide, tree-lined lane. A shadow slipped from behind one of the last buildings and vaulted over the side of the slow-moving vehicle. A girl squealed and her young man laughed. "You come and go like the devil himself, Earl," the boy said. Karen's head popped up at the sound of Earl's name, and Sarah's mouth went tight with annoyance.

"Hello, Mr. Sneaky B." The girl had recovered from her start. Earl made a place for himself in the hay and the two boys fell into conversation. Earl struck a match, the flare shadowing his lean, handsome face. Karen rustled in the straw.

"Let's pay him no mind," Sarah whispered. "He's just showing off."

"I don't care a fig for Earl Beard," Karen said in a voice meant to carry. It caught Earl's attention.

"Now look what you've gone and done," Sarah hissed. "He's coming over."

"We'll just pretend he ain't here." Karen threw a pert glance over her shoulder and turned her back resolutely on the approaching figure. Earl sat down, leaning back against the planks.

"Fine evening, Miss Cogswell."

"Lot you know." Karen wriggled in the hay, a plump shoulder and rump pushed up.

Sarah settled back into the straw, staring resignedly out over the tailgate. The moon climbed until it was no bigger than a thumbnail, and the stars shone brighter. The wagon had grown quiet as the horses plodded their steady way, circumnavigating the town. Sarah leaned back into the corner, watching the stars flow through the dark skeletons of trees overhead, Karen and Earl a single lump of shadow several feet away. Karen sucked in her breath sharply, making a tiny sound in her throat, and Sarah looked over at them. Karen's cloak had fallen back, and the bodice of her dress was unbuttoned. Earl worked his hand under her clothes, his fingers closing over her breast. Sarah jerked involuntarily, her elbow striking the wood. Earl looked up and saw her staring.

"Well, Little Miss Hot Eyes," he said softly, "why don't you run along and play?"

Karen grabbed her shirtsleeve. "Don't you tell," she hissed.

"You oughtn't to do what you don't want told," Sarah said, and levered herself up until she was sitting on the top plank. She swung her legs over and jumped to the ground. Her knees buckled and she fell, she had been sitting still too long. Scrambling to her feet, she ran alongside the wagon.

"Mr. Ebbitt? Can I ride up here with you?"

Sam looked startled, then pleased. "I've been wanting some company," he said, then reined in and extended an arm to her.

"Here, put this over you. Nights are getting cold." Sarah pulled the proffered robe over her lap, moving closer so she wouldn't pull it off his knees. Her skirts brushed over his boot tops, and his beard bristled into a fan as he smiled.

6

SATURDAY NIGHT BEFORE CHRISTMAS, THE STREET OUTSIDE THE schoolhouse was alive with people. To celebrate the season and the new windows the town had provided for the school, Imogene had held a spelling bee and potluck. The whole town had turned out, even those without school-aged children. Mrs. Tolstonadge and several of the women had stayed to clean up, by way of thanks, they said, insisting that Imogene go home.

Men seeing to teams and wagons, and women holding toddlers and skirts up out of the snow, made their way down the street. People shouted "Merry Christmas!" and held lanterns high, lighting neighbors and townsfolk into wagons and over icy spots.

Lugging a basket, Sarah picked her way through the cut in the snow to the schoolmistress's house. "Sare, you riding back with me?" Sarah looked up to see Sam Ebbitt smiling down from the seat of his carryall. "Your pa said it'd be okay."

"I got to see Miss Grelznik," Sarah excused herself.

"Suit yourself," he said shortly, then shook the reins and drove out past Joseph Cogswell's shay, where it was pulled up near the school. Karen stood nearby, adjusting her fur-lined hood.

Sarah saw her and started to call out, but the "Merry Christmas!" died on her tongue as Earl Beard materialized from the shad-

36

ows. He held Karen's waist as, simpering, she clambered heavily into her father's shay.

"Karen! You come away from there," Joseph Cogswell hollered from the school steps. His daughter gave him a stare of such contempt that he finished lamely, "Sarah Mary's wanting to talk to you."

Earl sauntered off in the direction of the town.

As her beau deserted her, Karen shot Sarah a mean look. "What do I care? Sarah Mary's such a child."

Sarah looked away, pretending not to have heard, and hurried to Miss Grelznik's door.

The little house at last looked like a home. Imogene's furniture had arrived from Philadelphia intact; the dining table and the chest of drawers bore scars from the journey, but nothing had been lost or destroyed. The high-backed mahogany rocking chair from which her mother had ruled the house sat in its place before the fire; heavy oak trunks stood guard on either side of the fireplace, collecting knickknacks; a squat rolltop desk in the corner under the window harbored writing supplies; the rickety table and broken ladder-back chairs had been replaced with a cherrywood table and two graceful chairs with thin, curved arms. The cot was gone from the bedroom, and the old, well-oiled furniture Imogene had had since childhood crowded the small space. There were two pictures: over the bed, a portrait in an oval frame of her mother as a girl, and on the chimney above the mantel, a painting of Ralph Waldo Emerson.

Imogene lit the lamps and put the kettle on. As she settled down with her tea, there was a timid knock at the door; Sarah Tolstonadge stood on the front step, holding in both hands the same basket she and her mother had brought Imogene the first morning.

"Sarah. Come in where it's warm." Sarah stepped over the doorsill and tripped on the hem of her dress. She would have dumped the contents of the basket onto the floor if it hadn't had a new lid, a homemade wooden flap hinged in the middle and fastened on both ends. Sarah righted herself and the basket and stood tongue-tied. Imogene reached out to help her but she clutched the handle tightly, her eyes fixed on her hands, and didn't see the gesture. "Would you like to set the basket down? It looks pretty heavy," Imogene suggested.

"Oh! Yes, ma'am. It's for you—the inside—Mam wants the basket back." Sarah thrust it at her, blushing. Imogene set it on the trunk under the window. Sarah made no move to go, but stood near the door, pleating and unpleating a fold of her cloak. Imogene smiled.

"Would you stay for a cup of tea, Sarah Mary?"

"I gotta stay till Ma's done cleaning up." She looked up. "I didn't mean it like that, like it sounded." She stumbled over her words. "What I mean is yes, please, I'd like a cup of tea, ma'am."

Imogene left her alone and went into the kitchen to fetch another cup. "You can hang your cloak by the door if you like," she called back. "and take a look around. You've not been here since I got my things."

"No, ma'am. I mean, yes, ma'am, I will." Sarah took off her wrap and draped it over the nail. The sleeves of her bodice were frayed and too short for her arms; the hem of her dress had been let down, and a dark circle ringed the skirt where the old crease had been. Sarah pulled at the cuffs, trying to make them cover her wrists. Giving up, she clasped her hands behind her back as though they might dart out and break something of their own volition, and look around curiously. Her eyes lighted on the basket and she carried it a bit nearer the fire. "There you go," she whispered, setting it down carefully by the hearth.

Imogene came out of the kitchen with the tea things and a hot-pad. She lifted the kettle off the hook and poured hot water over the tea. "Honey?"

"Yes, please."

They sat by the fire, Imogene in the rocker and Sarah Mary on a small stool near her. Imogene looked at the basket.

"It's from Mam and me," Sarah said into her teacup, "and everybody else." There was a pitiful cry from the direction of the fireplace. Imogene looked perplexed and knelt by the fire, peering up the chimney. Sarah laughed delightedly. "There's a little cat in the basket."

Imogene stared stupidly at it. There was another cry, louder and more long-suffering. "A kitten?"

Sarah laughed again.

"Let's let it out, shall we?"

The girl scrambled after the basket and dragged it onto the hearth rug between them. "I bet she's mad; Pa wouldn't let me bring her in 'fore the supper and the bee. She's been hid under the wagon seat. Gracie wrapped a horse blanket around her so's she wouldn't get too cold—that'll account for any wrong smells," Sarah chattered on, forgetting herself for a moment. She lifted the lid half an inch and immediately a yellow paw was thrust out. Imogene laughed and ran her finger along the straw so the kitten would reach out for it.

Sarah lifted the lid, took out a short-haired orange tiger kitten, and set it on Imogene's lap. "She's rare because she was born in November, and cats hardly ever litter in the winter like that."

Imogene stroked the fat little belly and instantly the cat began to purr. "I've never had a cat." She tickled it and laughed as it tried to catch her fingers. "What do I feed it?"

"Milk and scraps. When she gets older she'll catch mice for herself. She was Pa's idea. Pa said you ought to have a cat because you might have mice and you were an old—" Sarah turned brick red.

"An old-maid school teacher."

"Yes, ma'am." The girl whispered. She was all thumbs again and slopped her tea when she picked it up; she set it back on the hearth untouched.

Imogene smiled. "Cat got your tongue?"

"I don't know, ma'am." Sarah started picking at the fabric of her dress; her voice was so low that Imogene had to lean forward to hear her.

"You're shy, aren't you?"

"I guess so."

"Is that why you misspelled 'house' at the spelling bee just now? So you could sit down?"

Sarah looked up. "How did you know?" Imogene smiled and petted the kitchen; it had gone to sleep curled up in her lap. "I was afraid you'd just think I was stupid or something," the girl rushed on. "Everybody does, except maybe Mam and David. Sometimes I think I really am stupid."

"You mustn't ever let anyone tell you you're stupid," Imogene declared. "You're a very bright young lady." Her vehemence startled Sarah, and the girl's face firmed into the finer lines of womanhood for a moment. Imogene took her chin in her hand. "And you're going to be very pretty. I have a gift for you as well. I was meaning to give it to you as soon as school started again. Shall I give it to you now?"

"If you'd like," Sarah murmured politely.

Imogene laughed. "That wasn't a fair question. I'd like." She handed the kitten to her guest and left the room. A minute later she returned with an oblong wooden box, the surface scratched and dulled with use. She joined Sarah on the hearth rug. "Here, you open it."

Sarah took the box gingerly in both hands and lifted the lid. Rows of bright colors, arranged in the spectrum from white through the deepest midnight blue, bordered a narrow trough containing two fine-tipped sable brushes.

Sarah let out a long breath. "Paints. Real paints." Her eyes lit up as she ran her fingers over the box and delicately stroked the brush tips. "They must have cost a lot." The thought caught her up short. "I oughtn't to take them . . ."

"Take them, Sarah. You're an artist. You need good tools. I never had the talent for watercoloring. They were wasted on me."

Sarah smiled. "An artist," she repeated, pleased. "Can I show you something?" she asked suddenly, and pulled a bundle from her pocket: two flat bits of wood, a couple of inches square, fastened together with string. The wood protected a small square of paper. "It's a miniature," Sarah explained. Drawn in pencil was a three-quarter view of Imogene's face. The drawing was beautiful. In the tilt of the chin and the angle of the jaw, Sarah had captured Imogene's strength and intelligence.

"Sarah, you are truly an artist," Imogene marveled. "This is exquisite. May I have it?"

"I'll make you a better. Would you sit for me?" Sarah asked shyly.

"Of course."

"You would! Miss Grelznik, it will be truly good this time. With colors." Impulsively she kissed the woman's cheek.

There was a sharp rap on the door. Imogene jumped to her feet, her skirts upsetting the teacup. The kitten ran underneath the rocking chair, and Sarah dabbed at her tea-soaked dress.

"Dear me." Imogene took out her handkerchief to help mop up, but her hand was shaking and she let it drop to her side. "I'm terribly sorry. Are you all right?"

"Yes, Miss Grelznik. Mam'll get the stain out fine."

It was Mr. Tolstonadge calling for his daughter. Imogene thanked him for the kitten and wished them all a merry Christmas. She stood at the door watching as they helped Mam into the wagon.

Mrs. Tolstonadge's considerable weight rocked the wagon and set
the bells on it ringing. The rocking and the ringing had Margaret
Tolstonadge laughing, and when she laughed, the children couldn't
help but laugh with her. Sarah pushed from behind and Emmanuel
and the little girls tugged from the wagon, calling out encouragement. Walter steadied the team and looked miserably self-conscious.

Imogene closed the door on the families and the couples going
home to their Christmas trees and fires. She turned her back and
leaned against the wood. A tear rolled to the end of her nose and
she rubbed her face vigorously and sat down at her desk in front of
the window. Lighting the lamp, she started to write. The kitten
crept out from under the chair and jumped onto her lap.

My beloved Mary Beth, she began in a clear, bold hand, *I have
been so cold, so alone, without you next to me, warming my heart.* Imogene read the words back and barked a humorless laugh. "Don't
commit your soul to the public post, my girl," she said aloud. "Darrel Aiken's cry of 'unnatural woman' will hound you to the ends of
the earth. Which cannot be too awfully far from Calliope, Pennsylvania." She balled up the paper and began again in cramped, school-
marmish script: *Dear Mary Beth, I hope this letter finds you well and
in good spirits . . .*

When she was finished, she signed the letter, looked down at
the sheets of foolscap covered with her neat, restrained handwriting,
then crushed them and stared into the lamp for several minutes with
dry, unfocused eyes. The kitten stirred on her lap and she looked
down. "I'll get you a little something to eat soon." She scratched
the soft ears. "You're a dandy present for an old-maid schoolteacher, aren't you?" The cat yawned audibly and she smiled.
"Dandy." The kitten stretched, peeping over the edge of the desk,
ears flattened against some unseen enemy. A yellow paw shot out,
patting at the foolscap still wadded up in her hand. "Discerning
little creature, aren't you?" Opening her fist, she smoothed the pages
and, folding them, thrust them quickly into an envelope.

She scribbled *Mary Beth Aiken, 72 Elm Street, Philadelphia, Pennsylvania* on the face. She printed her return address in the upper
left-hand corner, then hastily crossed it out, marking and overmark-
ing until it was illegible. Having sealed the envelope, she slipped the
letter into her pocket and let herself out into the night.

7

STUDYING HARD TO EARN TIME TO WATERCOLOR, AND TO PLEASE Miss Grelznik, Sarah passed the winter quickly. Imogene's attention and Sarah's added zeal made up for the sketchy education of previous years, and by May, Sarah, at fifteen and a half, was ready to graduate from the eighth grade. She was second in her class.

There were six graduates, and the small school could scarcely contain the friends and families that had come to attend. They spilled outside, visiting with one another and watching the black clouds, big-bellied with rain, make their slow advance. The storm that had been just lace on the horizon at noon now covered half the sky. A breeze, rich with the smell of rain, ruffled the women's light shawls and teased at their bonnets.

By the time the people were assembled indoors and quiet, the rain was falling. It came down in torrents, pounding against the roof and darkening the windows. Imogene raised her voice to be heard over the din and formally introduced the graduating students; each stood as she said his or her name.

"It is traditional at commencement to ask those who have received the best grades to give a speech. Jana Jenkins is our valedictorian, and Sarah Mary Tolstonadge our salutatorian. Salutatorian will go first." Shyly, Sarah stared at the floor. "Sarah?" Imogene urged. Shooting Imogene a last, frightened glance, Sarah stood and stared at the crowd of familiar faces. She stepped forward slowly, the color draining from her lips. Her hands were shaking, rattling the sheets of paper on which she had written her speech. She bent her head over the page and began in a low, dry voice. "The class of 1874 . . ."

"Teacher's pet!" Karen hissed over the drone of the rain, and smiled sweetly at Imogene.

Sarah looked up.

"Go on," the schoolteacher said quietly. Sarah stared blindly at the sheets of paper clenched in her hands, desperately trying to find her place. The silence grew and stretched taut. Sarah's throat was working as though she were trying to swallow, her eyes hard and frightened. The blood drained out of her cheeks and she started to sway. Sam Ebbitt began to clap, then Mam took it up. A wave of palpable relief swept the room as applause caught on and built. Sarah stumbled to her seat. She didn't raise her eyes even when Imogene gave out the diplomas, and when the ceremony was over, she pushed her way through the congratulating hands and darted out into the rain.

Imogene found her huddled by the firewood under the lean-to behind the school. She rested her hands on the low crossbeam and leaned down to look in, rain darkening her dress. "Sarah Mary," she said gently, "why don't you come out of there? It's awfully cold and wet." Sarah covered her face with her hands, and her sobs broke out afresh. "May I come in, then? I'm getting soaked to the skin." Sarah nodded wordlessly and Imogene crawled under the low shelter, dragging her skirts through the mud, and sat silently by, hugging her knees and watching the rain. Sarah wiped her eyes, sniffling.

"I'm sorry, Miss Grelznik." Her voice was a thread of sound, rough with crying.

"What for?"

Sarah looked at her with red-rimmed eyes. "You're not ashamed of me?"

"No, never ashamed." Imogene stroked her tear-streaked cheek. She took Sarah's wet head and rested it against her shoulder, smoothing her hair. "You mustn't ever think that." Sarah started to cry again, quietly, without the wrenching sobs. Imogene held her, murmuring soft words.

"I don't want to graduate," Sarah burst out. Imogene tilted the girl's face up so she could see it.

"What do you mean, Sarah?"

"I won't see you anymore if I'm not in school. There'll be no one to teach me about painting. Miss Grelznik, you're the only one that understands me," she cried.

Imogene suppressed a smile. "Nonsense. You'll see me. I've grown very fond of you." She stroked the soft hair.

"Miss Grelznik, I'm real fond of you, too," Sarah declared.

Imogene laughed nervously and pulled herself free from the girl's warm embrace. "Now that you're no longer a student, you must call me 'Imogene,' " she said, to change the subject. "We'll be peers."

Sarah didn't know what a peer was, and didn't ask. She wasn't to be comforted. "Will I really still see you?" she insisted.

"I will tell you what," Imogene replied. "I'm going to Philadelphia in a few days—I've business there—but as soon as I come back, I want you to pay me a call. Will you do that?"

"The minute I hear you've got back."

"Will you come inside with me now? The people have all gone," Imogene reassured her.

Sarah dried her eyes with her sleeve, pushing the hair back from where it lay plastered to her forehead as Imogene eased out of the shed and pulled herself upright. She extended her hand to Sarah, helping her to her feet.

"You're strong!" Sarah gasped.

"It compensates for being so tall," she said wryly.

Sam Ebbitt was sitting under the canvas of his covered carryall. He started over as soon as he saw them.

"Is Margaret gone?" Imogene asked.

"I told 'em to go ahead on, I'd stay for Sare." He combed his beard with his fingers; he wasn't quite forty, and already it was streaked with gray. He hefted Sarah onto the front seat. She lurched, catching hold of his shoulders, her sodden skirts fettering her legs.

The rain poured down, pulling hanks of Imogene's hair free form her bun and pasting them to her cheeks. She laid her hand on Sam's arm. "Could I have a word with you, Mr. Ebbitt?" she asked. He looked at her expressionlessly, water dripping from his hat brim. "It'll only take a moment." He followed her from the wagon.

"Thank you for starting the applause this afternoon," she said.

"Women ought not to be in schools. Making a spectacle of themselves. Embarrassing everybody. It goes against good sense."

Imogene's breath went out of her as though he'd slapped her.

She pulled herself up straight and looked down at him. "I am a woman, Sam Ebbitt, and I make my living as a teacher. In school."

"You couldn't get a husband," he said bluntly, "and you got a right to live. That's a different thing." Imogene bit her bottom lip until it showed white around the edge of her teeth. Abruptly she turned and went into the house.

Sam slogged through the mud to where Sarah waited, small on the wagon seat. As they drove out of town, the rain let up and a crack of blue sky showed in the west.

"Looks like we'll have a clear sky by sundown," Sam said. The wind gusted, spattering the rain against their faces, and Sarah looked up. He pulled off his coat. "Put this on."

The bright tear in the storm widened, chasing the black-bottomed clouds overhead. Sam nodded in time with the dull sucking of the horse's hooves pulling clear of the mud. "You're all done with your schooling now, you got some kind of paper. That's more than enough for a girl," he remarked after a time.

Sarah felt her pocket. She had shoved her diploma in it when she bolted from the schoolroom. She took it out and pressed it flat on her knee: a bright border of wildflowers and vines in watercolor, and the neat hand of Miss Grelznik in heavy black ink. Water had gotten to it, and the ink had run into the colors.

"Don't go thinking on that speech or whatever it was supposed to be," Sam said. "You made a fool of yourself, but it's spilt milk now, and nobody thinks the worse of you for it." Sarah let the ruined paper fall under the wagon's wheels.

They drove on in silence. The rain stopped falling and rattled from leaf to leaf in the trees. Sam sat hunched, with his forearms resting across his thighs, staring between the horses' ears. Sarah, beside him, was curled down in his coat. One of the horses stumbled, and Sam straightened and spat over the side. "How old're you, Sarah?"

"Almost sixteen." She looked up at him. His brow was contorted, his thick eyebrows pulled together above his flat-bridged nose. Sam held her eyes searchingly.

"You're a young woman. Time you had a family." Sarah pulled herself deeper into the folds of his coat, putting the collar between herself and his eyes. He watched her. "What do you think you're goin' to do with yourself? Your pa hasn't much—David's run off,

and Gracie and Lizbeth are girls. Four females and only Walter to
help out."

Sarah squirmed uncomfortably. "I could teach," she said at last,
her voice small and uncertain. He snorted.

"I don't have to look far to see where you got that idea." He
glanced at her, hunkered down in the oversized coat. "Teach!"
He laughed.

Sarah looked at the smeared ink on her hands and the mud
caked on her skirt from hiding in the dirt behind the school, and
hid her face with her hair.

"You're no schoolteacher," Sam said.

Saran nodded, then shook her head. "No, sir," she said into the
rank wool.

"I got a farm to run. I been running it alone, but a man owes
it to himself to get some sons. I been talking to your pa; it's time
you were out raising a family of your own."

The setting sun poured down through the ragged blue hole, and
a rainbow materialized from one side of the sky to the other, tethered to the ground by dark hills. Sam turned the wagon into the
Tolstonadges' short drive. Sarah jumped to the ground and ran
inside without a word. The porch door slammed behind her, catching the sleeve of her coat. He sat in the carryall, waiting. The door
opened again and she came out. She walked timidly back and set
the heavy coat on the seat beside him. "Thank you, Mr. Ebbitt."
He nodded approvingly and she ran to the shelter of the house,
plummeting headlong into Walter and Emmanuel on their way out
to do the evening chores.

"Watch out," Walter said as she stumbled into him. He caught
her upper arm and steadied her.

"What's got into you?" her father asked. "You look rode hard
and put away wet." Sarah pulled away from them and ran into the
bedroom she shared with her sisters. Closing the door behind her,
she leaned against it, her breath coming in dry sobs.

The ceiling sloped away, the far wall only four feet high. Against
it bumped the head of a wide bed, its foot thrust into the middle
of the room; on either side of it were bright oval rag rugs that Mam
had made to protect bare feet from the cold planks in winter. The
sun had gone down and the room was full of twilight shadows. One
of the shadows broke away from the wall and moved slowly toward
her. Sarah heard footsteps and jerked her head up. Mam moved

into the half-light from the window, and took her daughter in her arms, pressing the girl's head to her breast. Sarah clung to her, trembling.

"I've been waiting for you. Your pa said Sam had talked to him." Sarah held tight, her teeth beginning to chatter. "You cold, hon?"

"I—d-don't—know," she stuttered.

Mrs. Tolstonadge stripped the wet clothes off her daughter and, bundling her into an old flannel nightgown, put her to bed. She tucked the covers close. "There. Our Mam's going to get you something hot to drink. It'll be just you and me for a while. I knew you'd be coming home full of news, and sent the little girls to Mrs. Beard's." Mam lit the lamp over the dresser and left her, carrying her wet clothes into the kitchen to spread by the stove. She returned with a steaming mug of hot milk, nutmeg grated on top. "Sit up, honey, so's you don't spill." She sat on the bed and put her arm around her daughter. Sarah sighed, settling against the familiar shoulder. "Blow on it a bit, or it'll scald your tongue," she warned as Sarah took the cup.

"Mam?"

"Hmm?" The room had grown dark; the single lamp by the door burned unevenly, dancing the shadows.

"Am I going to marry Mr. Ebbitt?"

"Do you want to marry him?"

"What else can I do, Mam?"

"What else can any woman do?" Mam rocked her gently, humming. "Sam's a good man; has a farm that's paid for."

"How old were you when you married Pa?"

"I was sixteen. Your pa was twenty-three. I remember how scared I was. I missed out on my sixteenth birthday because it was the day before the wedding and Ma was flustered. Just slipped her mind, I guess, and she never baked a cake up."

"You like being married, don't you, Mam?"

"Marriage isn't to like or not like, hon. A woman's got to get married if she can. That's the way of things. I like it now. I can't picture how I'd go on without you and David and the little kids." Margaret smiled and nuzzled Sarah's hair. "The babies make it all worth while. There's nothing I'd trade my babies for. It's why life isn't just coming and going and cleaning up after folks in between. If a woman doesn't have children of her own, she can be awful lonely."

"If I get married, will I have babies?"

"I expect you will. I had David less than a year after I was married."

"I'd have to go live at the Ebbitt place."

Mam laughed and bounced her comfortably. "You sound so sad. The Ebbitt house is big enough to put this little place in and rattle it around."

"It's dark."

"That's 'cause Sam doesn't have a woman to look after him. 'Course it's dark. I don't think those windows have seen a pail of washwater since Sam's ma died."

"Pa wants me to marry him, doesn't he?" Sarah's eyes were closed. She snuggled closer in her mother's arms. Margaret took the cup from her hand and set it on the floor.

"Your pa'd like to have you married off safe, and he thinks a lot of Sam."

"You want me to marry him, Mam?" Sarah's voice was slow with sleep.

Her mother stroked her hair, singing softly. Sarah's hand slipped from Margaret's shoulder. She had fallen asleep. Mam lowered her carefully to the pillow, still humming. She pushed the hair back off her forehead and kissed her before stealing from the room.

8

EARLY IN JUNE, IMOGENE PACKED TWO VALISES AND LEFT FOR PHILA-
delphia. Her train arrived five hours late, but William Utterback was
there to meet her, standing on the sun-drenched platform, his years
pooled in arthritic knobs on his fingers, his back straight and proud.
Imogene saw him as the train heaved into the station, a great cloud
of steam engulfing him as he returned her wave. She pulled the
small valise out from under the seat and took her place at the end
of the queue of weary travelers waiting to detrain.

Mr. Utterback stepped through the crowd, unruffled by the heat
and the noise. "Imogene, it is good to see thee."

Imogene took his hand like a man, then kissed him on the cheek.
"You look wonderful! I don't know why I sound so surprised, it's
not been so long—not a year." She looked around her, breathing
the thick air appreciatively, her head cocked to the side. The street
was alive with people and wagons, the traffic sounds punched over
one another: bells and shouting, creaking harness and rumbling
wheels. "It seems like a lifetime."

When the crowd had thinned, Imogene picked out her suitcase
from the other luggage on the platform. Mr. Utterback took it from
her as they walked into the shade of the elms lining the street. "I
know thee can carry it," he said as she started to protest, "but I'd
take it as a favor if thee would let me." Imogene let go of the handle

and fell into step beside him. "I hoped thee would come for the used textbooks thyself. Mrs. Utterback so looked forward to thy visit she all but forbade me to send them."

Over the weekend, Imogene relaxed, enjoying the company of the Utterbacks. But first thing Monday morning, she was outside her old schoolhouse. Her eyes traveled down from the neat belltower and over the shingled roof to the clean white walls with their skirting of foliage. "I love this school. I'm almost afraid to go in. I'll remember what I've been missing." Mr. Utterback held one of the doors open for her and she smiled, shamefaced. "Thank you. I've allowed myself enough self-pity for a day."

Rows of coathooks ran down the sides of a gloomy central hallway above low benches built onto the walls. Two doors opened to each side: Imogene pushed open the first door on the right. "I can smell the chalk. I think if a child hadn't set foot here for a hundred years, there would still be the smell of chalk." Orderly rows of wooden desks, holes for inkwells black in the upper right-hand corners, awaited the autumn's crop of children. Imogene walked between them, trailing her fingers over the scarred wood. She stopped at an unremarkable desk three rows from the front of the room, pressing her palm against the wood as though its history could come up through the oak.

"How is Mary Beth?" she asked. "And that boy she was to marry? Kevin, wasn't it? Kevin Ramsey."

"She is with child. Mrs. Utterback says it is due the end of July."

Imogene smiled and leaned back against the desk. "A baby! God bless her. She'll make a wonderful mother." She was still for a moment, smiling, her eyes soft. Mr. Utterback folded his crippled hands in front of him and looked away, leaving her to her private thoughts. She laughed aloud. "Mary Beth a mother. That is good news." Straightening, she dusted one hand against the other. "I'd best not see her. Will you tell her I asked after her?"

"Of course I will. I seldom see her, but Mrs. Utterback sometimes calls."

"Could I leave something with you? For the baby. If it would be awkward, perhaps you might say it was from you." Imogene's face puckered with concern, making her look younger.

"Thee may leave anything but the textbooks." He preceded her out into the hall. "There are thy children to think of as well."

Imogene spent every morning for the next several weeks immersed in the storeroom's dusty treasures. William worked with her when he could, and sometimes Mrs. Utterback came by with cool drinks and conversation. In the afternoons, when the wet heat of July weighed heavy and the close room became intolerable, Imogene walked through the streets and lanes of Philadelphia, visiting the places she had known as a child. She spoke to no one. She went alone to the house that had been her home. The garden was little more than dirt, and one of the shutters on the gabled window hung crooked, the hinge wrenched and broken by the wind. Two grubby children, apparently untended, poked at an anthill near the gate. Imogene stopped and the toddlers left their game to stare up at her with solemn eyes. She gave each a penny and bought two smiles. As she left, one of the bright coppers disappeared into a dirt-streaked mouth.

In the fifth week of her stay, she and Mrs. Utterback were in the backyard at a table under the spreading branches of an oak, surrounded by the glue pots and papers. Piles of mended books lay drying in the late afternoon sun, boxes of broken and torn primers were scattered under the table and around their chairs. Mrs. Utterback delicately dabbed glue onto the spine of a *Webster's Speller* that had been new when she was a girl in school. Imogene had just started for the house to fetch more lemonade when the side gate banged and a disheveled Negro child ran into the yard--a little girl not more than seven years old. Gulping for air, she pulled herself up short in front of Mrs. Utterback, too much out of breath to talk coherently. Imogene stopped on the back steps.

"It all gone bad," the child gasped. "an' she been cryin' for you. It all gone bad an' Momma sent me."

Mrs. Utterback took the child by the shoulders and pulled her through the tangle of boxes and onto her lap. "Melissa, sit quiet until thee can breathe." She held out her glass and the little girl drank the last swallows of lemonade. Her thirst quenched and her excitement abated, she started again.

"Mary Beth Ramsey havin' her baby an' Momma 'fraid it go bad. She go over to help, but Missus Sankey say she don't want no nigger woman around, so Momma stay under the window 'cause she like Missus Ramsey. Momma said it all gone bad." Melissa had worked herself back into a fright; she leaped off Mrs. Utterback's lap and pulled at her hands.

Imogene ran down the steps. "Quick, child, run. I can keep up." She turned to the older woman. "I've got to get to her."

Mrs. Utterback was halfway to the house. "I'll get Dr. Stricker and follow you."

Melissa grabbed Imogene's hand and darted out the gate. It was more than a mile across town to the Ramseys' house, and when the child tired, Imogene carried her, her long strides throwing her skirts before her. The shady lanes, with their tidy border of homes, grew ragged, the fences leaning and unpainted. Dogs wandered unconfined, sniffing at corners and poking their noses into refuse dumped in the street. The air was foul with the odor of rot, and clouds of flies buzzed over the garbage.

"There!" the girl cried finally, and pointed to a small house near the end of the street, the unfenced yard overgrown with weeds and only the memory of paint still clinging to the weathered wood. Imogene broke into a run. Melissa's mother, a heavyset woman of indeterminate age, was there to meet them.

"I told you to git Miss Utterback!" she scolded.

"She's coming with the doctor," Imogene intervened.

"You better do somethin' now," the Negro woman warned, "or there goin' to be no need for the doctor; Miss Sankey goin' to kill that child." She took Imogene by the arm and propelled her up the steps. "You get in there an' you do somethin' now, you hear? This nigger's goin' to wait here by the door an' she want to hear somethin' happenin'."

The spare front room was empty. The bedroom door stood ajar and Imogene pushed it open slowly. The last light of the sun poured through the window, flooding the room with orange light. A double bed, piled high with clothes and rumpled bedding, took up most of the space. A narrow-faced girl lay amid the covers, her eyes closed. In the corner, by the head of the bed, a sluggish, blowzy woman jabbed at something and there was an angry cry.

Imogene stepped to the foot of the bed. "Is she all right?" she whispered. The woman stared at her with glazed eyes. The air was heavy with the smell of whiskey and blood. Her mouth was slack, and she held a pin in her hand, poised above the protesting form of a newborn infant almost hidden behind a mounded blanket. The baby's hair was slicked against its head, and a gelatinous mass of afterbirth extended from it like a snail's trail. The umbilical cord, uncut, disappeared into a fold of heavy wool behind the infant's head. The baby turned milky eyes on Imogene and smeared its mouth with a tiny, bloody fist.

The sun dipped below the sill, and the orange light drained from the room. Without the food of color, the blankets showed their black banners of blood, and Mary Beth's white face was staring in contrast. Imogene leaned over the bed, her hands hovering above the still figure.

"Mary Beth," she whispered, stroking the girl's cheek with the back of her hand. "No. No, Bethy." Jerking back the covers, she pressed her ear to the girl's chest.

When she looked up, her face was like slate. Her nostrils flared slightly, two white dents appearing on either side of her nose. The midwife still poked drunkenly at the whimpering baby, trying to diaper it before the cord had been tied off or the blood and afterbirth washed away.

"Get out," Imogene said quietly. The woman looked up stupidly, focusing with difficulty. She pawed the hair away from her eyes.

"*You* git," she said thickly. "Nobody tellin' me my business. You git! Cow." She snorted and a thin line of mucus ran from her nose.

Imogene was around the bed in three strides. She clamped her hand on the woman's wrist and the midwife cried out, dropping the diaper pin on the bed. Imogene jerked her away from the baby, slamming her into the wall. Her fingers clenched into a white fist, Imogene raised her arm.

"You got no call to go hurtin' me," Mrs. Sankey blubbered. Her flaccid, puffy face quivered and crumpled. Imogene dropped her hand and, grasping the woman by the dresstail and the back of her neck, ran her from the bedroom.

Melissa and her mother crowded the narrow steps, peering in. When they saw Imogene, stonefaced and bloodless, drag the midwife from the bedroom, they scattered like chaff before a storm. They were just in time. Imogene wrenched back on the woman's hair and the seat of her dress, hauling her just off the floor, and hurled her though the door. She landed in a bawling heap at the bottom of the steps.

Imogene caught sight of Melissa and her mother cowering in the twilight.

She pointed at the Negro woman. "You! Get me some warm

water and soap. Send that girl for clean linens." She yanked a leather coin purse from her pocket and flung it toward them. "Clean. Do you hear me?" The woman picked the purse out of the dirt and handed it to her daughter.

"You do like she say, Missy. You git yourself to old Julie's, she get laundry from white folks, she have somethin'." Melissa ran off, clutching the purse. The woman planted her fists on her ample waist and glared at the darkened doorway where Imogene had been. "Eunice is gettin' that water," she said, "but it ain't fo' you. It fo' that baby an' her baby."

Eunice carried the pail of water into the Ramseys' house, setting it down in front of the bedroom door. "You in there?"

"Come in." It was a command.

The big Negress pushed the door open. The bedroom was dimly lit by a lamp and two candles. Imogene sat stiffly beside the bed, her bodice and skirt streaked with blood, the baby lying naked in her arms. "Bring it here," she demanded.

Eunice brought the bucket over and set it down hard, slopping the water onto Imogene's dress. Then her eye lighted on the still figure in the bed and she let out a long, low moan.

"It too much fo' that baby." She laid her hand, black and strong, against the narrow white brow and murmured a prayer, tears welling up in her eyes and coursing down her cheeks to drop unheeded on her wide bosom.

Imogene mechanically dabbed water from the pail and flicked it onto the inside of her wrist. "Water's too cool."

The black woman turned from the bed. "She dead an' don't need no doctor, so I got no use for you." She jabbed a finger at Imogene. "Eunice is goin' to take care of that baby. Here, you holdin' it all wrong." She scooped the sticky bundle off Imogene's lap and examined it deftly, crooning all the while. "You a fine baby, fo' all you bein' so little." She turned to Imogene. "You move yo'self. Find me somethin' big enough to wash this child in." Imogene stood slowly; she was unsteady on her feet and clutched at the back of the chair. Eunice looked at Imogene's stricken face and softened. "Honey, you just sit."

There was a clatter and Melissa appeared, peeking timidly through the bedroom door, an armload of white cloths pale in the dark. Eunice took the bundling from the little girl. "Fetch y' momma the tub." She tweaked the round chain. "You bein' such a big girl today, your momma be surprised if you ain't wearin' long dresses tomorrow mornin' when she get up." Melissa vanished noisily into the dark.

Eunice laid the cloths and the baby down on the bed. "You hold that lamp close." Imogene picked up the lamp and crowded near the bed as the black woman dug through the few implements the midwife had left behind and found a serviceable knife. She soaped it thoroughly and sluiced it in the pail.

Imogene stepped between her and the baby. "What do you mean to do?"

"I'm goin' to cut that cord an' tie it off neat." She shouldered by Imogene. "I delivered more babies than you can shake a stick at. An' most of them live just as robust as you please. They was most nigger babies and they hardy, but this baby, she want to live, too."

Mrs. Utterback and the doctor arrived as they were bathing the baby. Doctor Stricker formally pronounced Mary Beth dead and commended Eunice on her care of the infant girl. Mrs. Utterback said a quiet prayer for the dead woman and pulled the cover over her face. The doctor left soon after and, because Imogene asked it of her, Mrs. Utterback left as well. Eunice took the baby.

Imogene stayed alone with the dead girl. She pulled the tangled bedclothes straight, and tenderly cleaned Mary Beth's face with a damp cloth. She brushed the light hair until it lay smooth over the pillow and lifted the fine-boned hands, pressing them to her as if her body could warm them. On the girl's left hand, with her wedding band, she wore a simple circle of jade. Imogene slipped the dark ring off and onto her own ring finger; it wouldn't be forced over the joint, so she put it on her little finger. Folding the dead girl's hands, she laid them carefully on the silent breast.

When the room was tidy and the floor swept, she knelt by the bed, resting her head near Mary Beth, and wept.

A raucous shout snatched Imogene from a doze. The candles had burned down, one guttering near extinction. She looked wildly around the room until she saw the composed face on the pillow. There was a crash, and Imogene hurried to her feet. Laughter and shouting poured into the house. The flimsy door to the bedroom rattled as a heavy hand pounded on it.

"Hey!" More pounding. "Hey, in there! My boy here bred himself up a son yet?" Laughter and another crash. Imogene jerked open the door and Darrel Aiken all but fell into the room.

"Drunk." Imogene's teeth clenched on the word.

Darrel clung to the doorframe. "My baby sister made me an uncle? Where's that goddamn midwife I got?" Leaning dangerously, he narrowed his eyes and squinted into the room, then shouted over his shoulder to the shadow of another man standing in the dark, "No nigger woman for my sister!"

"No nigger!" the shadow echoed.

Darrel noticed Imogene for the first time. "We've been celebrating." Recognition crept into his eyes. "Jesus Christ! If it ain't Miss Grelznik. Im-o-gene Grelznik." He sobered up a little and his lips curled back from his teeth. "I ought to kill you. Sneakin' in here to make love to my sister when her man—man, goddamn it, not you, layin' on her like you was her man—that got a son on her's out celebratin'. You better not've had your hands on her. If you've so much as laid a finger on her, there'll be hell to pay." He peered drunkenly into the darkness over her shoulder and raised his voice. "You'll get the beating of your life! You hear me, Mary Beth?"

"Mary Beth is dead." Imogene pushed him away from the bedroom door and pulled it close behind her. "Please leave."

"Ramsey!" Darrel shouted. "This is your house or ain't it?"

Kevin Ramsey stood stock-still, his arms loose at his sides. "Dead?" he asked dully.

"Ramsey," Darrel growled.

Kevin Ramsey started to sob, huge gasping cries squeezing out of him. He sank to the floor and, supporting himself on his hands and knees, vomited, permeating the room with the stink of regurgitated whiskey. Imogene grabbed Darrel by the arm, taking him off balance, and escorted him to the front door. He lurched helplessly along beside her, flailing. She let go and he lost his footing, tumbling down the steps. The door slammed behind him and the bolt shot into place.

Darrel pushed himself to his feet, staggering back several paces. "Whore!" he cried, "You goddamn bitch. I ain't lettin' you off easy this time. You ain't fit to live with decent folk. You can't run so far but I'll find you and warn God-fearin' folk against you." He stumbled in the rutted street and fell to his knees, cursing savagely. Crying out like a wounded animal, he pressed his palms to his ears. "My baby sister's dead." He groped about in the dirt and, taking up a stone, hurled it at the dark house.

*   *   *

The week after Mary Beth's funeral, the Utterbacks took Imogene back to the train station. Surrounded by the crates of mended books, Imogene took her leave of them, and as the train puffed into view she pulled out her purse and snapped it open.

"Could you give this to Kevin Ramsey for the baby?" She pressed a five-dollar bill into Mrs. Utterback's hand. "And please . . . don't tell him who it's from. I'll send more when I can."

"I think he should know. He'll want the address to write and thank thee. He's a good man—it's just that he's so taken in by Mr. Aiken."

"You must never tell him my address!" She startled Mrs. Utterback with her urgency. Racketing wheels poured a flood of noise over the platform, washing away all other sounds. Mrs. Utterback kissed her again and William took her hand.

"Thee must come again soon," he shouted.

"I will," she promised, and boarded the train.

9

MAM LOOKED UP FROM HER BREAD DOUGH, HER FACE FLUSHED AND
hot. She pushed her hair back with her forearm. "Gracie, that your
pa?" Gracie was sitting on the front porch with Lizbeth, peeling
potatoes. The wagon Margaret had heard came around the barn
and into view.

"It's Pa," Gracie hollered back. She threw a half-peeled potato
into her sister's sack and ran out, banging the door against the porch
post as the wagon creaked into the yard.

"Finish the 'taters," Margaret shouted too late. Wiping her
hands on her apron, she came onto the porch to hold the door open
for her husband. "Never seen the flies so bad," she commented.
Lizbeth slipped under her arm to follow Gracie into the field and
away from the chores.

"Pretty thick already," Emmanuel said as he squeezed by her.
"Heat, I guess." He set a box of groceries down on the kitchen
table. "That ought to hold you for a while."

Sarah came in, carrying a freshly killed and plucked chicken by
the feet. Her hair was pulled into a knot at the nape of her neck
and she wore an apron dotted brown with old blood. Mrs. Tolstonadge took the bird and examined it thoroughly. "Good job, Sare.
Hardly a pinfeather left." She laid it on the table and started to
unpack the groceries.

"Sarah?"

"Yes, Pa?"

"Sam's going in to town this afternoon, asked me to tell you he'd be willing to come by and fetch you if you've any trifles you're needing."

"I'm okay, Pa. Mam's got chores for me."

Emmanuel pumped water into a mug and drank deeply. "Saw Miss Grelznik—she'd just got back from Philadelphia. Had more boxes than a dog has fleas."

"Miss Grelznik's back?" Sarah turned eager eyes on her mother. "Can I go into town, Mam? I can get everything done before bed if I get back early. Please? I haven't seen her since graduation."

Mam shoved her balled fists into the dough she'd left to rise. "Ask your pa."

Emmanuel looked at his daughter, her eyes bright, the color rising in her cheeks. "I thought you were too busy to go anywhere this afternoon." Sarah clasped her hands tight behind her and held her breath. Emmanuel pumped himself another cup of water and drank it. "Sam'll be by around noon. You'll ride with him if you're goin'."

Sarah ran into the back room and shut the door behind her.

"You leave that open," Emmanuel snapped. "Heat's bad enough without you closing out the breeze."

"I'm dressing, Pa," came the muffled reply.

He started for the door, but Mam laid a hand on his arm. "Let her primp up, Manny, she's old enough to want to look pretty for town."

"Primping for that schoolteacher." Emmanuel went to the bedroom and set the door ajar. "You can fuss with the door part open. There's nobody here wants to look at you."

Mrs. Tolstonadge shaped the dough into loaves. "Things'll come right. They always do." When Emmanuel snorted, she said, "You got a bee in your bonnet?"

"Maybe I do." He jammed his hat on and left the house.

Imogene's door was open to catch the afternoon breeze. She stood with her back to it, unpacking a crate. Boxes and piles of books were strewn about the room. She lifted out a stack of McGuffey's Readers and counted them. Their bindings were battered and covered with ink marks but she handled them as if they were fine china. Despite the summer heat she wore a heavy black dress with the suggestion of a train that swept the floor when she moved. Against the dark cloth her face showed pale, and gray shadows smudged her eyes.

Sarah stopped halfway up the path, her shadow thrown before her. She was bareheaded and the sun had burned color into her unprotected cheeks. Smoothing her hair back nervously, she pushed in the pins that had worked loose, and watched Miss Grelznik through the open door.

Imogene stopped and turned suddenly, as though she had heard someone call her name. "Sarah?" She came to the top of the steps, her eyes narrowed against the light. "Is it you?" Imogene swiftly descended the steps and, bending down, hugged her, kissing her warm cheek. Sarah rested against her shoulder for a brief moment before Imogene held her away. "Cat got your tongue?"

"Miss Grelznik! I never said good-bye."

"It seems like a long time, doesn't it?" Imogene hugged her again. "How you've changed in these eight weeks!" She turned Sarah a little one way and then the other. "You've done your hair into a bun and your mother gave you a dress that goes long to the ground. You have become such a young lady in such a little time." Imogene's voice broke and she covered her eyes with her hand.

"Miss Grelznik, you all right?" Sarah reached up and took away the hand; it was shaking. "You look awful poorly. Maybe you oughtn't to be in the sun."

"I'm a little tired is all. I'll be fine in a minute."

"Your hand is so cold." Sarah chafed it gently between hers.

Imogene managed a smile. "You cannot imagine how glad I am to be home." She looked at the square, weathered box she lived in, and laughed. "It is home now. Come in. I've things to show you and lots to tell you."

Sarah followed her inside. "Miss Grelznik, I got something to tell you, too."

Imogene held her hands out to the girl. "Imogene."

Sarah smiled, pleased. "Imogene."

"Thank you. Now what have you got to tell me?"

"I'm going to be married!"

The schoolteacher's hands clenched on hers and the girl cried out, her face going pale under her sunburn.

Imogene dropped Sarah's hands, pressing her fingertips hard against her temples. "I've hurt you, haven't I?"

"No, Miss Grelznik." Sarah sat on her stool beside the rocker as Imogene sank into it. She looked at her hands, working the fingers open and closed. "See. They're fine. It didn't really hurt. You looked so strange, I was afraid for you a little."

"And I was afraid for you." Imogene rocked slowly, the murmuring of the summer day and the creaking of the chair on the floor keeping the silence company.

At length the schoolteacher forced a smile. "We must celebrate. You are to be married." Imogene pulled Sarah to her feet. "It is too nice a day to be inside, rummaging through old books. I shall take you to the dry goods and buy you something frivolous—ribbons and candy. And I haven't asked you any of the proper questions. Who is the groom? You didn't seem sweet on any of the boys."

"Mr. Ebbitt. In September."

Imogene's forced calm deserted her. "Sam Ebbitt? Sam Ebbitt is—I don't doubt that he is a good man in his way—but he is—"

"Miss Grelznik," Sarah interrupted her. "Imogene," she amended carefully, lending the name music, "I don't mind marrying Mr. Ebbitt. Honest I don't. I could never teach or do anything, not like you. You know I couldn't. And I never was sweet on anybody, so I'd just as soon marry Mr. Ebbitt."

"You have time, Sarah, you're only sixteen."

"Pa wants me to."

Imogene wet her lips and pressed them together, her eyes wandering. Sarah watched her, her brow furrowed with concern. Then Imogene shook herself as though shaking off a bad dream. Sarah's hairpins had worked out again; Imogene pushed them in securely. "Let's go get those ribbons."

Jenkins's dry goods store was hot and close with the smell of pickles and warm wood. Sunlight streamed in through the windows, and flies buzzed lazy circles in the shafts of light. Jana, the second of Mr. Jenkins's daughters, leaned on the counter between two candy jars, fanning herself. She was an amiable-looking girl, her horsey face made interesting by wide-set blue eyes and an abundance of brown hair frizzy with the heat. Along one wall, by the counter, was a rack of sewing notions: thread and buttons and ribbon and trim displayed to their best advantage.

Imogene held the mirror for Sarah as she tried the ribbons

against her hair. They set aside a satin ribbon of rich teal blue and one of soft yellow. Jana measured a yard of each and cut them. "They're real pretty," she commented as she wound them carefully around her hand and folded them in a bit of paper. "You got a beau?" Her eyes twinkled at Sarah. "Look at you coloring up!" She laughed and handed the package to Imogene. "That going to do you for today?"

Imogene gave Sarah the package, watching her face light up as she opened it immediately, taking the ribbons out and letting them play through her fingers. "They're so pretty. There was always something we needed more than hair ribbons," she said. "Thank you, Imogene. Nobody's ever bought me toys. Even when I was little."

Imogene fished her black coin purse out of the depths of her skirt pocket and unclasped it. "Some candy sticks too, Jana. We're celebrating today."

The bell on the shop door jangled loudly and Jana smiled at someone over Sarah's shoulder. " 'Lo, Karen. Haven't seen you in a while." Sarah looked around and promptly turned her back again, her eyes on the counter and her mouth pulled tight. Imogene stared.

Karen, always a substantial figure, weighed a good twenty pounds more than she had in May. Her wardrobe had not kept up with the increase, and her dress was stretched tightly across her chest and upper arms, giving her an overblown look. There were food stains on her bodice, and her hair fell frowzily over her shoulders. Under Miss Grelznik's eye she tried ineffectually to tidy it, then stopped abruptly, thrusting out her chin.

Imogene found voice. "Karen, I'm sorry. I didn't mean to be rude. It took me a moment. You look very different. Hello."

"Hello. Hello, Sarah." She threw her greeting at Sarah's back, like a challenge, and Sarah winced. "Aren't you going to talk to me?" An edge of loneliness sounded through her surly tone, and Sarah turned around.

"Hello, Karen."

"We were just leaving. Won't you walk with us?" Imogene offered her the candy. Karen took a stick and bit the end off. Imogene gave one to Sarah and Jana and kept one for herself.

"I guess," Karen conceded.

The main street of the town was slow and sleepy in the quiet of the afternoon. Several men sat in front of the blacksmith's, under a

generous maple tree, their backs to the smithy wall. Two were playing checkers, while the third watched. The blacksmith's hammer
was silent and the forge cold. "H'lo, Karen, Miss Grelznik," Clay
Beard called from the shade.

"Good afternoon," Imogene returned. "You are working hard
today."

Clay laughed good-naturedly. "Mr. Rorvack's been called up to
the mine. A cart broke. I'm watching the place."

"Watching it do what?" Karen asked.

"Just watching it, I guess." He grinned without getting the joke.
"You seen Earl?"

"No, I ain't seen Earl!" Karen snapped.

One of the old men playing checkers, wrinkled and white-haired,
one arm ending in a stump above the elbow, cackled. "Question is,
has Earl seen you?"

His opponent, some years his senior, spat contemptuously and
wiped his rheumy eyes on his sleeve. "Kirby, you playin' checkers
or gabbin'?" The one-armed man returned to his contemplation of
the board.

Clay walked over to the women. "If you see him, will you tell
him Ma's looking for him? He ain't been to the mine more days'n
he has been, lately. Ma's afraid he's goin' to get himself fired. You'll
tell him, won't you?"

"I ain't seeing him, Clay, I told you."

"But if you was to?"

Karen rolled her eyes and swished her dress, ignoring him.

"That's a pretty dress you're wearing." Astounded at his own
boldness, Clay giggled.

Karen stopped switching her skirt tail. "It's nothing but an old
housedress."

"Oh." Clay stood dumbly for a moment. "It's sure pretty on
you, just the same." He ducked his head several times. "Good
seeing you, Miss Grelznik. You too, Sare." He ducked again, this
time into his cap, and went back to the checker game.

Karen took another stick of the wedding candy Imogene had
bought for Sarah. "Me and Earl are engaged," she confided.

Sarah snorted.

"Hush, Sarah," Imogene said quietly and, chastened, Sarah
dropped back half a step as the three of them walked on. Imogene
stole glances at Karen, noticing the thickened waist, the high color,

the glow of her skin even through the accumulated layers of dirt. Karen was pregnant. Imogene's heart went out to the girl and she unconsciously touched the jade ring she had taken from Mary Beth's hand. "Karen," she began delicately, "it has been a while since you were a student of mine, but if—for any reason—you need someone to talk to—"

"Why would I need to talk to somebody?" Karen interrupted suspiciously.

"Sometimes people need a friend," Imogene replied. "Just someone to talk with."

Karen's eyes narrowed and her hand strayed to her swelling belly.

"For any reason, Karen. Please come." Imogene laid a hand gently on the girl's arm.

Karen recoiled at the knowledge she read in the schoolteacher's eyes. "You keep your mouth shut!" she hissed. "You better keep quiet. No matter what I done, it's better than what you're doing. You and Sarah make me sick. Since you come, she's been mooning around you and now you're buying Sarah ribbons. Like an old dog suckin' around the chicken coop 'cause no man'll look at you."

Imogene slapped her. The print of her hand stayed white on the girl's face, then filled with blood until it burned red on the pale cheek. Sarah sucked in her breath, her hand over her mouth. For a moment they stared at one another, their faces frozen; then, with the suddenness of a frightened rabbit, Karen turned and ran. Imogene called after her, but she didn't stop or look back.

Back at the schoolmistress's house, Imogene brushed Sarah's long hair and divided it into two parts. When she had plaited the ribbons into the braids, she wound them into a crown around Sarah's head. The ends of the ribbons fluttered prettily down behind the girl's right ear. Both made an attempt to be gay.

Imogene looked out the open door as she tied the last bow. "We're just in time. Your mother and Mr. Ebbitt are here. Run along and show them your ribbons."

Sarah slipped into the bedroom to put away the brush and the looking glass. "Thank you for the ribbons," she said. "They're the nicest present I've ever gotten. Almost," she amended, and smiled at the beautifully framed miniature of Imogene she'd done with the water colors—the schoolteacher's first gift to her. It was hung in the place of honor over the mantel.

Imogene came to the little door. "You are welcome." She ducked through and stood behind Sarah, looking over the girl's head at her image in the mirror. The braids made a soft yellow circlet shot with gold and blue. With the hair swept off her cheeks and temples, Sarah's hazel eyes dominated her face, and her small mouth and pointed chin lent her an elfin look. Imogene laid her hand gently on the coiffed hair. "Better go now. Sam's waiting." She walked with Sarah to the carryall.

"Get a move on, Sare. Be milking time before we get back, as it is." Sam nodded curtly to Imogene. "Welcome back, Miss Grelznik."

Sarah stopped short. "My candy!"

"Well, go get it, goose," Imogene laughed. "It's on the kitchen table." Sarah ran back to the house. "Good afternoon, Mrs. Tolstonadge."

Mam smiled and fanned herself. "Hope the heat hasn't made you sorry you're back. Must have been cooler back in Philadelphia. That's by the ocean, ain't it?"

"Not much cooler, and I'm glad to be home."

Mrs. Tolstonadge leaned forward to look past Sam at Imogene. Her brow creased sympathetically. "Why, you're wearing mourning!"

Imogene's throat tightened when she heard the kind words, and she nodded. Tears started in her eyes. "A very dear friend, a student of mine, died in childbirth. She was such a little thing. She looked very like Sarah Mary."

Sarah came out of the house with her bag of candy as Mam started to speak. Imogene waved her to silence and smiled shakily. When she turned to Sarah, her eyes were dry.

"Mam, Imogene bought me ribbons." She turned a pretty circle for her mother; then, catching Sam Ebbitt's dark eye, she stopped.

"Get on in, Sare," Mam said gently. "Sam's got chores to get back to, and so do we."

Imogene watched the wagon roll away, the setting sun dyeing the dust orange in its wake, and shuddered. "Someone's trod on my grave," she murmured, and laughed to cheer herself.

Several weeks later, Earl Beard left town abruptly. Shortly thereafter, a piece of slate was hurled through the window of the schoolhouse, the words *I'll get you for telling* scrawled on it in chalk. Imogene recognized Karen's handwriting, but pitied the girl and, paying for the new window herself, said nothing.

10

THAT AUTUMN WAS A LANDMARK TIME FOR THE GOSSIPS OF CALLIOPE.
The little church had two weddings in as many weeks. The first
was the marriage of Karen Cogswell to Earl's brother, Clay. Judith laced her daughter tight in a whalebone corset, but Karen's
pregnancy still showed. Halfway up the aisle, the bride, wild-eyed
and sweating, clamped her hand over her mouth and bolted for the
side door. Her father held her veil out of the dirt while she vomited.
"Ought to have known better than to have a morning wedding,"
someone grumbled.

Clay alone, of all the wedding party, was happy. His broad face
was radiant as he took Karen's hand from her father's and closed
it reverently in his.

The second wedding was that of Sarah Tolstonadge and Sam
Ebbitt.

They were married September 29, 1874, and with a box of clothing and two dozen cookies tied up in a borrowed cloth, Sarah moved
out of the little bedroom she had shared with her sisters for as long
as she could remember.

The Ebbitt house was a two-story log building. The second
story, larger than the first, jutted out over the squat lower rooms,
throwing the few windows into deep shade. Sam had lived alone in
the house for twenty-six years. No homely appointments warmed it;

no curtains hung at the windows, no rugs brightened the dark floors, no cloths made the plain tables and heavy chairs less dreary. Twenty-six years of dust hardened in corners and crevices, twenty-six years of flyspecks darkened the window glass, and twenty-six years of dinners were burnt to the stove. A new wire brush and a new store-bought broom were in the pantry; Sarah had begun married life.

She and Sam quickly settled into the routine their days were to follow. Sam altered his life very little; he ate and he worked, and in the evenings he read from his Bible or sat silent by the living room stove. Sarah cooked and cleaned and lay still in the bed nights when Sam climbed on top of her. There was plenty to eat, and for the first time in Sarah's life, there was money for sturdy shoes that fit, and warm woolen dresses for winter.

December passed cold and dry, the new year blowing in on icy rains that turned the barnyard into a mire. Arms full of kindling, Sarah slogged back from the woodshed, eyes wide against the night. The dog growled, lunging at her in the darkness, straining at his chain. Sarah ran quickly by. Balancing the wood against her hip, she wrestled with the kitchen door latch. The cold metal gave grudgingly and she backed in and dumped the kindling into the woodbox. It still looked pathetically empty. Pulling out a few sticks, she opened the maw of the stove. Wind caught in the chimney and puffed a cloud of sparks out the open door. Emitting a shriek, she dropped the wood and leaped back, batting at the burning embers on her apron and skirts. Only one had burned the fabric and it was scarcely noticeable.

Quickly she collected the scattered firewood and peeked around the door into the main room of the house. Sam sat undisturbed before the potbellied stove, the Bible open on the table, his hands folded on his stomach, knees wide and feet planted, staring into the empty air in front of him. Sarah let the door close softly and, standing carefully to the side, stoked the stove. When the water was hot, she poured it into the sink, wincing as the steam hit her chapped hands, and busied herself with the supper dishes.

Sam pushed open the kitchen door soundlessly. Sarah hummed softly under her breath, swaying slightly in time with her song, her slender hips swinging from side to side, her skirts sweeping the heels of her small boots. Sam hitched up his trousers and combed his beard with his fingers.

"Sare."

She jumped, startled, and resting her dripping hands on the edge of the sink, she looked over her shoulder. "What is it, Sam?" His eyes were narrowed and his face taut. Sarah's eyes flicked down over the bulge in his pants. "Let me finish these dishes," she said wearily. "They'll stick if I leave them."

"It's time for bed. Let 'em go till morning." He held the door open as she dried her hands and took off her apron. His bulk almost filled the doorway and Sarah pressed by him. He followed her up the stairs with the lamp, closing and locking the bedroom door behind them.

Sarah waited on the edge of the bed, the coverlet pulled over her shoulders for warmth. Sam had shut himself in the little room adjoining, and she could hear him getting undressed. The bedroom, like every other room in the house, was larger than it needed to be and was impossible to keep warm. A small stone fireplace gaped against the end wall, dark and free of ash. Sam wouldn't waste wood to heat a room used only for sleeping. Dark walls built of squared-off tree trunks climbed up out of sight into the gloom beyond the rafters. The bed, too, was oversized and Sarah's feet didn't touch the floor. Bed, dresser, and washstand were the only furnishings; without rugs on the floor, the pieces looked adrift in a sea of wood that vanished into dark walls and darker corners.

The dressing-room door opened and Sam emerged in his night-shirt and cap, his feet still in his wooden work socks. Without the heavy outer garments he wore summer and winter, he was not imposing—his nightshirt bulged out over his pot belly and his legs were white and bandied. He brought the candle with him, setting it on the washstand. Sarah jumped down from the bed and snatched up her old flannel gown. Sam stood between her and the dressing room. "It's cold, what with the window in there. You'd best be changing here."

Sarah looked at him oddly. "There's windows here too, Sam. I don't see—"

"It's cold," he said flatly.

She chewed her underlip. "I don't mind the cold." She started past him, but he put out his arm.

"I'm telling you, Sare, you'll be undressing in here tonight."

"Sam—" Sarah looked up at him and broke off; his eyes were hard and wet, like those of a man with a fever. He got into bed, his back against the heavy headboard, the covers tucked around his waist.

Poised on the balls of her feet, holding her nightgown to her chest, Sarah looked uncertainly from the bed to the dressing room. She unfastened the top button of her bodice awkwardly. Her hands fumbled and she broke for the shelter of the darkened dressing room.

"Sare!" Sam's voice caught her. Tears sprang into her eyes and she wiped them on the soft flannel before she turned around.

"Sam, you want me to put out the light?" She reached toward the washstand.

"Leave it be."

She stopped at the edge in his voice, and turning her back to him, she began unbuttoning her dress. On the wall her shadow leaped and danced; Sam had turned up the lamp. Sarah faltered and a button clattered to the floor.

"Get on with it. It's too cold to be dawdlin'." His voice was thick.

She pulled the dress off over her head and laid it on the chest of drawers, hugging herself against the cold and the light. Goosepimples stood out on her bare arms, and her small breasts, their nipples hard, showed against the thin cotton of her chemise. She hiked her skirt over her knees and rolled her black stockings down. Sam's breathing quickened, audible in the silent room. In the mirror she could see his face; his lips were slightly parted and his eyes glittered in the moving light. She shivered, a prickling between her thighs, a warmth catching her breath and filling her throat. She paused, her arm outstretched for her nightgown, and watched his eyes devour her. Her breath escaped in an aching sigh. Leaving the gown where it lay, she untied the ribbons of her chemise slowly, deliberately. Sliding her hands under the cotton, she cupped her breasts a moment, her palms warm against her skin, then shrugged, letting the chemise slide free of her shoulders. She stepped out of her petticoats and stood naked, feeling the cold on her thighs and the heat inside her. Her narrow shoulders sloped gently away from a round neck; her breasts, pointed and firm, threw their shadow on the wall behind her. The lamp by the bedside warmed her body with yellow light, catching the soft hair at her nape and groin in a golden mesh.

Sam sucked in his breath. "Come to bed," he said hoarsely. Sarah slipped on her nightdress as he blew out the lamp, and crawled under the covers. He rolled against her, fumbling with the edge of her gown, pulling it up. His callused hand slid up over her thigh, pressing her groin. Fingers, working their way up her belly, kneading the soft flesh, closed roughly on her breast, pinching the nipple. She closed her eyes tight and gasped. There was a tearing sound as Sam ripped her nightgown; his mouth, wet, groping, worked down her throat. His lips closed around her breast and he sucked greedily, like a hungry child. Sarah's fists clenched on the sheets and her eyes widened, staring sightlessly at the ceiling. Sam's mouth searched out the other breast as he forced her thighs apart with the side of his hand. Yanking his nightshirt up, he pulled himself on top of her. Sarah's knees fell wide to receive him. He grasped his thick penis and thrust it into her, letting his weight fall against her. Whimpering, she arched her back to meet him, a small, animal cry deep in her throat as she grabbed his buttocks to pull him into her.

Sam froze, his body gone rigid, his weight crushing down on her.

Sarah moaned and shoved her hips hard against his, grinding for her own release. He wrenched himself up off of her as if he'd been burned. Sarah emitted a stifled sound, following his body with hers, and he jerked away, pulling himself free with a sucking sound. Sarah fell back on the bed, opening her eyes like a sleepwalker.

Limp and flaccid, Sam's penis shrank away under the overhang of his belly. His face twisted with anger, and he slapped her. "There's a whore in you," he cried, and slapped her again, snapping her head from side to side. "Crying like a bitch in heat." He spat at her contemptuously, but his mouth was dry. Sarah flinched. "You be afraid and you go on being afraid." He threw back the covers and stared down at her. Her nightdress was rumpled above her waist, her legs and loins bare. He backed away from the bed and pulled his trousers on over his nightshirt. He pointed a blunt finger at Sarah. "You stay in that bed and you think on yourself."

The sound of his footsteps receded down the stairs and the back door banged as he slammed it behind him. Sarah lay listening, her face crumpled in a soundless cry. Fear numbing her fingers, she pulled at her nightgown, working it from under her back and tugging it down until it covered her nakedness. She was shaking. She clenched her teeth to stop their chattering, and stared into the shadows over the bed until the muffled tread of Sam's stockinged feet sounded on the stairs. Sarah pulled the coverlet under her chin and squeezed her eyes shut as the bedroom door opened. He lit the lamp.

"Get out of bed," he said coldly. Sarah didn't move. He crossed the room and jerked the covers off her. Her hands still clutched, clawlike, at the air where the blankets had been, her teeth clattered, and she sucked air noisily through closed jaws.

"Get up."

Sarah gasped; her breath had gone out of her and she gulped at the air. Abruptly, Sam rolled her over, putting her feet on the floor, her face and torso still on the bed, and grabbed up the willow switches he had dropped inside the door. Frozen into rods, the willows sang through the air as he slashed at her legs. Pain loosened her jaws and she screamed. Scrabbling at the covers, she tried to crawl over the bed. He grabbed her collar and dragged her back, whipping her until her nightgown was ripped and ribboned.

He threw down the rods and lifted her up by the shoulders, turning her to face him. "Quit your howling." A scream tore open her throat, and he shook her. "Quit it now!" Sarah choked and coughed. He held her until she was done. "You feel those welts on your legs and you think on yourself." As he let go of her, her knees gave way and she sat down hard. Sam pulled off his trousers and, extinguishing the lamp, got into bed, settling the covers around his shoulders. Steam issued from his mouth, the room had grown so cold. He looked at his wife's narrow shoulders hunched in the dark. "Pull some covers over yourself," he said, not unkindly. "No sense freezing to death." There was no response, and he rolled onto his side, away from her.

Sarah sat facing into the dark, her little reddened hands folded in her lap and her small white feet dangling beneath the hem of the tattered flannel. She stared at nothing; her eyes were dry and as blind as the windows made opaque by frost.

An east wind sawed under the eaves, the windows silvered with moonlight and dimmed again. Finally she stirred. Pushing herself stiffly from the edge of the bed and creeping into the dressing room, she lowered her head over the chamber pot and was sick.

Sarah woke up alone for the first time she could remember, and cried out for Lizbeth and Gracie. Her own voice roused her and she sat up blinking in the blue half-light. Sam's side of the mattress was cold, and his trousers were gone from the footboard. She eased her feet over the edge of the bed, holding the weight up off her legs.

Her clothes were tumbled over the dresser top, the black stockings draped down to the floor. Sarah looked at them and her face flushed. She picked up the dress and petticoat, avoiding her reflection in the mirror, and pulled them on over her nightgown. Dressed, she faced herself in the glass. Her thin hair was matted at the back of her head and stuck out like straw. The collar of her nightgown poked out above the somber brown of her bodice. She ran from the room.

The fireplace grate was cold and the stoves hadn't been lit. The kitchen door was open and there was a thin layer of ice in the pail she used to heat the dishwater. Sam's Bible lay open on the table. Sarah eyed it with alarm as she closed the door and sat down on the edge of a chair. Crumpled petticoats gouged at her torn legs; she grimaced, holding in the pain.

Sam had opened the Bible to Proverbs, Chapter Five. At the top of the page was the heading: "The Mischiefs of Whoredom." The faded satin ribbon lay in the crease to mark the place. Sarah leaned her elbows on the table and, digging her fingers into her hair, read:

"For the lips of a strange woman drop as a honeycomb, and her mouth is smoother than oil:

"But her end is bitter as wormwood, sharp as a two-edged sword.

"Her feet go down to death, her steps take hold on hell."

Tears drowned the words; she threw herself from the chair and lay crying on the floor until she exhausted herself and was still.

Imogene dismissed class at three-thirty and cleared her desk. The wind, which had been rising steadily since noon, howled under the eaves, making the room creak and the windows rattle. The schoolroom emptied quickly, the children running home like late leaves scudding before the storm. Imogene closed the stove's damper and sat on one of the small desks, listening to the wind cry and the stove click and pop comfortingly. By four o'clock the light was going. She gathered up a pile of texts and let herself out, hurrying home, head down and shoulders hunched against the cold. Someone called her name and she faced into the cutting wind.

Sarah was huddled in the lee of the school, leaning on the rough wood of the building, her cloak held tight around her. Matted hair half hid her face, but Imogene could see that her eyes were red from crying.

"Sarah Mary? Sarah, what in heaven's name are you doing here?"

Sarah stumbled away from the shelter of the schoolhouse. Her knees started to buckle. Imogene dropped the books, catching her before she fell. Sliding one arm around Sarah's waist and the other behind her knees, she lifted her, carrying her like a child. The girl's cloak fell open and trailed over the ground, riffling the pages of the scattered books. Loose pages, freed, flew up and over the buildings like wild things.

She set Sarah down in the rocker in front of the fireplace. Still in a faint, Sarah slumped against the back, setting the chair rocking. Imogene steadied it with her foot and felt Sarah's face and hands; they were like ice.

Putting the girl's hands back in her lap, she started to tend to the fire. Sarah cried out and reached for her, and Imogene held her again. When she was quiet, the schoolteacher knelt in front of her. "Here, blow your nose." Sarah obediently took the proffered handkerchief, blew her nose, and wiped her eyes. Finished, she held it out. "You keep it," Imogene told her, smiling. "Will you be all right long enough for me to build a fire?" Sarah nodded and wiped her nose again; it was red from the tears and the cold.

When the fire was burning high, Imogene coaxed her out of her cloak and sat her near the blaze with a mug of hot tea and honey. Sarah held it in both hands, blowing on it. "Drink that slowly. I put a bit of rum in it to drive off the chill you took." Imogene pulled the footstool near Sarah's feet and sat on it, her dark skirts settling around her like stormclouds. Sleet started to fall and the fire hissed as the first drops blew down the chimney.

The heat and the rum were bringing the color back to Sarah's cheeks. "Feeling better? You look a little less peaked."

"I'm better."

"Do you want to tell me about it?" Sarah looked up from the fire into Imogene's gray eyes, and the tears welled up, spilling down her face. Imogene took the tea from her trembling hands and set it on the hearth. "My dear." She took the weeping girl to her and hugged her close. Sarah clutched at her, hiding her face in the soft woolen pleats of Imogene's bodice.

"Sam—Sam wanted the marriage—" She choked on her tears and coughed. "—the marriage act, and I liked it." She held tight to Imogene's waist, her eyes squeezed shut. "I liked it like a whore and Sam whipped me. I want to die. I can't go home."

"Hush now. Hush. That's my girl." She stroked Sarah's hair, murmuring. "Come on now, sit up. You can lean against me." The girl rested her head on Imogene's shoulder, hiccoughing, and Imogene took up the rum-laced tea. "Here, drink this. It'll make you feel better." Sarah drank and relaxed against Imogene's shoulder, flinching as the cuts on the backs of her legs opened.

"He whipped you."

Sarah nodded.

"Let me see," Imogene said gently.

Sarah pulled her skirts up and picked gingerly at a black stocking. The wool stuck where the blood had dried. She yanked it partway down, sucking in her breath at the tearing. The back of her thigh was crisscrossed with marks from the willow switches, the broken skin curled back, white and bloodless, from long, shallow cuts. Tufts of black wool stuck to the wounds, and where the flesh was not lacerated, it was bruised. Imogene looked at the leg and her face hardened. Sarah saw and was ashamed.

"Am I bad, Imogene?"

"No. Lie down here by the fire where it's warmest. I'm going to tend to those cuts." She helped Sarah out of her clothes, hanging her dress and petticoat on the pegs in the bedroom. The nightgown Sarah had worn underneath was so tattered that Imogene shoved it into the ragbag under the bed and gave her an old wrapper of her own to wear, rolling up the cuffs and pulling the skirt up through the sash so it wouldn't drag the floor. She brought her another cup of tea and rum, then soaked a cloth in warm water and laid it over Sarah's stockinged legs, wetting the wool until it pulled easily away from the wounds. Sarah's legs were slashed from ankles to buttocks.

"What did Sam whip you with?" Imogene's voice was controlled.

"A willow switch."

Imogene wrung the cloth with a vicious twist. "This will hurt a little." She washed the injuries tenderly. "I never knew a willow whip to cut this bad."

"I guess it was froze."

"Frozen."

"Frozen."

When the cuts were clean, Imogene spread a thick layer of salve over them and helped the girl into an old pair of cotton pantelets. Sarah lay down again by the fire, watching Imogene clean up the pots and rags. "Sam said I was a whore."

"You're not a whore, dear."

"He said I acted like one."

"He shouldn't have. Love sometimes expresses itself that way."

"I don't think I love Sam," Sarah said after a while. "Not like I do you or Mam or David. I just felt funny, kind of buzzy inside, and I closed my eyes so I couldn't see him—just nobody—and feeling that . . . like when I used to climb the rope in the barn when I was little. I don't feel funny when I think of Sam." Sarah finished her tea and stretched her toes under the rocker. Her voice was slow and sleepy. "Sam just grabs at me like I was an old plow."

Imogene crossed to the window and, pulling aside the curtain, stared out into the dark. The storm was moving east, the sleet pounding against the back of the house. Rivulets rutted the main street, carrying slush down to the ditches that served the town as gutters.

Sarah had fallen asleep in front of the fire. The girl's face was turned toward the flames, and was clear and rosy in the warm light. Her lashes, darker than her hair, curled against the soft skin, fragile and vulnerable. The sleeve of the wrapper had unrolled and claimed one of her hands; the other lay open on the hearth rug, the fingers slightly curled. Imogene leaned down and tickled the palm with her fingertip. Sarah murmured in her sleep, and the schoolteacher smiled.

Imogene cleared the tea things from the living room and washed them before she roused the sleeping girl. Sarah stirred at her touch and opened her eyes, her lashes dried in dark spikes.

"Can I stay with you?"

"No!" Imogene said, suddenly sharp.

Sarah bit the insides of her cheeks and swallowed hard, but still her eyes filled. She pulled herself awkwardly from the floor and looked vaguely around the room for her clothes.

Imogene caught her by the hand. "I'm sorry," she said, and glancing at the door, laughed nervously. "The night's got me in fidgets. I didn't mean to be harsh."

Sarah's legs were shaking so that she could barely stand, and under the pink of the fire and alcohol, her face was pinched. Imogene checked her watch for something to do; it was after eleven. The storm pounded, unabated, outside. Steepling her hands, Imogene pressed her fingertips to her lips and nodded to herself shortly. Then, to Sarah, still waiting, still watching: "You can stay—as long as you like." She smiled and turned Sarah by the shoulders. "Go along to bed now. I'll be there in a minute."

As the girl left the room, Imogene bolted the door and checked the windows. The curtains were all drawn tight. A log fell and the fire hissed and sparked. Imogene gasped, starting involuntarily.

"Don't be a goose," she said quietly. She set the screen in front of the fire and carried the lamp into the bedroom.

Sarah was already fast asleep. Imogene sat on the edge of the bed and stroked her hair absentmindedly. The last of the firelight from the other room played on the watercolors over the window: fragile yellow buttercups in meadow grass, the tiny white flowers that the people of Calliope called Johnny-jump-ups.

Imogene watched until the fire had burned down to embers and no longer cast its light upon the wall, then rose with a sigh and, taking a blanket from the closet shelf, made herself a bed on the living room floor.

Sam came before dawn the next day, cold and quiet. Imogene said nothing. She wrapped Sarah in her cloak and helped her into the wagon with exaggerated care. Sarah was too frightened to talk, and dully accepted Imogene's kiss on her cheek. The wagon pulled away, sluggish in the mud, its tracks filling with water. The storm had passed.

They reached the farm as the sun rose, a chill gray light in the east. Sam jerked on the reins and the cart horse stopped, rearing in the traces, trying to back away from the bite of the bit. He pulled the horsewhip from the seat beside him and held it across his knees.

"You'll not be running off like that again."

Sarah felt the sting of the salve in her wounds, felt her own fragility next to the bulk of her husband. In the summertime, before her marriage, she and Imogene had looked up the word "husband" in the teacher's dictionary: to cultivate, to nurture, to husband.

Sam cracked the whip against the footboard and Sarah jumped half a foot. "Sarah, you'll not be running off again." His eyes bored into her, and she could feel the tears hot in her throat. With an effort, she swallowed them; she was done crying in front of Sam Ebbitt.

"I won't, Sam," she managed.

11

SAM NEVER RAISED HIS HAND TO SARAH AGAIN, AND SHE NEVER GAVE him cause. When he took her she lay as still as a corpse, her lips forming silent numbers as her eyes slid methodically from crack to crack down the roof and walls. Sam was not unkind to her, and had a neighbor woman in once a week to help with the cleaning until her legs healed.

Walter worked at the Ebbitt farm nearly every day through the winter months, walking the miles to and from home in most weathers. He was learning to be as taciturn as Sam and, except for the brief messages he carried for Mam, proved to be no companionship for the young Mrs. Ebbitt. Finally spring came, and the lonely days of being confined by the weather were past.

On a Saturday in early June, Sam Ebbitt's carryall rattled down the narrow track into the Tolstonadges' yard, the dog trotting behind on a long lead. Mam came out of the house and hollered a welcome.

"Come in. I'll see if there's not something cool to drink." The dog, pulling loose lips away from his teeth and growling, slunk under the wheels into the shade of the wagon. Mam stayed well out of reach. "You oughtn't to bring that dog, Sam. One of the little girls could get bit bad."

"Dog don't bite," he returned.

Sarah jumped free of the wagon. Her face had filled out, her cheeks rounded. Her figure, too, was fuller, more womanly than it had been the year before. The bosom of her neat shirtwaist swelled attractively and was balanced by the merest trace of a bustle. "We're going to town, Mam. I got some shopping to do, and Sam said I could charge yardage at the dry goods if I saw something I liked."

"I expect you'll find something in that store to buy." Mam smiled over her head at Sam. He grunted.

"Where's Emmanuel?"

"To the mine. I expect him home any minute," Mam replied.

"I guess I'll go on down the road a ways. Meet him."

"That'd be good of you, Sam. He's not so young as he used to be, and come weekend he's wore out."

"Walter?"

"He's off being a boy somewhere, I expect."

Sam shook the reins and the shade rolled off the dog, warning him to his feet before the tether jerked.

Sarah followed her mother sedately into the house. Margaret watched her out of the sides of her eyes. Under the girl's bonnet, wisps of hair, escaping the coronet of light braids, framed her face. A quirk of a smile dimpled in the corners of her mouth. "You look like the fox been in the chickens," Mam said. "Here, spread this over your lap and make yourself useful." She handed her daughter a dishcloth and shoved a bowl of peas to the center of the kitchen table. Sarah opened a pod and, picking out the peas one by one, popped them into her mouth. "Don't you go eating these," Mam protested. "Not so many you can go eating them raw. It's early yet." Margaret dragged the bowl away, but not before Sarah had grabbed a handful. "What's got into you?" Mam chided.

A dog barked and Mam leaned to see out the door. Emmanuel was riding in with Sam. "Guess your pa was just about home." She looked at her daughter. "You and Sam seem to be getting on better." Sarah shrugged indifferently and ate another pea. "It'll come," Margaret said.

Walter, wearing a long-sleeved flannel shirt and wool trousers that fell down over his boots, emerged from the shade behind the shed. His boyish grace was gone, and at seventeen he was a stocky, lumpish young man already red in the face and turned down at the mouth. He joined his father and Sam by the gate.

Mam sighed. "Walter's a good boy, works harder than any boy

I know, but somehow Davie got all the fire. Maybe burnt himself up with it—I ain't heard." Sarah quit eating the peas and started shucking them properly.

"Mam, I missed."

"Well, pick it up and dust it off. A little dirt never did anybody harm." She pushed the half-filled bowl nearer Sarah.

"No, Mam. I missed."

Margaret looked up and Sarah nodded. "I been expecting it!" the older woman crowed. "Lord! No wonder you look so pretty, filling out." She laughed, dumping the unshucked peas off her lap and back into the bucket. "How you feeling? You sick mornings?"

"Some. Not much, though."

"Who'd've thought it? Not sick much." Mam glowed. "You're going to have a baby, hon. I'm pretty sure."

Sarah clutched her mother's arm. "You think so, Mam? You really think so? I thought maybe that was it, I been feeling so good. I feel full inside, like there was a hole in me that I never knew was there, and now what was missing ain't." Jumping from her chair, she caught her mother unawares and swung her around. "I can't believe it! I been praying every chance I got." Suddenly worried, she stopped herself. "Mam, ought I be doing this? I mean jumping around?"

Margaret hugged her. "Well, you might stop a bit, as much for me as for the baby. You use your head, and your stomach will tell you when you should stop doing what. It'll just plain get in the way."

"I'm going to have a baby." Sarah sat down with her palms on her cheeks and as quickly bounced up. "I've got to tell Imogene."

"Don't you think you better tell Sam?" Sarah looked blank. "If he's going to be a father, he might want to know. You don't think you got that baby all by yourself, do you?" Mam teased. "Sit down now. Another minute's going to make no difference. We've got some figuring to do. When did you last bleed?" Sarah's eyes rolled toward the ceiling as she ran over the weeks. "You weren't at Easter service. Sam said it was female trouble," Mam suggested, and Sarah looked immensely relieved.

"That was it, the last of March."

Mam counted on her fingers, naming the months. "Looks like December, or maybe even November."

Sarah hugged herself. "Maybe the winter won't seem so long."

Sam called from outside, and Mam gave Sarah another quick squeeze. "I'm so happy for you, Sare. For you and Sam."

"Don't say nothing, Mam."

" 'Course I won't. The news is yours to tell, and rightly so."

"Grandma Tolstonadge."

"Oh! My, I hadn't thought. Sounds just right. Old—but good to my heart."

Sam called again.

"Will you two quit pulling taffy?" Emmanuel added. "Man's got business in town."

Mam helped Sarah into the wagon with elaborate care, twittering and poking her daughter gently in the ribs. Once she caught Sam's eye and winked broadly; Sam jerked his head back as if she had spit in his eye, but never changed expression.

Sarah untied her bonnet strings and let the breeze carry them. The sky was a flawless blue, and the fullness of summer swelled under it in shades of brown and green. Underbrush crowded the edges of the wagon track, rustling with small birds foraging for their young, hidden in nests overhead. Oblivious of the damage to her complexion, Sarah lifted her face to the sun and breathed deep of the warm, scented air. Cupping her hands over her stomach, she petted it. Sam stared out between the horse's ears, his eyes fixed on nothing, his chin echoing the dogged tread of the cart horse. Glancing at him, Sarah smiled a secret smile to herself.

As they approached a ragged burst of rock, thrusting through the creepers, a cottontail bunny, frightened by the noise of the wagon, darted out from the safety of the brush. The dog bounded from between the rear wheels and caught the terrified animal in its jaws.

"Sam." Sarah grabbed his arm. "You've got to stop."

Sam Ebbitt looked over at his young wife and pulled up on the reins.

"Dog's got a rabbit, Sam."

He leaned across her to look. "His rope tangled in something?"

"Take it away from him," she pleaded.

"Rabbits are thick this year, Sare. Be eating the crops."

"Please."

"Why're you taking on over a rabbit? You've cleaned and et 'em plenty of times." He clucked to the horse.

"Please," she begged.

Sam blew air noisily out between loose lips and, shaking his head and muttering, climbed out of the wagon. "C'mere, boy. Lemme see what you got." The dog looked suspiciously over the inert form of the rabbit and growled. Sam cuffed him. "You don't by-God growl at me." The dog dropped the rabbit and ran under the wagon. "Looks like the neck's broke, Sare. No sense wasting it." He whistled and the dog pricked up his ears.

"Wait." She jumped from the wagon and scooped the little body from the ground. "It ain't dead, Sam, feel." He laid a finger on the rabbit's neck where a pulse beat rapidly. "Just stunned, you think?"

"We been long enough now. Leave it be."

"Let me take it. It ain't dead, Sam."

"Leave it be now. We fiddled enough of the day." Sarah held it cradled in her arms. "You don't have to let the dog have it if you don't want to," he conceded. She walked back down the road and put the bunny out of reach of the dog, under the overhanging brambles of a chokecherry bush.

"Sare," Sam said without looking back, "I said enough now." She ran back to the wagon and scrambled onto the seat.

Sam let her off in front of Imogene's. As soon as his back was turned, she caught up her skirts and ran up the path. Clay had pounded planks into the earth that spring to give Imogene footing through the mud, and Sarah's boots rang loud on the wood. Pulling up the latch of the door, she threw it open. Imogene was standing in the middle of the room; she turned when the door banged.

Sarah was through it and in her arms in a moment. "Imogene!" she cried. "We're going to have a baby!"

"Sarah, that's wonderful!" Imogene hugged her and held her away, resting her hands lightly on the girl's narrow hips. "We're going to do this right." She pulled her nose thoughtfully, her face grave. Sarah waited while Imogene paced, lost in thought.

"Shall I put on some water to boil?" Sarah asked in a timid voice.

"Not yet." Imogene looked at her and smiled for the first time since she'd received the news. "I think we've got a few months yet. We will learn. Everything."

"I meant for tea."

Imogene went with her into the kitchen and was measuring tea into the pot while Sarah put the kettle on. She put the canister down with a bump and turned to the young woman. Sarah was kneeling in front of the stove, striking a match. "Sarah, you must promise you will send for me the minute you feel anything. The moment. You must promise to make someone come for me."

The kindling caught and flared up. "I'll send for you, Imogene."

Imogene knelt and took her by the shoulders. "Promise."

"I promise."

"There are other things, too. We should start now. You mustn't let Sam make you do heavy work. And maybe you should eat certain things. I don't know." She stood and brushed off her skirts. "I'll find out. I'll get books."

Sarah put the kettle where the blaze was highest. "Women have babies every day. You oughtn't to worry so." She pulled her small mouth into a stern line, but still she looked pleased. "I'm going to have to call you Papa Grelznik."

They carried their tea into the front room and settled themselves near a window where the breeze blew in.

"I've wanted this so much," Sarah said. "When I was coming into town today, sitting up there beside Sam, I couldn't help thinking I'd stole something from him. All those times he thought he was taking from me, I was really taking from him.

"Something's mine. My baby. I look at everything—trees and birds, everything—and I feel a part of it. Like I was always skimming along just above, and now I'm down in it." She smoothed her hands over her belly. "Do I sound crazy? I don't talk like that in front of people."

"You sound a little crazy, but it is lovely. I wish everyone were as crazy as you." Imogene laughed uncertainly. "Papa Grelznik will take care of you, then it will be my baby, too. Would you mind?"

Sarah took the spinster's hand and pressed it to her stomach, though it was far too soon for life to show. "I wouldn't mind."

Sam came for Sarah at six o'clock, and she took her place beside him. Imogene watched until a bend in the road took them.

"You forget your packages?" Sam asked. "I ain't going back for them now. It'll have to wait till next trip."

"I never bought anything." She waited for a reply, but none was forthcoming. "Don't you want to know why?"

"You don't want a new dress, that's your business." Sam sounded nettled.

"I never got to the dry goods. I was talking with Imogene. The whole time." Sam wouldn't take his cue. He squinted uninterestedly, eyes front. The sun's last rays, knifing through the trees, barred the road with orange light. "Don't you want to know what we talked about?" Sarah asked.

"You're going to tell me anyways."

"I'm going to have a baby."

Sam looked over at her and a slow smile illuminated his beard. He slapped his knee and the horse put its ears back. He reached over and slapped Sarah's knee. "Good girl." Smiling, he lapsed back into silence. As the sun touched the horizon, he addressed her again. "You going to have a boy?"

"I don't know." Sarah's brow furrowed. "I don't know, Sam."

"You have a boy and I'll get you a present. A cart and your own pony to pull. You have a boy." Smiling, he slapped her knee again.

The wagon jolted around a bend in the road, bypassing the rock that had sheltered the rabbit earlier. The dog ran to thrust his long nose into the tangled underbrush where Sarah had hidden the cottontail. Whimpering with excitement, he pushed his face deep into the bushes but emerged empty-mouthed.

"Something must've got it," Sam said.

"Nothing got it. It came to and ran away."

Stars were starting to appear low in the sky; pinpricks of light in the summer-green evening. A chorus of crickets fiddled to the song of the frogs. Sarah untied her bonnet and pushed it off, letting it dangle down her back.

"Nothing got it." Leaning against the low backrest, humming softly to herself, she watched the stars come out.

12

THROUGH THE SUMMER AND INTO THE AUTUMN, SARAH'S PREGNANCY progressed. Sam, excited by his coming son, hired a woman to take over the heavy chores. Sarah spent the free hours the woman afforded her with Imogene, sewing tiny shirts and gowns and walking in the woods near town, planning and dreaming for the child she carried.

The memory of Mary Beth's lifeless face haunted Imogene, but she hid her fears and gloried in Sarah's good health and joy.

In the middle of a November night, a sharp rapping woke Imogene. Groping in the dark, she dragged a shapeless blue robe over her nightgown and hurried to the door. Walter Tolstonadge stood on the steps.

"Is it time?" Imogene asked.

"Sam said she's been having the pains for an hour, maybe two. Mam sent me to fetch Mrs. Thomas. I'm sorry to be getting you up like this, but Sam said Sarah's wanting you to come." Though Walter had learned stoicism over his father's knee, he couldn't keep the tremor of nervous excitement out of his voice.

"Quite right. Thank you for waking me. I'll be just a minute." She left the young man standing at the door and, lighting a candle, ran back into the bedroom. Beside the bed was a small bag, already packed. Imogene dressed hastily, snatched up the bag, and joined Walter outside. "A half-minute more," she told him. In her bag was a placard reading NO SCHOOL TODAY. She tacked it onto the schoolhouse door.

Lizbeth sat in the back of Sam's carryall, wedged between Mrs. Thomas, the midwife, and her daughter, Valerie. Imogene rode in the front beside Walter. A freezing wind scoured the night clean, and stars, undimmed by a moon, hung close to the earth. Several inches of old snow covered the ground, crunching under the wheels. Imogene buttoned her cloak beneath her chin and turned the collar up. Walter offered her half of the coarse blanket tucked around his knees. As she took it, Lizbeth crawled over the seat to sit with them.

Leaning against her mother's shoulder, Valerie snored, a purring sound. "Wake up now," Mrs. Thomas said testily. "Ain't it just like a baby to come along in the middle of the night. It must be close on one o'clock."

"It's somewhat past ten," Walter corrected.

"Hmph. Feels later. Will be, before this baby is ready to come into the world, I can tell you that. First baby. Mightn't be born till late tomorrow. Maybe not even then. Not much hips on the Tolstonadge girl. I guess I'd best be saying 'young Mrs. Ebbitt,' considering. Hardly enough room for what's been in, let alone room for a baby to get out." The midwife had a good laugh at her own joke. Valerie snorted herself awake under her mother's prodding. "You stay awake, girl. Time you was learning midwifing. A trade's a good thing for a girl that mightn't marry young." Unoffended, Valerie settled her fat behind more comfortably on the seat and looked around with sleepy eyes.

"My Val's helped out before." Mrs. Thomas directed her stream of chatter at Imogene's back. "But it was all easy birthings. She ain't never seen what can go wrong. Baby all 'round the wrong way and not wanting to come out at all—sometimes the little things get theirselves so twisted up they just tear the life out of them that's having them. Make themselves orphans before they're rightly born. You ain't seen nothing go wrong," she told her daughter, "and that's, of course, what a midwife's needing to know. The rest of the time you need hardly be there. Folks'll have them by themselves if you're late. I've seen it happen. They'll holler for you loud enough if something goes wrong. Except the fever, there's nothing you can do for that. Fever's God's will, is all. Gets a lot of babies and their mamas with them." Valerie had pulled a bit of bread from one of the pockets in her cloak and now munched it placidly. Imogene, her spine growing rigid under the flow of words, swallowed hard and wiped her hands on her handkerchief. Lizbeth had snuggled close to her for warmth and comfort.

"Sister going to die?" she asked, near tears.

"No. She will not die," Imogene declared. Her vehemence startled the child and silenced the voluble Mrs. Thomas.

At the farm, lights were burning in the kitchen and the upstairs window. Imogene jumped to the ground before the wagon came to a full stop, and hurried into the house.

Upstairs, lying in state, propped up by pillows, Sarah was talking cheerfully with her mother and Gracie. She wore a new bed jacket and her hair was tied back in the blue satin ribbon Imogene had bought for her. A fire burned merrily in the little fireplace at the end of the room, and lamps and candles brightened the walls. Sarah had a patchwork coverlet over her lap, and on the dresser were teacups and little cakes her mother had made. Mam knitted in a broad chair by the fire.

The bedroom door banged open, setting the dresser mirror swinging, and Imogene stepped over the threshold. With her hair still disheveled from her bed, and her lips squeezed white between a frost-red nose and chin, she looked fearsome. Conversation stopped and three pairs of eyes turned toward the door.

"Miss Grelznik, you look like the devil himself been chasing you," Gracie exclaimed.

"What's wrong?" Alarmed, Sarah pulled herself farther up in the bed. "Is there something wrong?"

Shamefaced, Imogene closed the door and shrugged off her cape. She crossed to the bedside to take Sarah's hand. "I had myself worked into such a fluster that by the time we got here I was ready to deliver the baby myself the moment I stepped through the door."

Mam smiled. "It'll be a bit yet. Edna here?"

"And Valerie," Imogene replied.

"I'm glad you're here," Sarah said. "I guess Walter did drag you out of bed. I told Sam to make him promise, but I thought Walter'd go scaredy-cat anyway. Would you like some tea?" Imogene nodded gratefully. "Gracie, would you run down and brew up a fresh pot? Make plenty; I hear Mrs. Thomas and Valerie on the stairs, and I expect they could use a little warming up." Sarah was serene in the role of hostess.

"It feels like a party." Imogene squeezed her hand. Margaret smiled but said nothing.

A great deal of wheezing and puffing announced Edna Thomas and her daughter. A timid knock on the door was drowned in a gust of voice. "For heaven's sake, Sam, there's no need to knock at your own bedroom. You been here before, or you'd not be needing my services now." Mrs. Thomas pushed through, and Sam retreated back down the stairs, into the company of Emmanuel and Walter.

Mam called him back. "Sam, would you tell the boys they can go on home now? Most likely I'll be here all night and a good part of tomorrow. There's no sense in them losing sleep. They have to work in the morning."

"Ma, one's coming," Sarah cried and, holding her breath, clutched Imogene's hand. The schoolteacher held tight and stroked the young woman's arm.

"They're coming right along," Mam said to Mrs. Thomas.

When it had passed, Sarah lay back against the pillow and smiled. Imogene was visibly shaken. "It's not so bad. Not for a baby," Sarah reassured her.

Gracie returned with the tea, Lizbeth carrying the cups, and the women settled in. They talked quietly, giving Sarah the support of their affection and the comfort of their experience.

Sometime after midnight, Sam, armed with blankets Mam had unearthed from the hall closet, bedded down on the living room floor.

The hours crawled by and Mam sent Lizbeth across the hall with a comforter and pillow to make herself a nest on the cot Sam had slept in as a child. The room would serve as the nursery when the baby was older. Margaret let her take a lamp to leave burning low to chase the goblins from behind the piled boxes and dusty trunks.

Through the dark morning hours, Sarah strained and cried. Just before sunrise, Sam left the house. Imogene watched him from a high window—a small, dark figure under sullen skies. He was burning brush today. Mam sent Mrs. Thomas and Valerie downstairs to get some sleep, and settled in the chair by the fire to nap. Imogene wouldn't leave the room. She read aloud to Sarah, sitting on a hard stool so she wouldn't doze.

Lunch came and went, Sam eating cold meat alone in the kitchen, Mam and Imogene eating sparingly in the bedroom and trying to coax Sarah to take a little food. Downstairs, the Thomases still slept. Grace and Lizbeth, grown tired of waiting, had wandered outside to play.

Near three o'clock that afternoon, Sarah's labor neared its end. Gray had replaced the red in her cheeks, and her damp hair lay close to her head. Another contraction wracked her; she bit down, trying not to scream. When she lay back, Imogene wiped her forehead with a cool cloth. Mrs. Thomas folded back her nightgown and kneaded her stomach, her dusky fingers, engrained with the dirt of years, expertly prodding the strained flesh. Sluggish with sleep and a natural dullness of mind, Valerie watched over her mother's shoulder, obeying commands to feel here and notice there. The girl's plump hands were less grubby than Edna's, but only from lack of time. As the examination progressed, Imogene grew increasingly agitated. Finally she laid her hand on Mrs. Thomas's arm.

"I must ask you to wash." Edna looked up without comprehension. "Your hands. You must wash your hands and arms. Valerie too, if she's to touch her."

"For heaven's sake," Mrs. Thomas huffed, "of all the nonsense . . ."

"You must wash before you touch her again," Imogene insisted quietly, her fingers closing on the other woman's wrist. Mrs. Tolstonadge looked on in silence, and obvious disapproval. Sarah sucked in her breath as another wave of pain built.

"It ain't long now," Mrs. Thomas cautioned Imogene. "Baby's coming."

"Don't send her away," Sarah cried. The wave broke and she screamed.

"Now look here, Edna's been—"

Imogene cut Margaret off. "Wash. Quickly." She locked eyes with the midwife, and Mrs. Thomas, grumbling, retreated to the washstand. "Use some of the hot water there in the fire. There's a brush in the drawer. Above the elbows." Imogene issued instructions from the bed as Mrs. Thomas rolled up her sleeves and soaped her arms thoroughly. Sarah was screaming again, holding fast to Imogene's hand.

"Mam!" she gasped and her mother was beside her, holding her other hand as she bore down. Margaret glared at Imogene over her daughter's head.

"Fine time to get persnickety," she said under her breath. The midwife was back with them, shoving the blankets from the foot of the bed, her hands still dripping.

"Pull her up there some," she ordered. "Let her hold on and push against you. Give her some help." Valerie, as white as a sheet, crept up close behind Margaret and, unnoticed, hid her eyes.

Knees held wide by the midwife, Sarah pushed with all her strength. Sweat beaded on her forehead and ran down the side of her face, wetting Imogene's cheek where it pressed against hers.

"Push now," Mrs. Thomas urged.

"I can't," Sarah sobbed. "Please. I want to go home, Ma. Please. I don't want to do this anymore." She writhed against Imogene. The teacher was behind her, a backboard of flesh and bone.

"Come on, my dear," Imogene breathed in her ear. "Just once more." Taking a deep breath, Sarah pushed and the sweat ran in rivulets. Her knuckles turned white as she clenched her hands.

"It's coming. Thata girl. Thata girl." Mrs. Thomas talked her through. The baby's head was emerging; the mirror over the chest of drawers reflected the round mass pushing through. Sarah's skin ripped under the strain, and blood poured around the baby's skull. Valerie looked up, saw the image in the glass, and stopped breathing. "It's huge," she cried. "It's too big."

"You hush!" Mam hissed.

"The baby's head is out," Mrs. Thomas called cheerfully. "The worst's over. One more." Again Sarah caught her breath and strained until the veins stood out on her temples, and the infant was delivered into the midwife's waiting hands. Exhausted, Sarah fell back against Imogene. "Mam?" she whispered.

Margaret looked at the squirming, blood-covered bundle in Edna's hands. "A boy. He's beautiful, hon." The tears welled up in Sarah's eyes as Mrs. Thomas laid the newborn child on his mother's stomach. She put her hand on her son's tiny head and smiled. "He looks like a wee, wise, little old man."

Tears also streaked Imogene's face as she reached timidly to touch a little clenched fist with her finger. "He's perfect."

The cord stopped pulsing and Mrs. Thomas cut it, Imogene insisting that she soap and rinse the knife beforehand, the way the black woman had in Philadelphia. Sarah was delivered of the afterbirth, but she still bled where the flesh had been torn around the birth canal. Mrs. Thomas packed the boiled rags that Sarah used during her menses against the tear and made Sarah as comfortable as possible. Mam changed the bed with the help of a sick and shaky Valerie.

When the baby had been bathed and lay at Sarah's breast, and Imogene had washed the new mother's face and brushed her hair back into its satin ribbon; when the soiled bedding had been spirited downstairs to be burned on the trash heap and the bed was fresh and clean; when all traces of the agony and the blood and the sweat were cleared away and hidden like the secrets of female necromancers—only then did Mam call Gracie and send her to the field to fetch Sam.

The girl returned out of breath. Sam wouldn't come. He said he had some burning to finish, and he'd be in around six o'clock. Angry, Mam stomped about the room, straightening the night's undoings.

Lost in the wonders of the new child, Sarah and Imogene were indifferent to Sam's absence. They lay on the bed, the baby between them, counting his fingers and toes and expressing delight at his every move and sound.

Mam finished tidying. "I'm going downstairs to get a bite to eat. Edna, Val—I expect you could use some food, too." As they left, Mam paused in the doorway. "Sarah, you try and rest some." It was an admonishment directed toward Imogene as much as it was an instruction for Sarah.

A red sun peeked over the windowsill and the fire burned low in the grate. Side by side, the child safe in the crook of Sarah's arm, she and Imogene slept. Two faces, one pretty, the other strong and lined, rested beside the bland and rosy face of the newborn baby. Sam stood uncertainly at the foot of the bed. He cleared his throat and Imogene awoke. "Sarah," he said. His wife opened her eyes. Sam looked at her and his son. The spinster slipped from the bed to occupy herself winding some yarn that had tumbled from Margaret's lap.

"It's a boy, Sam." Sarah pushed the blanket down so he could see the child's face, pink against her breast.

"You got yourself a pony cart," the man replied.

Imogene sniffed audibly.

Sam came around to sit on the stool, looking at the wizened

little face, wrinkled and red. "We'll call him Matthew." The baby hiccoughed and the nipple slipped from his mouth. Sarah adjusted him nearer and he nursed again, gurgling his contentment.

"Matthew. I like that." She smiled at her husband. "You want to hold him, Sam?"

He scratched his beard. "No, you do the holding." Carefully, Sam touched his son's face. His fingers were immense beside the minute nose and tiny, round chin. Embarrassed by his oafishness, Sam drew his hand back. "Ugly little fella. Seems healthy, though." He stood up. "Miss Grelznik, I'm running the girls home. If you need a ride, we'll be going in a few minutes."

Imogene stopped to kiss Sarah's cheek before following Sam downstairs. "He's a beautiful baby," she whispered.

13

"NOT A THING, MISS GRELZNIK." JACKSON POKED HIS YELLOW-stained fingers through a pile of mail. "You've been here religious since you got that letter from Philadelphia last week. You must be expecting something special. It's a bit of a walk out here."

Imogene smiled and ignored the stationmaster's hints. "Good day, Mr. Jackson."

"Don't you go trusting to the weather this time of year; March is a funny month," he warned as she stepped outside. "Wouldn't do to have the schoolteacher froze to death."

Joseph Cogswell crossed the tracks to meet her as she left the station. "Good morning, Joseph. Aren't you needed at the mine office this morning?"

"Morning," he returned. "I saw you coming in here and quick came down for a word with you. The payroll's been done, there won't be much clerking until Monday. I'll be back before the men start coming for their pay." He pulled his hat off and scratched behind one ear. Uneasiness radiated from him like heat from a stone. "Imogene, I had a letter from Philadelphia." The school-teacher's back stiffened and she seemed even taller than she was. "It pretty much concerns you."

"I've been expecting it," she said, half to herself. "Of course it wouldn't come to me. He sent it to you."

He met her eye reluctantly. "I'd rather we didn't discuss it here."

"I won't be in most of the day," she said, and left him, hat in hand, standing in the middle of the road.

"Imogene! I'll come by after work!" he called after her, but she didn't slow down or turn.

Jackson had come out on the station steps. "What's the row about?"

Joseph jerked his chin at Imogene's retreating back. "Schoolteacher."

"She's had a burr under her saddle all week," Jackson said.

Imogene closed the door of her house and slid the bolt home. Pulling the chair away from the window so she couldn't be seen from the street, she picked up a letter from the desk. She had read it so many times the folds were in danger of tearing.

17 February 1875

My Dear Imogene,

Mr. Utterback and I have had some rather bad news. William's brother has taken ill; he's an old man and William feels he may not recover this time. We will have left for Holland by the time this arrives. I'm sorry we shall miss our summer visit. Heaven knows when we will be home again.

I have taken the liberty of giving Mr. Ramsey your address. I know thee forbade it, but Mary Beth's little Rosemary is such a frail child and I'm afraid to leave him with no one to turn to—he is so grateful for the money you send.

Affectionately,
Alice Utterback

Imogene pressed the heels of her hands against her eyes to blot out the leering image of Darrel Aiken. If Ramsey had her address, Darrel Aiken would have it. Now Joseph Cogswell's demeanor proved it. The cat jumped onto the desk and sat on the letter, swishing her tail for attention, and Imogene stroked the yellow fur. "Hello, Dandy cat," she said wearily. Dandy began to purr. "What am I going to do?" The cat batted at her hand as she rubbed her eyes again. "Oh, for a little cat mind." She scratched the outthrust chin. "A little cat mind like yours." Dandy butted her head against the teacher to get her ears scratched. "I can feel the foundations shaking again. He means to drive me even from here. But you needn't worry your little cat head. I am your world, aren't I?" Suddenly, Imogene pushed herself to her feet, the cat forgotten. "I've got to get out."

Outside, a pale winter sun shone from a sky full of white mare's tails. There was no wind to sway the naked tree branches, and the day was unseasonably mild. February's snow was beginning to melt in patches, and people were out of doors taking the air, knowing that winter was far from over, tomorrow might bring another blizzard.

Staying near the edge of the road where the ground was driest, Imogene set off west, out of town, at a brisk pace. Bits of earth, kicked up by her heels, speckled the hem of her dress, and the half-frozen mud caked on her boots and wedged under her heels. Several wagons stopped, calling offers of a ride, but she waved them on with thanks.

By the time she reached the Ebbitt farm, she had walked off some of the anxiety that gripped her. She stopped at the gate to smooth her hair back into its pins. The dog saw her and set up a ruckus that brought Sarah to the window and then to the front door. She was dressed prettily in bright blue checks, her hair tied up in a rag.

"You stop!" she hollered at the dog. The barking grew shrill and Sarah lobbed a piece of wood at his head to obtain silence. "I hate that awful old dog. I wish Sam would get rid of him. Especially now, with the baby." She kissed Imogene on the cheek. "Did you walk all that way?" Sarah ushered her in and took her wrap. The house was warm and smelled of food and babies. A fire roared in the big cookstove and another, smaller fire blazed in the potbellied stove in the front room. Imogene went straight to Matthew. He waved his tiny fists from a basket set among piles of dried beans on the kitchen table; Sarah was in the midst of culling.

"I needed some air," Imogene said. "And I needed to see new things today. Old irritations were getting me down in the mouth."

"Old irritations?"

Imogene looked at Sarah; her young face was smooth and happy, her cheeks still softly rounded from the weight she had gained when she was carrying Matthew, the hazel eyes wide, innocent, vulnerable despite the hard year behind her. The teacher looked away. "It's nothing, really. Silliness. I'm sure it will all blow over." Sarah still looked troubled, so Imogene brightened her voice and smiled. "Really. It's nothing. I needed to see the baby."

Pushing her face near Matthew's, she rubbed his nose with hers and was rewarded with a heartfelt gurgle. She scooped him out of the basket and cradled him. The baby's soft brown curls feathered onto a moon face. His nose and mouth were clearly defined, and his blue eyes bright and interested. He looked gravely over Imogene's arm at his mother and wiggled his feet. "He'll have to go East to school," Imogene said seriously. "There will come a point where my teaching won't begin to be enough. And you meet people at the University that help to smooth your way in business."

"Sam wants him to take over the farm."

"That's nonsense. If Sam wants someone to take up with the carts and cows when he leaves, then let Walter do it."

Sarah's eyes lighted up at a sudden thought. "You said you wanted to see something new. Do you?"

"Why? What have you got that is new?"

Sarah threw her apron on the table and pulled on an old coat of Sam's. "Better get your coat on. It's turning nasty, looks like." Imogene nestled the baby back into his basket, and having shoved it so far from the edge of the table that nothing short of an earthquake would dislodge it, she followed Sarah out the kitchen door.

Inside the barn it was dark and cold. Along the sides, where the cattle fed, the heat of the livestock softened the air. Summer's mountain of hay had dwindled to the height of a man, exposing twenty feet of plank floor. A cart sat in the open space, a square wooden box with a bench seat just barely large enough for two people. It had a fresh coat of dark blue paint and the seat had been padded and covered in sandy-colored canvas.

"The pony's in the paddock out back. He's the color of the seat, with a lighter mane and tail," Sarah said as Imogene admired the little conveyance.

"So this is the chariot for the firstborn son. I had forgotten."

"I had too, but Sam remembered and about a week ago he came home with the pony tied on behind the wagon and the cart just sort of tumbled in the back. It was broken in a couple of places and all rough and splintery, but he fixed it up nice for me. I've already driven it twice, before the thaw made the roads so sloppy. Maybe Sam'll let me drive you into town."

"Have you gone so far alone?"

"No. Just to home and back. And Walter was with me on the way back. But I could do it. Driving a cart's just fun, but it ain't hard. *Isn't* hard."

"You wouldn't dare take the baby would you? The seat is so narrow, I'd be afraid he would fall off."

"Look behind." There was a wedge-shaped crate made of sturdy slate and nailed to the cart bed. "Sam put that in for me so Matthew could ride. Sam's going to be a good father, maybe. Mam says he's sure showing the earmarks. He's different now that the baby's come."

However, Sam said the roads were too bad to take the cart out, and Sarah solaced herself by walking a little way with Imogene before saying good-bye. Imogene did not tell her of the letter.

The wind had come up and the day had turned cold. The schoolteacher wrapped her scarf over her nose and mouth, walking as fast as the uneven footing would permit to stay warm. She had gone nearly half the distance when Mr. Jenkins happened by with a load of goods he was bringing from the depot, and gave her a ride. The closer they got to the town, the more withdrawn Imogene became, losing the glow that Sarah and her child had given her. By the time Mr. Jenkins let her off in front of the dry goods store, she was as agitated as she had been when she left Joseph that morning.

"You'd better get yourself home and indoors," Mr. Jenkins said. "Looks like maybe you're coming down with something. You feeling all right? One of the girls'll make you something hot to drink."

Imogene came out of her reverie at the sound of his voice. "No, thank you. I'm fine. A bit chilled. Perhaps you're right, I'd best take myself home straight away."

"Sure I can't drive you the last bit?"

"No. Thank you."

He watched her walk away. She was a little unsteady and stumbled over the snow, which had refrozen into lumps. "Coming down with something," he said, and nodded to himself.

Joseph was waiting for her when she came up the walk. He declined her offer of refreshment and sat down on the edge of a straight-backed chair, dangling his hat nervously between his knees.

"This is not a social call, as I've said," he began. "There's been a letter from the East, from a Mr. Aiken."

"Darrel Aiken."

"That's right. Darrel Aiken."

"May I see the letter?"

"I don't have it with me. Judith has it." He had the grace to look ashamed. "I'm sorry. Anyway, it's not fit for a decent woman to see."

"Judith has it," Imogene repeated.

"Judith picks up the mail. She opened it by mistake." Imogene waited, her hands folded in her lap. He seemed at a loss for words and sat turning his hat.

"Go on," Imogene said.

"He makes a lot of accusations."

"Do you believe them?"

"No, I don't."

"Well, then." Imogene started to rise, dismissing him.

"It's too serious a thing to ignore," he went on, and she sat back down. "The letter says you lost your post because you were morally unfit to teach."

"I see. What are you going to do?"

"Nothing for the present. As I said, I don't believe any of it to be true. If you want to give me an explanation, I'll listen." He gave her a moment to reply, but she said nothing. "That's it, then."

Before he reached the door she stopped him. "Am I to stop teaching?" she demanded.

He smiled disarmingly. "I've not arranged for a new teacher, Imogene. I've written the school where you taught in Philadelphia. I expect to hear in a week or so. I'm sure it'll all get cleared up and no harm done."

"Mr. Utterback is in Holland."

"I didn't write William. There's a Mr. Thresher there now. If he says it's not true, and I expect he will, then you'll still be teaching here. I'll destroy the letter and that'll be the end of it, as far as I'm concerned. As far as anyone is concerned. I'll see to that. I just wanted you to know what had happened and where I stood."

"The town meeting for the school-board elections are April third. Will I preside?"

"I'm sure I'll hear before then, Imogene."

She held herself together to open the door for him, and when he was gone, down the walk and into the street, she slammed it with all the force she could bring to bear. Dandy, asleep under the table, raced into the bedroom, her tail fuzzed into a bottlebrush.

14

EVERY DAY, IN THE EVENINGS, WHEN THE MINERS STREAMED DOWN the main street like a river of coal, blackening the snow with the dust from their clothes, Imogene watched for Joseph to come up her walk. Sometimes she would meet him on the street or in a shop. If they were alone he'd say, "Nothing yet. Perhaps tomorrow," and smile or touch her arm in silent reassurance.

The third of April came, the day of the school-board elections, and still Imogene had not heard. In the late afternoon, smart in a navy skirt and a white shirtwaist, she checked her image in the glass one last time. A black fitted jacket was folded on the chair beside her; she put it on and pulled her sleeves straight. Outside the window, the sky was dark and low. Gusts blew scattered pellets of snow against the panes. People hurried in from the street, holding on to their hats, their mufflers and collars turned up against the cold. The school was filling up.

Imogene opened the door and the cat darted in, nearly tripping her as she stepped outside. The lilac bushes in front of the school had only just started to bud. The sudden cold would kill the blooms this year.

Her name was shouted on the wind; from far down the street, Joseph Cogswell was hailing her. Imogene waited, making no move to meet him, and he broke into a trot.

"I've got to talk with you," he said as soon as he'd recovered his breath. "Can we go inside?"

"You can tell me here," Imogene returned. Her gabardine skirts snapped like whips in the wind.

"Very well." He rubbed his nose and looked around uncomfortably. "Very well. I'm sorry to do this, Imogene, but I'm going to have to ask you to resign your position as a teacher. I got a telegram from Philadelphia."

"I'm not to teach anymore?"

"I'm sorry." He handed her the telegram.

TO JOSEPH COGSWELL
CALLIOPE, PENNSYLVANIA

IMOGENE GRELZNIK WAS FIRED ON SEPTEMBER 21ST 1873
FOR IMMORAL CONDUCT TOWARD A FORMER STUDENT.

SPENCER THRESHER
ACTING PRINCIPAL
SOUTH PHILADELPHIA PRIMARY SCHOOL

Imogene crushed the paper and dropped it in the slush. The wind rolled it under the steps.

"I want you to come to the meeting, Imogene. I'll just say that you've decided to take your leave and you can say whatever you like for the reason. There's no need for anyone to be hurt more than need be—you've done well by us, and that's not changed. We'll make it a farewell and you can go or stay as you see fit." He talked quietly, comfortingly, lightly holding her elbow as though he were merely escorting her to dinner or the theater. Numbly, she let herself be guided the short distance to the school.

Someone had lighted the stove, and with the fire and the press of people, the schoolroom was pleasantly warm. Sarah sat with her mother near the front, the baby playing happily on his grandmother's lap, his bright eyes seeming to miss nothing. Clay and Karen sat with Mrs. Beard. Karen, silent and lumpish between clay and her mother-in-law, looked as though she had not bathed or washed her hair since the wedding. Clay held their daughter on his lap. Her little fist patted his hand, barely big enough to close on his sausagelike fingers.

Mrs. Cogswell stood apart. Her gaze fixed on her husband the moment he entered with Imogene.

"Joseph . . ."

"You stay out of this, Judith." And he was past, smiling, greeting people, leading Imogene to the head of the classroom.

There was a smattering of applause as Imogene reached the front of the room. Sarah waved, but the schoolteacher didn't see her. Joseph seated her near the wall and, stepping behind the desk, rapped for silence with a ruler. Mothers gathered toddlers off the floor and onto laps, where they couldn't get into mischief, and people shuffled expectantly.

"Before we start with the elections and whatnot," Joseph began, "there's something I'd like to say. Imogene Grelznik has been the teacher here for three years. Three years is the longest spell we've had a teacher. And in that time, Miss Grelznik's turned the school from a drafty shack used by subscription teachers who charged two dollars a head—and drank most of that—into a warm, fit place for us to send our children. And if words and energy could have done it, she'd have built a brand-new school. For the first time, youngsters coming out of Calliope can stand up beside their cousins schooled in the East and not be ashamed. I think we're all willing to admit Miss Grelznik's responsible for all this."

Mrs. Cogswell's face was growing a deep shade of crimson. Every time her husband looked toward the back of the room, she'd tried to catch his attention and he'd avoided her eye. Finally she broke her aggressive silence. "This has gone far enough," she declared.

There was a confused silence; the people looked from Judith to her husband and back.

"Judith," Mr. Cogswell warned, "before you say anything, let me finish."

"I will not. I've stood here and listened to this long enough. You and that schoolteacher of yours have been pulling the wool over the eyes of this town. People have a right to know." The words snapped out like thrown stones, and no one had time to respond. In her hand was a brown envelope with the words *Head man at school Calliope Penna* scrawled across the face. She took out a folded sheet of paper and opened it.

"Judith, that's enough," Mr. Cogswell shouted, but all eyes were on his wife.

"This letter came in the mail over a week ago, and I kept my tongue in my head, but I think the time's come it would be a wickedness to keep quiet. This letter came over a week ago, like I said, and I take no pleasure in reading it. It's from a Mr. Darrel Aiken of Philadelphia."

Mrs. Cogswell had everyone's attention. She began to read: " 'I would have wrote sooner but Imogene Grelznik made so careful to keep her whereabouts a secret it's took me this long to find her. If she's teaching in your school then whatever she told you about leaving here is a lie. She was run off for behaving indecent and immoral toward a young girl, my sister, who is now dead. I found her acting with my sister the way only a man ought to act toward a woman who is his lawful wedded wife.

" 'I wrote to warn you against her that she craves unnatural things and I don't want no brother or father to have to see what I saw betwixt them two and live knowing it. Respectfully yours, Darrel Aiken.' "

Judith finished. People continued to look at her because they couldn't look at Imogene. Mrs. Cogswell folded the page, creasing it sharply between her thumb and forefinger, and laid it down on a desk. "Somebody had to do it," she said, "and I waited longer than was right."

Sarah held Matthew to her, her lips against his hair, and watched Imogene. The schoolteacher sat erect, spots of color burning in her cheeks. As people found voice and a confused babble arose, Imogene crossed to the desk and picked the ruler out of Joseph's hand. It cracked on the desktop, and there was quiet. Holding the eyes of the people she knew, she looked from one to another: mothers and fathers of the children she taught, merchants from the shops where she traded, former students—she held them and she began to speak.

"Mary Beth Aiken was one of my students and a very dear friend. I was there when she died." Imogene's voice was strong, defiance clipping the edges. "Darrel Aiken is a drunken ne'er-do-well. If on the strength of this man's letter you would condemn me . . ." People were settling back into their seats, the power in Imogene stilling their fear.

Karen looked around the room. People were relaxing; Miss Grelznik was winning them back. Her eye lit on her husband, and the handsome face of his brother flashed through her mind. Hatred filled her, she jumped to her feet, her chair crashing over against the floorboards. Pointing at the schoolmistress, she cried, "I saw them!"

All eyes turned to her. Karen swelled with the attention. "I saw her kissing Sarah Tolstonadge," she lied viciously. As one, the townsfolk took a quick breath. Pleased, Karen embroidered on the lie: "They was doing it when they didn't know I was there. I was looking through the window—the bedroom window."

Sarah's eyes grew wide. "Karen," she cried, "that isn't true! You know it isn't!"

"Imogene was kissing on her like a man. In the bedroom. And Sarah pregnant out to here," Karen insisted and, looking pleased with herself, maintained a smug silence while Sarah's world unraveled.

"You're lying," Sarah breathed, then screamed, "You're lying!"

Chairs were scraping, people coming to their feet.

"No!" Imogene shouted. "It is not true. Not Sarah. No! Please, God, listen to me!" Her words were swallowed up; everyone was yelling at once. Sam Ebbitt pushed through the milling crowd and grabbed his wife by the upper arm, jerking her to her feet. Sarah cried out and held tight to the baby. Sam plucked her son from her arms, handing him, shrieking, to Margaret. "Look after the boy," he commanded, and half-led, half-dragged Sarah toward the door.

Curtains drawn and the door bolted, no candles lit against the night, Imogene rocked herself before a cold grate, her eyes open but unseeing. Unsettled by her strange behavior, Dandy had given up crying for her dinner and vanished into the bedroom.

Around midnight the snow turned to sleet and the wind drove it against the windows and down the chimney in icy drafts. Roused by the cold, Imogene lay down in the bed fully clothed and pulled the covers over her. Dandy came to nestle against her warmth, kneading at the pillow with her claws and purring.

Several hours before dawn, Imogene was snatched from an uneasy doze by a low thump. Motionless, she lay listening. Her breathing rushed loud in the dead air of the room and she could hear her heart pounding against her ribs. She held her breath. There was nothing—then a soft, sliding sound. Throwing back the covers, she crossed to the bedroom window and, pulling the curtains apart a bare half-inch, put her eye to the slit. The storm had blown itself out. The night was moonless and the shadows protected their secrets. She settled the curtains closed again. A barely audible cry, seeming to have no place of origin, came to her through the close darkness. It sounded like the muffled wail of a baby. The hairs prickled on the back of her neck as she groped her way to the bedroom door. "Who's there?" she whispered. Her voice was higher than usual, and she cleared her throat. Nothing. Slipping her shoes off, she padded silently into the kitchen and grabbed the matches from the stove. Back in the living room, she struck one and held it over her head. The room was empty but for the two glowing eyes of the cat, watching curiously from the bedroom. The match burned to her fingers and she shook it out. Again in the dark the sound was there—the soft shush of something rubbing against the house. She grabbed up the fire tongs. Creeping on noiseless feet, she made her way to the door and pressed her ear against it. A faint sound of scratching could be heard through the planks. Holding her weight against the wood to relieve the bolt, she drew it back, careful not to let the metal rasp; then, grasping the handle, she raised the fire tongs and jerked the door inward. It pulled out of her hands as a shapeless bundle of humanity fell against it, and Sarah Ebbitt crumpled to the floor. Faint starlight picked out her features above the cumbersome layers of an oversized man's coat.

Imogene lowered the fire tongs and dropped to her knees beside the prone figure.

"I came in the pony cart," Sarah mumbled. Her eyes were lost and she was nearly senseless.

"Shhh. Shhh." The schoolteacher lifted her to her feet, helped her inside, and rebolted the door.

Imogene shoved the pothook to the back of the fireplace. The kettle was heavy, full of molasses boiling down for candy. Quickly she built a fire and lit the lamps. Sarah wouldn't sit, but leaned woodenly against the mantel, her forehead resting on the stone; she trembled until her skirts quaked. Sam's old mackinaw hung loose on her small frame, the sleeves falling over her hands. Her long hair tumbled in a mat around her face, hiding her eyes.

"It'll be warm in half a minute," Imogene said. Gently she took the coat from the young woman's shoulders. As it slid down, she saw that her blouse was dark with blood, the red stain feathering under her arms and trailing in colored streamers down her skirt, where the shirred cloth soaked up the blood. "Oh Lord. Oh my Lord." Imogene whipped the coat to the floor.

"He whipped me." Sarah slumped against the stone. "I came here in the pony cart." She was slurring her words, her hands clamped on the mantel for support. Imogene had to pry them loose. One was swollen, the fingers puffy and discolored. Imogene took it between her own hands as gently as if it were a wounded bird. "Your hand," she said softly. "The one you paint with. What did he do to your hand?"

Sarah looked at it, noticing it for the first time. Painfully she flexed the fingers; they were not broken. "Oh." She blinked to clear her thoughts. "I must have hurt it on Sam's face."

"You hit Sam Ebbitt? My dear, whatever possessed you?"

Sarah hung her head. "He called you a name."

"My little love," Imogene whispered.

Sarah's knees were buckling. She could no longer stand. "Can I sit down now?" She pleaded.

"Of course! I'm not thinking right. Of course you can." Imogene helped her kneel on the rug before the hearth.

Sarah's mouth was dry, and she tried to swallow unsuccessfully. "My back. He made me take my clothes off and hold to the bedpost."

"Let me look." A dozen small wooden buttons, sticky with blood, closed the back of Sarah's shirtwaist, another ten or twelve hung loose where her fingers had not been able to manage them. The blouse fell open and Sarah held it over her chest. Imogene turned the girl's back to the firelight. A whip had cut heavily, the lash splitting the flesh every time it was laid on. Five slashes clawed from her right shoulder to her waist, like the track of an immense cat. Blood had poured down, obscuring the skin and making odd patterns where the fabric of her shirtwaist had left its mark.

Imogene stared at the ruined back; the fine white skin cut to ribbons, black knotted blood puckering the edges of the gashes.

Sarah would carry these scars with her always.

"My poor darling." Tenderly, Imogene ran her finger down the line of Sarah's neck and shoulder, the young woman's skin like silk to her touch. "Oh, my poor dear."

Sarah let her blouse fall and the firelight played over her breasts. They were heavy with milk, the nipples large and dark against her skin. A long, tremulous breath quivered deep in her chest; she turned to Imogene. "He hurt me bad."

The older woman's eyes were bright with unshed tears and there was a streak of blood on her face where she had brushed back a lock of her hair. "I know he did," she said softly, and gathered Sarah to her, stroking her hair and talking quietly. Sarah tilted her head back, eyes closed.

"Dear girl, I wish I could keep you safe. Here with me," Imogene whispered. "But you must go back to Sam. My love, you've a baby now." Sarah locked her hands behind Imogene's neck and held so tightly that the schoolteacher had to fight for breath. "You will heal. Go home. People will forget." Sarah clung to her as a man holds to a raft in stormy seas.

The latch rattled; the women froze and instinctively Imogene's arm came up to protect Sarah. With sudden violence the door burst open. The bracket that held the deadbolt ripped from the jamb, spraying splintered wood across the room. Red-faced, neck swollen with anger, Sam Ebbitt filled the doorway.

"I thought you might've run here." Paying no more attention to Imogene than he would to a cat, Sam pulled his wife from the floor and shoved her toward the rocker. "Get your clothes on." Sarah fell to her knees, toppling the chair. He booted her in the rump, and her face smacked into the wood. A thin line of blood traced down her chin from a split lip. Sam grasped her by the back of the neck and, forcing her left arm behind her, wrenched off her wedding ring. Then, shoving his wife's face near the hot metal grate, he said, "in the Bible they brand whores. I ought to brand you, let you wear what you are on your face."

Imogene pushed by him and snatched the pothook to her. As she closed her hand over the iron rod, her palm sizzled, and the smell of burning flesh was in the room. She lifted the half-filled kettle from the hook and slopped some of the boiling sugar syrup down Sam's back.

With a roar like a wounded bear, he released Sarah and fell back. Imogene held the pot high, ready to throw the rest in his face. Sam started forward and she cocked her arm. "I'll blind you, Sam Ebbitt. I swear to God I will."

"You're the devil's own." He spat, and the spittle struck her shoulder, hanging there in a gob. "You've taken her; take her to wife and burn in hell." He hurled Sarah's wedding ring at her where she cowered on the floor. "God forgive you, because I won't!" And Sam was gone. They could hear the pony cart drive away, his horse tied on behind; the silence he left was so absolute it rang in their ears.

Imogene put the kettle back on the hob and closed the door, pushing a chair against it to keep it from swinging open. The fire brushed Sarah's face with orange light as she crouched, half-naked and sobbing, by the hearth. In the fold of her skirt, something glinted dully. Imogene knelt beside her and lifted the wedding ring from where it had fallen. The gold shone warm and worn.

She worked the circle of jade from her little finger and replaced it with the gold. Her palm and fingers were blistered, and the rings pulled away the burned skin. "Give me your hand, Sarah." She slipped the jade ring onto the third finger of the girl's left hand.

Sarah's fingers closed on hers, and her tears broke out afresh. "I'm afraid. I'm so afraid. Don't ever leave me, Imogene."

"Not ever."

SUNRISE BURNED OUTSIDE THE BEDROOM CURTAINS, THROWING A patch of figured gold across the coverlet; a single stripe of hard blue sky divided the drapes. Awake at first light, Sarah blinked vaguely at the ceiling. The calm mask of sleep evaporated as she remembered where she was. She pushed the heavy woolen blankets aside and they folded in a wave, looking as though there were still someone under them.

Her back was still from shoulder to hip. Easing her legs over the edge of the mattress, she sat up slowly, pulling herself upright with the bedpost like an old woman. Using the headboard as a crutch, she stood. Fever flushed her cheeks and burned bright behind her eyes. The schoolteacher's borrowed nightdress trailed out after her, disappearing into the tangle of sheets and bedclothes. She pulled it free and inched it off over her head.

Pantalets, black stockings, and homemade bandages of soft, clean fabric swathed her from hip to shoulder, leaving only her chest and arms naked to the cold. Gingerly, Sarah felt her breasts, wincing from the touch of her own fingers. Milk leaked from her swollen nipples, and her skin was stretched taut.

As the sun climbed, a narrow bar of sunshine striped the floor; she stepped into it, shivering and rubbing her bare arms. Wind rattled the window glass and the curtains parted slightly with the draft. The early-April sun was as cold and ungiving as the light of January. Sarah hugged herself and looked around. All her outergarments were soaking in a tub of cold water in the kitchen. After a minute's hesitation she took down one of Imogene's skirts and dropped it over her head. By rolling the waistband until it bunched thick around her middle, she managed to get the hem clear of the floor. Blood was seeping through the bandages on her back. She dressed quickly, oblivious of the pain, checking over her shoulder every few moments to see that Imogene still slept on her pallet of blankets before the fireplace in the living room. Sarah pinned up the sleeves of Imogene's shirtwaist to free her hands, but she couldn't manage the buttons up the back. She put on the jacket the teacher had worn to the meeting the night before. Having dressed, she picked up her shoes and tiptoed from the bedroom.

Sam's coat hung on the high peg by the front door. It was a struggle to unhook it and lift it down, and afterward she rested for a moment on the chair that Imogene had used as a doorstop. Leaning forward to keep her injured back from touching the chair back, she watched the sleeping form before the hearth, starting whenever Imogene stirred or made a sound. Then, quietly, Sarah moved the chair and let herself out. The hinges had bent when Sam kicked in the door, and it wouldn't stay closed. Silently, Sarah wrestled with it until tears of pain and frustration formed in her clear eyes and rolled down her cheeks. "Imogene, you can't know I've gone yet," she whispered to herself.

After a while she gave up and crept away. The main street was empty. Though the sun had scarcely cleared the trees in the east, the men who worked the mines were already underground. Without looking right or left, Sarah hurried in the direction of the Ebbitt farm.

Weather had taken its toll on the hard-packed roadway, and at the outskirts of town Sarah stumbled and fell. She struggled to her feet and, rolling the skirt back up to where she could walk unhampered, glanced anxiously back toward the houses. Smoke came from chimneys, and children were beginning to stir out of doors. Across from the school, one of the Beard children, a little girl, barefoot and coatless despite the cold, darted out from the house to gather an armload of kindling from the woodpile. Sarah turned and ran.

Before she reached the Ebbitt farm, two wagons had passed her. Neither had offered her a ride. She had not raised her eyes until they were gone, but her cheeks had colored a deeper hue and the feeling of their eyes on her back had stooped her shoulders as much as the pain of the lashing. Off and on, she cried to herself. Her eyes and nostrils were red-rimmed where the wind and tears chapped her skin, and her split lip was dry and cracked, too dry even to bleed.

The farm was quiet—no smoke from the chimneys, no movement at the windows. Sarah crossed the field and stood on the stile. Her knees shook and she sat for a moment on the top step, the barn sheltering her from the wind, and watched the house. The wind died, and in the sudden stillness she heard Sam calling to his plowhorse. Made bold by the knowledge he was already in the field, she climbed down and, keeping the barn between herself and Sam, crossed to the kitchen door. Her hand was on the latch when she stopped, arrested by the sight of a loose chain. The dog's tether lay across the yard like a snake dormant with the cold. The hook that clipped it to his collar was broken and the dog was nowhere to be seen. Hand on the door handle, ready to bolt inside, Sarah looked for him. Both of the barn doors were closed. Underneath the woodshed, the pile of old blankets the dog slept on was empty. With a sigh of relief she opened the door.

Lips pulled back and hackles rising, Sam's dog waited for her inside the house. Sarah gasped and jerked the door shut again. She backed away as quietly as she could and quickly ran to the front door. A clicking of claws on a wooden floor warned her that the dog had gotten there before her.

She gazed up at the windows. "Matthew," she called uncertainly. She pressed her palms to her temples to cool them, and walked around the house, holding her head and calling her son's name, looking up at the blank upstairs windows—the bedroom, the dressing room, the nursery. "Matthew! Matthew!" Back at the front door, she fell to her knees and rested her cheek against the wood. "Please, dog. I've got to get my baby. Please." She pleaded, her lips pressed near the latch. The dog paced inside, growling. Sarah pulled herself to her feet and opened the door a crack. The pacing stopped and dull yellow eyes turned on her. The growling deepened, grew sharper. "I'm going to open the door real slow. Good dog. Shhh. Shhh. Don't you be afraid. It's just me. Sarah. Hush now." Slowly she pushed open the door. Forelegs stiff, hindquarters coiled near the floor, the dog waited. "I'm going to be coming in now. Hush. Good boy. Hush."

She stepped over the sill and he lunged. Instinctively, Sarah threw up her arm to protect her face as the dog's body hurtled into her, smashing her against he wall. She screamed as her flayed back hit the wood. Strong jaws closed on her arm. His teeth caught in the fabric and he worried the frail girl like a troublesome bone. With a tearing sound the sleeve let go, and they both staggered back. The animal scrabbled on the wood for an instant, found his feet, and flew at her face. Shrieking, Sarah retreated through the half-open door. He threw himself at the opening, spittle flecking his muzzle. She slammed the heavy door, catching his head in the jamb. With an angry howl he shoved ahead, his powerful chest forcing the door out, his teeth slashing at her hands and wrists. But she held tight to the handle.

Sobbing, Sarah leaned back, her eyes closed to shut out the black gums and yellowed teeth with their streamers of saliva. With all her strength she pulled, holding him pinioned in the door. In a frenzy the dog wrenched his head sideways to get at her wrists. As he turned, he exposed the underside of his throat to the door's edge. It closed another inch, and Sarah jerked back with a frightened cry. The oak squeezed the dog's windpipe, and with a choking sound he stopped growling and writhed frantically, his nails scratching loudly on the floor.

Eyes shut tight, head thrown back, Sarah held on and cried. For a long time she pulled, her sobs drowning out the struggles of the animal. Minutes passed, and finally there was only the sound of her own whimpering. At last she looked. The dog's head was wedged crosswise in the door, his dull eyes wide and bulging, his tongue lolling between his teeth. He looked as terrifying in death as he had in life. Sarah let go of the door and he slid silently to the floor. She screamed and ran.

When she had recovered her courage in the warm comfort of the barn, she returned to the kitchen. Refusing to look at the inert form crowding the front door, she climbed the stairs. She pulled herself along with the handrail and stopped to rest once before she reached the top. Despite the cold, sweat curled the tendrils of hair at her temples and throat.

The nursery was empty, the crib made up as she had left it the afternoon before. Several of the dresser drawers gaped open, their contents in disarray. Matthew's diapers and gowns were gone. Sarah stared around the small room as though the baby might somehow have hidden himself in a corner or under a chair.

"Matthew, it's Momma."

On unsteady legs she groped her way down the windowless hall, her hand trailing along the wall for support. The bedroom door was open and she slumped in the archway. Beside her, on the washstand, an inch of water still stood in the pitcher. She drank thirstily, the wide brim spilling it over her face and neck.

The room was as it had been, with one exception: everything of hers was gone. There was no pillow on her side of the bed, the few things she had brought from home were off the walls and the dresser, none of her clothes hung in the closet, the drawers had been emptied of her stockings and underthings; even her hairbrush had been taken from the night table. A bachelor's room, rough and unkempt. It looked just as it had the first night she had come there, a bride.

Sarah rushed from the room and down the stairs. She tripped and fell the last two steps into the living room. Picking herself up, she pulled her skirt high and ran again.

Sam was on the far side of the field, walking in the furrow behind the plow. Brown earth turned from the blade, folding back, dark and rich. Birds wheeled behind, eyes sharp for worms and grubs in the new-plowed soil. He was coming toward the farm buildings, looking directly at Sarah over the horse's rump. He gave no sign that he saw her. Able to run no farther, she stopped and waited. She rubbed her eyes and pressed her hands to her chest to still her rapid breathing. The plow pulled the land under its blade until there was less than fifteen feet between them, and still Sam gave no indication that he was aware of her.

"Sam!" she cried, and a gull, circling overhead, cried in raucous answer. Reaching the boundary of the field, Sam heaved on the plow handles and worked the lines. The horse turned and pulled back the other way. Sarah ran after him. "Sam!" She was no more than three yards from him, but he didn't turn or seem to hear her call. She stumbled out across the furrows to walk beside him, keeping up as best she could. "Sam, you've got to hear me. Please, Sam, you've got to talk to me. I want to come home. Please, I want to come home. I want my baby, Sam. Let me come back."

He clucked to the horse and called out, "Steady there," as it shied at a weed tumbling before the wind.

"Sam!" Sarah screamed. "Where's my baby? Where's Matthew?" He plodded on, his eyes fixed on the trees at the end of the field. "Where is he?" Frantic, she threw herself at him, her thin hands clawing, her small fists glancing harmlessly off his round chest and beefy shoulders. The stone of his face broke and he flung her off.

"You're an unnatural woman. You've got no child." He picked the reins out of the dirt and called to the horse.

Sarah lay where she had fallen, the wind blowing her hair out over the ground like winter wheat. Twice more, Sam's plow passed her before she dragged herself to her feet and limped back to the road. Sam never looked at her.

It was nearly midday when Sarah reached the Tolstonadge home. She turned off the road and came slowly up the drive. Inside, Lizbeth was laughing and Mam was visible through the kitchen window. The porch door slammed behind her and there was a murmuring within, followed by silence. Sarah turned the knob. The door was locked.

There were no more tears; she leaned wearily against the familiar wood of home and rested. Behind the door, someone started to speak and was hushed.

"Mam?" Sarah said softly.

No answer came. Sarah turned from the thin comfort of the porch and, looking back every few yards, returned to the road.

Mam Tolstonadge overtook her before she'd gone half a mile. Pulling her to the side of the road where a thicket sheltered them from the wind, she hugged her and cried over her. "Sam's been over," Mam said, "and your pa says you're an Ebbitt now if you're anything, and we're not to interfere by so much as talking to you. Emmanuel hasn't the right to lose another child to me, husband or not, so I came after you."

"My baby, Mam."

"Sam took him this morning, long before sunup. I don't know where he's got him. Sam said as how he'd found you and Imogene like the letter had said. But I don't believe he's got the sense he was born with. That man! He sees just as far as the end of his nose and makes the rest up to suit himself." Sarah's knees gave way. Mam caught her to her breast and held her close. "Hon, Sam's bound to give him back to me. Lord knows, he can't care for him alone, nor go paying some woman. I'll take care of him like he was my own till you get Sam turned around and go home."

"There's no turning him, Mam. He's set."

"Maybe not," Mam said comfortingly, but above her daughter's bent head, her eyes were bleak. "Here," she said after a while, setting Sarah away from her. "I got ways of doing things your pa don't know nothing about. If you need anything, you just leave a note by Mrs. Thomas's and I'll get it. I'm not losing another child to that man's mulishness." Margaret held her close again, her wide, pillowed frame supporting Sarah easily. "You're burning up, Sare. You'd best get yourself back to the schoolteacher's quick like a bunny and get in out of the wind. She oughtn't have let you go out, hot as you are."

Sarah held on to her mother, her face buried in the soft bosom. Gently, Margaret put her arms from her neck. "I've got to go. Walter's home and he'll be wondering where I'm off to and go telling his pa. I got to go now. I've been gone longer than's smart already." She kissed Sarah and left her. "You get yourself to Imogene's now," she called over her shoulder.

Calliope was bustling with people and wagons when Sarah reached the edge of town. A band of boys had collected in front of the Beards' house and played at hitting a fist-sized rock with sticks, whooping and swooping at it as though they were mounted on swift ponies. A wagon lumbered down the middle of the street and another, its team unhitched, awaited repairs in front of the blacksmith's shop.

Sarah stood by the side of the road, the weight of her outsized garments and the wind bearing her down until it seemed she would fall. She looked from the boys at their game to Imogene's door, to the wagon driver with his children on the seat beside him. The town was too full of eyes. Losing her courage, she crawled on her hands and knees up the dirt embankment and into the underbrush until she was out of sight.

It was after sunset when she ventured from her hiding place. A cloud cover had blown in, obscuring the early stars and warming the evening. She had secreted herself less than a quarter-mile from the school buildings, and although she was stiff from the cold and confused with fever, she was there in a few minutes. Imogene had the door open and was out on the steps at the first sound of her tread.

Sarah stopped at the foot of the walk, a dark shape swaying in the last light. Imogene ran to her, arms outstretched, ready to catch her if she fell.

"Don't touch me!" Sarah croaked. "Please, God, don't touch me!" Her frightened eyes darted to the windows of the neighboring houses, but they were all closely draped to keep out the night air. Imogene dropped her arms as though she had been struck, and abruptly returned to the house, leaving Sarah to follow unaided.

The place was a jumble of crates and boxes. Some were half-filled, piled on top of others already sealed and labeled. A trunk took up the middle of the floor, its lid propped open. Sarah's clothes, dry but for the seams, hung from a line stretched from the mantel to the peg by the door. The desk was covered with old letters sorted into untidy stacks.

Imogene threaded her way through the confusion and poked up the fire. The door shut softly and Imogene put the poker away. When she turned to Sarah, the anger and hurt were gone from her face. "I've been so worried. I woke up and you were gone."

Sarah hadn't come into the room, but stood with her back to the door. "You're packing," she said. "You're leaving. You're going to leave me." With startling energy, she grabbed things from the trunk and hurled them to the floor. She pulled the boxes of letters from the desk and dumped them over. "You sneaked all the boxes in. You were getting everything ready to go when I wasn't here." She laughed as tears poured down her cheeks, and collapsed in the mess she had made. Imogene fell to her knees and tried to gather the young woman into her arms, but Sarah flailed at her. "You're leaving me!" she cried. "You're going away."

"No, my dear. No. Not now, not ever." Sarah wouldn't be comforted, but continued to cry.

Imogene left her and ran into the bedroom. She jerked a hatbox from the closet shelf and reached behind it to pull out a metal box the size of a book. She ran her hand down the length of the shelf, dislodging some half-dozen boxes and a lamp chimney that shattered when it hit the floor. Finally her fingers found what they were looking for: a small key on a nail driven into the back of the closet. Haste making her fumble, she unlocked the box and hurried back into the other room. Sarah still lay amid the clothing and papers.

Imogene knelt in front of her and spilled the contents of the box onto the floor between them. Coins rolled off under the chairs. The cat, perched on the mantel, roused herself to chase one but it settled quickly and she lost interest. Bills tumbled out in a heap. Imogene picked up a fistful and pressed them into Sarah's hand, folding the narrow fingers around them. "The money left from the sale of my house. Take it." She pushed another handful of money into the pocket of Sarah's coat. "Everything I have is yours." She unpinned the silver brooch that closed the collar of her dress and pinned it on Sarah's bodice. "Everything. I won't ever leave you." Sarah stopped crying, her interest caught like a child's. "I would never hurt you," Imogene said. "I love you. You needn't earn it or even deserve it, it's just there. No matter what you do, it won't change. If I never saw you for a hundred years. It just is."

"Like air?"

Imogene smiled at her. "Like air."

Sarah sat up, both hands full of money, money spilling from her pockets, her tangled hair falling over her face. Imogene held out her hands and Sarah put the money aside to take them. "I'd like to go to sleep now," she said. "I'm real tired."

Imogene helped her to bed.

"Will you unpack?"

Imogene settled the covers over the girl's shoulders and tucked them smooth. "You sleep, we'll talk in the morning."

16

SARAH WAS SLEEPING FITFULLY, ROCKING HER HEAD BACK AND FORTH against the pillow. Occasionally her hands jerked and she'd cry out.

Already awake and dressed, Imogene stood by the bedside. She laid her hand on the girl's forehead, and for a moment Sarah was still. Then, quietly, Imogene left her.

Yesterday's bitter wind had blown itself out and the weather was mild. Imogene unbuttoned her wrap and stood for a long moment on the front steps, the sun on her face, her head to one side, listening. Birds rustled in the lilac bushes in front of the school, their subdued twittering and stirring deepening the stillness of the morning. No tardy children hurried down the main street, none of the righteous scuffled before the school door in celebration of a last minute's freedom. With a sudden spasm, Imogene straightened her shoulders. "Bash on regardless," she said, and smiled crookedly.

The sound of a hammer's clanging rang from Hugh Rorvak's forge; Imogene turned her steps toward the smithy. Sweat rolled down the blacksmith's temples and darkened his collarless shirt. With iron tongs he held a red-hot crescent against the anvil. His hammer, swinging in short, regular arcs, pounded the end of it flat. At the back of the shop, where it opened into the stable, Clay Beard stooped, his back to a sorrel mare, holding her hoof between his thighs, plying a three-cornered rasp.

Imogene's shadow fell across the door and Clay looked up, smiling and gesturing a greeting with the file, before bending to his task again. Hugh Rorvak had seen her as she walked up from the street, and looked away without acknowledging her. She waited quietly just outside the door for him to finish shaping the wagon shoe. For fifteen minutes he worked on, heating the metal, pounding. Occasionally he looked her way from under lowered lids and, finding her still there, worked with renewed vigor. At last he plunged the metal into a tub of water. A hiss, a cloud of steam, and the pounding of the smithy was exorcised for a moment. He pulled the metal shoe for the wheel of a wagon from the black water and held it over a wooden wheel propped against the wall; it fit close. Imogene started to speak but he turned his back, reaching down another piece of metal for the forge, and she ran out of patience. Stepping over the threshold she said, "Excuse me, Mr. Rorvak, I've come to hire a wagon."

With unnecessary clatter he hefted the tongs over the lip of the furnace. "Got none. They all been let."

"What about that one?" She put herself between him and his anvil. Forcing his attention, she indicated a small wagon visible through the stable door.

The blacksmith never looked where she was pointing. "It's busted. Nobody can take it."

"What about tomorrow?"

"All been spoke for." He pulled the iron from the forge. One end glowed a dull red. "Better stand back. You'll get yourself bad burned."

Imogene retreated toward the door. "Is there nothing you can let me have? It'll only be for an hour or so in the evening."

"Sorry."

Imogene watched him as he laid the metal on the anvil. He seemed to feel her eyes on his back. "Sorry," he said again.

Clay hailed her as she crossed the stableyard, motioning her to him. "Didn't mean to go flapping my arms at you like that," he apologized. "I was afraid Mr. Rorvak'd see us together if I was to come over to you."

"That wouldn't do, would it?" Imogene said sarcastically.

"No, ma'am. Wouldn't do at all. You be needing a wagon?"

"Yes."

"That one there," he jerked his chin at the wagon Imogene had pointed out to the blacksmith, "ain't hardly broke. Mr. Rorvak'll be up to the mine late this afternoon. Maybe five, six o'clock, I could bring it by. I'd like to do it for you, ma'am. And little Mrs. Ebbitt."

Imogene's eyes softened and she laid a hand on Clay's arm. Hard muscles met her gloved fingers. "Thank you, Clay, you're very good. But won't you lose your situation here?"

"I'm not smart, Miss Grelznik, but I'm real strong. Stronger even than Mr. Rorvak. When comes something he can't lift, he calls for me. But I'm not so smart and maybe I don't know no better'n to let you have that wagon for a bit." He tapped his temple with a sooty forefinger, and a look as close to cunning as he could muster sparkled in his guileless blue eyes.

Imogene laughed. "Thank you, Clay. You are a strong man." Bright blue skirts and running steps caught Imogene's eye. Her hand fell from Clay's arm as a gawky girl in her early teens flitted from the side door of the Beards' house and down the street. She was wearing a blue-checkered dress and carrying an armload of clothes. Imogene looked from the girl to Clay. "Your sister, Jillian, is wearing Sarah's dress."

Clay shifted uncomfortably. He stared at the ground and squeezed his cloth cap in both hands. "Yes, ma'am. Mr. Ebbitt brought 'em before dawn this morning. Gave them to Ma to give out. Said there was no sense decent women going cold. Ma saved some things for the girls, but they're pretty little yet. And Karen, though I see her pretty as she ever was, well, she likes her food and she's not the little spit of a thing Sarah Ebbitt was."

"Is."

"Anyway, Ma's given the dresses and whatnot to folks as can use 'em."

Imogene inhaled slowly through pinched nostrils. She sucked in her cheeks and nodded to herself. "The baby?"

"Ma's looking after him."

The clash of the smith's hammer stopped and Clay looked nervously over his shoulder. "It won't do to have Hugh see us talking, he'll sure tell me how I can't let you have that wagon, and as it ain't mine, I couldn't take it then." Clay put on the cap he'd been mangling, and hurried back into the stable.

In the street, people turned away, whispering, as Imogene passed. It was after ten o'clock when she reached home. As he opened the door, Sarah flew at her, Imogene's voluminous night-gown trailing over her hands, the hem dragging on the floor.

"Where were you?" she wailed. "Where've you been?" Laundry, strung across the room on a makeshift clothesline, got in her way and she became entangled in the line. "You left me alone!" Sarah cried, and broke into noisy sobs.

Imogene went to cradle her in her arms, but she threw her hands up, warding the schoolteacher off. "Don't touch me." Then, "You left me alone!"

The schoolteacher caught her by the shoulders and shook her. When the frenzied look left her eyes, Imogene held her close and Sarah clung to her.

"You left me alone," Sarah said again, when she'd quieted. They were sitting together on the hearth, Sarah resting her head on Imogene's shoulder.

"I had to. I've got to take care of us now, don't I? I wanted to let you sleep. You feel a little cooler now than you did this morning. Would you like something to eat?" Sarah shook her head. "Maybe you'll feel like eating a little something tonight."

"Maybe."

Imogene stroked her hair. "Where's the cat?"

"I put her out."

"We'll have to find something to carry her in. Why don't you go lie down now, I can finish up here. Clay's coming by for us around five o'clock."

Sarah raised her eyes. "Why?"

"We've got to leave Calliope," Imogene said gently. "We can't stay here now."

"We can't leave. Matthew . . . Mam . . . my clothes . . ."

Imogene took her hands.

Sarah jerked free. "No! My baby, I can't leave him. He's so little. No!" The thin arms flapped in the big sleeves, and a look of determination flitted across the small face.

Imogene caught her and forced her to be still. "Listen to me. We can't stay here. I can't work here, and I must make a living for both of us. They won't let us stay."

"You go," Sarah cried. "You go. I can stay here. I'll live here and I'll take in wash, or cook maybe. I'll—" She broke off and hid her face in the folds of the nightdress.

"You can't live here anymore. This is school property, Sarah."

As gently as she could, Imogene said, "You have nothing. Even Matthew is not yours. He's Sam Ebbitt's boy. If we could find him, steal him away, then he, too, would have nothing. Sam will let you go—he'll never let his son go. He'd hunt you down. You don't want that for Mattie. Nothing is yours."

"You're lying!" Sarah cried.

"Nothing," Imogene went on inexorably. "You haven't even a change of clothes. I saw that girl Jillian wearing one of your dresses this morning. Sam's given them away."

"They're mine!" came the muffled cry.

"No, they aren't. They belong to Sam. Even what you had before you were married. It all belongs to Sam. If he wanted, he could have you arrested and sent to jail for stealing the clothes you had on your back when you ran away. That's the law. It's all Sam's." Imogene pulled Sarah's shirtwaist from the clothesline. "This is his." She jerked the skirt and draped it over the rocking chair. "And these." She snatched up Sarah's underthings from where they'd been heaped when Imogene changed her bandages the night before. "These are his stockings."

Sarah held up the frilled pantalets and smiled a little. "These are Sam's pantalets?"

"That's my girl. We're going to be all right. You'll see." Imogene hugged her. "You go rest. I'll finish up here and wake you so we can get ready ourselves." She helped Sarah to her feet. "It will be all right. I promise." Sarah didn't move. "The leaving is for Mattie as much as for you," Imogene said, and the girl allowed herself to be led.

While Sarah slept, Imogene packed, parceling the scattered bits of her life into boxes and closing them up with itemized lists carefully pasted to their lids. Then, mopping, dusting, scrubbing, she worked her way from room to room, cleaning away the last traces of her residency. When the house was bare but for the molehill of her possessions piled near the door, and the rooms smelled of soap and water—the homier smells of coffee and lavender having been washed away—Imogene carried in the bathtub. She filled it half-full of cold water and put the kettle on to heat. The water began to boil and she went to wake Sarah.

Groggy and feverish, Sarah shambled out of the bedroom, guided by Imogene's steady hand. The tub of water waited before the fire, cold and uninviting. Sarah looked from it to Imogene.

"I'll pull the curtains so you can undress, then in you go." Imogene smiled reassuringly.

"It's only April."

"April's a good month for bathing."

"It's still winter outside." As if to corroborate Sarah's sentiments, wind rattled the window glass.

"It's much warmer today. Almost spring. Best bathe now while the afternoon sun is at its warmest."

"Washing too much is unhealthful. Mam says." The unanswerable authority called down, Sarah turned for the bedroom.

"Nonsense. In you go." Imogene closed the drapes and poured boiling water into the tub, great clouds of steam engulfing her.

Sarah allowed herself to be led to the tub and sat limp and unprotesting in the water, her legs crossed tailor-fashion. Warm water cascaded over her neck and shoulders. She winced as it found the lash cuts.

"I'll be as easy as I can," Imogene promised. "I have some ointment that will help, but I've got to clean the wounds first." Blood—dried, broken open, and dried again—scabbed over most of the slender back. Pus gathered at the torn edges, and the narrow strips of flesh between the slashes were beginning to show an angry red. "You've not tended to yourself and I've been remiss. Running about, you've opened these a dozen times."

"I had to look for Matthew." Her son's name dulled Sarah's eyes, and tears ran down her cheeks. Imogene said nothing.

Deftly she swabbed the cuts clean, dabbing at the torn skin with a soft paste of soap. That done, she began the task of shampooing the fine blond hair. It fell, lank and wet, below Sarah's waist. Gathering it up and rolling it into a knot, Imogene squeezed the excess water out and secured it with pins from her own hair. "There. That will hold it for the time being." She handed Sarah the bar of soap. "You get soaped up; I'll get the rinse water." Sarah held the soap but made no effort to clean herself.

"Sarah!" An edge of fear sharpened Imogene's voice, and slowly Sarah looked up. "Don't think about it, Sarah. There's nothing to be gained. Try not to think. Oh, Sarah, I am so terribly sorry," Imogene whispered, her eyes full of the fragile, uncomplaining girl. Sarah started to rub the soap against her skin. "That's right. I'll get the rinsewater before you get a chill."

Wrapped in a blanket, Sarah sat near the fire while Imogene brushed her hair dry.

"Where are we going to go?" she said, breaking a long silence.

Imogene leaned over the back of the rocker to catch the barely audible sound. "Hmmm? Where? Reno. It's in the Nevada Territory. The state. It's a state now. Nevada." She kept her voice cheerful and light.

"Nevada," Sarah repeated hollowly, and Imogene laughed.

"You make it sound as though it were Hong Kong or Calais. It's not so far. The railroad runs right to it." She hesitated for a moment. "An old friend of mine lives there with her husband. She said they had need of schoolteachers." She reached into her pocket and took out the letter she had taken from her piles of correspondence—the letter William Utterback had given her to read on the trail two and a half years before. She glanced quickly at the first page: *17 September 1873. Dear Mr. Utterback,* the letter began. Imogene put that sheet back into her pocket and handed Sarah the page beginning, *There's a dearth of teachers here, and new people arrive to stay every day . . .*

Sarah started to read but lost interest after a line or two, and let the paper fall to the floor.

"Reto," she said.

"Reno. With an *n*. Read the rest. She goes on to say how beautiful it is there and how nice the people are." Sarah gave no sign that she heard. "Here. Let me read it to you." Imogene picked up the page and snapped it straight: " 'There's a dearth of teachers here, and new people arrive every day to stay. A lot of good family people. One of the railroad men told Jim'—that's her husband— 'Reno had stayed the same size because every time a woman got pregnant a man left town. Now you sometimes see a father pushing a pram.

" 'Mountains ring the meadow that Reno is built on, some so high there's snow almost all year round, and when the wind blows you can smell the pine trees. I love it here; it's such a world of odd bits and surprises. Almost all the stores lining the main streets have false fronts a story taller than the real buildings. The men are rough and often dirty, chewing tobacco and spitting indoors, yet when I go out they'll step off the boardwalk into calf-deep mud and hold their hats to their chests until I've passed. Good women are a treasure here.' "

Sarah was rocking herself back and forth, humming. It was a lullaby. Imogene stopped reading and watched her for a moment, lines of worry, like hatchet marks, between her brows. "There's not much more, just some about the weather. And her signature, Isabelle Ann Englewood. I knew her as Close."

As good as his word, Clay Beard was outside the schoolmistress's house at five o'clock. Their scant belongings were quickly loaded into the wagon. Alone in the house, Imogene ran her hand lovingly over the dark wood of the rocking chair that had been her mother's, before leaving it to the mercy of the person who was to come after her.

"Clay," she said as she climbed up beside Sarah on the wagon seat, "Dandy hasn't come home. Would you take care of her when she does? She's a good mouser."

"She'll turn up, Miss Grelznik. I'll watch for her. One more won't be noticed at home."

It looked as if everyone in town had come outdoors to stare after them as the wagon rolled through on its way to the depot. As they passed the church, a stone struck the side of the bed, spooking the horse. Imogene turned in time to see a boy of ten disappear around the corner of the building. He was one of her students. She fixed her eyes on the road and never looked back again. Sarah stared sightlessly down at her black-gloved hands.

The trail was five hours late. Both women sat outside on the station platform, perched amid their boxes and luggage, Sarah beyond caring and Imogene unwilling to face the people who lingered inside. Jackson had come out several times to ask them in, and once he'd brought them some fruit he said his "missus" had "packed extry."

It was after midnight when they boarded. Imogene led Sarah to a seat by a window and slid in beside her. The young woman hadn't spoken all evening and now slumped against the seat as though there was no feeling in her damaged back. Pulling off her glove, Imogene laid a palm on Sarah's brow. She twitched away to lean her forehead against the glass.

"You're warm. How do you feel?"

She didn't answer and Imogene dropped her hand to look past Sarah at the warm lights of the distant town. "The unmitigated gall of these people to call themselves Christians." The word *Christians* hissed. "They are so afraid of love. They strike out against their own children and snigger behind the back of anyone who dares reach out to another. Warding off the evil eye!" Imogene struck her fist against the hard wooden armrest. The knuckle of her little finger dimpled and reappeared as a tight knot half an inch from where it should have been. The hooting of the trail whistle drowned her cry.

17

THE TRAIN RATTLED THROUGH THE COUNTRYSIDE, THE NIGHT TER-rain invisible behind blackened windows. Blankets and pillows were heaped in a rumpled mound over Imogene's and Sara's knees. In a basket between their feet, the food that Imogene had packed remained untouched. Sarah hunched forward, resting her head against the seat in front of her. Her eyes, wide and dry, looked at nothing. Imogene dozed fitfully, clutching the edge of the blanket up out of the muck of dirt and tobacco juice even in her sleep.

In the shadowlessness just before dawn, Imogene was startled from her sleep by Sarah's cries. The girl was whimpering, her injured back wedged into the corner where the seat and the carriage wall met. Dried spittle flecked the corners of her mouth. Twitching, she cried out again. Imogene laid a hand lightly on her arm. "Sarah, you are having a bad dream," she said softly. "Wake up." Sarah jerked violently at her touch and screamed. Several passengers rustled in their sleep, one turning to cast a concerned glance in their direction. "Wake up, Sarah. It's Imogene." She shook her gently. Sarah's head snapped up as though it were on a spring. Crying, she reached blindly for Imogene and pressed her cheek against the older woman's neck. "There, there," Imogene soothed. "You've been having a nightmare."

"I couldn't wake up." Sarah said brokenly. She was trembling, and though she cried, her cheeks were dry. "I couldn't move and I was so afraid. I had to wake up and I couldn't." She shuddered and cried again.

Imogene held her, rocking her. "It was a bad dream. That's all. Fever makes people have funny dreams."

"It meant something. Like in the Bible."

"No. You woke up, didn't you? Can you eat something?"

Sarah had retreated back into herself and turned to stare out the window without answering. Imogene pulled the basket from between her feet and, rummaging inside, drew out two hard-boiled eggs and an apple, its skin wrinkled from a winter in Mr. Jenkins's cellar. "You must eat. I'm going to peel a hard-boiled egg for you. You've got to eat something." Her voice had a hard, bright edge. Quickly she shelled the egg and pressed it into Sarah's hand. "Eat it. You'll feel better." The girl continued to look out the window, her fingers lax, her face empty. After a moment, Imogene took the egg from Sarah's lap and ate it herself, chewing and swallowing with difficulty.

Over the following days the fever worsened; Sarah lay back against the seat, breathing shallowly, her lips white and dry. Imogene took money from her dwindling purse to procure a sleeping compartment.

As the train crept across the Midwest, Sarah lay in the sleeper with the curtains pulled close. The stale air, smelling of sickness and unwashed bedclothes, sometimes forced Imogene to the somewhat fresher air of the sitting cars, but mostly she stayed with Sarah, reading or staring out the window at the endless prairie. Occasionally, herds of buffalo dotted the green and brown expanse. Whenever they passed a herd of the shaggy creatures, shots cracked from the windows of the train; puffs of dust would explode from the rough hides and the great beasts would crumple. The train never slowed; only carrion-eaters and sportsmen enjoyed the kill.

The train's last over-night stop was Elko, Nevada. Imogene booked a room in the Grande Restaurant, Hotel, and Chop House. The train wouldn't be leaving for Reno until morning. Their room was simply furnished with a bed, a chair, and a washstand; homespun curtains of faded cornflower blue hung over the single window, and no wallpaper or paint softened the bare walls or floorboards.

Before Imogene would let Sarah lie down, she made a thorough inspection of the mattress and bedclothes. Pronouncing it "clean enough," she helped Sarah out of her gown and fetched water to clean her wounds and change the dressings. The unhealthy red was fading from the skin around the whip cuts across Sarah's back, and the shallower marks were beginning to close.

"You rest," Imogene said as she tucked Sarah in the bed. The middle sagged and the frail girl looked as though she were lying in a trough. "I'm going down for our suppers. I won't be long."

Sarah said nothing. She hadn't said more than a dozen words in three days.

Imogene left one candle burning and descended the narrow stairs. Everything was new and bare. Downstairs, a single room ran the length of the building; trestle tables with rude wooden benches were set in rows along both walls, an aisle between. The school-teacher paused in the doorway. The eating house was filled with coarse-looking men, indifferently bathed and shabbily dressed. Neckerchiefs took the place of shirt collars, and strange tricks of thread and bits of odd-colored cloth attested to inexpert mending.

As Imogene made her way down the central aisle, she was as-sailed by the smell of hearty stew. A stocky man carried the entire pot and a ladle from table to table. The miners, each with his own tin plate, often dented in a dozen or more places from years of packing, shoveled the food in rapidly, taking huge mouthfuls. They ate without speaking, and the scraping of spoons on plates was loud. When the men finished, they wiped up the gravy with bits of bread or their fingers and held the empty dish upside down out over the aisle if they wanted more.

At the far end of the room a woman with thick, light hair and a red face was handing out baked potatoes from a basket; they were so hot that even the callus-palmed miners tossed the potatoes from hand to hand and cursed under their breath.

When Imogene returned with the food, Sarah couldn't eat. Imo-gene finally gave up coaxing and ate her own supper, the tray bal-anced across her knees. Near the bowl was a periodical with a worn cover. "The proprietress loaned me this." Imogene indicated the paper-covered book. "She thought we might like to read it, since we are going to be living in Nevada. She's never read it herself—she speaks English moderately well, but she never learned to read it. She's from Vienna. A man from the East left it here six months ago and she set it aside for him in the event he should ever come back for it. That's nice, don't you think?" She waited hopelessly for Sarah to reply. "I want to read you something," she went on. "It's by Mark Twain. I used to read Mr. Twain to the class sometimes, remember? It's about Virginia City, that's near Reno. 'How they rode! The Mexicanized Americans of Nevada. Leaning just gently forward out of the perpendicular, easy and nonchalant, with broad slouch-hat brim blown squire up in front and long riata swinging . . .''

"Tell me about Mary Beth," Sarah said suddenly.

Imogene put aside her tray and wiped her hands on the towel that served as her napkin. Fear was souring the food in her stomach. "She was a student of mine. A lovely girl," Imogene began carefully. "She was about your age. What do you want to know about her?"

"Is it true what the letter said?" Sarah stared at the bare wood of the wall. "Please tell me," she whispered.

To gather her thoughts, Imogene carried the remnants of her supper across the room and set the tray in the hall, her mind running through the quiet year she had spent in the company of Mary Beth Aiken.

Mary Beth was sixteen when they'd met; it was her last year in school. She was outgoing and pretty. Students had had crushes on Imogene before and she had come to recognize the symptoms, but this time it was different. Mary Beth had fallen in love with her.

What first drew Imogene to Mary Beth was her obvious intelligence and the eager way she had devoured life, wanting to know everything, to experience new sensations. At sixteen, Mary Beth knew things that Imogene, at twenty-eight, never even guessed existed. Much later she told Imogene that she had loved a black servant girl. They'd been lovers until they were found together in the back pantry of the master's house. Half-dressed and shrieking, Mary Beth had been chased into the street by a knife-wielding cook. The fracas had brought the mistress downstairs, and Mary Beth's lover was sent away. Both girls had been fourteen.

Imogene closed the hall door and looked back at Sarah's slight form, hardly noticeable in the hammock of the old mattress. Sarah reminded her of Mary Beth. She was shy but pretty, and there was the same quality of need, a hunger for love and touching.

"I was infatuated with her at first," Imogene said to Sarah's back. "Then slowly it ripened into love. I think Mary Beth was the only person who ever truly loved me. Loved me for exactly who I am, and what I am not." Imogene smiled unconsciously, remembering her seduction. Mary Beth had decided that they were to be lovers. "One evening, just before fall term was to start, she invited me to picnic with her on the bank of the river. When we met near the water, on the outskirts of town, I sensed a peculiar excitement in her. She was wearing a new dress, borrowed for the occasion, and she was still damp and rosy from a bath." The scent of lilac and soap came strongly to Imogene's nostrils and she leaned against the splintery door of the hotel in Elko, remembering.

"I took the picnic basket from her. I remember being startled at its weight; it contained more wine than food. I followed Mary Beth to a secluded clearing, close to the water and screened by trees and underbrush. There was enough breeze that the mosquitoes didn't bother us. The night was full of stars and the murmur of the river.

"I was very naïve," she said, "though I was twenty-eight, almost twenty-nine. I had never felt the stirrings that Mary Beth did. But that night we became lovers. I was lost in her. Obsessed. I would have done anything to make her happy. That fall we were together was one of the happiest of my life. We walked for miles through the hills, watched the leaves change color and drop from the trees. Mary Beth was very bright, like you, and read. We talked about books.

"We were together all that winter, too. We'd sit by the fire in my house, doing needlework or just being quiet together. For nearly a year I was happy. We laughed a lot, and talked. And made love.

"Her brother, Darrel, the man who wrote the letter that lost me my post in Calliope, came in on us one evening. He had been drinking and had run out of money before he felt he was drunk enough. He knew she would be with me and he came to my house, came in without knocking. Mary Beth and I were on the couch in the parlor.

"He was very ugly. Mary Beth was afraid and wouldn't leave with him. He waited for her outside, hidden in the dark. He caught her when she finally left, and beat her very badly. The next day he reported me to the school and I was let go. That is about all." Imogene left the door and pulled a chair near Sarah's bed. "Sarah?" Sarah lay like one dead. "Sarah, talk to me. Do you hate me now? Very much?"

"I can't hate you, Imogene," Sarah said after a while, but she wouldn't look at Imogene and her voice was cold and flat. "Maybe I've felt it too. It's just like Sam said, we are abominations in the sight of God!"

"No, Sarah," Imogene began, but Sarah covered her face with the bedclothes, holding her hands over her ears like a child, as if trying to hide her feelings even from herself.

They arrived in Reno the afternoon of the following day. A cold wind blew down from the mountains to the west, but it was warm enough in the shelter of the station house. Imogene settled Sarah in a sunny corner and went to find their luggage.

The Reno station was immense; three sets of tracks cut a swath between rows of shed-roofed warehouses. The constant wind sent eddies of dust like small waves over the rails. Nearly twenty shiplike freightwagons, with eight to twenty-two mules in the traces, were scattered amid the storage sheds. Men scurried to and fro like ants, with great weights on their backs, transferring goods from wagon to storehouse and storehouse to freight car. The town itself stretched away to the north and south along a wide main street bordered by wooden walks. Stores lined the sidewalks, one snug up against the next as though the valley were not large enough. Each had its sign hanging over the door or painted on the false front above the wooden awning: V. MILATOVICH GROCERIES AND LIQUORS; PIONEER HALL BREWERY; BATHS; TOBACCO; J. B. PHILLIPS STATIONERY & MUSIC STORE; STOVES & TINWARE; DRUGS. At the southern end of the street, a silver ribbon streaked across where the Truckee River ran through town. Beyond, the sharp ragged blue mountains rose like a wall circling the meadow to the south and west. Lower, dun-colored desert mountains completed the circle to the north and east.

Imogene located their belongings on a far platform in front of one of the storage sheds. The warehouses were open to the weather, the roof on the open side sloping down above a raised platform and out over the tracks. Imogene ducked under an angled support beam and climbed the steps.

The men who were working there stopped what they were doing and eyed her askance, clearly undecided what the occasion of a woman visitor called for, not to mention the visit of a woman of Imogene's stature. One of them spat decorously over the side of the platform, two pulled their hats off. Two others, fortunate enough not to be confined to the platform, scurried off, leaving their companions to fend for themselves.

Imogene had no difficulty procuring storage space for her furnishings. She promised to call for them as soon as she had found permanent lodging, and offered to pay a rental fee in the interim, but the man in charge refused, insisting that they took up no more room than a cat.

On her return she found Sarah huddled on top of the suitcases, hunched almost double. Vomit stained the front of her dress. "Oh, my poor dear," Imogene murmured, ineffectually dabbing at the dress with her pocket handkerchief.

Sarah looked at her listlessly. "I'm sorry," she said.

"I'll get you someplace you can lie down," Imogene promised, and hurried into the shadowy recesses of the station.

Behind a long counter partitioned off into several working areas, three men, wearing collars, their sleeves held up with garters, went about the business of the railroad. A knot of men at the counter were arguing vehemently over a missing shipment of harness leather. Imogene skirted them and located the clerk who seemed least concerned with the fray.

"Pardon me." She raised her voice to get his attention. "I am just arrived with another lady. She's ill. Is there a place nearby that would be suitable? We'll be staying here indefinitely."

The young man she addressed was absorbed in the argument. "Where's your menfolk?" he said absently.

"We're traveling alone."

"They ain't come to meet you?"

"We are not expecting to be met."

His face crinkled into a practiced leer and he turned his eyes to her for the first time. Immediately the half-smile disappeared with all thought of fancy ladies. He was all repentant respect under the unflinching gaze of the definitive Schoolteacher. "I beg your pardon, ma'am. I was woolgathering. Expecting those fellas might come to blows. Two lone ladies, you say. I expect the Broken Promise'd be the place. Fred and Lutie run a nice clean house, and nobody'd think the worse of you for staying there. Lutie'd see to that. It's just down the main street to your right. Everything's on Virginia Street, pretty much."

Imogene thanked him and left the hand luggage in his car. With Sarah leaning heavily against her shoulder she set out for the Broken Promise. It was about a quarter of a mile from the station, set back from the street behind a white picket fence. A weathered rocking chair graced the narrow veranda, and an ample woman with faded brown hair and a friendly, fleshy countenance was stooped over, planting bulbs along the lattice skirting. The woman straightened up and pulled off her gardening gloves as Imogene opened the gate.

"The mite looks a bit poorly," she clucked, and without further ado she shored up Sarah's other side and bustled them in out of the wind. She settled them in the second room off the top of the staircase, saying, "I only got a couple of rooms at present, and this'n is the nicest."

Sarah's skin was hot to the touch and she shook with chills. The two older women stripped off Sarah's soiled outergarments and put her to bed. The stocky innkeeper was Lutie Bone; she and her husband, Fred, owned and ran the Broken Promise. Lutie sent a boy to fetch their luggage and went down herself to find a cot that Imogene had requested.

Imogene looked at her watch. It was just half past four. Sarah was dozing. For a few moments she regarded the sleeping girl indecisively. Then she wrote a quick note and pinned it to the cloth cover on the bedstand, where Sarah could not fail to see it if she awoke.

The wind had picked up, scouring a fine dust from the streets and driving it against the wooden façades of the buildings. Imogene let herself out the gate. To the right, Virginia Street petered out into scattered homes and disreputable-looking shops. To the left was the bulk of the town, with its stores and eating houses. Holding on to her hat, she turned resolutely left in search of Isabelle Anne and her husband.

It took an hour to canvass the post office, the courthouse, and finally the stationer's where Isabelle Anne Close's husband had worked. The Englewoods had moved to Sacramento.

Letting the wind snatch her hat awry and whip her hair from its pins, she trudged back to the hotel. Mount Rose threw its shadow across the wide valley floor, and without the sun, the wind lost every vestige of spring and blew bitterly cold. Exhaustion drew down Imogene's cheeks and deepened the creases around her eyes and mouth; she looked like a woman in her forties.

Several people were gathered around the fireplace in the parlor: a man and his wife and an elderly woman with thinning white hair piled elaborately, if inexpertly, on top of her head. Avoiding their curious glances, Imogene went straight up to the room. There was no light showing under the door and she turned the knob slowly, careful not to make too much noise. The room was deep in dusk and shadow. "Sarah, are you asleep?" she whispered. There was no answering rustle. She closed the door quietly. Without lighting a lamp, Imogene unpinned her hat and sank into a chair, her shoulders stooped. She rubbed her eyes tiredly. "What to do, what to do," she muttered to herself. Gray in the evening light, her face in the looking glass caught her attention and she stared at her reflection. Hair stuck out from her head like straw, one strand falling down over her eyes. "Double, double, toil and trouble," she said wryly, and turned her back on herself, massaging her temples.

When Imogene's eyes had adjusted to the half-light, she noticed that Sarah was not in the bed. "Sarah?" she called, and stood to walk around the footboard. A candle was extinguished on the floor, a scar burnt in the hardwood. Sarah was sprawled beside it, her petticoats tangled around her knees, her hand outstretched toward the candle. Imogene knelt and cradled her in her arms.

Sarah's eyes fluttered open and she looked around her with the gaze of a stranger. "I fell," she murmured. "I have to get Matthew inside before the storm hits; I can hear the wind."

Imogene pressed her cheek against the girl's burning forehead, rocking back and forth. "Oh dear God," she whispered. "Oh dear God."

18

SARAH THRASHED IN A PRIVATE NIGHTMARE, SOMETIMES RECOGNIZ-
ing Imogene but more often calling for people who were familiar to
her childhood. Always she cried for her mother and David and
begged for her son. Imogene stayed awake through the nights,
watching the thin, tortured face by the light of a shielded lamp.

At dawn of the third day, Imogene sat near the window. The
dark wool of her dress was rumpled; she had not taken it off in four
days. The white hair at her temples showed stark in the blue light,
and in her lap she twisted a handkerchief, grimy with use. Outside
the window, the sun touched the peaks of the Sierra. The rosy hue
spread down over the snow and turned at last to gold.

"Imogene." Sarah's voice, mostly air, sounded far away. The
schoolteacher turned slowly, reluctant to leave the pearly glow of
sunrise for the sickroom. Sarah's face was still flushed with fever,
but the delirium had lifted and Imogene saw recognition in her eyes.

"My dear," Imogene whispered. "You are back with me." She
brought Sarah water from the nightstand and stayed, holding the
hot, dry little hand, until the girl slept.

Imogene looked from the helpless white fingers to her own blunt,
capable hands, and a heavy tiredness blanketed her features. Lying
down on the cot by the far wall, she let herself sleep.

When she awoke, the afternoon sun was throwing the shadow

of the hotel across the backyard. Sarah was still sleeping. Imogene levered herself stiffly out of her cot and sat down near the window to write Margaret Tolstonadge a brief account of their journey and Sarah's illness, ending with: *Please write Sarah Mary of Matthew and of home. She is still very ill and is not a strong woman. I think news of home and family would be so good for her now. As ever, Imogene G.* She addressed it in care of Mrs. Thomas and, with a last check on Sarah, slipped out of the room.

Having posted the letter, Imogene walked slowly up the boardwalk, her heels making a hollow sound on the wood. The sun shone under the wide overhang of the wooden awning, and Imogene tilted her face back to catch the light. Brown-and-white sparrows perched in the rain gutters, and the bright yellow-orange breast of a Western oriole flashed over V. Milatovich's grocery store.

Outside Willamette's Dry Goods and Feed, two men lounged in a warm square of sunlight, their shoulders braced against the building. One was young, around thirty, with thick brown hair that curled boyishly over his ears. Large features crowded his face, and one side of his mouth drooped a little, giving him a puckish look. The other, gnarled and grizzled and in his fifties, was not over five feet seven inches tall, even in his thick-heeled boots. A sharp beak of a nose dominated his face, and bright blue eyes twinkled deep on either side of it. As Imogene drew near, the older man pushed himself out from the wall and tugged at the brim of a battered old hat. His right hand was missing all but the middle finger and thumb.

"Afternoon to you, ma'am."

"Good afternoon." Imogene nodded, giving them both a cursory glance.

"You be the lady come in with the little sick miss the other day?"

Imogene stopped. "Yes, I am." She waited. The man had his hat off and was standing respectfully enough. He had to look up to talk with her. His companion had relinquished the support of the wall at Imogene's approach and pushed his hat back in deference to her sex.

"If you're a spinster lady or a widow, I'd like to suggest we get hitched." The man rubbed his grizzled head with the stumps of his fingers in an overabundance of humility. Imogene stared at him uncomprehendingly. "I'm proposing matrimony," he explained.

Imogene touched her drawn cheeks, her hair; then, with an obvious effort at self-control, she dropped her hands to her sides. Blood rose in her face to the roots of her hair, only her lips and the edges of her nostrils retaining their former pallor. "Excuse me." Holding her dress back so it wouldn't brush against him, she stepped around the man as though he were a pile of manure.

Undaunted, he called after her, "You ever change your mind, name's McMurphy. Willamette'll know where I can be found."

The younger man laughed. "Now you've torn it, Mac. You're too little. Gal like that throws the little ones back."

Mac hit him with his hat. "Go on. Mouth off. You got yourself a woman."

The younger man snorted derisively.

Sarah was asleep. Still warm with fever, she had thrown off her covers and her small feet showed pink beneath the hem of the nightdress.

Quietly, Imogene unpacked the rest of her bags and put her things away. She saved out ink and a dozen sheets of white paper. When the room had been tidied to her satisfaction, she sat down again at the window and carefully wrote in large letters across the top of each sheet: LAUNDRY AND MENDING. I. GRELZNIK—INQUIRE AT THE BROKEN PROMISE. She waited several moments for the ink to dry, then took them downstairs.

Lutie was busy in the kitchen. But for the parlor, the kitchen was the largest room in the hotel, with the stove and pantry at one end and a long plank table flanked by benches at the other. The hotel residents ate in the kitchen along with two railroad men who lived near the station and boarded with the Bones. Lutie was cutting potatoes into cubes with a meat cleaver when Imogene came in.

"Pardon me, Mrs. Bone."

"Lutie. We're not so formal as all that." She waved the cleaver in the direction of the bench opposite. "Sit yourself down. How's little Mrs. Ebbitt?"

"Still sleeping." Imogene slid in between the table and the wall.

"That'll do her more good than anything. What've you got there?"

Imogene had laid the papers out on the table. "That's what I've come to ask you about. Until I can find a position, I've got to turn my hand to something to earn our keep." Lutie's face clouded as she read the leaflets. "I still have enough to pay the rent," Imogene added quickly.

"I'm not worried about that, hon. I expect Fred and I aren't going to starve if we have to carry you a bit, till you're settled. Taking in laundry just maybe isn't the best way."

"There will be no teaching positions until fall term, and I want to pay our way."

"Chinese do most of that kind of work. Some white folks do it, it's just that a Chinee'll work for less money. I don't know how they live, but they do. It kind of puts the squeeze on everybody. I don't think you can get by charging less, and nobody's going to pay you more."

"I need to do something." Imogene poised her pen over the ink bottle. "How much should I charge?"

"Fred and I can carry you for a bit."

"A nickel per shirt and ten cents for trousers?"

"Whatever you make it, six Chinese will go you a dime better."

Imogene penned in REASONABLE RATES under the name of the hotel.

The laundry did not pour in. Fred said the people in Reno who were genteel enough to wash their clothes didn't like asking a white woman to do it for the pittance they could pay a Chinese.

Sarah was bedridden, her recovery progressing so slowly that at times Imogene feared her health had been destroyed by the fever and the shock of being driven from her child and home. Most of every day, Imogene sat with her, reading or writing letters. Propped up in bed, small against the bulwark of pillows, Sarah spent the days uncomplaining, watching the shadows move across the wall.

Imogene coaxed her with books and lively talk, and spread breadcrumbs on the windowsill so the birds would stop there, but Sarah seemed too tired; the books would slip from her hands and her mind wandered from conversation.

Mid-May brought a letter from Mam, and with it the first spark of interest Sarah had shown.

Dear Sarah,

I'm hoping this letter finds you on your feet again. There's not a lot of news from here. Gracie's taken to going over to Sam's once or twice a week to do his housekeeping for him. He gives her a little pin money for it and she wants to do it. He doesn't allow talk of you, she said; I guess he's made his mind up on it.

The baby's still with Mrs. Beard. I've seen him a time or two when I've been in town, and he's as fat and happy as can be. I've bent Sam's ear on the subject and just got grunts out of him, but I think he's softening. I expect to have little Mattie here at home by the end of summer. Big news is— Mattie talked. Not ten months and a word! He can stand, too, Mrs. Beard says, if you give him a finger to hang on to.

There's no new schoolteacher as yet. Joseph stepped down from the board and people have kind of let it go. I'm working on your pa to step up, we've got Lizbeth to school yet, but she's such a pretty little thing your pa says she won't be needing it.

Tell Miss Grelznik I asked after her. There's still people here speak kindly of her.

Love,
Your Mam

Enclosed in the letter were four one-dollar bills.

Over the next few days, Sarah read the letter again and again until Imogene teased that she could repeat it by rote. The letter gave Sarah no pleasure and there was an unhealthy sense of urgency when she pored over it.

One evening after reading it through again, Sarah lay back on the pillows. "When last I saw him, Sam called me an abomination in the sight of God." Imogene looked up from her book. Sarah was tearing soundlessly at her sunken cheeks, her nails raking the skin red. Imogene held her hands until she slept, and stayed at the bedside long into the night, afraid to leave her. After that, the letter was put away and Sarah never asked for it.

The four dollars went to Lutie in partial payment of May's room and board. Lutie was a gracious creditor, but her mother-in-law, Evelynne, never missed a chance to remind Imogene that she lived at the Broken Promise on "Bown-yay" (as she insisted Bone was pronounced) charity.

In June, Imogene had a caller. She was upstairs with Sarah when Lutie came up to announce that there was a man waiting in the parlor. "Looks like a beau." Lutie winked at Sarah. Embarrassed, Imogene shook her head a curt "no" and preceded Lutie down the stairs.

Evelynne had come in from the porch to cross-examine Imogene's guest, and he stood by the hearth, parrying the old lady's questions with a guilty air. He looked up with relief when Imogene came into the room.

"How do, ma'am. I'm McMurphy. You probably don't remember me."

"I remember."

"You do?" He looked sheepish. "I've been meaning to talk to you about that, but what with one thing and another . . ."

Mrs. Bone hung on his every word. Annoyed, Imogene checked him with a look. "Is there something I can do for you, Mr. McMurphy?"

A tattered piece of paper was crushed in his hands along with the hat. He spread it out apologetically. "I found it all messed up like this or I wouldn't have mashed it." He smoothed the page. "Did you write this?"

Imogene glanced at the sheet briefly; it was one of her handbills for laundry. "It's my advertisement."

"No, ma'am. Did you write it yourself? The letters?"

"Yes. I wrote it myself. Please make your point, Mr. McMurphy."

"Mac." He pulled some crumpled dollar bills out of his shirt pocket and held them out to her. "I was wondering if you'd write a letter home for me. My writing is not so good as yours, and I want it to be a good letter."

Imogene fetched pen and ink and led McMurphy into the kitchen, where there was a steady writing surface. "About that other . . ." Mac began when they were alone.

"There's no need, Mr. McMurphy. A joke is a joke and it's done."

"Oh no, ma'am! That was the straight goods. I'm sorrier'n hell if you took me wrong. I don't blame you for getting your back up, but it's dead earnest. A big, handsome gal like yourself might not get around to looking at a wart of a fellow like me if I was to wait for the natural course of events. I wanted to get my bid in first, is all. No offense meant, none at all."

McMurphy's manner was frank and open, his head bowed over his fisted hat, his eyes as clear as a mountain lake and as blue.

Efficient and businesslike, Imogene dipped her pen and readied the paper, but her cheeks were warmed by the gnarled little man's sincerity. "It's quite all right, Mr. McMurphy. Please sit."

She was at a loss where to look. With an abrupt gesture of annoyance, she brushed her belated girlishness aside and snorted. Meeting Mr. McMurphy's eye, she said, "I am flattered and I thank you for thinking so well of me, but I don't think I will marry. Not in this lifetime."

Halfway through the dictation, old Mrs. Bone found reason to busy herself in the kitchen—a part of the house she avoided at all costs on most days. Neither Imogene nor Mac took any notice of her until the letter was finished and Mac had asked Imogene to sign his name for him. When the ink was dry he folded the page reverently and tucked it into his wallet. Then he hovered near Imogene, standing stiffly by the table, looking pained and pulling absently on his bottom lip. Imogene stoppered the ink, wiped the nib clean, and waited.

"There's something I want to ask you," he finally muttered. Imogene inclined her head. "In private, I mean." Imogene started to say no, but caught Evelynne Bone cocking an eager ear. She escorted Mac out onto the front porch.

"I wasn't exactly straight with you. I said I didn't write so well. Truth is, I don't write at all. Do you think you could teach me? Enough to sign my name? And maybe to read some. I can pay for it."

A light kindled behind Imogene's tired eyes and she smiled. "Teach? Yes, I think I could teach."

19

WITHIN A MONTH, IMOGENE HAD FIVE STUDENTS AND WAS PAYING for half of her room and board. Lutie had volunteered the parlor for lessons, but the men were so self-conscious that they preferred taking their instruction in the rough hominess of the kitchen and agonized over their second-grade primers among the potato peels and onion skins rather than risk someone catching sight of them through the parlor windows.

Sarah Mary was not any better. Sometimes she would sit up, away from the window in her borrowed nightdress, looking out on the town and the river beyond, but mostly she lay abed. She was terribly thin; white skin stretched over the fine bones of her hands, and dark-ringed eyes dominated her face. The recurring fever continued to sap her strength. Her greatest comfort was listening to Imogene tell of the goings-on in the hotel and the town she had never really seen. Imogene found in Sarah a haven from the pressure of earning their keep and the noise and dust of Reno. Together they would watch the change of light on the mountains or talk quietly.

After sunset on July Fourth, 1876, the Centennial, Imogene and Sarah sat in the security of their room. The two women were watching fireworks from their window, the distant explosions carried to them on a soft night wind, when Fred Bone knocked and stuck his head in.

"Lutie sent this up," Fred said, "for nerves." He left them with a jar of homemade wine. In a moment he was back, peeking around the jamb. "By the way, Miss Grelznik, if you like this teaching you got yourself into, you ought to pay Bishop Ozi Whitaker a call. Today I drove by that fancy girls' school he's a-building, and it looks darn near ready for business." Imogene thanked him but said no more about it.

Rockets and noisemakers were joined by drunken shouting and gunfire. Later, down by the Riverside Hotel, some shanties caught fire, sending showers of sparks and flame into the air that paled the gaudiest rockets. The two women sat by the window, hand in hand, until long after midnight, sipping Lutie's nerve medicine.

When they were too tired to watch any longer, Imogene brushed out Sarah's hair for the night and helped her into her nightgown. The scars on her back were still livid against the pale skin, and ridges ran from shoulder to hip.

"Are you going up to that school?" Sarah asked.

"I thought I would."

Sarah closed her eyes and Imogene smoothed the lids with the tip of her finger.

"Sing to me?"

Imogene sang softly, an old lullaby imperfectly remembered from childhood.

Early the next morning, Imogene ate a hasty breakfast and left the hotel. It was clear and cool; the day's traffic had yet to fill the air with dust. She walked half the length of town, turning off Virginia Street when she reached the Truckee River.

Down the river, about a fifteen-minute walk through the sage from the railway station, a three-story building stood on a knoll, facing south over the Truckee. A fancy cupola graced the top, and there was an ornate, pillared, porticoed entrance. The building was not yet completed; it lacked paint, and the front door was leaning against the stair railing, off its hinges. Piles of dirt and brick took the place of lawn and landscaping.

Impeccably groomed and dressed in a short black jacket over a gray bustled dress, Imogene climbed the knoll, carrying her skirt up out of the dust. The clean, pungent smell of sage was swept up by her trailing skirts to mix with the scent of pine borne down from the mountains.

When she reached the summit, she turned and looked back over the river while she caught her breath. It was an ideal place for a school, within walking distance of town but not crowded around with shops, private homes, and other noisy distractions.

No one came out to greet her and there was no sign of life visible through any of the windows. She climbed the long staircase and rapped on the doorframe. Above it, balanced on the sill, not yet nailed in place, was a brass plaque reading BISHOP WHITAKER'S SCHOOL FOR GIRLS.

Imogene knocked again and called out, "Hello! Excuse me! Hello!"

Her voice echoed through the unfinished building. She stepped inside and called again. The room was spacious and well lighted; sawdust covered the floor, and several of the window sashes were propped against the wall waiting to be installed. The smell of new-cut lumber filled the room. Through the window openings, the river sparkled below the deep blue wall of the Sierra. A shadow fell across the rectangle of sunlight on the floor, and Imogene turned.

"I'm Kate Sills. How do you do." The woman in the doorway shifted the cardboard box she was carrying to her hip and thrust out her hand in the manner of a man.

Imogene took it. "I'm Imogene Grelznik. There didn't seem to be anyone here. I apologize for letting myself in. I was told this was to be a school for girls, and my curiosity got the better of my manners."

"Understandable. This may be the last time you'll see it so quiet; we've forty-five girls coming in October. Do you have a school-aged daughter?"

"I'm a teacher. I just came west . . . from Philadelphia. I'd like to apply for a position."

Kate Sills studied her with new interest, and Imogene looked back frankly. Kate was a short woman, squarely built, with a fine, strong head set solidly above broad shoulders. She was thick-middled, in her early forties, with glossy brown hair untouched by gray; she seemed a warm and capable woman.

"I don't expect you've many discipline problems," Kate said, enjoying Imogene's towering height.

Imogene laughed. "Not many."

"Unfortunately, I'm not the one to talk to. Bishop Whitaker does the hiring. I can give you his address if you like; I'm sure he'd be amenable to talking with you if you stopped by. I think all the positions are filled, but you should give it a try." Kate scribbled on a slip of paper with a silver pencil she wore on a chain pinned to her bodice, and handed the note to Imogene. "Would you like me to show you around?" she asked. Imogene accepted and followed her into the cool recesses of the building.

Kate Sills led her through the maze of rooms on each floor—schoolrooms, recitation rooms, music rooms, dormitories, the receiving parlor. The harsh lines of worry carved into Imogene's brow began to ease; she forgot herself in the halls of the school, with its fine rooms and offices, all so new they still smelled of the trees they had been built with. She took off her gloves and ran her palms over the smooth wood of the pianos. "There are five," Kate said as she, too, admired the workmanship. "Tuned."

Bishop Whitaker's school was to have everything: art, music, French, cooking, mineralogy, trigonometry, Old Testament history, astronomy, croquet, painting, philosophy, and bathrooms. Imogene forgot the Broken Promise, the bills, and Sarah Mary.

Talking steadily, comfortably, calling each other by their Christian names, Kate and Imogene rested in the cool of the kitchen over glasses of cold tea. "My mother used to have an old cook," Imogene said. "She was the fattest woman I had ever seen. She could eat more than any two men. I used to sit down in the kitchen with her, afternoons in winter. I remember watching her consume enormous quantities of food and follow it with half an apple pie. Then she'd lean back, pat her stomach, and wink at me. 'I think I've died and gone to pig heaven,' she'd say." Imogene looked around the wide, windowed dining room. "That's how I feel. I'm in pig heaven."

She stopped at Bishop Whitaker's on her way back to the hotel. He was out, Mrs. Whitaker said, but she was welcome to wait. Imogene sat in the dim parlor, chatting with Mrs. Whitaker until her husband returned.

Ozi Whitaker looked like a picture out of the Old Testament of an illustrated King James Bible: a snow-white beard cut in the shape of a spade, a fringe of white hair around a bald dome, and features as sharp and unyielding as chiseled granite. Imogene stood automatically as he strode into the parlor; he was not a large man but he dominated the room. His thin-lipped mouth opened like a trap: "Mrs. Whitaker," he said, "we seem to have an unexpected guest."

Before Imogene could find voice, the bishop held out a cupped hand—a cottontail rabbit, not more than five inches from nose to tail, shivered there in his palm. Mrs. Whitaker lifted the little creature from her husband's outstretched hand and, excusing herself, left the room. "One of the dogs had gotten it," the bishop explained. "I'll let it go out in the meadow when it's old enough to fend for itself." He smiled and gestured to the dusky green settee. Imogene sat abruptly, not quite recovered from his entrance.

The bishop sat down opposite her, completely at ease with the silence, watching her with kindly eyes and waiting until she was ready to speak.

"I was up at your school today," Imogene began, and Ozi Whitaker leaned forward in his chair like a child about to hear a favorite story retold. "It's the most beautifully thought-out school I have ever seen. Ever imagined."

"Ah." He sat back, smiling.

"I'm a teacher."

He thrust out his beard. "Are you a good teacher?"

Imogene thought for a moment. "Yes." The one word carried the weight of her life's worth.

The bishop seemed pleased. "I have hired six instructors and the matron." The bishop regarded her for a minute. He was thinking. He sat across from her as solid and easy as a tree. Imogene, too, was still, but the line of her back and the set of her jaw indicated that it was more a matter of control than of nature. A pendulous ticking sounded from a dark, ornate clock on the mantel behind the bishop's chair. Imogene did not look at it.

"My girls will be Nevadans, most from small mining towns in the desert. Many, I hope, will be given scholarships according to need. They'll come from all walks of life. A lot of them won't have a primary education that's up to our standards." His pale eyes twinkled. "When we're old enough to have standards," he amended.

"Bishop Whitaker's is a high school. We'll need a teacher to take these girls from the desert and bring them up to entrance level—a preparatory school the girls can attend while they're enrolled in other classes, until they've caught up. I've not yet found a teacher for my preparatory classes."

"For the last three years I taught first through eighth grades in a one-room schoolhouse in Pennsylvania."

"I'll need your references."

Imogene sat like a stone. Her jaw jerked once before she spoke. "Of course." She was overly loud. "I'll bring the address by tomorrow, if that would be convenient."

Ozi Whitaker escorted her to the front hall.

"Forgive my manners," the bishop said as Imogene started down the porch steps. "I haven't asked your name."

"Imogene Grelznik."

"Tomorrow then, Miss Grelznik."

Sarah was out of bed, sitting by the window in her nightgown, when Imogene got back to the hotel. Imogene apologized for having been gone so long, and hurried down to the kitchen to bring up a cold lunch. While they ate, she told Sarah of Bishop Whitaker's School For Girls. Some of the light that had come into her face as Kate Sills was showing her the rooms returned as she talked. Sarah left off picking at the food and watched her intently. Imogene was laughing, telling of the bunny and the bishop when she broke off suddenly and her smile faded as she told Sarah, "He wants a reference."

The significance of the request slowly registered on Sarah's face. "You want this, don't you?"

"Very much."

"What are you going to do?"

"Write one myself?" Imogene smiled wryly.

"You can't! It's not honest!"

"No, I suppose I can't. Bishop Whitaker's going to write to Philadelphia. I'll have to write to Mr. Utterback and tell him Mr. Aiken's venom has done it again. I hope that he has returned from Holland, and that my letter reaches him before the bishop's. I'll post it this afternoon."

When she finished writing the letter, she read it to Sarah. The younger woman listened quietly, her eyes fixed on her folded hands. "What do you think?" Imogene asked. Sarah shook her head without speaking.

Imogene sat aside the letter. "I'm sorry. I've made you go through it again, haven't I?"

Sarah waved her hand, a frustrated, negative little gesture. "It's not just that." She looked up and the tears made her eyes seem enormous. "It's that you'll be teaching again and they'll all be so bright and pretty and sure to love you."

The schoolteacher sat down on the bed. "You mustn't worry. It hurts me when you do, as if you don't believe in me. Or think so little of me you think I could forget." She stroked Sarah's cheek. "You can be a little jealous to flatter me, but you mustn't ever believe it."

20

WEEKS PASSED AND THERE WAS STILL NO WORD FROM WILLIAM
Utterback. The money that Imogene was able to earn by teaching
her adult students was inadequate and inconsistent; they paid by
the lesson and often didn't come at appointed times. Lutie and
Fred, though openhearted, began to feel the financial drain; the
summer months were their busy time, and a room and two places
at board paying only partial rates would be felt when money got
tight the following winter. They were too kind to say anything, but
it showed in their faces when Imogene returned from the bishop's
with no news. They, too, were waiting for the letter.

The last week in July, the bishop took Imogene into the formal
parlor and closed the door. "I'm seeing a young man about the
position today. As fond as Mrs. Whitaker and I have grown of you,
I can't in good conscience hire you without references, not when
everyone else was asked to give them."

Imogene nodded abruptly. "I understand." She did not tell
Sarah.

The young man was given the job.

William Utterback's letter came the second week in August.
There was a glowing recommendation addressed to the bishop, and
a sealed note to Imogene so full of un-Quakerlike denunciations of
Darrel Aiken that it warmed her heart to read it.

On September fourth, five weeks before Bishop Whitaker's School was to open its doors, Kate Sills paid Imogene a call at the Broken Promise. There had been a gold strike twenty miles south of Reno, in the Washoe region. Rumors were stampeding the miners from older claims. It was said to be the biggest strike in Nevada's history. The bishop's young man had come to him full of contrition. It was the opportunity of a lifetime, he had said, and he couldn't live with himself if he passed it up. He was terribly sorry if there was any inconvenience, but he'd already bought his kit.

He had been bitten by the gold bug and Imogene had a job. Eighty-five dollars a month. Imogene stayed up half the night, too excited to sleep, writing lesson plans by the light of a lamp turned low so that the glare wouldn't keep Sarah from her rest.

From then on, Imogene spent her days at Bishop Whitaker's School, helping Kate prepare for the fall term. Sarah was alone much of the time. Most days she rose and sometimes she dressed herself, but the sickness had taken its toll and she showed little interest in life.

Disturbed by her apathy, Imogene went to the railroad station and unearthed Sarah's watercolors, bought two new camel's-hair brushes that they could ill afford, and borrowed a generously upholstered parlor chair from Lutie so Sarah would be comfortable.

On a hot day in mid-September, Sarah sat curled up in her chair. A dry desert wind blew incessantly, bringing on a fever and sawing at her nerves. Despite the heat, she had closed the window to escape the wind, and the room was airless and dull. In front of her, propped across the chair arms, was a scrap of board that Imogene had begged of Fred, with a fresh white sheet of watercolor paper tacked onto it. Beside her, on the sill, were her colors. Before Imogene had left that morning, she had set the paints by Sarah and nestled the drawing board across her knees. "You watercolor beautifully," she'd said. "You used to find such pleasure in it. You'd spend hours in the field behind the schoolhouse, lying on your stomach in the sun, painting wildflowers."

Sarah had looked at the board and tiredness had claimed her. "I can't paint anymore."

"Please, Sarah," Imogene had insisted. "It would do you good. One painting. Promise me. Paint a self-portrait. That's bound to be pretty."

And after a minute Sarah had promised. Now, hours later, the paper was still untouched. Wind rattled the pane in a sudden gust. As Sarah shifted in her chair, her paintbox was knocked from the sill and she looked at it for the first time since morning.

Just then footsteps sounded in the hall and knuckles rapped lightly on the door. "Sarah, are you there?" Lutie called. "I got something for you." Sarah pushed the board away and struggled to her feet, to open the door. "Hope you weren't sleeping." Lutie used hushed tones whenever she talked with or about Sarah. "A letter came for you and I thought you'd like it right off."

It was from Mam. Sarah tore it open before the door closed behind Lutie. Margaret's characters, round and thick, sprawled across the page, allowing only four or five words to a line.

> *Dear Sarah (& Imogene),*
>   *Your Pa's going to take me into town today & I'll get a chance to mail this. Things here at home are pretty much like always. A bit emptier maybe, I miss you & I miss Davie more now you're gone too.*
>   *I know you're wanting to hear news of the baby. He got sick, nothing to be scared by, and it did a good turn—Sam brought him here to stay. Gracie's took to that baby like a cow to a calf. She takes care of him like he was her own. And he gets around some. His fat little legs are pumping all the time getting him into this or that. You'd think Gracie'd thin down with all the running after him she does but I think she's going to be a big woman like her Mam. The other day he grabbed her around the knees & said "Mama?"*

There was more to the letter but Sarah didn't read it. She read that last paragraph a second time. Then she stopped reading and rocked herself, Mam's letter crumpled in one fist. Sarah set it carefully on the dresser and walked to the window.

Her toe struck the board to which her watercolor paper was tacked. Sarah snatched it up. "A self-portrait," she said, and started to laugh.

It was after supper when Imogene came home. An untouched tray of food blocked the door outside the room. Imogene pushed it aside and went in.

On the windowsill a candle flickered in the draft, burning unevenly, a pillar of wax towering over the wick. Sheets of paper littered the floor. Pages hastily scrawled with paint, the water curling them into phantom leaves, were scattered over the bed and made piles on the chest of drawers. In the midst of this macabre scene was Sarah, bent over the parlor chair, her drawing board propped against the back. Her color box rested on the chair arm in a dark stain, with a cup of dirty water balanced precariously beside it.

Imogene lit the lamp. "Sarah?" Sarah looked over her shoulder at the sound and fixed Imogene with a blank stare, then turned back to her painting. In the lamplight her dress showed stains where the bodice and skirt had been used to wipe her brush. Lutie's parlor chair was similarly streaked. Imogene watched Sarah for a moment, the little hairs on the back of her neck prickling with fear. She picked up one of the paintings from the floor, a picture done in purples and blacks. She held it to the light. It was a crude watercolor of a naked woman.

Imogene snatched up several more. All were depictions of women. Some were missing arms or legs or features. Most were nude.

Oblivious of everything, Sarah went on painting. Imogene quietly left the room and ran downstairs on tiptoe.

Everyone was gathered in the parlor, close to the fire. Lutie and Fred were engrossed in a game of checkers, and Evelynne, her party manners pitching her voice higher than usual and her thinning hair piled in a particularly intricate nest, was spinning her web for a distinguished-looking guest from San Francisco.

Imogene slipped by the open door unnoticed and, feeling her way through the darkened kitchen, lit the lamp on the pantry shelf. Back behind the applesauce she found the whiskey. Wrapping it carefully in a dishtowel, she hurried back up the stairs.

Sarah had finished another painting; she was trying to affix it to the mirror over the washstand with soap. The glass banged against the wall as she jabbed at it with the bar.

Imogene poured several inches of the whiskey into a tin cup. "Sarah?" She crossed the room and laid her hand on Sarah's shoulder. The girl jerked convulsively, cracking the corner of the mirror.

"Sarah, put that down now, it's time to stop." She worked the soap bar out of Sarah's hand. "Put the painting away," she said gently. "We're done with painting for today. I want you to drink this." Imogene pressed the rim of the cup against Sarah's lower lip.

Most of the whiskey ran down her chin, but Imogene managed to get her to take a few mouthfuls.

"That's the girl. We're done with our work for today. Can you take a little more? Here, drink a little more." Imogene spoke soothingly, pouring the whiskey down Sarah until nearly a quarter of the bottle was gone. The collar of Sarah's dress was soaked and the room stank of whiskey, but at last the rigid muscles in the young woman's face and back began to let go.

Imogene set aside the bottle and eased Sarah onto the bed. Sarah rolled her head on the pillow and smiled lopsidedly. "I been watercoloring." Sudden tears drowned her eyes. "Don't look," she pleaded. "Promise me you won't look. I think I've been crazy," she confided. "I'll be okay now. Don't look."

Imogene promised.

"A self-potrit," her words were slurred. "Potrit-potrit-potrit." She made a little song of it, wagging Imogene's hand in time with the music.

"Gracie's Matthew's mamma now," she murmured when she was near sleep. "Mam said."

Imogene said nothing; the words came as nonsense to her, and she sat grim-faced and scared, her eyes never leaving Sarah's face until the girl slept.

The wind buffeted the hotel, pawing at the eaves and setting the house to howling. Dry clouds raced across the sky, making ghostly shadows under a gibbous moon. Imogene spread the coverlet over Sarah and crossed to the window, taking the whiskey with her. With a chemist's precision, she poured the cup one-quarter full and set the bottle on the sill. The ruined parlor chair still carried its share of Sarah's artwork; pale legs and blood-black breasts leered obscenely in the silvery light. Imogene turned her back on it and, sipping her whiskey, watched the night. The dusty streets rolled away like white velvet, the trees silver and black. In the distance, a lone man leading a mule walked in from the sage. The desert hills behind him were stark and mottled in the moonlight.

Imogene finished her whiskey and turned from the window. She gathered up Sarah's paintings, twenty-five or thirty in all, shredded them into the washbasin, and put a match to them. The paper curled and blackened, the flames leaping as high as the mirror. As quickly, it died away to nothing and Imogene scraped the ashes into the chamber pot.

Deep in a drunken sleep, Sarah did not stir.

Mam's letter turned up the following morning when Imogene took the washbasin downstairs to clean it. Sarah was hung over, but Imogene made her sit up while they read the letter together. Finished, Imogene set it aside and put her arm around the girl's shoulders. "Margaret ought to have known better than to say what she did," Imogene said. "Sometimes when people love you and you leave them, even when it isn't your fault, they say and do spiteful things without meaning to. I think your mam was just missing you very much and her hurting made her mean. It may not even be true."

"He doesn't remember me," Sarah said dully. "I guess it made me crazy for a little while. I'm okay if I don't think about it. I'll be careful."

Imogene hugged her, her cheek pressed against the tangled hair. She held her, thinking. Mam's letter stared up from the mess of blankets.

"We won't let Matthew forget," Imogene said suddenly. She lifted Sarah from her shoulder. "We will write every day. You write a letter to Matthew every day and at the end of every week I'll post them."

Sarah's eyes brightened for a moment, then dimmed. "Matthew's a baby."

"Mam will read them to him. He'll not understand much, but you'll always be there with him. He'll know he has a mother and when he's older he'll know you always thought of him, always loved him. I'll help. We'll start today." She got ink and paper. "Sit up." Pillows were pushed behind her and covers tucked around her until Sarah appeared upright and stable. Imogene spread the paper over a book and dipped her pen. "Dear Matthew?"

Sarah bit her underlip and then began, "My Dear Son Matthew . . ."

It was a short letter, filled with warmth and caring. When it was finished, Sarah signed her name, a shaky, spidery hand under Imogene's sure black strokes.

The parlor chair and the washbasin were ruined. Imogene overruled Lutie's protests and they were added to her bill. She replaced the broken looking glass herself, smuggling in the new one wrapped in a shawl, rather than face the same odd looks occasioned by the chair and the burnt basin. An hour's scrubbing had gotten the worst of the soot off the ceiling above the washstand where the paintings had been burned.

Evelynne Bone, who had seen the paint-smeared chair and the charred basin, gossiped of it. One evening she made the mistake of cornering McMurphy while he waited in the parlor for his lesson. She told him what she had seen. "It smacks of necromancy," she whispered with satisfaction. For her pains, the old miner told her she might put it in her pocket and ride on it; he didn't know what "neck-romancing" was, but he'd bet the old bat had never had any herself.

Two days later, Imogene came home from school at an unaccustomed hour to collect some books she had forgotten. Evelynne Bone was rummaging through the top drawer of the dresser in their room. The old woman scuttled out, snapping a whispered explanation of "seeing to the poor child, alone all day." Sarah was asleep. Without waking her, Imogene kissed her forehead and whispered, "I'll find us a home."

21

SARAH'S FEVER SEEMED TO HAVE BURNED UP WITH THE PAINTINGS; morning after morning she awoke with a cool brow and clear eyes. Imogene began to hope she was finally mending. Weak from the long illness, Sarah stayed in their room much of the time. The first jewellike days of autumn, she had ventured out to sit on the porch in the sun, but the overzealous ministrations of Evelynne Bone had driven her back inside.

With her health, her spirit began to recover. Letters to her son, Matthew, were her chief joy. As she grew stronger, she delighted in keeping house for Imogene. The room was always tidy and a new painting or a spray of sage, carefully arranged, would cheer the schoolteacher's desk. And Imogene's undergarments were mended with such delicate stitchery that Lutie said it was a shame she couldn't show it off to the menfolk.

Both Imogene and Lutie looked for a day when they could take Sarah to the mountains. On a Saturday in Indian summer, they borrowed Fred's vegetable cart and drove Sarah to the meadow west of town. Though there was already snow on the peaks, the air was soft and the sun warm on their backs. Birdsong played with the rush of streams. The summer's last warmth brought out the smell of the pines.

Tethering the pony in the shade of a white pine, they spread their blanket on the bank of a stream that cut through the new grass of the meadow. Sarah, imprisoned so long in her convalescence, turned her face to the sky like a sunflower. In the fresh mountain air she was persuaded to eat half again what she would have at the Broken Promise.

After lunch, Imogene and Sarah left Lutie to doze over her crocheting and walked arm in arm along the creek. Stands of willows bowed over the water, dappling the light with thin, bladelike leaves.

Sarah held tight to Imogene's arm, breathing deeply of the sweet air. "There's no smell like this in the world, Imogene. It makes me feel that if I could only breathe in enough, I could float—like those hot-air balloons you read to me about from the newspaper."

Imogene pressed her hand. "It is good to be out of doors. I think we both had a touch of cabin fever."

For a few moments they walked in silence. Overhead, geese honked, flying south. Golden aspen leaves gilded the mud along the creek.

Sarah slowed to a stop, her face blank in thought.

"What is it?" Imogene asked.

"I was wondering what I would have done without you these past months. What I would do without you now. You were always there."

"I always will be."

Fear touched Sarah like a shadow and she shook herself to be rid of it. "I'm younger than you," she said sadly, then brightened. "But I'm not terribly healthy. Maybe I will die first."

"Sarah!" Imogene laughed. "That's a morbid fancy." She started to stroll again along the stream.

"Wait." Sarah stopped her and took her face between her small hands. "I want to thank you. Lean down." Softly she kissed Imogene's mouth. Sarah's knees gave way and the schoolteacher had to support her in the crook of her arm.

"My dear! Are you all right?" Anxiously she laid a hand on Sarah's forehead, but it was cool to the touch. "Your eyes are feverbright."

"I'm fine," Sarah said breathlessly. "I'm singing inside." Her face quickly sobered. "Maybe we'd better go back to Lutie."

"Let's sit a minute," Imogene suggested. "Let you rest—let me rest." She smiled at Sarah. "Sometimes I don't know if my old heart can take you. It's pounding like a stampede of wild mustangs.

Besides, I have some good news. I wanted to wait till we were alone to tell you." Imogene sat on a fallen log and Sarah perched obediently beside her. "I have found us a house. It is quite small, but it is dear. And we can afford it with what I'm making at the school."

"Imogene, you don't mean it? Just the two of us?"

"Just the two of us."

Sarah hugged herself. "You can't guess all the hours, when my eyes were still too weak from the fever to read, I passed the time pretending we had our own home. Little dreams—like me calling to you from another room and nobody else to hear, us puttering around the kitchen. Mam'd never believe this, but I'd think how I'd like doing the dishes and filling the icebox with food. How long have you known?" she demanded suddenly, and pounced on Imogene, tickling her for keeping such a secret.

Imogene captured her hands and held them in her lap. "I found out this morning. Our landlady, Mrs. Addie Glass, sent over a note that I'd been found satisfactory."

"Tell me everything—how many windows, how many doors, how many nails in the walls—everything."

"Sarah," Imogene asked earnestly, "are you happy?"

Sarah looked long into her friend's face before answering. "It means a lot to you?"

"More than the world."

Sarah hesitated, choosing her words. "Knowing that you love me makes it so things can't ever get as bad again as they could before I knew that," she began. "Your love is a net under me. I still fall but now I can never hit bottom."

Imogene said nothing.

"Yes, I'm happy."

"It would be good to hear you laugh again."

"I will."

On the second Saturday in October they moved their belongings from the Broken Promise. A breeze blew rich with the smell of a mountain autumn. Fred's wagon was out front, already loaded with the boxes that had been so long at the warehouse down by the tracks.

Sarah was on the porch, apart from the bump and bustle of moving. Sitting still and pale in the fall sunshine, her blond hair in close, neat braids, she looked like a porcelain doll. Her skin was smooth and translucent from the months indoors, her white hands folded small in billowing skirts. Around her, people spoke softly, were a little kinder, and when they looked at her they smiled.

Mac carried a valise past her. It was his third trip to the wagon, and each time he tipped his hat to Sarah, tugging on the battered brim with the two remaining fingers of his right hand. The young man Imogene had seen with him the day he proposed to her was helping with the move. Mac had introduced him as Nate Weldrick. Nate was of medium height and build, with a wide face. Thick, wavy brown hair and a boyish grin made him look younger than his thirty-two years. He seemed even more ill at ease with Sarah than Mac did, afraid to come near or speak, and giving her a wide berth when he crossed the porch so his heavy footfalls wouldn't jar her.

Imogene was in high spirits as she loaded the last of their things into the wagon. "Sarah," she called, "are you ready?"

Lutie came out carrying a box covered with a dishcloth. "Something to take with you." Imogene pulled back the cloth and laughed at the wealth of food Lutie had packed.

"We shan't starve on the crosstown drive. Thank you. I'll bring the box back as soon as we're settled in."

"Never mind." Lutie waved her hand in a dismissing gesture, and gave Imogene a hug. Sarah came down from the porch and Lutie patted her cheek tenderly. "Are you sure it's not too soon? Who's to get Sarah's lunch?" she demanded.

"I'll get it for myself," Sarah replied. "I can, Lutie, it's just that I forget." Lutie hugged her and both women looked a little misty until Lutie laughed and reminded herself they were moving less than a mile away.

Nate Weldrick jumped down from the wagon as the three women approached. Unobserved and uninvited, a fourth woman was coming as well. She weaved unsteadily across the road, thin graying hair falling around a heavy face mapped with age and broken blood vessels. A boy, scarcely two years old, was clutched under her arm and jounced against her fat middle uncomplainingly, his square dusky face grave, his straight black hair tumbled over his eyes. The woman rounded the end of the wagon and grabbed Nate's arm.

"Hey! I'm talking to you, Weldrick." She fell against the side of the wagon. The little boy wriggled free, landing on his round behind in the dirt. He didn't cry, and as soon as the scuffle of feet permitted, he pulled himself up with the aid of a wheel and toddled off.

"I ain't been paid!" The woman jerked Nate's arm like a pump handle until he pulled away.

"Hattie, get away from me. Go on. Git. You're drunk. You been paid."

"I ain't. You want that half-breed kid of yours looked after, I got to have more money. He eats more'n any three white kids."

"Wolf ain't eating it, you're drinking it, you old cow."

"You watch who you're callin' a cow! I got better things to do than look after your half-breed brats."

She was hanging on the front of his shirt as much from instability as from anger. He pushed her away and turned to Imogene and Lutie. "This ain't no kind of scene to be having before you ladies, and I'm sure as hell—begging your pardon—sorry." He turned viciously on the hag still plucking at his elbow. "Hattie, get that damned brat out of here!" He dropped his voice and shot another embarrassed look over his shoulder. "Get that kid out of here. What're you thinking, bringing him here?"

Hattie hadn't lost her head of steam. "I'll bring him anywhere I want," she retorted. "I got to spend my own money on that kid. You ain't give me enough—"

A gurgling laugh, a rich, high sound Imogene hadn't heard in a long time, turned her attention from the argument. Sarah was sitting on the porch steps, her skirts falling into the dirt on either side, laughing and playing pat-a-cake with the baby. Wolf lifted his pudgy little hands to mirror hers, playing the game with solemn intensity. The child was dirty, his hair and clothes ragged and unkempt, but his eyes and skin were clear and the flesh firm over his stocky frame.

"I'm sorry about this," Nate said to Imogene's back, and pulling out a leather purse, he turned on Hattie. "You get that kid away from these people," he hissed. "I've told you before."

Hattie eyed the closed purse blearily. "I want four dollars."

"What you want ain't necessarily what—"

"Mr. Weldrick," Imogene cut in.

"I'm sorry, ma'am. I'm holding you good folks up."

"Is that your child?" She looked to where Sarah and Wolf played on the steps.

Nate's face reddened. "Wolf! You get away from that lady, you hear me? Wolf!" Imogene shushed him as Sarah looked up. Wolf, ignoring his father's orders, sat down promptly and began playing with the hem of Sarah's long skirts.

"Never mind, Sarah," Imogene called. "Mr. Weldrick, is that child yours?"

"Yes, ma'am," he admitted.

"And this woman cares for him?"

He nodded.

"Four dollars—" Hattie began.

Imogene cut her off. "What do you pay her?"

Lutie looked shocked. Nate was taken aback as well, but the force of Imogene's personality made it impossible not to answer.

"Three dollars a week."

"We'll take him, Mr. Weldrick. Sarah and I. Mrs. Ebbitt is home during the day. She has some experience with small children. Three dollars a week, with careful husbanding, will pay for his food and clothing. Is that acceptable to you, Mr. Weldrick?" It was more a statement than a question. Nate looked helpless in the face of her rapid-fire reasoning. "Then it's settled." She thrust out her hand and he pinched the ends of her fingers awkwardly.

"Hey! Hey, you, lady!" Hattie stumped belligerently after Imogene as she walked back to the yard. "What about me?"

Imogene stopped. "You are not fit to care for a child," she reasoned. "I suggest you go home and sober up." And she left Hattie sputtering at the gate. Nate Weldrick had to give her two dollars severance pay before she would leave.

Their new house was small, set behind an old Victorian home on the banks of the Truckee, in a yard planted around with elm trees. The cottage nestled amid a small grove at the end of the yard. At one time it had housed Chinese servants. The windows in the main room looked out across the lawn to the big house where the widow Addie Glass lived alone. She was small and white-haired, and as energetic as a woman half her age. Mrs. Glass had met Imogene, the last in a long line of prospective tenants, and finding her plain dress and forthright manner appealing, she had let Imogene have the place for fourteen dollars a month.

The cottage had two small bedrooms, a living room, and a kitchen. Thirty yards through the trees and out into the sage stood the outhouse. In the kitchen and the bedrooms, the ceilings were just over six feet high, and though Imogene would not have bumped her head, she stooped. "The Chinese," Mrs. Glass had explained, "are a small people. Mr. Glass didn't want to waste the lumber."

The wagon came up the drive beside the big house, Nate Wel-

drick walking alongside, Imogene and Sarah sharing the seat with
Mac. Wolf, perched on Sarah's knees, her arms around his middle
so he couldn't fall, watched the proceedings with the same serious
demeanor he'd worn while playing pat-a-cake. Mrs. Addie Glass
waved to them from her parlor window but didn't come out; she
was sitting with a young woman draped in the black of mourning.

"Cora Ferguson," Mac said, making the gossip sound like news.
"Husband killed by Indians up Susanville way. Fella on watch deserted—fella named Fox—and the Indians snuck in and killed five
soldiers. Sleeping. The whole patrol. Hear she's going back to
New Orleans."

Wolf was unaware he was half Indian, but Nate wasn't and
looked disgusted as he lifted the child from Sarah's lap to the
ground. He handed Sarah down with gentlemanly deference, then
spoke over her head to Imogene. "I don't think I ought to be leaving
Wolf. Mrs. Ebbitt here's weak as a kitten, she can't hardly lift that
kid, and he's about half-wild, according to Hattie."

To everyone's surprise, Sarah spoke up. "I can lift Wolf."

"She'll hurt herself trying, Miss Grelznik," Nate insisted. He
leaned down and put his hands on his knees. "Mrs. Ebbitt," he
said gently, "you'll go hurting yourself, trying to lug that boy
around, and I'd feel real responsible. Old Hattie's fine for him. You
look after yourself and get your strength back. He's a dirty little
beggar; you don't want him all over you."

"I can lift him," Sarah said, but the fear that she could not care
for a child clouded her face and she sounded uncertain. Imogene
climbed down to stand between Sarah and Nate. Nate had to
straighten up and step back to look her in the eye.

"Mr. Weldrick, we shook on it. I've heard a handshake is legal
tender in a court of law out West. Sarah, why don't you take
Wolf inside?"

Sarah wavered a moment, vague and unsure. "It'll be fine,"
Imogene said, and Sarah led the child away.

Nate looked after them while Imogene busied herself with the
unloading. "Mac," he said, "somebody once gave me brandy in one
of those long-legged glasses that ping when you flick them. I bit
right through it, the glass was so fine. Just took a bite right out of
the rim. Cut my lip. That little gal makes me think of that."

To add to their small store of goods from Pennsylvania, Fred
and Lutie had given them two cots, Addie Glass had brought several

chairs and a small table down from the attic to put in their living room, and Mac had pressed an old Colt .45 on them. "Law here's often as not settled by the authority of Judge Colt," he said.

While Imogene opened her boxes of books, dishes, and household goods, Sarah made a soft bed of blankets for Wolf in the room that was to be hers. Often, with Wolf pattering at her heels like an affectionate puppy, Sarah sought Imogene out with questions. Did they have a washtub for the child? Was there enough money for a new suit of clothes? Where were the scissors to trim his hair? Had Imogene seen the soap dish? Imogene had to settle the two of them in a comfortable corner with a picture book lest Sarah wear herself out.

They were both napping when Imogene finished cleaning their new home. Wolf sucked his thumb as he slept, a fold of Sarah's dress clutched in his fist. Imogene tiptoed past them, outside, to dump her washwater.

"We're a family," she said. She tilted her head back and looked up at the patch of sky framed by a delicate golden tracery of leaves. "Thank you."

22

OVER THE WINTER, SARAH GREW STRONGER. BAD WEATHER AND WOLF gave her an excuse not to venture out much, and except for Imogene and McMurphy, she saw no one. When summer came around, Imogene gave her the task of the household shopping to get her to go into town so she could overcome her shyness around strangers.

Sarah made Mac go with her.

"It smells summery."

Mac flared his big nostrils and took a noisy sniff. "You're the smellingest gal I ever knew, Mrs. Ebbitt."

"I can smell the sage when it's hot, and the horses, and the sun on the wood. Summer. Back home it's not so dry, and the air's got so many smells you mostly can't sort them out."

"It's dry, I'll give you that. Maybe later we'll get some rain. August sometime'll bring down thunderstorms." They walked in silence for a while, Wolf at Sarah's side, kicking up little puffs of dust for the pleasure of watching them fly. The wooden buildings soaked up the sunlight and sent it back into the air in shimmering waves. Sarah wore a sunbonnet to protect her face, and a new peach-and-brown plaid dress that Imogene had made for her on the Singer sewing machine at the school.

Mac had given up prospecting in late spring and had taken a job caring for Wells Fargo's draft animals. Mostly he worked after-

noons and evenings, currying and bedding down the teams in from
the run across to Pyramid Lake and the Smoke Creek Desert. "I
ain't going shopping with you," he said. "But I'll be waiting around
to carry. Find me. Don't go trying to carry things yourself."

He left her in front of the stationer's. Imogene's credit was good
in any shop in Reno, and consequently so was Sarah's, and the
storekeepers were used to the shy young woman with the half-breed
Indian boy. After leaving the stationer's, Sarah went to the grocery
and the dry goods, leaving her purchases to be called for at the
counter. After a week's letters to her son were posted, she looked
for Mac.

The boardwalk that fronted most of the stores harbored scattered
idlers in its shade, the sun sweeping them farther and farther under
the overhang. Mac's gnomelike figure was not among them. Above
the town, the mountains faded to cardboard cutouts in the summer
haze, with a speck of white here and there, where a pocket of snow
escaped the sun's detection. Shading her eyes, Sarah searched the
far side of the street.

"Where do you think Mac's got himself to?" Sarah asked Wolf.

Without hesitation the toddler thrust a round arm out and
pointed across the street. "Saloon." In his limited vocabulary, "saloon" was one of the few two-syllable words he used. Wolf was not
given to much talk.

The doors of the Silver Nugget were open, the shade an even
stronger draw on an August afternoon than whiskey, gambling, or
women. After the dazzle of the day, nothing was visible inside. A
howl, a human coyote baying at the moon, sounded from the darkness behind the open doors, and Sarah blanched. "I get him." Wolf
disengaged his hand from hers and started resolutely across the
street, as though routing men from saloons was not a new experience
for him.

Sarah caught up with him. "We'll go together."

Inside the double doors, the saloon floor had been cleared of
tables. Men, talking and shouting, formed a tight circle around the
open space, the beer in the mugs they held slopping onto the sawdust and other patrons. In the ring were two men and two dogs: a
squat, beefy fellow in his mid-fifties straddling a black dog and
sporting a bowler pulled down against his ears so that his snow-
white hair thrust out in waves below the brim; and a long-legged,
long-haired man with a red beard that covered his neckerchief,

crouching on his hands and knees, face to face with a shaggy brown and gray mutt.

The bearded man stuck out his tongue and began licking his dog's broad chest. Owners were expected to "taste" their dogs to assure the bettors that poison had not been spread on their fur before the fight. Quiet fell on the gathering as they watched intently. "That's enough," said the man who'd called for them to begin. "Manny ain't poisoned."

Sarah stood dumbstruck in the open doorway, clasping Wolf's hand in hers. "He licked that dog!" she said half to herself, half to the boy. She spoke softly, but her words fell in a sudden quiet and the bearded man's eyes rolled up from the dog to her. He let out an earsplitting roar and charged toward her. Mac, standing to the back of the ring of bodies, upon a chair so he could better witness the proceedings, dropped his beer and threw himself after the charging man.

He was too late. The dog-licker had cleared the saloon in three strides. His long arms wrapped around Sarah and swung her high into the air. Wolf sat crying in the dirt, and Sarah was screaming.

"David!" she cried when her breath returned, and standing on tiptoe, holding tightly to his neck, she sobbed happily. Mac, having brought a barstool out with him, stopped brandishing it when he saw that the two of them were acquainted, and perched on it instead, rubbing his jaw with his finger stubs.

David turned to the faces crowding the doorway. "My sister," he announced. He whooped again and tossed her into the air, eliciting a little, breathless scream. When he put her down they stared shyly at each other, neither knowing what to say.

David offered her his arm. "Front of a saloon's no place for a man's sister. Come on, Manny." He whistled and the dog trotted out to wait at his heels. "Sorry about the fight, boys. You understand. Another time."

Brother and sister walked up Virginia Street toward the river, Sarah's arm held firmly under David's, Wolf doggedly clutching Sarah's skirts, virtually forgotten. "It's good to see you, Sarah Mary. I get lonely for family. Doggone, but it's good to see you!" He threw back his head and laughed. Sarah wasn't saying anything, but she clung to his arm, smiling up at him and giving him a shake and pressing her head against his shoulder now and then as though to convince herself he was real.

"I never thought I'd see you again," she said as they left the main street. Tears started and he held her, laughing down at her and patting her back with his big hands.

"I promised when I left, didn't I? Well, there you are." He surveyed her critically. "You're just a little bit of a thing. No bigger'n a girl. And shyer than I remember."

She tugged at a strand of his long hair. "You're just like I remember you. Exactly."

Addie came out on the porch with disapproval wrapped around her like a cloak. Her eyes raked David's considerable height, from his balding head to the heels of his heavy railroad boots. Sarah introduced him as her brother, and the formidable little lady graciously let them pass into the backyard.

They sat under the elms, talking. David recounted his adventures, changing them where necessary to make Sarah laugh. He had started for the silver mines of Virginia City as he had planned, to strike it rich. A year had passed before he arrived. On the trip across the country, he had struck up a friendship with an engineer who worked for the railroad, surveying track, building bridges, and digging tunnels. They had sat up all night, passing a bottle between them and swapping tall tales. David admitted that as the younger and less experienced of the two, he'd invented most of his contributions. By morning it had been decided that David would travel with the engineer and learn engineering.

"Now I'm a regular railroad typhoon." David laughed at his own joke and went on, "Danny's dead, blew himself up tunneling through the gold country in California, but I'm building bridges the same way he would've done." He was silent for several minutes, remembering his friend.

He asked Sarah what had brought her west, and had to be satisfied with the answer, "I came with Imogene." She avoided the subject and looked so miserable when he tried to pursue it that he let it go.

In midafternoon Mac came by, carrying the parcels Sarah had forgotten in town. At first he was gruff and disgruntled, jealousy making him peevish. But a little coaxing from Sarah cheered him and he joined them on the grass. He and David knew a lot of people in common; the subject of family being exhausted for the moment, the conversation moved on to embrace people and events further afield.

Wolf was over his first fear of David and played close to the big man, missing no opportunity to get a good look at his beard. Finally, David invited the little boy to touch it. After a tentative pat and a tug or two, Wolf, evidently satisfied as to its texture and authenticity, wandered off to play in Addie's rhododendrons.

"Where'd you come by the Indian kid?" David asked.

"I take care of him for his pa," Sarah replied. "Wolf's a good boy."

David looked at his sister, warm and maternal, smiling at the baby as he played.

"Look!" Wolf crowed, waving a perfectly ordinary twig, and Sarah laughed and clapped her hands.

David winked at Mac. "Some Indian's kid landed in a pot of jam."

"He's only half Indian," Mac said. "Pa's a miner up Virginia City way, though he gets around. Does a lot of things. Right now he's over to San Francisco doing some damn thing."

"Wife die?"

"I don't know as they were rightly married, when it comes down to it. I don't know if a white man can marry an Indian in Nevada. They had some Indian mumbo-jumbo, I remember. Me and Nate was pretty drunk. But not a marriage proper like you think of."

"Did she die?" Sarah asked this time.

"No, Weldrick run out on her. Last I heard, she was shacked up with some miner up near Carson."

"Wolf's mother is alive?" The odd tone in Sarah's voice caught Mac up short in his gossiping. Imogene and Sarah were close-mouthed about their personal affairs, but Mac had seen the changes the Indian boy had brought about in Sarah.

"You getting at something I'm missing?" He cocked a wary eyebrow.

"Wolf ought to be with his mother," Sarah said flatly.

"Now that ain't so. After Nate lit out she took to the booze, can't leave it alone. And besides, she run off and left the kid—guess her new fellow didn't take to half-breeds not of his own making— and last November she left him outside a flophouse Nate was staying at. Naked as the day is long, and tethered to the horse trough with a piece of rawhide. If he hadn't shied a horse by wiggling, nobody'd have found him till he froze to death. I guess the little fellow never set up a caterwauling like most kids would've done. That's the In-

dian in him, I expect. You keep that boy, Mrs. Ebbitt. You take
him back to his ma, he'll die as sure as if you put a gun to his head
and pulled the trigger." Mac's exaggeration had the desired effect;
the haunted look left Sarah's eyes and she watched Wolf like a
young lioness would watch a lone cub.

"Mrs. Ebbitt?" David looked at his sister.

"I married Sam Ebbitt."

"That pigheaded, psalm-singing son of a bitch!" David exploded. "Jesus Christ, why?"

Sarah looked ready to cry.

Mac shoved himself to his feet, saying he had to see a man
about a horse, and, excusing himself, hurried from the yard.

"Why?"

"I just did," was all she would say. Another avenue of inquiry
was closed and they sat without speaking, watching the clouds
change shape overhead. With Wolf's busy hands busied elsewhere,
Manny came out from under the porch where he'd hidden himself,
to lie between Sarah and David. He flopped down with a mournful
sigh and rested his chin on his paws. Sarah scratched his ears for
him.

"You like Manny?"

She nodded. The dog pricked up an ear at the sound of his
name.

"I named him Emmanuel after Pa. He's a fighter, takes offense
at everything and starts in snapping."

"You miss Pa?"

"Nope."

"Remember Sam Ebbitt's old yellow-eyed dog?"

"That damn dog bit me once. I like to killed him, but he got
under that woodshed."

"I *did* kill him."

"You're joking me!"

"No, I'm not. I choked him in a door." Sarah smiled a little in
spite of herself. "And I'm not sorry, either."

David laughed so loud it brought Mrs. Glass to the window.

When Imogene came home from school, Sarah, David, and Wolf
were indoors preparing dinner. When it was ready, Sarah said a
simple grace: "I thank You, Lord, for my brother."

After supper she asked David to stay with them while he was in

Reno, and Imogene added her welcome, but David declined, making his excuses. "It's just nine—way before my bedtime," he said. "I'll likely still be visiting with some of the boys long after you're asleep. I can sleep anywhere. Besides, I've got to be in Auburn—over the Sierras—tomorrow, but I'll come by in the morning and say good-bye. I'm in these parts a lot," he assured Sarah. "I'll be on your doorstep so much you'll wish I'd stayed lost."

He wouldn't change his mind and so Sarah hugged him, said good night, and went in the bedroom to tuck Wolf in. David and Imogene could hear her singing to the boy through the door. David paused on the porch steps. "Could you walk with me a bit, Miss Grelznik? There's some subjects I'm not clear on."

The night had turned cold. Even in summer a wind came down off the mountains and cooled the valley at night. In the clear, dry air, there seemed to be half again as many stars as shone in the Pennsylvania skies. They walked in silence for a while, following the footpath along the river, David's silhouette only slightly taller than Imogene's.

"How do you come to be out West?" he asked. And Imogene told him of Darrel's accusations and Karen Cogswell's hysterical outburst, of Sam whipping Sarah and breaking into Imogene's house when Sarah had run there for protection.

"Was it true about you and Sare?"

Imogene answered with an icy stare.

"I'm sorry," he said after a moment. "There was no call to ask that."

"I'm sorry too." They walked on, Manny padding softly at David's heels.

"Do you need money?" he asked, ending a long silence.

"No. I have a good job. We can take care of ourselves."

Before they parted, Imogene gave him the address they used to send letters to Mam, and he scribbled down the address of a bar in Virginia City where he received his mail.

23

SUMMER STAYED LONG INTO SEPTEMBER AND CAME AGAIN FOR A WEEK in late October. The bishop's girls returned, a year older and anxious to lord it over the new students. Imogene immersed herself again in her beloved school, and Sarah tended to the household and to Wolf. Sarah spent her days with him, and the child brought her out of herself.

Nothing was seen of Nate Weldrick, but the money for Wolf's upkeep came every few weeks by way of Mac.

David passed through Reno twice more and spent a day each time with Sarah. Wolf learned to ride Manny, much to the dog's annoyance, and Sarah made David forbid it for fear that Manny would bite the boy.

With Indian summer, the last of the warm weather disappeared and geese honked overhead in black, southbound vees. At Thanksgiving, the bishop gave the school five fat Canada geese and Imogene persuaded Sarah to join the girls for Thanksgiving dinner. Shy and retiring, Sarah said little and ate sparingly. The girls were enchanted and made up romantic stories about her for half the night.

A fire burned in the potbellied stove, the flames devouring the wood with a shirring sound, making the room cozy. Outside, a thin, hard winter sun shone, its cold light glinting off bare branches and winter-brown grass. Only the white pine in the far corner of the yard retained its greenery, unperturbed by the passing of the seasons, grander even in winter.

Sarah sat near the stove, her head bent over a tiny red flannel shirt, her narrow hands plying the needle deftly. Wolf had left a pile of wooden blocks behind to climb up on a chair. Kneeling on the seat, he pressed his cheek against the pane, squeezing his eyes to the right. A little fir tree leaned against the porch, its boughs tied up with twine.

"I can see the tree," he said solemnly.

"Mmm-mm." Sarah didn't need to ask which tree; the fir had been a favorite topic of conversation since Fred Bone had brought it by several days before.

"We're going to put the tree in here with us."

"That's right," Sarah assented. "It's a Christmas tree."

Wolf lost interest in it; Christmas Eve was almost a week away, and the little boy lived entirely in the present. He jumped off the chair and waddled over to a bookcase under the far window. Suddenly he chirped with excitement, "Somebody coming."

Sarah set aside her sewing and joined him at the window. "It looks like your pa."

Nate rode up the drive past Addie Glass's house and tied his horse to one of the bushes. The horse was a sleek claybank stallion with a white diamond on his forehead. Horse, saddle, and bridle were new, the leather still bright and creaky. Nate wore stiff new dungarees—"reach-me-downs," the creases sharp from where they'd been folded on the store shelf—and a new shirt. Grease flattened his unruly curls, and the corner of his mouth bled a little from a recent shave.

Sarah backed away from the window.

"He's coming up the walk," Wolf announced.

Sarah picked up her sewing, looked around the room, and put it down again.

"He's at the door," said the little sentinel. The knock came and Sarah jumped.

"He's knocking on the door," Wolf reported. Reluctantly, Sarah opened it. The overwhelming scent of pomade and new leather greeted her. Nate pulled his hat off; his shining cap of hair was dented where the band had been.

"Afternoon, ma'am. I'm Nate Weldrick, as you may recall."

"I remember." There was an uncomfortable pause. "Wolf's pa."

"That's right." He shifted his weight and looked past her into the house. "I'd have been by sooner, but I been over San Francisco way these last six, eight months."

"Won't you come in?" she said belatedly.

Nate sat in the lookout chair, turning his hat between his knees. The boy had disappeared. Sarah sat down on her sewing, bouncing oddly when she realized what she'd done. Too embarrassed to remove it, she spread her skirts to the sides so the red flannel wouldn't peek out from underneath.

"You've come to see Wolf?" Her voice was high-pitched and airy. She cleared her throat.

"You could say that."

Sarah's eyes searched the small living room as if a three-year-old child could simply have been overlooked. "He was just here. Let me check the other room." She escaped into her bedroom and closed the door. Wolf was sitting quietly on the box bed she and Imogene had bought for him, not doing anything, just sitting with the air of an adult resigned to waiting. Sarah knelt beside him. "Wolf, your pa's here to see you."

"I ain't s'posed to stay in the room when he's with ladies."

"That's silly. Don't you want to see your pa? Come on." Sarah held out her hand and he accompanied her unenthusiastically back into the front room.

Father and son stared at each other.

"Why don't you say hello to your pa?" Sarah whispered.

"Pa." Wolf tasted the word. An alien sound.

"You know better," Nate said. "Nate." He smiled at Sarah, a charming, boyish smile showing off straight, healthy teeth. One side of his mouth was slightly paralyzed, and the stiffness lent him a rakish air. "Taught him to call me Nate. 'Pa' sounded kind of funny somehow, coming from an Indian kid." Sarah nodded as though she understood. Wolf stayed obediently in front of his father, awaiting further instructions.

"Looks like you been taking good care of him. I mean his clothes are clean and whatnot."

"He's a good boy."

"You get tired of looking after him, you let me know. Hattie'll take him back." Again the boyish grin. "Hattie'll do anything for a fifth of whiskey."

"I won't get tired of Wolf." The boy was still standing in front of his father, solemn and unblinking.

Nate looked down at him. "Ain't you got something to do?"

Recognizing a dismissal, Wolf went to the blocks he'd left tumbled under the window and was instantly absorbed in the construction of a doomed tower.

"It ain't a bad day," Nate said when the silence had grown too long. "I got a horse in San Francisco. Maybe you'd like to see him? It ain't a bad day; out of the wind it's above freezing."

Sarah considered his proposal for a moment. The cold winter light was not inviting, but Nate's bulk made the house uncomfortably small. "I'll get my things."

In a few minutes she reemerged from the bedroom, wearing a cape and gloves, a small wool coat over her arm. "Get your coat on, Wolf. It's nippy out." She held the coat ready, its stubby arms outthrust as though an invisible child were already inside.

"The kid'll be okay here by himself," Nate said.

"I don't leave Wolf home alone. He's too little," Sarah returned quietly. Her soft eyes reproached Nate and he squirmed.

"That horse of mine ain't never seen a kid; I don't know how he'll take to him."

Sarah showed no inclination to leave without Wolf.

"Bring him along. What the—the hay." Nate shrugged and pulled on his hat.

Nate's new horse was seventeen hands high, with a wide, powerful chest. He pranced and threw his head up, whinnying nervously when the three of them approached.

"Easy there, settle down, Hellion." The name did little to reassure Sarah, and she hung back, keeping Wolf with her. "Easy there, settle down. Attaboy." Nate got a grip on the bridle and jerked. The heavy spade bit dug into the animal's mouth and the proud head came down. "Come on up to him. He ain't going to hurt you, I got him." Sarah wouldn't have moved, but Wolf tugged her ahead fearlessly. "Go on and pet him. But keep an eye on him, he's been known to bite. Stay back from his front hooves," Nate warned Wolf. Sarah lifted the boy with an effort and let him stroke the velvet nose.

"I'll take you for a ride, ma'am," Nate offered.

"No, I'd be scared." Sarah set Wolf down and held him firmly at her side.

"Come on. It ain't nothing. I'll be holding his head. With a spade bit, he can't do nothing. Get on, I'll give you a ride." The horse whinnied and rolled an eye down at Sarah; white showed around the black, and Sarah paled.

"No, I don't ride. I'm afraid of horses."

"Now look, I told you I was going to be right here. I ain't going to leave, and with me holding him there's nothing to be afraid of." He held out his hand. "Wolf, get yourself clear."

Finally, Sarah let herself be lifted onto the horse's back. She sat there trembling and holding onto the saddlehorn with both hands. Hellion danced a little and twitched his hide as though to rid himself of a fly.

They'd gone an eighth of a mile, nearly to Virginia Street, when Hellion shied at nothing and skittered, sidestepping perilously near the river's edge. Sarah cried out and Nate laughed, gentling the horse.

"Could I get down now?" Too frightened to move, Sarah looked helplessly at the stirrup dangling below her boot.

"He was just feeling his oats. I had him. You're as safe as houses up there."

"Please, I want down. Please." Nate shrugged ungraciously and lifted her out of the saddle. She immediately put him between her and Hellion. Wolf scampered up to take her hand and the three of them walked on without further conversation. At Virginia Street they turned back, keeping to the river path.

"I brought you something from the city." Nate pulled a paper parcel from his jacket and held it out to her. "For you and the kid," he said, and Sarah accepted it.

"Is it a Christmas present?" she asked shyly.

"It's near Christmas, ain't it? Yeah, I guess you could say that." Sarah started to tuck it away in a pocket of her cloak.

"Open it."

"It's a Christmas present."

"Hell. No, it ain't. It's just a *present* present. Open it."

Sarah peeled back the brown paper; there was crinkly white confectioner's paper inside and she tore it open.

Nate laughed at the look on her face.

"What are they?" she asked. The package contained flat, withered, orange-brown circles, their edges curling up all around.

"Eat one."

She took one out gingerly. Nate pinched two from the package and popped one in his mouth; the other he gave to Wolf. The little boy nibbled an edge off and chewed contentedly. "Candy," he said to Sarah.

"You know what these are, kid?" Wolf looked suspiciously up at his father. "These are dried ears. They cut them off little Indian boys and dry them out in the sun. They dry up sweet as anything." Wolf put his hands over his ears and hid his face in Sarah's cape.

"Stop it," Sarah said. "You're scaring him."

Nate bridled at the uncharacteristic authority in her voice. "Don't be a crybaby," he snapped at the boy. "Nobody likes a scaredycat." Wolf buried his face deeper in the folds of the cloak. Nate bent over, his hands on his knees. "Come on now, I was just teasing. What's the matter, can't you take a little teasing? Them's just dried apricots is all. Little bitty pieces of dried fruit." The child refused to be cajoled. "Come on, kid, you want a horseback ride? I'll give you a horseback ride." Wolf was not proof against the temptation of a ride on horseback, and came out from behind Sarah to be lifted into the saddle, where he gazed happily around, delighted with his new vantage point, his short legs sticking out to the sides.

"You warm enough?" Nate asked Sarah after a minute.

"Yes."

"Don't talk much, do you?"

"No."

"Cat got your tongue?"

"No."

Nate let the conversation rest for a while before he tried again. "I mean no disrespect, but you're a fine-looking girl." Sarah blushed and he smiled at the red in her cheeks. "I've a mind to ask if I can come calling another time."

"I'm married."

Nate snorted. "Mrs. Ebbitt, ain't it?"

"Yes. Mrs. Sam Ebbitt."

"I don't recall seeing a Mr. Ebbitt."

Sarah said nothing.

"He run out on you?"

"No," she almost whispered.

"Well, it ain't natural, a young, good-looking girl like you living holed up with an old-maid schoolteacher. Nobody to talk to. Nobody to look pretty for. It ain't the way the Lord intended. A pretty little gal like you—"

"We've got to be getting home," Sarah burst out. She darted back and pulled Wolf from the saddle, her fear of the animal forgotten. "We're going home now," she explained to the startled child. "Thank you for the ride, Mr. Weldrick." Wolf was big for a three-year-old, but Sarah picked him up, carrying him awkwardly across her chest.

Nate started after her. "Here! Let me take you home."

"No!"

Lugging a protesting Wolf, Sarah ran from him.

Imogene left school just after four o'clock; she had stayed late, working on a fitted wool coat of soft robin's-egg blue—Sarah's Christmas present. Mac had donated two white rabbit pelts to line the hood and cuffs.

Columns of smoke rose from chimneys all over town, particles of soot and ash catching the thin sunlight. Above the railroad station, black smoke billowed from engines coaling up for the haul over the mountains. Walking quickly to keep warm, Imogene passed through the quiet residential neighborhood and across Virginia Street to the railroad station.

"I'm expecting a parcel from Philadelphia," she said to the clerk. "Books." Tired of waiting the many months it often took for books to arrive after ordering, Imogene had taken to sending William Utterback lists of materials she needed. He bought them for her in Philadelphia and sent them out. If Kate felt that the school could use them, Imogene was reimbursed; if not, she paid for them out of her own pocket.

The books had arrived in two big boxes. Imogene pulled one over the counter and cut it open with a single-bladed jackknife she took from her purse. There was a letter from Mr. Utterback inside; she took it out, then tied up the box again and lifted it experimentally. "I can't carry both by myself. Is there someone here who can help me?" she asked the clerk on duty.

"It's an off time; I'm the only one here. I can't leave or I'd do it myself." The clerk leaned on the counter and sucked his teeth thoughtfully. "Might try over to the Wells Fargo. Judge Curler's got an errand boy over there not good for much."

Imogene thanked him and sat down to read her letter before walking the short distance to the Wells Fargo office.

3 November 1877

Dear Imogene,

Here are the books thee ordered but for The Old
Curiosity Shop. *I shall keep looking and send it when I can.
Mrs. Utterback is in as good health as our years will allow,
and sends her best.*

*Kevin Ramsey has remarried, to quite a nice girl, Mrs.
Utterback says, and is moving west to Illinois to be a farmer.
It will be a better life for Mary Beth's child.*

*I have news of an old friend of thine, Mr. Aiken. He left
Philadelphia with Friend Oakes's cashbox and the hired girl—
the young woman was just turned fourteen and a very slow
thinker. The girl is back now, heavy with child; he left her just
outside of New Orleans. No one has heard from Mr. Aiken.*

*I hope that this finds thee well and content, and that the
books are all in order.*

Peace,
William Utterback

Imogene folded the letter and put it in her purse. "I'll be back
for my parcels," she informed the clerk.

She proceeded to the Wells Fargo office. Judge Curler sat at an
oversized desk behind a railing, steel-rimmed glasses pinched on the
end of his nose, poring over a pile of receipts. By the woodstove
lounged an ungainly fellow in his early twenties, his pimpled cheeks
covered with fine, sparse hair. He was thick without any evidence
of strength, the flesh heavy and slack. A second desk in the back
was empty but for a sign reading R. JENSEN. DIZABLE & DENNING.
In one corner stood a telegraph apparatus.

The judge looked up as Imogene opened the door. "What can
I do for you?" He removed his glasses and laid them carefully beside
the book he was working on.

"The clerk at the railroad station said you had a boy here who
might be able to carry some parcels home for me. It's not far."

"Harland!"

The young man toasting his feet swung his chair around.

"This is Harland Maydley, ma'am. He'll get your things home
for you. Harland, make yourself useful for a change; give this lady
a hand with her boxes."

Harland pushed himself laboriously from his chair and pulled on his coat with a lethargy that bordered on insolence.

Imogene walked quickly, with long clean strides, and Harland Maydley, with his shorter legs, had to skip every few steps to keep up.

"You're Miss Grelznik, ain't you? Teacher up to the school?"

"I'm Miss Grelznik."

"Mac McMurphy told me when I pointed you out once. That girl your daughter?"

"No." Imogene closed her mouth behind the word with a finality that would have daunted even an only slightly more sensitive individual.

"She's a looker, in a hoity-toity kind of way," Harland went on.

"The young lady is married."

"Yeah? I seen her out riding today with Nate Weldrick and that half-breed kid of his." The sneering insinuation brought Imogene up short, and he stumbled to avoid bumping into her. They were several hundred feet from Addie's house.

"Thank you, Mr. Maydley, that will be all." She dug in her purse, took out a nickel, and tipped him. "Just set the boxes down. I can take them the rest of the way without your assistance."

He looked her up and down impertinently in an attempt to regain face, but she was too tall, too unbending. He dropped the boxes in the dirt.

"You tell that *married* lady that Harland Maydley said hello." And with the air of an unanswerable wit, he turned and sauntered down the street.

Imogene watched him go, her lips compressed, two white dents on either side of her nose appearing and disappearing as she breathed. "I so detest little men," she muttered, and without taking her eyes from Maydley's back, she bent down to grasp the twine of the boxes, clenched her teeth against the bite of it, and carried them the rest of the way home.

The smell of cornbread baking and beans simmering on the stove met her at the door. She shouldered her way in and set down her burden.

"That you?" Sarah called from the kitchen.

"It's me." Taking the chair by the stove, Imogene pulled off her gloves. Dark red creases marked the places where the twine had bitten into her fingers. Across one palm, the scar from the burn she'd received in her confrontation with Sam Ebbitt showed ridged and redder than usual. Imogene made a fist and then slowly spread her fingers; the hand no longer opened completely. She turned her hands palms down so she needn't look at them, and held them near the stove.

Sarah came in from the kitchen, wiping her hands on a dishtowel. The heat from the stove pinked her cheeks prettily. "Look what Wolf and I did," she said, pointing to a small feathery wreath over the bookcase. It was of pine, and the long needles thrust out in all directions, making it far from round. Nestled in the needles were bright scraps of fabric sewn into fat butterfly bows.

"You've had quite a busy day, haven't you?"

Sarah ignored the edge in Imogene's voice. "I asked Mrs. Glass, and she said that big old pine would never know me and Wolf had taken anything."

"Wolf and I."

Sarah looked dubious. "Are you sure?"

"I'm sure."

"Anyway, do you like it?"

"It's lovely," Imogene said without much enthusiasm.

"You don't like it."

The schoolteacher heaved a sigh. "I'm sorry, my dear. I'm just tired, I suppose. I like it."

Sarah walked to the window, rubbing her already dry hands with the towel. The sky was the clear gray of winter twilight, the bare elms etching it with black. Through the dark branches an early star twinkled. The yard had already gone into night, and Addie's Victorian home loomed up out of the darkness like a lighthouse on the shore of a dark sea.

"It gets dark so early now."

Imogene didn't reply.

"Nate Weldrick came by to see Wolf today."

"Ah. How paternal. Where is Wolf now?"

"Napping." Sarah came over to perch on one of the boxes beside Imogene. "We went out for a ride with him. He gave me those."

Imogene glanced at the bowl of dried apricots on the table. "Did you have a nice time?"

"I'm scared of horses, I didn't want to ride it. It was one of those big ones that rolls its eyes at you." Sarah stared out the window as she talked.

"Do you like Mr. Weldrick?"

Sarah pulled her thoughts back from the riverbank to look at her companion. The teacher's face was carefully composed and gave no clue to her thoughts. Sarah picked up Imogene's hand and pressed the scarred palm to her cheek.

"You're so cool. It feels good."

"Are you feverish?" Imogene asked in alarm.

"No, it's from the stove. I don't think I like Mr. Weldrick," she went on, to answer Imogene's original question. "He was nice, though. Not to Wolf. If I didn't know already, I'd never guess he was Wolf's pa by the way they act around each other. But maybe I like him okay. He's a man." Sarah waved her hand as if this explained all.

"Your brother and Mac are men; Lutie's Fred is a man too," Imogene reminded her. "If Mr. Weldrick is boorish, his sex is no excuse."

"I don't know." Sarah played with Imogene's fingers, arranging them, crablike, on her knee. "He said it was unnatural, two women alone with nobody to talk to—you know."

"Yes. I do know. No man to talk to. How empty our lives must be without the intellectual stimulation that the likes of Mr. Weldrick could provide. I suppose his sparkling wit and fascinating manner kept you spellbound?" Imogene had risen to stalk about the room; she snapped a picture book shut and turned to Sarah.

"No-o," Sarah said carefully, choosing her words, "but I know what he meant. We're just women."

Imogene said nothing.

"It's unnatural."

Imogene forced herself to be still and returned to the chair beside Sarah. "Do you like him?" she asked gently. "Being with him, does it make you happy?"

"No," Sarah said.

"Then there's an end to it."

Sarah bit her lip and gazed out through the dying light to the river.

≋ 24

SNOW WAS FALLING IN TINY DRY FLAKES, A DUSTING OF WHITE
already on the ground. The wind swooped down from the mountain
slopes in sudden gusts, sending the snow into white whorls and
pushing wavelets of white across the frozen lawn. Slate-colored
clouds hid the mountain peaks, and the Truckee River ran gray
in sympathy.

Sarah watched out the window, the snow quietly cloaking the
brown grass and leaving a white tracery on the tree branches.

Wolf pushed up beside her, nudging under her arm. "Can we
play at Mrs. Whitaker's today?"

She stroked the coarse black hair. "Not today, today is for staying indoors. Home." She looked around, eyes soft with contentment. The bare makeshift look of the rooms was gone, and homely
touches warmed the house: a rag rug on the floor, crocheted doilies
on the chair arms, white-and-blue sprigged curtains in the windows.
"I like being inside when it snows; I always have, even when I was
a little girl. I could be warm and snug and look out the window
and watch the snow come down."

"Can I go outside?"

"A little later. Imogene has half-day on Saturdays, maybe she'll
take you out when she gets home. If the snow gets deep enough,
maybe we'll make a snowman."

The snow was ankle-deep by the time Imogene, red-nosed and smiling at an all-white world, came home from school. She and Sarah bundled Wolf in sweaters, coats, and scarves until he could scarcely move, took him out near the banks of the Truckee, where the drifts were deepest, and taught him to make angels in the snow.

Nate's clayback stallion was tethered in the drive when they got home. Around the horse's hooves the snow had been churned black, and a blanket was thrown over him. Wisps of smoke came from the stove pipe, rising straight up until they were as high as the main house, then feathering off sharply to the east.

Imogene shifted Wolf to her other hip; he'd been too tired to walk. "Evidently Mr. Weldrick is here. He's been to call on Wolf a half-dozen times since the new year. Fatherhood seems to have hit him hard, if rather late."

Sarah looked confused and depressed, an expression she often wore when Nate Weldrick came to call. "He's not on the porch."

"It seems he's invited himself in and built a fire," Imogene said sourly. She strode to the front door and jerked it open, banging it against the side of the house. Nate, who was crouched before the stove, poking kindling into a growing fire, started at the crash.

"Mr. Weldrick. What a surprise." Imogene stood in the doorway without coming in.

"How do, Miss Grelznik." He reached to take his hat off but it wasn't there; he snatched it from the chair beside him. "Come in, come on in."

"Thank you." She was painfully polite.

"I nearly froze to death riding over from Carson. Just got here maybe a quarter of an hour ago. You gals were out, so I just kind of let myself in."

"So I see."

"Didn't figure you'd mind, what with it snowing and all."

"You're here, it seems, so it would certainly be a waste of time to mind. If you'll excuse me, Wolf is wet and tired. We all are." Imogene carried the boy into the room he shared with Sarah, and closed the door.

Quietly, Sarah shut the front door and lit the lamps. A lamp flared, brightening her cheeks and eyes for a moment before she turned down the wick.

"You look real pretty. That's a pretty coat," Nate said.

"Imogene made it for me."

"You look pretty in it. You ought to wear it more often."

"I wear it when I go outside." Sarah fingered the fur on the collar, then, at a loss for anything else to do, took it off, though the room hadn't taken any warmth from the fledgling fire.

"That blue looks good, better than all the drab gray stuff she's got you in most of the time. You ought to get yourself some bright-colored things."

Sarah hung up the coat and smoothed the sleeves of her charcoal-colored gown self-consciously. It was another of Imogene's dresses cut down and resewn to fit Sarah's slight frame.

"Get yourself something pretty." Nate dug into his pocket and took out a small leather purse.

"Please, Mr. Weldrick." Sarah glanced anxiously toward the bedroom door.

"You're afraid of her, ain't you?"

Sarah laughed, a light surprised sound.

"She don't like me much, does she?"

"I don't know. We never talk about you."

Her answer seemed to annoy him.

It was late when he finally left. Imogene stood in front of the stove, heating sausage cakes in the skillet. At the kitchen table, perched on a stool, Sarah peeled and sliced boiled potatoes. Neither had suggested supper while Nate Weldrick was there.

"Wolf never got his supper," Sarah said. "Should I wake him, do you think?"

Imogene pushed at the sausages with a wooden spatula. "I think not."

Sarah dropped the potatoes into the hot grease and watched them brown. A companionable silence flowed around them, warmed by the sizzling.

"Mr. Weldrick thinks you don't like him. Do you?" Sarah asked.

Imogene spooned their dinner onto the waiting plates. "I don't think he's a good father," she replied carefully. "But mostly I suppose I don't care for him because he makes you so unhappy."

"Mr. Weldrick's nice to me," Sarah protested.

"Yes and no."

Sarah waited.

"He's pleasant and complimentary," Imogene continued, "and he seems to care for you, after his fashion. But since we've moved to this house you have come so far. I remember those first months at the Broken Promise—you are so much stronger now, more sure of yourself. Mr. Weldrick takes that away from you."

"I don't know," Sarah said, suddenly tired. "I don't know anything anymore."

Imogene looked up at the hollow sound of her voice—the confusion, the depression. *"Demonstratum est,"* she said.

Before Sarah could reply there came a sound of bells, of pots and pans crashing together in the icy air, of shouting and the beating of makeshift drums. Faint at first, a long way off, then growing louder, the din swelled as the noisemakers came up Virginia Street to the river. Hooting and wild laughter cut through the winter night.

Grabbing wraps, the two women stepped outside, leaving their supper to grow cold. Addie Glass was on her back porch, a heavy dressing gown thrown over her bed clothes. She was carrying a lantern.

"Miss Grelznik, Mrs. Ebbitt—I was just coming to fetch you," she called excitedly, waving them over. "I thought, being so new to the West, you maybe hadn't seen a charivari." The lantern cast ample light and they hurried over the snow.

Addie led them through the dim corridors of her house and into the front parlor. "It's better if it's dark," Addie said when they reached the bay window overlooking the street, and blew out the lantern. In its last light her weathered face looked as rosy as a young girl's, and her eyes shone. "They'll be by in a few minutes. I remember my charivari like it was yesterday. Rupert was the drunkest of all." She laughed at her memories. "My Rupert was the sweetest drunk in the state. He loved everybody. If I'd come late, he would've married the best man."

Across the water, the first dancing lights came into view, and individual voices could sometimes be distinguished from the general tumult.

"They're grander here than anywhere," the old lady said. "The Chinese sell fireworks beforehand."

The parade of torches and lanterns snaked like a dragon along the road following the river. Snatches of song floated out across the water. Addie Glass leaned forward and opened the window. "Never mind the cold," she said. "Look, there's the bride and groom."

Pushed along at the dragon's head, a buckboard covered in homemade decorations carried the newlyweds. Running alongside the groom were the loudest merrymakers, whistling and banging spoons and pails against the wagon. The bride, all in white, her veil falling off, clung to the seat, radiant even across the width of the Truckee. The buckboard was pulled by a mass of men in lieu of horses. Those too tired or too drunk would stagger away to be replaced by fresh pullers.

"Look at them!" Addie said. "Just look at them! That's the way it ought to be."

Entranced, Sarah watched the torches weaving and dipping through the night like winter fireflies, mirrored by running reflections on the river's surface.

"Like it should be," she murmured.

Throughout the spring and summer, Nate came to call on Sarah, and though she showed little pleasure at his attentions, she always received him. For Wolf's sake, she said.

Imogene would sniff and purse her lips and say nothing.

❧ 25

ELMS AND OAKS WERE FROSTBITTEN TO RED AND GOLD, AND THE warm yellow autumn leaves of the cottonwood trees lined the streets. Imogene stepped out of the stationer's and heard a train whistle in the distance. "Most trains will be carrying Bishop Whitaker girls," she said to herself. "They'll be trickling in all week." The thought brought a smile.

A gust of wind fluttered her shawl. She looked to the west, where the tips of stormclouds were visible beyond the mountain peak. As Imogene watched, the front grew and darkened. She hurried along the boardwalk.

McMurphy was lounging against the side of the stable across the street from the Wells Fargo office, his back against the sun-warmed wood. He jerked his hatbrim as she approached. "After-noon, Miss Grelznik."

"I haven't seen you since August, Mac. Have you gone back to prospecting?" Imogene asked.

"No, ma'am, I got put up from stablehand to swamper. I been mostly on the run to Pyramid and Round Hole."

"What does a swamper do?"

"This one reads." He pulled a yellowed magazine out of his hip pocket, showing off to his teacher. The cover featured a cowboy and several dozen Indians. "I'm reading right now." He tapped the magazine.

"After a fashion," Imogene said dryly.

Mac laughed and folded the cowboy book back into his pocket. "What I do is ride along on the stage and see to the livestock, changing teams, hitching, unhitching, and feeding and whatnot. We've got horses at every stop, pretty near."

Lightning flashed to the west, a great forked tongue licking down the mountain side. Half a minute later the rumble of thunder reached their ears.

Mac sniffed the air. "Whoo-ee! We ain't long for it now."

"It looks as if I'd best be going." Imogene pushed her hatpins in. "Congratulations on your new position, Mac."

"I hope you're not thinking to go home," Mac winked.

"Why not?" Imogene asked.

"Not more'n twenty minutes ago, Nate come by. He was slicked up and pomaded till a skunk wouldn't have him. I asked him if he was going courting. He said, 'Not today I ain't. Today I'm going asking.' He wasn't just beating his gums, neither, he meant to do it. Figured he could talk little Mrs. Ebbitt around if they was alone. She's a docile little gal. Maybe you want to hole up over to the office for a while, let them kids do their lovemaking. The judge's got the stove going."

Sarah was behind the house on the path, collecting colorful sprigs of leaves, when she heard Nate's claybank on the drive. She stood poised for an instant like a doe ready to run, her basket of branches under her arm. Gusts heavily scented with the coming rain blew fire-colored leaves around her skirts.

Nate rapped smartly on the door. There was no answer and he opened it partway. "Anybody home?" Silence. He closed it and came around the end of the house. "Hello! Guess you didn't hear my hullabaloo. I figured you might be to the outhouse."

Sarah blushed. "I was collecting leaves, Mr. Weldrick." She showed him her basket.

"Be your last chance, this storm blowing up's going to pound them off." He walked with her back to the house. In the closeness of the living room the smell of his pomade was overpowering. Sarah started to open a window and then stopped, embarrassed.

Nate grinned. "Guess I'm pretty ripe, ain't I? I told the barber I was calling on a lady and he got kind of heavy-handed with the stinkum."

Sarah smiled. She looked at the clock over the bookcase.

"You expecting Miss Grelznik home anytime soon?"

Sarah dropped her eyes. "Not for another hour or two."

"Where's the kid?"

"He was cranky. I think he was feeling a little peaked, so I put him to bed."

Nate absorbed this information, nodding. "I'll get right down to what I come about. I been calling pretty regular these past months, haven't I?" He looked at Sarah. "You'll give me that?"

"Yes, that's so. You come to see Wolf."

"You know that ain't it; I come calling on you. You know that the same as you know I'm sitting here."

Sarah didn't say anything.

"What do you say to that, Sarah?"

It was the first time he had ever called her by her Christian name, and she looked up, startled.

"The way I figure it, I got no call to go on calling you Mrs. Ebbitt. Either Mr. Ebbitt's dead or run out on you, and either way, according to my way of thinking, he's lost his claim. You leave a property unmined for a while and pretty soon your claim's no good. It's anybody's. So I figure you're just plain Sarah Ebbitt now." Nate was loud, argumentative.

Sarah sat in the straight-backed chair by the stove, pleating and unpleating her skirt between her fingers.

"You ought to have a husband and kids of your own," he went on. "Not living with a dried-up old maid, keeping house for her and raising a half-breed Indian kid. You ought to have a man to look after you."

A war look came into Sarah's eyes. "I like keeping house with Imogene."

"That ain't the point!" He made a chopping gesture and banged the end of his little finger on the chair. "Damn." He thrust the injured pinky into his mouth and got up to pace in front of the window. The storm had hit; rain drummed against the glass, obscuring the trees on the far side of the yard behind wavering curtains of gray. There had been no single drops to herald the downpour; it had come all at once, dinning on the roof and ringing down the stovepipe. It was dark enough to light the lamps, though it was just after two o'clock.

The bedroom door opened a crack, then all the way, and Wolf

came out. "Sarie? I'm having bad dreams." Sarah's relief was evident as she turned her attention to the sleepy child. She knelt and pushed the lank hair from his face.

"What's the matter, Wolf?" She laid the back of her hand on his forehead.

Nate turned from the window. "Damn it, Wolf, go on, get yourself back to bed. Don't be bothering us now."

Sarah folded Wolf in her arms. "Your pa doesn't mean it, honey. What kind of dreams?" When she talked to the child, her shy, uneasy look evaporated, and her hazel eyes were warm, her small mouth soft. Wolf nuzzled into her shoulder.

Nate picked the boy bodily off the floor out of the comfort of Sarah's embrace. "Come on, kid. This ain't the time." To Sarah he said, "You stay put. We ain't done talking yet." Before she could say a word he was out the door, Wolf with him.

The storm had broken before Imogene was halfway home, and she ran, her shawl pulled up over her head. Her skirts were heavy with water in a moment, and rain streamed off her face. Wet leaves blew against her, brown with the rain, clinging like seaweed.

As she turned off the river road, up the drive, thunder cracked overhead and a prong of lightning threw the cottage and the yard into sharp relief. Imogene slowed to a walk, clutching her side, panting for breath. Nate stepped out on the porch and slammed the door. Imogene recognized him and stopped. Instinctively she backed against the side of the main house, where she was half-hidden behind the stone chimney.

Nate carried Wolf under his arm; the boy's face was tight with tears. Nate reached under the canvas waterproof over his saddle and jerked out his hat and coat. He jammed the protesting child into them, pulling the hat down around the boy's ears. Then, carrying Wolf like a bundle of dirty laundry, Nate plunked him down on the top step of Addie's back porch, where it was dry. "You stay put, you hear? Don't you come in till I tell you." And with that he strode back to the house and let himself in without knocking.

"The nerve of that man!" Imogene whispered. Color rushed to her cheeks and she began to shake. She stepped from the shelter of the chimney and stared at the house. Her lips twitched, thoughts forming and changing as she watched the mute façade of the home she shared with Sarah. Rain formed icy rivulets and ran down her neck and collar.

A chirping sound distracted her. She looked over to the porch where Nate had left his son. Wolf had managed to wriggle out of Nate's mackinaw, and bareheaded and coatless, he played at boats in the overflow of Addie's rain gutter. He was as wet as if he'd been tossed in the river. Quickly, Imogene bundled the child in her sodden shawl and ran for the house.

The storm covered the sound of the front door opening.

Nate held Sarah by the shoulders, her narrow frame crumpled between his hands. His face was pushed close to hers. "What kind of a life have you got here? Answer me that," he was insisting. Sarah would not raise her eyes to his.

Thunder rolled overhead, the wind abated, and for a moment it was still. Into the stillness, Imogene spoke. "A very fine life, Mr. Weldrick."

She stepped over the sill and put the bundle that was Wolf into Sarah's waiting arms. "He's soaked to the skin, Sarah. Perhaps you will take care of Mr. Weldrick's son. It is clear he will not."

"Wolf!" Sarah cradled him to her breast. "No wrap." She fixed Nate with a hard look. "Mr. Weldrick, if he catches cold . . ." She never finished her threat, but escaped into the bedroom with the child and slammed the door.

Imogene turned to Nate. "Please leave, Mr. Weldrick. Your attentions are not appreciated here."

"Sarah!" He banged on the bedroom door and rattled the knob. She had locked it from the inside. "Sarah, that kid had a coat!"

"Get out!" Imogene turned him from Sarah's door with one arm.

"I'm proposing marriage," Nate protested.

"The young lady has a husband. You've been made aware of that."

"She can get a divorce."

"And live with her neighbors always pointing and gossiping?"

"Not out here, there ain't enough women. Nobody'd ask. Nobody'd know. A gal like Sarah'd get respect wherever she was. You're so damn jealous you can't see straight."

The blood drained from Imogene's lips and her hand clenched on their chair back.

"That's it, ain't it?" Nate sneered. "Jealous. I ain't blind. Mac ain't blind. Anybody with eyes can see. You go green when a man so much as looks at her. You're jealous because men ain't falling all over themselves to pay court to you. If anything wearing pants gave you the eye, you'd change your tune fast enough.''

Imogene laughed, not the hurting, humorless laugh of a frightened woman, but full-throated and easy, and Nate was surprised into silence. "Is that what you think, Mr. Weldrick?" The laughter still played around her mouth. "That I want a man of my own?"

"I do," he said sullenly.

She smiled and shook her head. "You cut a sorry figure for a courting beau—giving your attentions to a married woman, no land, no job, no prospects. What do you come to offer Sarah? You've demeaned the life she has here with me. Here she is respected and cared for, she has clothes and food and a decent place to live, friends that love her. What do you offer? Your manliness? Get out.'' Imogene held open the door, ignoring the rain that blew in on the rug.

"I can give her kids of her own."

Imogene's composure crumbled. "Get out!"

Unhurriedly, Nate crossed to the door. "I aim to get all them other things. I ain't intending to drag Sarah all over the country; I figured to quit jobbing and settle down. If I've got to do it first, so be it. I'll be back. And then you can prate your by-God, nose-in-the-air head off and be damned. I'm going to marry her.''

Imogene closed the door quietly after him and stayed for a moment staring at the wood. Low voices came from Sarah's room, murmuring in mellow accord with the rain. Imogene's wide shoulders sagged and she turned wearily. Sarah stood in the doorway. Rain drummed steadily on the roof and walls, filling the room with sound. Gray light, filtering through the streaming windows, ran down the walls and stripped the color from the rag rugs. Sarah crossed the room and put her arms around the schoolteacher's waist, laying her head against the wet ruffles on Imogene's bodice.

Imogene held her close. "I'm sorry, Sarah. I was so terribly jealous. So afraid I would lose you. I'm sorry. Do you want to marry Mr. Weldrick?'' Her voice, deep and hollow, seemed to bubble up from the depths of a well.

"I don't know."

"Hush now, don't cry, talk to me."

"It would be better, maybe. I guess I should. I can't go on forever like this. I just don't know. I'm so afraid.''

Wolf was crying, a thin, fretful whimpering.

"He's hot," Sarah said. "It makes him peevish. I think he's coming down with something."

"We'd better see to him," Imogene replied, but they stood a moment longer in the wavering half-light, holding on to each other.

ᕙ 26

THE LAMPS IN THE KITCHEN HAD BEEN LIT FOR HOURS. RAIN STILL pounded against the windows. Neither Imogene nor Sarah had mentioned Nate or his proposal of that afternoon.

"Wolf's a little under the weather," Sarah said, removing the boy's place setting and putting it away. "I'm going to put him to bed with a dish of bread pudding. I think he's taken a chill. That drenching Nate put him through seems to have aggravated it. He was feeling a little peaked before Mr. Weldrick came." She scooped a bowl half-full of pudding and took a spoon from the drawer.

"Take a candle?"

"No need." Slipping the spoon in her pocket, Sarah left the kitchen.

Imogene pushed the fried ham to the back of the stove, where it would stay warm, and took the potatoes from the oven. She squeezed them until their jackets burst open and put a chunk of butter in each.

Sarah returned, slipped into her place at the table, and said grace. Neither had an appetite, and after making a feeble attempt to eat, they cleared the dishes and went to sit by Wolf. The only light in the room spilled in through the open door from the living room. Wolf, round-faced as the moon, lay quiet, his arms at his sides.

Sarah smiled. "He's asleep."

"It's a good sign."

At the sound of voices, Wolf opened his dark eyes. "You sleep," Sarah said, and he closed them obediently. Imogene laid the back of her hand against the curve of his cheek. "If the fever is not gone of itself by morning, we'll call the doctor."

In the morning he was worse; his eyes shone with an unnatural luster, and the skin of his face was drawn and hot. The bed gave him no comfort and he complained ceaselessly that there were rocks and spiders in it.

The doctor came at midmorning. It was influenza. People died of it in the winter. He'd seen whole mining camps wiped out. "Keep him warm," he said. "As warm as he'll let you. Sometimes the fever breaks."

Imogene stood over Wolf. The little box bed came scarcely to her knees, and she loomed over it like a giantess. "I've been out in the rain, soaked to the skin a hundred times. When I was a girl at Elmira College in New York, I used to wash my hair Saturday afternoon before chapel. In winter it would freeze on the way across College Square and melt during prayers, dripping down my back. I never once caught cold."

"Wolf's a baby," Sarah replied.

"Who would think a moment in the rain without a coat could chill him so much?"

"It was more than a moment; Mr. Weldrick made him go outside before you came home."

Imogene shook as a tremor ran down her spine, and busied herself in the kitchen making strong broth.

They took turns sitting with Wolf, replacing the covers when he threw them off, and watching the fever consume him. Sarah grew pale and dark-eyed, mirroring the face of the child. She would not sleep even when Imogene sat with Wolf, and wouldn't stay out of the room long enough to eat a proper meal.

Near midnight on the third night of Wolf's illness, Imogene came in to sit with her.

"You ought to try to sleep, Sarah. You'll get sick."

Sarah shook her head. Her hair, plaited into one long braid, fell over her shoulder. She tied it in the sash of her robe to keep it out of the way. Wolf lay quiet in his little bed, the covers tucked up under his chin.

"He seems to be resting better," Sarah said.

Imogene looked at the hollow eyes, their pupils twitching under the lids, and laid her hand on his chest. The fragile cage of flesh and bone trembled under her palm as Wolf labored for air. "Maybe."

"Mr. Weldrick put him out in the rain with no coat."

Imogene didn't comment.

"I might have stopped him if I'd said something."

"Don't, Sarah. Nate Weldrick did what he did. You can't blame yourself."

In the early hours of morning, Imogene lay awake, the lamp turned low by her bedside. Sarah was sitting with Wolf in the other room. Too tired to concentrate on her book, Imogene lay listening. The rain had let up and the wind soughed through the wet and falling leaves. A low, piercing wail started. As if that had been the sound she was listening for, Imogene threw back the bedclothes and ran to the other room.

Hands clasped tightly in her lap, her shoulders hunched almost to her knees, Sarah keened a single, wavering, high-pitched note, and rocked herself. She looked up when Imogene came in.

"He's just gone. Burned up." She clawed at the air, trying to drag understanding from it. "Gone."

Sarah turned her face against the familiar planes of her friend's broad chest, and great gulping sobs tore out of her. Imogene held her, her own tears falling into the soft halo of hair.

Wolf was an Indian and so couldn't be buried in the Christian cemetery. The Indian cemetery was on the outskirts of Reno, and the gravediggers grumbled at having to walk so far in the rain. Drizzle darkened and smeared the wooden tombstones, and around the grave the mud was ankle-deep. Imogene stood close to Sarah, with Lutie and Fred beside her. Mac was at Sarah's other side, his grizzled old face as soft as a woman's around the mouth and eyes. He'd carried the coffin from the wagon, he and Fred Bone; it was scarcely half the length of a man, and its toy-sized dimensions mocked the living. Across from them, over the open grave, the bishop and Mrs. Whitaker bowed their heads. Sarah, dead calm, stood between Imogene and Mac, her face drawn and sunken around the eyes, but composed.

When it was over and the handfuls of wet earth had been dropped on the coffin, Sarah and Imogene rode home with the

Whitakers. Ozi's proud, matched bays, young and spirited, refused to suit their steps to the occasion and lifted their feet high out of the mud as if dancing. The cloud cover had begun to break and the sun came through in rainbowed fingers, touching the leaves back to gold.

"Will you come in for a bite?" Mrs. Whitaker asked as they drew abreast of the Whitaker house. "I'll bet you've not had a decent meal in a while. Come in and eat."

"Sarah?" Imogene asked.

"No thank you, Mrs. Whitaker, I couldn't."

"Won't help to go hungry," the bishop's wife advised.

Ozi shook the reins. "Bishop?" Imogene laid a hand on the seatback. "I'd like to walk the rest, if you don't mind. I need to get out and walk a little."

"It's wet. You'll catch a chill yourself."

"I'd like to walk too," Sarah said unexpectedly. There was a sense of quiet authority drawn around her like a cloak, the same sad sense of self-possession that had straightened her back at the graveside. The bishop bowed to the dignity of her grief and helped them both from the carriage.

Late-autumn sunlight shone warm on their backs, and the morning's drizzle sparkled on every leaf and blade of grass. The pungent smell of rain-washed earth and rotting leaves swelled up from the ground. A thin mist rose from the river and blew into translucent ribbons over the water. Arms linked, they walked side by side on the grassy bank, avoiding the mud of the path.

"Things aren't real yet," Sarah said. "Like Wolf's not being home when we get there. No more. Something that can't be fixed, won't ever be better. I can't believe that. How am I going to bear it when I do?"

"We'll bear it together."

"I should have married Mr. Weldrick like he wanted me to."

"Why?"

"I had another chance. Mam says folks don't often get more than one. Maybe God took Wolf because I wouldn't take it. If there was a life to be taken, it should've been mine."

"I can't believe in a God who would kill a child to prove a point," Imogene said.

"Imogene! Please don't!" Sarah glanced nervously up at the

clearing depths of the sky. "He does things like that in the Bible all the time."

"So he does."

Their skirts were wet and mud-spattered by the time they reached home. Wrapped in a dry robe, Imogene built a fire and arranged their petticoats over a chair in front of the stove, their wet shoes and stockings lined up like black attendants underneath. Sarah, clad only in bodice and pantalets, sat by the table, her eyes fixed on nothing.

By her chair, a picture book lay on the floor. Toys littered a corner of the room, a half-demolished castle of wooden blocks leaned against the bookcase, and a miniature jacket hung beside Sarah's blue wool coat on a peg by the door.

"Why don't you lie down for a while, Sarah?"

"Can I lay on your bed?"

"We can trade rooms if you like."

Sarah stopped in the doorway and looked back. "Nate Weldrick put him out like a stray cat," she said. "I might have married Nate. I wouldn't have liked it, maybe, but I know I've got to right myself with things. But he put him out without a thought. Drowned him like a kitten."

Imogene looked away, hiding her eyes with her hand.

Imogene boxed up Wolf's toys and tidied the house while Sarah slept, and later the two of them sat at the table, Sarah reading, Imogene plying her needle to the hem of a pillow sham. Scented autumn air came in through the open windows, and a small fire burned in the woodstove to take the chill out.

Kate Sills came up the drive with a basket of preserves—gifts from the staff and herself. Wet leaves muffled her footsteps and neither Sarah nor Imogene heard her until she reached the house. Imogene put the kettle on and the three of them sat around the table, the two teachers talking quietly.

"Imogene, Bishop Whitaker and I have discussed it," Kate said, "and we can get by without you for the first week or so of winter-term, if you'd like."

Sarah spoke up before Imogene could reply. "Go back Monday, Imogene, you know you should. Teaching always makes you feel better."

"I don't want you to be by yourself in an empty house."

"I'll be all right. I have some things to do. I'll have Addie and I can walk over to Mrs. Whitaker's if I'm lonely." There was a new firmness to Sarah and no trace of self-pity in her words.

Imogene stirred her tea.

"I think I would like to be alone for a while," Sarah said, and it was decided.

The last few days of the week, neighbors came and went, bringing things they thought would be needed. Lutie brought fresh linens from the Broken Promise so that Imogene and Sarah would be spared the bulk of the week's laundry, Mac brought a load of wood cut to fit the potbellied stove—though he'd brought them a cord in September—and Mrs. Whitaker brought over more food than the two of them could eat in a week. It was a relief when, in the evenings, there was time for the two of them to sit together, quiet with each other and their grief.

Trusting to the strength Sarah seemed to have found in her loss, Imogene left for school early Monday morning. Sarah walked with her to the river path. The sun hadn't been up half an hour, and shadows stretched long over the moving water. Their breath came in clouds, and the frosty air brought blood to their cheeks and noses.

"I'm afraid winter is here," Imogene said as they reached the path. "You'd better get back inside before you catch cold."

"I will," Sarah promised. "Let me walk with you a little further."

Pleased, Imogene slowed her steps, though she had been late leaving the house. Sarah hooked her arm through the older woman's and they walked without speaking. The storm had torn the last leaves from the trees along the river's edge, and bare branches painted a winter scene against the blue November sky. The two women walked on a carpet of mauve and purple. Sarah kicked a clump of leaves, but they were heavy with water and wouldn't take to the air.

"We used to make great piles of them when I was little, and dive into them. I like remembering then," Sarah said.

"My father didn't abide leaf-diving." Imogene hardly ever mentioned her childhood; all her talk of memories suggested she had entered the world through a schoolroom in her late twenties. "Not for young ladies anyhow."

They had come to the foot of the hill leading up to the school.

Sarah detached her arm from Imogene's and laid the schoolteacher's gloved hand against her cheek, but said nothing.

"Thank you for walking with me," Imogene said. "I enjoy things so much more when you're with me."

Sarah watched Imogene until she vanished from sight behind the school door. Then, running lightly over the sodden ground, she hurried home. In Imogene's room she dragged a chair over to the closet, climbed up, and rummaged through the boxes on the top shelf until she found the one she was looking for—a battered blue hatbox with an ill-fitting lid. She carried it to the bed and dumped off the top. Inside was the Colt .45 that Mac had insisted Imogene keep.

"By the authority of Judge Colt," Sarah said.

Using both thumbs, she pulled back the hammer and a mechanism clicked, holding it in place. She held the gun away from her and fired. A bullet smashed into the wainscoting and the pistol bucked backwards. Without hesitation, she pulled the hammer back again and turned the pistol around. She pushed the barrel of the .45 against her breast, feeling the cold metal through her bodice. Steadying the gun in her two hands, she tried to imagine life draining from her, pumping out with her blood, leaving emptiness and peace behind: a quiet, permanent stillness.

She would be with Wolf.

Never again would she see Imogene—not in the heaven that Sam's Bible set forth.

Suddenly the Colt was heavy; it required too much effort to hold her wrists rigid. Sarah set the gun down on the bed, stroking the metal with her fingertip. "God," she whispered, then slid to the floor and steepled her hands like a child. "God," she began again, "what do you want of me?" In the silence she could hear the pendulum clock in the front room. "Damn you, answer me!" she cried, and with an angry gesture, swept the .45 off the coverlet. The gun slammed into the wall and the hammer fell. The sound of the gunshot rattled the window glass and the bullet shattered a pitcher on Imogene's dressing table.

The silence in the room seemed palpable until a loud drip-drip ended it; water from the ruined pitcher had made its way to the table edge.

Sarah pulled herself to her feet and stole from the room. She stopped long enough to gather her coat and bonnet before leaving the house.

The day had warmed and she was flushed with walking by the time she reached the Indian cemetery. She stopped at Wolf's grave. Loosing her bonnet strings, she pushed it back and let the air dry her temples. "Wolf, my dear baby, I love you very much," Sarah said, and looked from the dark earth of the grave to the sky. "But I love Imogene too. Maybe more than's good. Maybe more than God."

She stood for a moment, searching the sky, before she looked back to the pathetic mound of earth. "Is that why you take my children, Lord?" she breathed. Her throat filled with tears and choked off the words. Hardening her mouth, she scrubbed her eyes with the tail of her coat. "If there is a God," she said defiantly. "Maybe there's only love." She looked into the depths of blue beyond the Sierra and grew afraid and lonely.

"Dear God," she prayed, "I know you mustn't tempt the Lord thy God and this isn't that, it's just business. If you could show me it wasn't true that Nate killed Wolf—in a way—I'd put Imogene behind me, marry again. Marry Nate Weldrick."

She squeezed her eyes shut and willed the words to heaven. When she opened them she was alone and small under the ring of mountains, the little grave at her feet. "If not, Lord, I'm going to cast my lot with love." The defiance returned and she added, "Half a year. I'll listen half a year."

For minutes she stood still, expecting to be struck to the ground, but there was nothing.

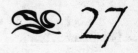

HAVING SWEPT UP THE SHARDS OF BROKEN PITCHER, PATCHED THE
bullet hole with baking soda, flour and water, and pasted a picture
postcard over it, Sarah waited for Imogene to come home from
school.

"I want to get a job," she said as the schoolteacher let herself
in. "I have to have something to do. It's time I pulled my own
weight, as Mac says."

Imogene closed the door and took off her coat. "We can live on
what I earn, you know that. We are even saving a little. You needn't
do this for me."

"I want to feel I'm helping."

Imogene warmed her hands at the potbellied stove. Enjoying the
warmth of the fire and the homey smell of supper from the kitchen,
she realized she'd grown to like returning at the end of each day to
a home kindled with another woman's work.

"You help me, Sarah."

"I suppose," Sarah said falteringly. "Yes . . . I suppose I do."

Guilt shook Imogene from her complacency. Even with the toys
cleared away, Wolf's presence was everywhere, from the scuffed
chairs to the smudged nose prints on the window. She turned from
the stove. "I've gotten spoiled, having you to come home to. What
kind of work are you thinking of?"

"Needlework is all I can do," Sarah replied. "So that's what I'm thinking of."

"I'll ask at school for you. Some of the girls come from well-to-do families."

In the next week, Sarah gathered up her courage and posted notices advertising needlework for hire in the stores, but got no response.

Her resolve had not weakened, but she was running out of places to post notices when Kate Sills came up with an idea. The youngest girls at Bishop Whitaker's were too young for the school and needed to be tutored. "What they need," Kate had said wryly, "is a wet-nurse. The bishop had no business taking them." There was no money in the budget to fund such a position, but if Sarah would work for a dollar a week and lunches, Kate said she would pay it out of her own pocket.

Imogene brought the news home like a gift.

"I couldn't!" Sarah exclaimed. "What if I can't do it? Oh, Imogene, what would Kate think of me? Needlework I can do here, with nobody watching me. Teaching? I don't think so. You're the teacher, Imogene, I couldn't teach."

"The oldest isn't even six," Imogene reassured her. "All you need do is care for them, play with them, take the time with them that the other teachers can't spare. It wouldn't be teaching, really."

Sarah squared her shoulders. "I'll do it," she declared, as if she were promising to rebuild the Colossus at Rhodes.

Seven girls at Bishop Whitaker's were under the age of six, girls that the bishop, in his softheartedness, had taken because their older sisters were enrolled and the mothers had pleaded. Sarah was to take them from eight-thirty in the morning until noon, the hours when the other teachers were the busiest. One of the recitation rooms was set aside for her use. "When the weather is better, you can take the girls out of doors if you like," Kate had offered. Secretly, Sarah felt she'd be let go before winter was out, but she put on a brave face.

The first morning, Imogene walked her to the recitation room and introduced her to the children assembled there. The little girls greeted Imogene with boisterous affection. Seven sober faces bobbed and seven stiff curtsies were dropped for Sarah. "See you at lunch," Imogene whispered as she left. "They are going to love you."

As the door swung shut behind Imogene, the eldest, Maybelle, a pigtailed child of five and a half, stepped forward. "Why do I have to be with the little kids?" she demanded. Two of the very little girls started to snuffle because their feelings were hurt.

Sarah's heart sank.

Nobody would talk except to say something spiteful. Finally, Sarah separated the two older girls and gave them each a stack of picture books. The youngest she let play together, happy to have them occupied and moderately quiet.

By ten o'clock the smaller children were bored with one another and had started to squabble. Before the morning was out, Sarah had all seven isolated, each scowling over her own pile of pictures.

Imogene rescued her in time for lunch. The moment she opened the recitation room door, seven voices piped, "Miss Grelznik!" and there was a mad rush of children to hide in her skirts. Sarah was not far behind.

"It was awful!" Sarah wailed over the soup. "They hated me. I'll never be a teacher until they invent rooms with more corners. I ran out of places to send them, they were so bad."

"You don't have to do this," Imogene reminded her. "Do you want to stop? No one will think less of you for it."

"No." Sarah took a spoonful of soup. "I want you to help me make up a lesson plan."

"Sarah, they are just babies—"

"I don't care. Maybe they don't need a lesson plan, but I do."

"We'll do it first thing after supper," Imogene promised.

That night it was Imogene who cleared up the dinner things while Sarah pored over sheets of foolscap. Near midnight, Imogene came to stand behind Sarah's chair, resting her hands lightly on the younger woman's shoulders. Sarah leaned her head against the schoolteacher and closed her eyes. "I'm almost finished," she sighed.

Imogene kissed the golden crown of hair. "Take care of yourself, Sarah. Your love is more than a net under me. It is the tower from which I shout down the world."

Next morning, armed with a basket of paints, paper, glue, and bits of cloth, Sarah again took possession of the recitation room. When Imogene peeked in before the noon break, all the children were happily absorbed in making Christmas ornaments. She mouthed a silent "Congratulations" to Sarah and closed the door noiselessly.

"They are warming to me," Sarah reported as she and Imogene ate in the school lunchroom. "The eight of us had a good time this morning. I taught them something, too. While we worked, I told them the story of Christmas and how it is celebrated in Holland and Italy. You told those stories to me, years ago. Remember?" There was a scuffle and commotion in the hall. Several of the teachers, including Imogene, left the table. Half a minute later, Imogene poked her head back into the lunchroom.

"Maybelle has skinned her knee on the ice. She says no one is to touch it but Mrs. Ebbitt."

Sarah stayed at Bishop Whitaker's School through the winter, and by spring she was teaching fine needlework to the older girls and assisting in the classroom during the afternoons. Sarah never spoke of Wolf, though she would sometimes talk to him when she knew she was alone, and she never forgot her pact with God.

ॐ 28

HEADS BOWED OVER THEIR BOOKS, BRAIDS AND CURLS TUMBLING over their cheeks, the bishop's girls scratched answers on their final examination papers. Occasionally they glanced up at the test questions Imogene had written on the board. Sunlight streamed through the windows, warm on Imogene's face and hands. Careful not to disturb her scholars, she slid the sash up and leaned out. Eva Quaiffe, the music teacher, had laughed, telling Imogene that spring was short-lived in the eastern Sierra. "It came on Tuesday last year," she'd remarked. But now the bitterbrush was in bloom on the mountainside, and the sweet scent of the yellow flowers drifted down, mingling with the sharpness of sage. Imogene breathed deeply and closed her eyes.

"Soon all your girls will be gone," said a voice at her elbow.

"They are your girls too, Kate. What will you do with the summer?"

The principal settled her elbows on the sill by Imogene's and looked to the mountains east of town. "I'll be here most of it. The bishop has finally gotten the money to have the drive landscaped, and I want to be here when it's done. Catch up on my back work. But I'm going back East for a month, I hope, to see my sister in St. Louis."

A chair scraped, drawing their attention back inside. The chair-scraper was a ten-year-old girl, small for her age, with an angular face and frizzy brown curls that pushed defiantly from under her hair ribbons. Her hand bobbed above her head and she periodically bounced herself several inches out of her chair, the increased height of her hand designed to bring the teacher more promptly.

From a small desk near the rear of the room, Sarah rose and crossed noiselessly to the little girl's desk. Imogene and Kate watched the two in whispered conference for a moment before turning back to their former positions. Imogene smiled as she leaned near Kate. "This ought to be good for discipline, the principal and one of the teachers hanging out of the window after we've scolded the girls about it half a hundred times."

"That's why it is better to be a woman than a girl," Kate returned. "Your new assistant seems to be getting on nicely."

"Sarah Mary is good with little children."

Kate glanced back at the young woman. "She will be a good teacher if she ever overcomes her shyness. The older girls adore her. How is she? It's been five months since the little boy died, hasn't it?"

"She seems better, but she's so quiet, even at home. She doesn't talk about it much."

"You're looking after her, Imogene. She'll come back to herself."

"Unless someone else starts working on her. Sometimes she talks of marrying Mr. Weldrick. He could press her into it, in the state she's in now. She sometimes thinks Wolf's death was God's way of telling her she is living wrong." Imogene smiled without humor.

"That's nonsense. God isn't a matchmaker."

"Tell that to Sarah. She talks of marrying Nate one minute, and the next of how he put Wolf out in the rain. I don't know how she will resolve the two things if Mr. Weldrick ever comes back." Imogene looked across the hills, blue with sage, toward the cemetery north of town. Flowers were planted on the little mound, and it was free of weeds; Imogene tended the sad little garden religiously. "It was good of you and the bishop to agree to take her on as my assistant—I don't like her to be alone."

Kate laid her hand on Imogene's for a moment. "She's turned out to be a great help to us."

Imogene looked at the watch pinned on her bodice. "All right, girls," she said, turning back to her students, "time is up. Put down your pens."

The Saturday after school let out, the Reno Wheelmen spon-
sored a dance, a fund-raiser, in the meadow south of town. Some
of the older girls were allowed to stay at Bishop Whitaker's an extra
day to attend. The bishop promised to drive them to and from the
affair himself with his wife, Miss Sills, Mrs. Ebbitt, and Miss Grelznik along to chaperone.

Saturday was beautiful. It was early summer, the grasses in the
meadow not yet baked desert-brown and the wildflowers at their
most abundant.

Fred Bone's grocery wagon was full of picnickers. He and Lutie
shared the front seat, Fred looking dapper in a new haircut, his
mustache freshly dyed, and Lutie resplendent in yards of pale yellow
gingham. Behind, in the open bed, Fred had arranged bales of hay
in a square and covered them with canvas to form makeshift seats.
Evelynne Bone sat on one bale, straight and proper and over-coiffed,
bestowing flirtatious glances on her seat partner, Judge Curler. The
judge, in his bowler and spectacles, a whiskey blush clowning the
end of his nose, was as dignified as she. He was holding forth on
the hair-raising adventures of a Wells Fargo employee. The latest
hullabaloo, he said, had involved one of the remote stations: the
wife of the stationmaster at Round Hole had gone out of her mind
contemplating another summer in the Smoke Creek Desert. Dizable & Denning, the firm that leased the buildings at the stage stop,
were searching desperately for a replacement.

Sarah and Imogene sat together on another bale. The two were
turned around almost backwards in an attempt to ignore the scrutiny
of the judge's assistant, Harland Maydley. Several picnic baskets,
covered with cloths to discourage the flies, bumped along between
the bales. One of the Wheelmen, his starched collar gleaming white,
his tie nattily in place, whizzed by them as they approached the
meadow. At the sight of a man on a bicycle, the horses shied and
showed the whites of their eyes.

Lutie clucked. "They just work their feet to death to give their
fannies a ride!" she declared.

"Lutie Bown-yay! What language. And in front of a gentleman,
too." Lutie's mother-in-law smiled coyly at the judge.

"It's Bone, Ma," Fred said mildly. "B-O-N-E. Bone."

The meadow was already filling with wagons and carriages.
Young girls in bright summer dresses dotted the landscape like wildflowers. Their mothers, only slightly less excited, stayed back in the

shade of the carriages or under the canvas roof of the pavilion. Men wearing colorful shirts, unstained by their day-to-day labors, hair dark with grease and combed close to the head, mustaches dyed and waxed, visited in groups, admiring one another's horses and equipage. The murmur of voices and the creak of wagons was punctuated by the staccato beat of the Wheelmen hammering together the dance floor.

As soon as the wagon rolled to a stop, Imogene excused Sarah and herself to find the bishop's party. Harland Maydley invited himself along, but Lutie, seeing Sarah's distress, called him back to help carry the picnic baskets.

In the afternoon, the Wheelmen, smart in their striped jackets and knickers, put on a show. They rode backwards, seated on the handlebars; four men got onto one bicycle, tangled together like affectionate acrobats, and pedaled an eighth of a mile down the wagon road; a line of cyclists coasted down a gentle slope by the creek, their bellies on the seats, their feet pointing out behind; they rode every way a person could contort and still manage to push the pedals and steer. The performance met with such success that they did several of the tricks a second time. Afterwards they gave free rides to the young ladies, filling their arms with chintz and white ruffled cotton as the girls tried to balance on the narrow handlebars.

Cowhands from the nearby ranches grew restless and green-eyed, watching the girls flock around the cyclists, crying prettily for another turn, and they set up a riding course of picnic baskets and tree stumps. Their show of fancy horsemanship brought the dimples and adoring glances back from the Wheelmen, but the cowboys' opposing offers of free horseback rides were not so well received; most of the girls had grown up around horses. The cowboys were deluged with tots anxious to grow into cowboys themselves, and spent a disgruntled hour or so riding ecstatic children down the meadow and back.

Near sunset the musicians took their places on the completed bandstand and tuned up. The soft lights and the discordant sounds drew the picnickers in from the meadow and the fringe of evergreens that flanked it. By the time the first star of evening had risen in a mother-of-pearl sky, and the breeze had died away to a zephyr, the people were all gathered around the dance floor, their blankets spread on the grass.

Imogene and Sarah were near the steps opposite the musicians' stand. Sharing their blanket were two of the bishop's girls, Fanny May Enor and Emma Hazlet. When the call to choose partners came, the two girls feigned great indifference and talked animatedly between themselves, watching the comings and goings of booted feet out of the corners of their eyes. Under the pressure of being chosen or left to sit, Sarah grew as nervous as the schoolgirls and confined her eyes to her folded hands. Boys nudged each other and giggled, but they were the choosers, and those fearing rejection could choose not to take the chance. Girls had only the power to veto, and for the ugly and the shy it was no consolation.

Couples passed, climbing the steps arm in arm, some stopping to plunk small children in a box behind the accordionist for safe-keeping before taking to the floor. On the blanket spread by the steps, only Imogene was at her ease with the frilly dresses and bouncing lights. And only Imogene was asked to dance. Mac entrusted his hat to Sarah and led the schoolteacher onto the floor.

Toe-tapping music and swaying lights finally overcame even the most reticent swains, and by moonrise all the girls were dancing. Evelynne Bone had even taken a stately turn around the floor with Judge Curler before one of the wags watching told her he was called "Judge" only because he could drink more than any two men and still look sober. Disappointed in love, Evelynne had retired to spend the rest of the evening pleading a headache.

Nearly everyone danced. There weren't enough women, so some of the men tied handkerchiefs around their arms to signify that they were "ladies" for a square, and, out of the way, under the lanterns, the children danced their own versions of what they saw. A burly shopkeeper, with his partner literally on his arm, danced a dignified square with his four-year-old daughter.

The moon, three-quarters full, flooded the meadow with silver light, and the dance floor, with its colored lanterns, shone like a fairy ring.

Sarah and Imogene were resting after a square, clapping in time with the music, watching the stars rise over the black bulk of the mountains, when suddenly Sarah stopped and clasped her hands to her breast. Beyond the dancers, pale and otherworldly in the moonlight, Nate Weldrick rode up the dirt track from town. In the cold light, the claybank stallion showed a dull pewter.

"Sarah? What's the matter?" Imogene asked. Sarah pointed a rigid finger toward the approaching horseman.

Nate rode out of sight behind the pavilion, reemerging into the moonlight a few minutes later on foot. Both women had forgotten the noise and the lights and the dancing.

"Miss Grelznik! You two moonstruck? This is the third asking."

They looked up into Fred's friendly face. He had his arm thrust out in a welcoming hook. "I haven't had a dance yet. Come on, as soon as they get swept, we'll be setting new squares."

Distracted, Imogene shook her head. "I'm tired. Thank you, though, Fred."

"Not enough dances in this part of the country for anybody to get tired. Especially the gals. In some counties it's the law they got to bring an extra pair of shoes, because the boys are going to dance them through one pair before midnight." Fred had pulled Imogene up and walked her halfway to the dance floor. The music started, and holding her arm firmly, he ran to form the side of a square.

Imogene swirled around the floor, her feet attending to the calls, her eyes and mind on the darkness beyond the lanterns.

Fanny May and Emma were gone to the dancers, and Sarah sat alone. She watched Nate as he worked his way around the circle of people. Spots of color burned high on her cheeks. Nate's eyes raked over the rows of blankets, searching from face to face.

Sarah pulled her knees up and hugged them, forcing herself to concentrate on the kaleidoscopic patterns of the square dance.

"Sarah?" Nate was beside her, his hat in his hand, the familiar smell of pomade mixing with pine pitch, sweat, and the fresh smell of the night. "Sarah, could I have the next dance?"

Sarah shook her head, her eyes steadfastly on the dancers.

"Mind if I sit down? I been riding all day."

"No . . . I mean . . . please . . ." Sarah hugged her knees tighter.

With a grunt, he sat down anyway, his feet stuck awkwardly in front of him where his boots wouldn't spoil the blanket. "It's a pretty night, no denying that." He watched her covertly, her smooth cheek rosy in the soft light of the paper lanterns.

"You look even prettier than when I saw you last time." He laughed. "It's been a while."

Sarah's little teeth nibbled at her upper lip.

"Of course, you were in a bit of a tizzy then." He laughed again, remembering.

"Wolf died." The words burst from her, loud enough that the people nearest turned to stare.

Nate stopped laughing. "Wolf died?"

"Your son. My Wolf. He's dead these six months." She watched him closely, her eyes fixed on his.

"Jesus." Nate rubbed his hand over his face. "Jesus, I'm sorry. That's too bad. He wasn't a bad kid. What did he die of?" he asked gently.

"He died because he was put out in the rain with no coat! Put out like a dog! He got a chill and he died," Sarah said coldly. "Because of you."

The dance finished and Imogene fled from the floor. In the spill of yellow light she could see Nate talking with Sarah. She reached the blanket just as Sarah sprang up and ran off into the dark confusion of wagons. She started after her, but Nate Weldrick caught her arm. "Miss Grelznik, Sarah will wait a minute. I got to talk to you. She's running away from me, thinking I killed that boy. You know that ain't so."

Imogene tried to pull away, but he hardened his grip and held her. "I got money now," he went on. "That's where I been. I got money and I bought a little spread south of here. Big enough to raise a family on and make a living. I been building her a cabin and it's done now. You tell her, by God!"

Imogene wrenched her arm free. "I don't know what you are talking about."

"You know."

Mac came out of the darkness from the direction of the wagons at the same time that Fred reached them from the dance floor. Mac spoke first. "I found little Sarah crying her heart out, all hid back there in the dark." His eyes lit on Nate. "Nate. You're back. It's about damn time. Have you been annoying Sarah?"

"Yes," Imogene said.

Mac's face darkened and he took Nate by the arm. Mac's remaining thumb and finger were as strong as a crab's claw. "Come on, Nate. You bother either one of these ladies again and I'll set the law on you. Hell—I may pin your ears back myself."

Nate stood his ground. "You tell her, Miss Grelznik."

"Come on, son," Fred said. "You're making a stink." Nate went, walking between the two men. They stopped on the far side of the wagons, out of earshot of the revelers. There were angry gestures and Nate broke away to join a group of young idlers who had been watching the festivities from a distance and passing a bottle between them.

Mac left Fred and spoke briefly with a big-shouldered, big-bellied man leaning against one of the pavilion posts. Mac pointed to Nate, then picked his way back to Imogene's side.

"I had a talk with Sheriff Graff. There won't be any more trouble. He said he'd keep an eye on Nate. If Graff says he'll keep an eye on somebody, it usually means both eyes and his boot heel. I don't think Nate'll make trouble; he's not a bad sort," Mac reassured her.

Imogene found Sarah leaning against the side of Ozi Whitaker's carriage. The schoolteacher led her back to the dance. They abandoned the blanket by the steps to sit in the cool darkness with the bishop and Mrs. Whitaker; the other teachers had gone back to town. Sarah was quiet and withdrawn, but Imogene chatted with the girls when they spun by, breathless and shining from the dancing, to fling themselves down a moment. Mac stood apart, gossiping with his cronies and watching Nate.

Nate Weldrick watched Sarah and drank. The bottle occasionally flashed in the moonlight as it passed from hand to hand or, empty, was tossed into the meadow grass, a new one then being dredged from one of the saddlebags. And Sheriff Graff watched the knot of men who'd come to the dance and kept themselves outsiders, drinking and joking beyond the circle of light.

When enough liquor had been consumed, a fistfight broke out. The sheriff broke it up as quickly as it had begun, arresting four men, Nate Weldrick among them.

Mac came over to the bishop's party after Nate and the others had been escorted back toward town, and asked Imogene for a word in private.

"Weldrick'll be cooling his heels in jail for a day or two," he informed her. "He give me this to give to Sarah. Seeing as how he upsets her, I figured you'd better have a look at it and give it or not give it as you see fit."

Imogene thanked him, and as soon as she was alone she unfolded the note and read it.

Sarah,
    I gave Wolf my own coat and set him in the dry. You ask Miss Grelznik what happened to them because I sure don't

know. I left him dry and wearing my coat is all I know. I got
a place now, I got it for you and me. I want you to marry
me. You can get unhitched from before if he is real and not
dead already which I ain't so sure of. You ask Miss Grelznik
about the coat and I'll propose proper when this is done.

Nate Weldrick

P.S. I'm real sorry about Wolf. Also, I love you and I ain't
never said that to nobody.

The hand was steady; he'd written it before he was drunk. Imogene folded it carefully and put it in her pocket.

"Do-si-do and swing your partner. Swing your corner 'round
and 'round," the fiddler called. Wearily, Imogene turned her back
on the music to return to the bishop's blanket.

"Sarah, would you go for a walk with me? You have been sitting
a long time." Imogene linked her arm through Sarah's.

The dance was beginning to break up, and the early-to-bed people were folding their blankets and packing picnic baskets back into
the wagons. Imogene stopped at Fred's wagon to get their shawls.

Away from the dance floor, in a swale in the meadow, a lone
boulder pushed its face into the moonlight. Imogene led Sarah to
it. Strains of the banjo and fiddle floated across the meadow with
the light, high sound of women's laughter, thrumming above the
beat of leather boots.

Imogene spread her shawl over the rock to protect their dresses.
"Sarah, would you be happier married?"

Sarah thought for a moment before she replied. "I should, I
know."

"Do you want to marry Mr. Weldrick?"

"He put Wolf out in the rain."

"What if he hadn't? I mean, what if he'd not been responsible
for what happened?"

"I would marry him. If I was sure. The six months are almost
gone." She said the last defiantly. Imogene didn't understand but
was too engrossed in her own thoughts to pursue it.

A night bird swooped low overhead, its wings whistling as they
cut the air. Imogene listened and it was gone. She pulled the note
from her pocket and stood to shake the dampness from her skirts.
The moon was at her back, full on Sarah's face. Imogene looked at

her, young and soft in the moonlight. Between her thumb and fingers she held the bit of paper with Nate's proposal and his declaration of innocence.

"My dear, would you love Mr. Weldrick?"

Sarah was quiet for a long time, then she replied, "No." She shook her head slowly. "I love *you*, Imogene."

Imogene started to cry and, hugging Sarah fiercely to her, she crumpled Nate Weldrick's note in her hand.

DUST MOTES DANCED IN THE SUNLIGHT AND THE ROOMS WERE UN-
naturally still. All the girls but those who'd stayed for the dance had
gone home for the summer. The others were in church, and Bishop
Whitaker's School was empty but for Imogene. She sat at her desk,
looking over the neat rows of inkwells, chairs, pencil trays. After
two years of use, everything still looked new and smelled slightly of
furniture polish. She sat motionless, her chin resting on her folded
hands, sunlight pouring in through the open door of the recitation
rooms on the east side.

"I thought I'd find you here." Kate Sills appeared in the doorway, her neat Sunday hat pinned squarely on her head, her white
gloves immaculate. "I met the bishop's wife before the service; she
told me you'd handed in your resignation."

Imogene smiled wanly. "Oh dear, I'd hoped to slip away without
good-byes. I'm glad I didn't. We're leaving Reno, Kate."

"You love Bishop Whitaker's."

"I love Bishop Whitaker's. But we're leaving today, on the morning stage."

Kate unpinned her hat and set it and her gloves on a desk.
"You're certainly not doing things by halves, are you? Where, may
I ask, is the morning stage bound?"

"Round Hole—among other places." Imogene laughed. "I'm going to be an innkeeper, Kate."

"At Round Hole? The stop on Smoke Creek? Imogene, you must be unbalanced! Have you ever seen the Nevada desert? It is truly a land God forgot." Kate gave Imogene a hard look. "You're in trouble. Let me help. I am not without influence in this town."

"I'm not in trouble. Sarah hasn't been very well—even before Wolf died. Innkeeping is something we can both do. Something we can do together. I used to think teaching was my life, but it takes me from Sarah and she needs me."

"We need you too, Imogene. You have a gift for teaching."

"There are other teachers in the world. Sarah Mary needs me."

"As an innkeeper? Just the two of you? You'll break your backs and your hearts."

"It's a stage stop. Mac says it's isolated; he goes through it twice a week on his run. It will do Sarah good to live out of town; she's too easily influenced by what people think." Imogene gave vent to a small bitter smile. "Or what she thinks they think. We need to get off by ourselves if she's to get away from that."

Kate sat on the edge of the desk, cool and unblinking, regarding Imogene. "Is that all?"

Imogene sighed and pushed impatiently back from her desk. "The sheriff is letting Nate Weldrick out of jail this afternoon. Mac told me."

"And Mr. Weldrick will push Sarah into marriage if you stay."

"It would be a mistake. Sarah won't stand up for herself; she'd be little better than a servant."

"So you're going to push her into innkeeping—stagestopping."

"That's right," Imogene said without remorse.

"The desert will make her little better than a slave. It is not work for a woman like Sarah," Kate said.

"I'm strong as an ox. I can do the work of a man. Two, if they are small." She won a dry smile from Kate. "Sarah needn't work herself to death, I will see to that. You have never seen her around Mr. Weldrick. The man reduces her to a child. In her own mind as well as his. Sarah can't fight that right now. It would destroy her spirit."

Kate heaved a sigh and reached out to take Imogene's hand. "My thoughts are with you, you know that."

"I know it, Kate. It's one of the many things that will make it hard to leave Bishop Whitaker's."

Dizable & Denning's representative shared the Wells Fargo office with Judge Curler and Harland Maydley. His name was Ralph Jensen. He was a slim man of middling height, sandy-haired and colorless, with watery blue eyes. He stood behind the counter, one hand splayed over the lease, the other holding a letter. When he'd finished reading it, Imogene asked for it back, folded it in a businesslike way, and put it in her purse. "Mr. Ebbitt has asked us to secure a position," Imogene lied easily. "He'll be coming out to join his wife within the month," she said.

"We're in a hell of a fix, with Van Fleet pulling out the way he is, or I wouldn't send you two out without this husband of yours showing up to do his business himself." Ralph Jensen pulled on his nose. It was long, the end flattened like a spade, as though he'd tugged it out of its natural shape years before.

As Imogene reached for the lease, he pulled it back over the counter. "Now wait a damn minute. I'm going to have Mrs. Ebbitt sign this, and you can give me the twenty-seven dollars. Harland or the Judge or anybody can witness. But it's not legal. A woman signing a lease won't hold water, even if she has got a letter from her husband with say-so. Take the lease with you and as soon as Mr. Ebbitt shows, have him sign it and send it to me. Understood?" He waited until Imogene and Sarah had nodded like obedient children before he removed his hand from the paper and shoved it and the ink across the counter.

"Round Hole's a ways from anywhere," he warned as Sarah stepped forward to take the pen, and she hesitated.

"Isolation won't bother us, Mr. Jensen," Imogene assured him.

"This ain't isolation, lady, this is right damn in the middle of nowhere." He took in Sarah's soft uncertain glance, Imogene's solid answering gaze, and he shrugged. "Go on, you're holding up the stage. Noisy'll tell you the particulars and the Van Fleets said they'd stay on a day or two and show you the ropes."

The leavetaking was subdued. Lutie and Fred saw them off. Fred was to send their things after them by freightwagon. Lutie and Fred were confused and hurt by the sudden departure, and Harland Maydley, newly promoted to the post of Jensen's assistant, puffed about officiously.

The two women climbed quickly into the mudwagon—a coach smaller than a Concord, with an even more jolting carriage. Mac was on top with the driver, Noisy Dave. Noisy was a rubber-faced man of middle years, with thinning blond hair. A belly as big as that of a woman eight months with child hung over his belt. A mustache of startling proportions, a soup-strainer, completely hid his mouth; the tips were waxed and pointed toward his ears. The driver hawked, spat over the side, wiped his mustache, and, with a bellow, shook the reins and the horses pulled the mudwagon down the main street.

Imogene and Sarah were alone in the coach, seated side by side so neither had to ride backwards. Dust boiled from under the horses' hooves and was churned into the air by the wheels. Sarah leaned back against the upholstered seat and pulled the shade down.

The ribbon of green that the Truckee unfurled through Reno was quickly behind them. Sarah raised the shade a couple of inches and looked out. They were traveling through a dry valley bordered by hills of sage and rock. "I'm not sure about leaving Reno," she said, and dropped the shade.

"It will be all right. As Mac says, 'I can feel it in my finger bones.' It will be better, we'll have something of our own. A lease is almost like buying," Imogene said with more confidence than she felt.

"We had teaching," Sarah said after a while. "You loved it."

"I'll learn to love innkeeping. *We'll* learn. This time we'll learn together."

Sarah looked out the window again. At the end of the valley, a mountain of rock reared shimmering in the heat, its broken sides supporting nothing but rust lichen and an occasional patch of sparse desert grass. "It's so dry," Sarah observed. "Mac says it's as bad at Sheep's Hole. Worse."

"Round Hole. There's a round spring there. The stop is close to a big lake. How bad can it be?"

Sarah tried to read to pass the time, but the jouncing moved the book so violently she couldn't follow the text, even using her finger. Eventually she leaned back to wait out the journey.

The coach road wound north through the Carson Range and a little east of Reno toward the Pah Rah Mountains and the western shore of Pyramid Lake. Desert mountains, devoid of any vegetation but the constant gray-black sage, crowded close. Old avalanches had tumbled rock down the mountain faces and lay like scabbed wounds below the ridges. Boulders the size of houses thrust out from the jagged summits. And always the terrain grew dryer, until at last it could scarcely support even the sage, and the bushes grew stunted, ten or fifteen feet apart.

Around three o'clock in the afternoon, a sharp rapping brought Imogene and Sarah out of their torpor. A ghostly face appeared upside down in the window, and Sarah squawked at the apparition before she recognized Mac behind the white alkali dust.

"Told you it was bad," he snapped, without preamble. "Look lively now, we're almost through the Pah Rahs. You'll be able to see the lake in a few minutes, and it's a beauty."

Revived by the promise of water and green growing things upon which to rest their eyes, the women sat up straighter and took an interest in their surroundings. But the approach to Pyramid Lake was as desolate as the land they'd been traveling through for the past hours. Alkali flats, blinding white in the afternoon sun, stretched away on either side until they reached mountains spotted with sage. There were none of the soft announcements that usually herald water, neither green foliage nor the soft feel of humid air.

"It's a little cooler," Sarah ventured as the stage came to the top of a barren rocky rise.

"Pyramid Lake," Noisy hollered down.

Below, spreading out across the desert floor, was a lake of the same hard blue as the sky. The shores were crusted with white and nothing grew. Even the sage and the coarse brown desert grass retreated from its shores. Gray, cone-shaped bubbles of stone frothed up fifty, seventy-five, a hundred feet in a skyline of fantastic castles at the north end of the lake. The eastern shore abutted against the foot of a mountain range, and in its shadow several more volcanic cones pushed up out of the lake.

"How bad can it be?" Sarah said.

The mudwagon jolted on, plowing up its plume of white dust. A hot dry wind buffeted the coach and drew the moisture from the lips and throats of the passengers. They rode in silence, occasionally passing each other the canteen Mac had provided. The water was tepid and tasted of metal.

They rounded the end of the lake at sunset. The mountains had turned rose, lavender, and gold. Shadows stretched long over the mountain faces, and the sage dotting the valley floor stretched out dark fingers five times its size. Mac rapped on the side of the coach and called on Sarah and Imogene to witness the mammoth bubbles and spires of rock. Pyramids of liquid stone, frozen in shape by the waters of an ancient sea, lay exposed on the lake shore. They clustered at the water's edge like a ruined dream of Baghdad. Bats circled the spires and turrets, streaming from hidden caves in black ribbons.

Apathetic with the dust and the rolling of their stomachs, the women stared blankly through the moving frame of the coach window, then fell back against the seat to look at nothing.

Past the lake, the road curved northeast up a sand and gravel hill to a pass in the low hills that marked the end of the Pah Rah Range, northwest of Pyramid Lake. Noisy Dave pulled up at the summit, bellowing boistrous whoas. "Sand Pass," he hollered. "There's Round Hole below. If you gals want to step out, take a look, and stretch a bit, go ahead." They climbed stiffly from the coach, not trusting their cramped legs to support them.

Winding down the shadowed side of the pass, a white wagon track snaked through a sea of sage; mountains, rounded and covered with the same coarse blanket of vegetation, rose to the northeast. To the south, rock-faced and sharp, the granite peaks of the Fox Range curved away in a jagged wall. Held between these pincers of rock and sand was the Smoke Creek Desert.

Near the middle of the broad valley floor, the sagebrush stopped abruptly in a wavy shoreline; beyond, there was nothing but the white glare of an immense alkali flat baked until the crust had cracked into a crazy network of lines. On the edge of the flat, in a blunt finger of sage that poked out onto the dead lake bottom, huddled Round Hole Stop. In an oasis of green the size of a postage stamp, its few trees looking like refugees in an alien land, three buildings, bleached the same drab gray as the sage, clung to the green skirts of a spring.

"Oh my Lord," breathed Imogene.

"You gals change your mind?" Noisy asked.

"I knew it was desert," Imogene replied crisply, but still she stared down on the desolate valley.

"Imogene," Sarah whispered, "nobody can live down there."

"Staying or not," Noisy put in, "we're going to be there tonight. There's no place else within a half-day's ride." He started talking to the team as Imogene and Sarah climbed back into the mudwagon.

Stars were shining in the long desert twilight when they at last pulled up at the stage stop. A low, open-faced building formed one side of a square of hard-packed earth. Flanking it were a stable and a long two-story building with a veranda and two chimneys. The fourth side of the quadrangle, across the coach road, was the spring itself, a barn, and a squat icehouse.

The spring was aptly named, a round hole about forty-five feet across, with high, grass-covered sides. Under the darkening sky the spring lay black and placid, but the sound of moving water was everywhere. In the parched desert landscape it fell on the ear like music. A windmill pumped water to fill a trough in the small meadow to the south—forty acres of green crowded on all sides by the thirsty Smoke Creek. A narrow irrigation channel gurgled in front of the house and down through the paddock beside the barn, and another ditch ran full behind the stables and out across the square of dirt between the buildings. Planks had been laid over it where the paths to the shed and the stables crossed it.

Noisy held the horses in a hard grip, shouting soothing words at the top of his voice until Mac could get around to the lead team to hold their heads. The animals had smelled water several miles out and were frantic to drink.

A small man appeared from the murk of the stables and hurried across the yard to help with the unharnessing. Noisy Dave climbed down from the box and pounded his thighs with the flats of his hands. "Long haul, that," he boomed, "but we brought you some passengers. I don't know if you can rightly charge them, Van. It's the folks took over your lease." Noisy called through the coach window to Imogene and Sarah, "This is Beau Van Fleet."

The man's face had lit up when the lease was mentioned, and he ran halfway to the house. "Elmira!" he shouted in a high, boyish voice. "Come on out, it's the folks took over the lease." He laughed. "You hear me, pet?"

A hard-faced woman, all angles, stepped out on the porch, half-hidden in the gloom of the veranda. "Well, it's none too soon for me," she called back, and hurried down the steps to meet them. In her eagerness she pulled Sarah bodily from the mudwagon and bustled her and Imogene into the house.

Several freightwagon drivers were eating supper; they sat at a bar that ran half the length of the room. At the far end was a large stone fireplace with a varnished wooden mantle. A rattlesnake skin was stretched on the stone, the gray and brown diamonds shimmering in the lamplight. Several tables, mismatched and without cloths, were set between the bar and a row of windows overlooking the coach yard. Near the fireplace a motley assortment of comfortable chairs were scattered about. The ceiling was low and unpainted, of the same planking as the floor. The walls had been papered, but it was peeling in several places and faded wherever the direct light of the sun hit it.

When Imogene and Sarah were ushered in, herded like ducks before the nonstop quacking of Mrs. Van Fleet, the men paused in their silent shoveling to glance at the newcomers. Tired beyond talk, dusty and bedraggled, Sarah and Imogene let their garrulous hostess take them where she would. After several indecisions and shufflings of chairs, she seated them at a table near a window.

"There. Got you a window seat." She laughed nervously, an exhalation of air through pinched nostrils. "Not that there's anything to see. You sit tight here, rest yourselves. Can I get you a little something?"

Imogene looked to Sarah; she was staring out over the baked earth. The forbidding wall of mountains beyond inked a ragged black edge to the translucent silver of the late-evening sky. The moon, rising, shone warm and golden between two peaks.

"Sarah?" Imogene lightly touched her arm.

Sarah shook her head.

"Just water for now," Imogene said to Mrs. Van Fleet. "We're still a little unsettled from the ride."

Elmira hovered near them a moment more, patting the chairbacks and making agitated chirping sounds as though afraid they would flee if left to themselves. Finally she left them alone. "These're the folks come to take over the lease," she said as she passed the men at the bar. The leather-faced diners looked curiously at the two women. Sarah and Imogene pretended not to notice.

"Hell of a place to bring your womenfolk, if you ask me," a short, thick-necked man grunted.

"Nobody asked you, Lyle." The scrutiny over, the men went back to their suppers.

Imogene pulled off her gloves and reached across the table to take Sarah's hand.

The moon cleared the mountains, bathing the desert with soft light. In the courtyard, men moved about at their chores, black shadows in the moonlight.

"There's just nothing," Sarah whispered, staring out the window.

Imogene pressed her fingers. "It will be all right, Sarah."

"I know it will." Sarah made herself smile and return the pressure of Imogene's hand.

Mrs. Van Fleet returned with a glass of water in each hand, both dripping from being thrust under the pump. Sarah thanked her and drank thirstily. Before she had taken more than a swallow or two, she gagged and shoved the glass from her so abruptly the water slopped on the table. She hid her mouth with her handkerchief, coughing and dabbing at her eyes. Imogene picked the glass up before Elmira could retrieve it, and put it to her lips. She recoiled at the smell.

"Smells like rotten eggs, doesn't it?" Elmira exhaled through her nose in a silent laugh. "Tastes like them, too. And the water isn't half of it. Hon, I should've warned you, but I've got so used to it I sometimes forget. Beau says he's got so he prefers it, but it still tastes like rotten eggs to me. Everything gets to tasting of it—coffee, tea, lemonade, even your baked goods. It's the alkali in the water, they say. But it doesn't seem to hurt you."

As she mopped at the table with her apron, she poured out a stream of talk that allowed no time for reply. Sarah recovered herself and sat clutching her handkerchief. "Made me just choke," the woman was saying, "but now I drink it right along with Beau. I've almost forgot what good water tastes like."

"All the water tastes like this?" Imogene pointed an accusing finger at the half-empty glass.

Elmira looked from one to the other. "Oh my," she murmured, "I go on too much. It's not so bad, you won't even taste it in a week or so. Sooner. You get used to it right off." She turned to Sarah. "You okay, hon?"

Sarah nodded unconvincingly.

"If you could show us our rooms . . ." Imogene said with a tired smile and a gesture at her dust-stained traveling clothes.

Upstairs, two long low-ceilinged rooms, imperfectly hidden behind dingy curtains, opened off a small landing. Mrs. Van Fleet left them just outside the doorways. "On your right," she said, and retreated down the stairs. Imogene raised the candle she'd been handed; WOMEN was scrawled over one lintel in chalk, MEN over the other. She pushed aside the curtain on her right and held it until Sarah had passed through. Their bags were already piled in the middle of the room. Five cots thrust their feet out into the middle of the floor. Two of them were made up; stained mattresses, cotton breaking through the ticking, covered the others. The room was hot and airless. Several flies, mistaking the candle's reflection for the last light of day, battered themselves against the glass in a last mindless attempt to reach it.

Imogene opened two of the windows and settled the curtain more modestly over the door.

"Where will we begin?" Sarah's eyes swept over the dreary walls and bare wooden floor. Even in the cheery light of the candle flame, everything showed the same dull brown of the desert.

Imogene sighed and shook her head. "The first thing we are going to do is clean."

≈ 30

MR. AND MRS. VAN FLEET REMAINED AT ROUND HOLE FOR THE better part of a week, helping Imogene and Sarah learn the needs of the stop. Stages came through twice a week. The stage from Reno, usually driven by Noisy Dave with Mac as his swamper, traded passengers with Ross, the driver of the northbound coach that ran up through Buffalo Meadows and Deep Hole, through Eaglesville, Cedarville, and Lake City to Fort Bidwell. Passengers on the night stage stayed overnight at Round Hole, but the main bread-and-butter of the stop came from the constant traffic of wagons hauling freight; Round Hole was a regular stopping place on most of their routes.

With Beau Van Fleet's help, Imogene renegotiated the agreements he had with the wagoners that supplied Round Hole. Food that couldn't be raised or killed in the Smoke Creek Desert had to be brought in from Fish Springs Ranch to the south or Loyalton to the north, and all manufactured goods were ordered from Reno. Imogene, Sarah, and the illusory Mr. Ebbitt—who figured strongly in all the business discussions—were responsible for providing the transient livestock with hay and grain. It was brought in three-hundred-pound bales from Sierra Valley via Portola, a town over Beckworth Pass eighty miles southwest. Dizable & Denning leased the stop a wagon primarily for that purpose.

Mrs. Van Fleet grew visibly calmer as each day passed and Imogene showed no sign of condemning the Van Fleets to another prolonged stay in the desert by changing her mind. By the time Elmira and her husband left on the Sunday stage for Reno, she was actually good-tempered.

An hour after the Van Fleets departed on the Reno-bound stage, several three-hundred-pound feed bales were brought in by freight wagon from Sierra Valley and Sarah and Imogene started inn-keeping in earnest. They fed the driver and saw him on his way, set to work breaking down the bales and storing the loose hay.

Sunlight filtered through the gaps in the barn walls in golden stripes, and the air was warm with the scent of hay and horses. Imogene and Sarah worked in their shirtsleeves, with bibs and tuckers hastily fashioned from old bedsheets protecting their clothes. Dust motes danced to the desert's silence in the still air.

Sarah lifted a forkful of hay and tossed it into the growing mound at the back of the barn. Straws sparkled like gold as they fell through the fractured light.

"Rumplestiltskin!" Imogene called as the straw turned to gold and spun to the floor.

Sarah laughed and suddenly threw aside her pitchfork. "Watch me, Imogene." Running headlong, she dove into the hay. "Come on," she cried, "oh, you whose father couldn't abide leaf-diving."

Imogene laughed self-consciously.

"Dive!" Sarah ordered. And, awkwardly at first, then gaining speed, Imogene ran for the pile of hay and flung herself on it. Sarah scrambled to the top, scratching straw down on Imogene. Grasping the rope tied over the beam, she began to shinny up as best her petticoats would allow. Halfway to the top, she let go and tumbled backward into the soft hay. Following her lead, Imogene climbed the wooden ladder affixed to the barn wall. Up near the high loading window, she called, "Look at me!" and hurled herself into space to fall fanny-first into the pile.

Scooping up double handfuls of hay, Sarah showered Imogene, keeping up the barrage until the older woman shoved half a mountain of straw down on her in retaliation. Sputtering, Sarah dug her way out only to be buried again as Imogene, at the top of the heap, yelled, "King of the mountain!" and kicked down hay. With renewed vigor, Sarah let out a roar and charged up the side of the stack. She threw herself on Imogene and they rolled over and over until their hair fell free and their petticoats tangled.

"That," Imogene laughed as she recovered her breath, "was all the childhood I have ever had. Thank you, Sarah."

Sarah brushed the straw from Imogene's face and kissed her eyelids. "My childhood is over," she said. "I'm not a bit sorry." She smiled into her old friend's eyes and, with a fingertip, traced the line of Imogene's mouth. "Lord, I think I'm going to like being a woman. You've always been my teacher; teach me to make love to you."

Imogene arrested Sarah's hand and held it. "Why now, Sarah?"

"God lost. We won."

Imogene didn't understand, but she answered the young woman's smile. "We'll learn together."

Sarah touched her lips to her old friend's, the sigh of her breath soft against Imogene's cheek, and the schoolteacher felt the warm rain of Sarah's tears. "My love," she whispered, "what is it?"

Sarah laughed. "I think I'm melting. I have been in love with you since I was fifteen. You've peopled all my dreams. Your face, your dear beautiful face." She kissed Imogene again and the strong arms folded around her. Lightheaded with the scent of Imogene's hair and the cut hay, Sarah felt her heart lifting, light as a dry desert cloud.

Imogene felt as though she had finally reached home.

A sense of celebration claimed Imogene and Sarah as they moved their things from the women's dormitory into the bedroom they would share.

Over the next week they cleaned every surface inside the stop, boiled every stitch of cloth—the curtains, the bedding, what tablecloths there were—and dusted and polished until the freight drivers retreated out of doors with their hastily prepared meals, grumbling that Round Hole wasn't what it used to be.

Fresh meat was a problem; the freighters were a carnivorous lot, and beef and lamb were expensive. Beau Van Fleet had saved himself a great deal of money by hunting venison, rabbit, and occasionally duck, pheasant, or even squirrel. Nearly three-quarters of a large doe had been left when he and Mrs. Van Fleet departed. The haunch of meat hung thirty feet above the ground at night, away from the flies, like a macabre flag, and was buried in a cool earthen pit lined with straw during the day. Mr. Van Fleet said the crust that formed over the flesh would keep the meat almost indefinitely if it was kept cool. Day by day the chunk of venison grew smaller. Finally, ten days after they'd taken over the stop, Imogene steeled herself to the task and took down the rifle she had purchased from the Van Fleets. In the cool of the evening, after they had eaten and seen to the needs of the one guest—a freighter from out of Salt Lake hauling cloth goods—Imogene and Sarah taught themselves to shoot.

The sun had almost set and the sharp smell of sage hung in the air. The road disappeared behind a ragged wall of scree twenty miles east. Above the mountains, the sky glowed sea green. About a hundred yards from the house, the fence that separated the meadow and the buildings from the desert was broken by a gate. Beyond, the world seemed more desolate and forbidding than the patch of ground they'd grown accustomed to, and they turned off the road just inside the fenceline.

The rifle was an old Henry Repeater; Mr. Van Fleet had shown them how to load it and fire it. With some difficulty, Imogene slid open the cartridge chamber and Sarah poked the bullets into the magazine. Fumbling one, she dropped it in the dirt and both women froze.

"It didn't go off," Sarah whispered.

Imogene picked it up gingerly, holding it between her thumb and forefinger. "It looks all right, but I don't suppose we'd better use it, it may be damaged inside." She set it gently on the ground at a little distance from them.

With infinite care, Sarah slipped two more bullets into the rifle. "No more will go in," she breathed.

"Do you think we should close it?" Imogene asked.

"I think Mr. Van Fleet said to close it."

"Sarah, stop whispering, it's making me nervous," Imogene responded.

Imogene choked the barrel with her thumb and middle finger and pointed it away. For a minute or two they simply stood, Sarah watching, Imogene holding, growing used to the idea.

Imogene took a deep breath. "All right. What shall I shoot at?"

"I could put a rock on a fencepost," Sarah suggested.

"Let me just try to hit the post first." Imogene pulled up the rifle and leaned her cheek against the stock.

"You're supposed to hold it tight to your shoulder," Sarah said. The schoolteacher pulled the Henry tight to her shoulder.

"And sight with both eyes. Open."

"I can't see with both eyes open."

"Well, you're supposed to."

Imogene opened both eyes.

"Squeeze. Don't jerk," Sarah warned.

Imogene glanced at Sarah over the rifle stock.

"Mr. Van Fleet said." Sarah smiled sheepishly.

Imogene laughed. "All right. Squeeze. Here we go." The rifle kicked a little but she'd kept it snug against her shoulder and the recoil didn't hurt. The fencepost, twenty feet away, was unharmed, but a tiny burst of dirt beyond showed she hadn't been far wide of the mark. After several more tries they were rewarded with a satisfying *thwack* as a bullet finally struck home.

"Could I try?" Sarah asked.

Imogene handed over the rifle. Half a dozen rounds were expended into the dirt before Sarah got the feel of it, then she, too, managed to hit the post. It was growing too dark to see, and they gave up their target practice for that night.

After that, most evenings found them out by the eastern fence. Imogene fired with steady dependability; the weapon was a tool and she worked with it doggedly until she had mastered it. Sarah either shot brilliantly, hitting everything she aimed at, or she was unable to hit anything and would quit, frustrated, after a few rounds.

Finally the deer carcass that the Van Fleets had left was gone, and the freight drivers began to grumble for red meat. So, on a hot afternoon when there was no one around, Imogene took down the rifle, Sarah filled her apron pockets with cartridges, and they went hunting rabbits. The smell of baked earth rose from the dust under their feet, and the sun burned through the high desert atmosphere. Sarah folded the scoop of her bonnet forward until the brim flopped on both sides of her face like outsized blinkers.

"I wish I'd worn gloves. This sun'll tan you like leather faster than the Pennsylvania sun. Back home I could stay out half a day sometimes and not show pink at all. If you don't take care, Imogene, you'll ruin your complexion. You're already brown."

"I know," Imogene replied. "I've never given my complexion much thought."

"It's better brown, I think." Sarah looked at Imogene critically and rattled the bullets in her pocket. "Yup, I like the way you look."

"As long as you like my face, I will be satisfied with it." Pleased, Imogene blushed a little under her tan.

"Now you are truly beautiful," Sarah said. Forgetting she had a fistful of bullets, she threw her arms around Imogene's neck and kissed her soundly.

"Sarah." Imogene put the young woman from her. "We must always be careful."

"This is the West—the middle of the desert. Who would care? Who would see?"

"Once burned, twice shy, they say, and I have been burned twice. The third time might be at the stake." Imogene smiled. "I'm overanxious. You may kiss me as long as there are no alien eyes within a hundred miles."

Sarah kissed her again.

This time Imogene kissed back. "I like this neighborhood," she said.

A fat cottontail, slow with the heat, hopped ahead of them, his white fluffy tail catching their attention. Oblivious of the huntresses, the bunny grazed in the shade of a sage bush.

Sarah pointed, but Imogene had already seen it. Silently she held the rifle out and indicated Sarah's apron pockets. Sarah counted out the cartridges and dropped them into the rifle. They always loaded the rifle together as they had the first time they'd fired it.

Imogene pumped a bullet into the chamber. At the click of metal on metal the rabbit ceased its eating and looked up at them. Slowly, Imogene pulled the gun to her shoulder. The rabbit took fright at the movement and darted into the road. Galvanized by the flight of her quarry, Imogene fired. The bullet struck the ground behind and a hundred feet beyond the rabbit, plowing a puff of dirt into the air. The rabbit scampered to safety in the high reeds along the irrigation ditch at the edge of the meadow. Sarah ran up the embankment and looked over the fence, her eyes raking the acres of grass.

"It got away," she said accusingly. "You didn't leave both eyes open."

"I don't think I left *either* eye open. I wasn't even close."

"Let me." Sarah bounded down the slope and took the rifle.

"Do you think you can do better?"

Sarah just laughed and pumped a cartridge into the chamber.

"My, it's exciting," Imogene said.

"It's real, not just a target."

"Be careful, you've got a bullet ready."

"I know," Sarah replied with a race of annoyance. "It'll be faster."

A second rabbit came into view as she spoke, not fifteen feet from where the first one had been grazing. Sarah sucked in her breath, stealthily pulled the rifle up, sighted down the barrel, and squeezed the trigger. The gun barked and the rabbit toppled onto its side in the dirt.

"I got him!" she cried, and Imogene clapped her hands. They ran down the roadway. Sarah reached the rabbit first and stopped just short of it. The bunny lay on its side, panting shallowly, its open eyes covered over by a milky membrane. Its lips were pulled back from its teeth and a ribbon of tongue showed pink between the blunt incisors. Blood ran from a neat round hole in the little animal's side, pulsing out with the rapid beating of its heart. Sarah fell to her knees with a cry. Frightened by the sound, the cottontail kicked its hind feet, the blood gushed out suddenly, and it was still.

Imogene stopped behind Sarah and rested her hand on the younger woman's shoulder. Sarah looked up. "I killed him."

"That was the object."

"I guess so." Flies had found the wound, and made a frenzied buzzing in the hot air.

Imogene urged Sarah to her feet. "You go back to the house. You got dinner, the least I can do is prepare it. Go on now." She watched as Sarah walked back toward the welcoming shade of the buildings. The gun was left on the bank; Imogene picked it up and balanced it over her arm. The rabbit stared sightlessly up at her. She grasped its hind feet, lifted it, and holding it as far from her as possible, she too walked back to the house.

By suppertime the rabbit was stew, and Imogene served it with pride.

Two wagoners had come in that evening, one tall and lanky, with a horse face and a head as bald as an egg, the other of middling height, broad-shouldered and barrel-chested, with a spiky shock of black hair. They shoveled the stew down in complacent silence and asked for seconds. They were regular travelers through Round Hole and loudly appreciated the reappearance of meat on the supper table.

Sarah managed a small bowlful but was withdrawn most of the evening. When supper was over, Imogene led her out onto the porch, away from the murmur of the freighters. The summer night was cool and the air so dry and clear that the stars seemed to hang within reach of the distant mountaintops. Imogene pulled two weathered chairs, used for sitting outdoors, close together and they sat quietly for a time, enjoying the soft sounds of the desert night.

"Do you want to tell me about it?" Imogene said after a while.

"I just feel bad about the rabbit."

"We have to eat."

"I know. I'm being silly."

Imogene smiled at her earnestness.

"I don't want to hunt anymore. Is that okay? I'll cook."

"Of course."

The door banged behind them and the tall angular wagoner joined them on the porch. He jerked a thumb over his shoulder. "I'm going to hit the hay. Dan'll be up awhile longer, but he said to tell you he won't be needing nothing. Good night, ladies." He ambled down the steps and out toward the barn.

"Good night, Curley," Imogene returned. "When are we going to have the honor of having you as an overnight guest inside?"

"When Farmer's Feed and Grain pays their drivers a decent wage and pigs fly," he called back good-naturedly.

They watched his lanky silhouette fold down out of sight in the high grasses beyond the spring as he bedded down for the night.

"I don't mind killing chickens," Sarah said suddenly. "I used to wring their necks better than Walter, Mam said. And I had some chickens at Sam's. They were all mine, I took care of everything. Chickens are different, they're just to eat."

"We'll order some chickens from Reno tomorrow when the stage comes," Imogene decided. "Is there a time of year for chickens?"

"I don't know. We'll want grown ones anyway; baby chicks might die on the way. Some hens and a rooster. Do we have money?"

"No. We'll 'run our face,' as Mac says. We may as well order some saplings too. In for a penny, in for a pound. I'm hungry for trees, shade trees."

"Are we too poor?"

"No, dear. I just worry. We're doing quite well. We should have most of the equipment I took over from the Van Fleets paid off by next year."

They ordered the chickens and the saplings the following day, and as soon as the passengers off the southbound coach for Bishop had been fed and settled into their lodgings, they set about constructing a chicken coop, assisted by two young men. Neither was yet thirty years old, adventurers from the shattered South, cadging rides from freight wagons to try their luck in California. One was lean and blond, his eyes aged by the war; the other was shorter, darker, and spoke very little. Attracted by Sarah's fragile good looks and a chance to break the tedium of an idle summer afternoon, they had offered their assistance with the building project. Dubbing Sarah "straw boss" because she was the chicken expert, they carried the motley assortment of lumber Imogene ferreted out from the piles of refuse behind the stable and shed. The Southerners would have built the coop by themselves if Imogene hadn't insisted they instruct her and Sarah in the fundamentals of carpentry, in return for which supper would be on the house. By evening an adequate coop was erected, Imogene and Sarah wielding the hammers, the two boys looking on and shouting directions and encouragement.

When it was finished, Sarah patted the corner of the low, sloping roof; she'd been too busy to be shy and now the new structure took her mind up completely. "We've done it," she said with delight. "And next time we'll be able to do it by ourselves."

Long after supper was over, while Imogene was still tending bar, Sarah sat by the window of her bedroom, looking out at the dark mountains and the small black hump on the north end of the stable that was her chicken coop.

Imogene came to bed after midnight, walking softly so she wouldn't awaken Sarah if she was sleeping.

"Imogene?" Sarah called softly.

"It's me."

Sarah pulled herself up and made a place for Imogene on the bed. "You're up so late." She took Imogene's hand and kissed it.

"Those boys stayed up drinking. I don't like to see young people drink so much."

"Maybe they're homesick."

"Maybe."

"I've been looking at our little shed. I haven't built anything before. It's easy."

"I sometimes think women are discouraged from doing men's work because they're afraid we'll discover how easy it is."

"I like it. Imogene, I don't hate it here as much as I think I should."

Imogene laughed. "Well, that's good. Maybe we're getting used to it. It's late, we'd best get some sleep." She slipped into her nightgown and crawled under the covers. "How did I stand a cold bed all those years?" she asked as Sarah snuggled close.

Before dawn, a wagon driver was banging on the counter in the bar and bellowing Imogene's name. Pulling on a heavy wrapper, she came quickly. It was still dark, with only the barest glimmer of light in the east, but Imogene recognized him by his barrel shape and low-crowned hat.

"What is it, Cracker?"

"Those reb boys I give a lift in? They fell in the drink last night. Too drunk to get out, what with the high sides and the grass slippery." Blunt and angry, he poked his finger into the air. "Fence that goddamn hole in! I mean it. I told Van Fleet and now I'm telling you."

"The boys drowned?" Imogene asked stupidly.

In the face of Imogene's horror, his anger dissolved somewhat and he mumbled a gruff affirmation. "They did. Me and one of the boys heading out Susanville way fished them out. They must've staggered into it when they went out to bed down for the night. I don't expect they had the price of a bed between them?"

Imogene shook her head. She stood silent for a moment, looking past him, then said, "I'll get dressed."

The young men lay side by side in the grass by the spring. The Round Hole yawned still and dark in the half-light before dawn.

"You can see where they tried scrambling out." Cracker pointed to where the grass was torn and pulled down. "The bank's high, and what with the grass growing out over the water the way it does . . ."

"Why didn't they call for help?" Imogene cried. "Didn't anyone hear them? I'm sure it would have awakened me. I've always been a light sleeper . . ." Her voice trailed off.

"No sense worrying it now, ma'am, maybe they were just too drunk, thought it was all in fun till they was spent. Maybe one passed out and tumbled in and the other got dragged down, trying to fish him out. There's no telling."

Another man, round-headed and thick-shouldered, arms soaked to the shoulders, searched the two dead men. Cracker jerked his chin toward him. "Lyle here pulled them out."

Lyle rocked back on his haunches, resting huge hands on his thighs. "They got nothing on them to say who they was," he said. "Just drifters, I guess. Like as not didn't have any folks to speak of."

The boys' faces, so animated and young the night before, were gray and old, wrinkled by water. Imogene held herself against the chill, rubbing her upper arms as the sun topped the mountains.

"If you can point us to some shovels, we'll bury them," Lyle offered.

"Here?" Imogene said, aghast. "Shouldn't there be someone— a graveyard—something?"

"The heat'll be on us in an hour or so," Lyle warned. "They'll start stinking. We'd as well bury them now."

"There are shovels in the shed."

While the passengers on the morning stage for Reno loaded their baggage and harnessed a fresh team, Lyle and Cracker quietly dug a grave in the meadow below the spring. Imogene had fetched two old sheets from the house, and the boys' bodies were wrapped head to foot in makeshift shrouds.

As the men lowered the corpses into their common grave, Sarah ran down from the house. Lyle saw her and waved her back. "Nothing you can do, missus. Go on back now."

"It's all right, Sarah," Imogene called. "There is no more to be done."

But Sarah came anyway. With short, determined steps she ran across the road and skirted the Round Hole spring. Her face was as pale as death, but her mouth was set in a firm line and her eyes were clear.

Imogene stepped between her and the open grave. "My dear, you needn't have come."

Sarah held out the book she had clutched across her bosom. "The Bible," she said breathlessly. "You would've forgotten it. Those boys would want the words said over them." Sarah held the Bible out to Imogene.

"Will you read it?" Imogene asked softly.

"The Bible's not for me to read or not read anymore," Sarah replied.

Imogene took the Bible and opened it to the Twenty-third Psalm. Sarah stood beside her, her eyes averted from the bundles in the bottom of the trench. The two wagoners bared their heads and stood quietly by as Imogene read aloud in a deep, sure voice. When she closed the Bible, she had tears on her cheeks.

Cracker cleared his throat. "That was right. Me and Lyle would've forgot entirely."

"Thank you, Sarah," Imogene said, and they walked slowly back to the house.

That afternoon, when the stop was empty, Sarah and Imogene, the younger woman gloved and bonneted against the rays of the sun, used their newly learned skills to erect a railing around the spring.

ᘍᘰ 31

THE CHICKENS ARRIVED, A ROBUST, STRINGY LOT WITH PARTICOL-
ored feathers. Only two had succumbed to the rigors of the journey,
and they were eaten for dinner. Imogene's saplings arrived on the
same coach; their wavering green tops, frosted white with alkali dust,
gave the mudwagon the look of a grizzled old head. Mac and Noisy
supervised the planting from the shade of the porch, giving sugges-
tions and speculating on their chances of survival. Noisy was pessi-
mistic, but Mac figured they'd live out the week.

Summer ended abruptly. Imogene's saplings, planted in a neat
line around the house's side yard, lost their leaves almost overnight,
and a biting wind blew out of the northwest all autumn and through
December. Slate-colored clouds scudded dry and cold across a
dome of scoured blue.

The valley was too dry for snow, but the mountain peaks were
white, and frost covered the ground through February and March.
Imogene made the trip by wagon the eighty miles to Loyalton to
get hay. She was gone nearly a week, and Sarah ran the stop alone.
On her return they spent the better part of two days breaking the
bales into manageable lots.

The weather stayed bitter through April but held a suggestion
of softness in the afternoons, and rain fell in cold scattered showers,
the progress of a lone thunderhead often visible as it carried its dark

streamers of rain over the face of the desert. High-voiced new frogs peeped from the spring, and the winter black of the sage was taking on a greenish cast. By the end of May, the bitterbrush was in bloom and spiny yellow and blue flowers half as big as a penny and close to the ground appeared along the road where the water settled in the swale. Jackrabbits and cottontails the size of a woman's hand grazed fearlessly on the short, coarse grass by the meadow's edge. Occasionally a coyote, tempted by the easy game and a winter's lean belly, would hunt them in the daylight, and the nights were filled with coyote song as they called to unseen mates over the Smoke Creek.

The coach out of Reno rattled through the crisp spring air, the dust from the horses' hooves and the wheels plumed up behind for three hundred yards. About a mile from the house, waist-deep in the fragrant sage, Imogene shifted the carcasses of two freshly killed quail and shaded her eyes to watch the mudwagon. Van Fleet's old coat hung from her shoulders down past her hips, its mottled blue-and-brown plaid stained with use and the blood of rabbit, squirrel, and deer. The sleeves were too short and her bony wrists stuck out several inches. The dress she wore was faded and patched, an old housedress she reserved for hunting; it had shrunk over the years and didn't quite reach the top of her wide-toed, lace-up, men's boots—her tramping boots, Sarah called them.

Noisy was the first to look her way; she waved and started for the road. Noisy Dave hollered and waved back. Mac, half-asleep beside him on the high seat, jerked upright. Head bare to the weather, the Henry Repeater held easily in the crook of her left arm, Imogene strode through the brush.

"You're a ways from home, Miss Grelznik," Mac said as Noisy reined up. Several passengers craned their necks out the side windows to catch sight of her. Imogene had become a character people talked about even in Reno.

"Can we give you a lift home?" Mac asked.

"That would be nice," Imogene thanked him. "Sarah ought to have lunch on; we'll get there while it's hot."

Mac jumped to the ground and handed her up, as gallant a gentleman as if she were in satin slippers and a taffeta gown. When she was settled between them, Noisy shook the reins and hollered instructions to the lead team. The horses, excited by the smell of water and the sight of the barn, needed no second invitation and started off at a good clip. Noisy, hunched forward, his round belly on his knees, the leather leads strung between his fingers so that he resembled a puppet master, looked over at Imogene. "You want to give it a try? Take the wagon in?"

"No, thanks," she laughed. "Two horses are enough for me, and it took me a while to learn to handle that. We must walk before we run. Maybe next year."

A rut, cut in the roadbed by an old wash and revived by flash floods during the spring rains, jolted the coach, and a gunnysack hung on a post by the seat yelped and whined. "I near forgot," Noisy said. "Mac and me brought you and little Mrs. Ebbitt a present." Spitting a graceful arc of tobacco juice over the side, he lifted the sack free and dumped it unceremoniously on Imogene's lap. "It's tied up tight, better leave it like that, he's a feisty little feller. I think he's too little to bite you through the sacking, but I wouldn't trust him far as I could throw him, if I was you." Imogene held the bundle carefully, trying to protect it from the jolting of the ride.

"It's a coyote pup," Mac explained. "Don't know if he'll live or not, he's pretty small. Noisy here spotted him off to the side of the road. The bitch had been shot—must've been near the den, because three pups had come out to her. The pups were no more'n three or four weeks old. This little fella was the only one left alive. Just bones, tail, and ears. He was so weak he couldn't hardly stand, but he bit old Dave a good one." Mac laughed.

"Damn pup," Noisy growled amiably. "Be a good dog if somebody don't kill him first."

The pup stirred inside the burlap bag and Imogene laid her hand on it. She snatched it back quickly. "He was trying to bite me through the sack!"

"He's quite a pup," Noisy agreed.

"Watch him, Miss Grelznik, pups've got teeth like needles. You want me to hold him?" Mac offered.

Imogene shook her head and arranged her skirts around the swaddled coyote so he couldn't reach her with his teeth.

The coach rolled into the inn yard and Noisy pulled up before the steps. "Sarah!" Imogene called as she climbed down. "Sarah Mary!" The door burst open and Sarah darted out of the house, her apron clutched up under her chin in both hands.

"Look who's come out to meet us! Maybe it's my birthday or something and I don't know it," Mac teased.

"Imogene," she gasped, grabbing the older woman's arm, "a rat chased me out of the kitchen. It stood up on its hind legs and jumped at me. It was huge." She held her hands, one above the other, about a foot apart. "This tall."

"A rat ran after you on its back legs?" Imogene tried not to sound incredulous.

"Jumped at me." The coach door opened and a round-buttocked man backed out. Sarah made a couple of little hops to demonstrate the tactics of her attacker.

Mac laughed. "Must've been a kangaroo rat."

"Mac," Imogene admonished, "it scared her."

He looked hurt. "I'm not fooling. Kangaroo rats come out around this time of year. About so high, big-bottomed, long tails—they hop around like kangaroos."

Imogene and Sarah eyed him warily.

"It's the truth if I ever told it," he protested.

Sarah glanced nervously over her shoulder at the passengers emerging from the coach, knocking the dust from their clothes. "I better be getting on with lunch," she murmured.

Imogene handed her the quail. "These ought to go in the ice-house unless we're having them for supper tonight."

"Just chase that kangaroo rat out with a broom or something," Mac hollered after her. "He'll leave you alone."

"She don't mix with folks much," Noisy said.

"Sarah's a shy little thing," Mac admitted, "till she gets to know you."

"She's better." Imogene held the gunnysack away from her. It was wet and beginning to smell. She hung it back over the post by the seat. "Sarah works herself to death, thinking she has to make up for letting me meet the coaches and take care of the customers. She's quite a cook. And she can skin a rabbit in half the time it takes me."

Imogene greeted the passengers as Mac and Noisy busied themselves with the livestock. It wasn't until after lunch had been served and cleared away that Imogene remembered the coyote pup.

The gunnysack hung slack on the post, looking empty. In the bottom, a slight widening indicated the pup. Imogene cupped the inert form in one hand and lifted the sack free. "Hey, little fella," she called softly. There was no answering squirm. She carried the puppy, still wrapped in the sack, into the kitchen, away from the noise of the dining hall. Sarah was doing the dishes, humming a song to herself in a sweet, high voice. Gently, Imogene set her burden on the plank tabletop and unwrapped it.

"What've you got there?" Sarah dried her hands and came over to the table.

"A coyote pup. I'm afraid I've killed it. I forgot about it and left it out in the sun." She freed the small form from its burlap prison and stroked the dirty fur. The puppy, light brown and feathery-tailed, was no longer than her two hands. He was gaunt, and his fur was caked with his own filth. "He's breathing, I think." Imogene rested her hand lightly on the tiny ribcage. "I'll put him someplace cool and maybe he'll come around."

Sarah got a wet cloth and squeezed a few drops of water on the pointed nose. A pink tongue flickered out. The fur around the pup's mouth was crusted with dirt and stood out in spikes.

"He looks as though he's got moss growing on his jaws," Imogene remarked. "The water seems to be helping." When the pup ceased to accept water, they laid him on the back porch, near the trap to a small cellar, where it was cool. They folded the burlap bag into a cushion and sat a bowl of water nearby. Sarah left the door ajar so she could listen for him.

In the middle of the afternoon, much recovered, the little dog tottered out of his nest. Sarah was at the kitchen table peeling and dicing onions. He growled, a sound so small it was almost a purr, and Sarah looked up.

"Hello, little moss-face," she said softly. He growled again. "Don't you growl. You're too little to growl." Talking reassuringly all the while, Sarah slid out of her chair and sprawled prone on the floor propped up on her elbows.

When Mac and Imogene came in from the barn an hour later, Sarah had coaxed the little animal onto her lap and was squeezing milk into its mouth from a badly chewed corner of her dishcloth.

Imogene pulled off her work gloves and knelt beside them. Mac, leaning in the doorway, pushed back his battered hat and wiped away the perspiration with his forearm. "Wish you gals would get yourself a hired hand. Bucking hay and mucking out ain't women's work. Nor an old man's, neither." He scrubbed his grizzled stubble with his finger stumps. "You'll bust something inside, you keep at it, Miss Grelznik."

"I'm strong as an ox, Mac, you've said so yourself. There's a lot of men that don't work as hard as I do."

"Still and all . . ."

Imogene reached out to stroke the pup's fur, but he growled at her, a funny gurgling sound through the milk. Sarah looked up. "Mac, will he kill my chicks, do you think?"

"He might. 'Less you teach him different. You maybe could teach him, coyotes are smart beggars."

"How do I teach him?"

"First time you catch him messing around the chickens, hit him between the eyes with a two-by-four. That's got to get his attention. Then just tell him real nice not to do it."

Dinner was over. A fire crackled in the stone hearth at the end of the dining hall away from the bar. Most of the clientele had left on the northbound for Fort Bidwell. Two wagoners played checkers at a table near the bar. Noisy was gone, opting to sleep outside to save money, though the temperature still dropped below freezing most nights. He was going to retire when he'd saved enough, he said, find the fat of the land and a rich widow, and live off them. Mac and Imogene sat near the fire, their chairs drawn up close to the blaze, nursing their after-dinner coffee. Except for a kerosene lamp turned low over the checker game, the fire was the only light in the room.

"Sarah still playing with her new dog?" Mac asked.

Imogene smiled. "I imagine. She set about making a bed for him out of an old crate so the little fellow won't get cold. She's good with small, timid things."

"She's got a feeling for what it's like being scared, maybe. Creatures can sense a person's insides that way. That little gal is doing fine. I never figured her for a life as hard as this, but she's doing okay."

"Sarah Mary is stronger than she thinks."

Mac slurped his coffee noisily and stared into the fire. The sound of the checkers slapping down mixed pleasantly with the pop of the burning pitch. A spark flew out and Imogene reached for the shovel.

"There is no Mr. Ebbitt, is there?" Mac asked.

Imogene scooped up the burning ember and threw it back in the fire. "That's right, Mac. I forged his name on the lease."

For a long time, neither of them said anything. The fire burned low and—more for something to do than from necessity, since it was warm so near the hearth—Mac threw another log on the grate.

"You two gals oughtn't to be trying to run this place alone. It's rough country out here."

"We're doing all right."

"I expect you are. Better'n some. Food's a damn sight better, but the place is looking rundown, needs some paint and nails."

"I can do it, Mac."

"I'll give you a hand when I can."

"You're not going to tell Mr. Jensen?"

"No, I ain't."

Imogene leaned back in her chair, her eyes resting on Mac's gnarled old face.

"Thanks, Mac."

"Mr. Ebbitt dead?" Mac asked after a while. "Or don't he exist? Nate was poking around the Wells Fargo office, asking questions, soon as Sheriff Graff let him out."

"Mr. Ebbitt is real and living, the last we heard. Sarah writes home every day, and her mother gets a letter to us every six weeks or so. What did Mr. Jensen tell Nate?"

"That Mr. Ebbitt was coming to join his wife and that was that. Nate got thoroughly drunk and got himself thrown back in the hoosegow. Soon as he was let out again, he unloaded that farm he bought and lit out for the mines down Washoe way. Weldrick ain't a bad feller. A girl could do worse."

Sarah came in from the kitchen, carrying an unlit candle.

"How is your coyote doing?" Imogene stretched out her hand and Sarah took it, perching on the arm of the chair.

"He's still pretty skittish. He won't really come to me unless he's hungry. But he's better—he'll be tame in no time. And he eats a lot."

"What're you going to name him?" Mac threw the last of his coffee into the fire, and there was a hiss and a momentary dark spot on the log. "What was that you were calling him this afternoon? Moss Face? That's a good name for a prickly-jawed little coyote."

"No. I'm going to name him something pretty. Maybe something Indian or something."

"Are you heading for bed now?" Imogene asked.

Sarah nodded and stifled a yawn.

"Need a light?" Mac asked. Sarah held out her candle. He struck a match against the sole of his boot and lit it for her. At that moment there was a banging on the door.

"Who the hell could that be?" Mac growled. "It's damn near ten o'clock." Imogene started for the door, but Mac stopped her. "Let me get it. Nobody just happens by this part of the country in the middle of the night." He grunted and pushed himself to his feet. The checker players paused in their game to see who the latecomer was.

Mac opened the door and Sarah screamed. Leaning in the doorway was a man with no pants. A grimy red plaid shirttail fell over the man's bare buttocks and gaped open at the front under his vest and short jacket, exposing a matted thatch of dark hair. His legs and thighs were burnt lobster-red, and tiny white blisters pushed through the skin like mushrooms. Both of his feet were bare and swollen to twice their normal size. Behind him on the porch, brown footprints in blood showed the way he had come. Blinking at the light, he dragged his hat off and clutched it respectfully in one hand. In the other was an army canteen. A short growth of beard shadowed his mouth and jaw, white streaked his hair at the temples. He was around forty years old, tall and lean. As they gaped, he slumped against the doorframe and fell to his knees. Mac caught him before he pitched forward onto the floor.

"Sarah, put on some washwater," Imogene ordered. "We'll see to him in the kitchen." Sarah tore her eyes away and ran from the room.

The wagoners left their checker game to help Mac carry the man into the kitchen. He was coming to his senses and they half-carried, half-dragged him between them, stopping just long enough to snatch a cloth from one of the tables and tie it around his waist. He was conscious enough to sit up while Imogene bathed his feet in warm water and Sarah made cold compresses for his sunburnt legs.

The man was slow of speech and stunned from the sun and the miles barefoot across the desert, but after drinking a generous glass of corn whiskey, he managed to tell his tale.

His name was Karl Saunders. He had been riding across country from Deep Hole to the Indian settlement at Pyramid Lake—not on business, he had a friend there. He carried only a little money and his saddle was old and cheap. Three young men, the oldest not yet twenty, had overtaken him southwest of the coach road about ten miles east of Round Hole. They had stolen his horse, his gun, and, as a joke, his boots and pants. They'd left him his canteen and told him there was a stage stop a few miles to the west. He'd walked barefoot through the desert to Round Hole.

Sarah tore an old bedsheet into strips, and Imogene bound his lacerated feet loosely. Kindness crippled him. When to walk was to live, he'd walked miles over rock and broken ground without boots, but under the compassionate ministrations of the women, he could no longer stand. Mac and one of the drivers carried him onto the back porch, where Sarah and Imogene had hastily improvised a bed of flour sacks and horse blankets. Sarah sent Mac upstairs to fetch a blanket and pillow from the men's quarters. The bright eyes of the coyote pup peered out at the proceedings from the hiding place he'd burrowed in his bedding.

In the morning, before sunrise, when Sarah came to start breakfast, there was already a light showing under the kitchen door. She pulled it open a few inches and peeked in. Karl Saunders stood hunched over the drainboard, his long legs spread wide so he would be closer to his work surface. He wore his blanket tied around his waist, and the shirt and vest they'd put him to bed in. His feet were still bound, mummylike, in the cotton windings. Sarah hovered, poised in the doorway, unsure whether to go in or run away.

He felt her eyes on him and turned slowly from his task. "Morning, missus." His smile was warm and childlike in the rough face. He was easily as tall as Imogene.

"Good morning, Mr. Saunders." Sarah slipped in, staying near the door. Karl had a belly that hung down over his twine belt; it began to throb and pulse independently, and Sarah stared, transfixed. The small pointed nose of the coyote pup thrust through Karl's open shirtfront, and Sarah laughed. Charmed, she crossed the kitchen, her fear of Karl gone. "He's took a shine to me," Karl said, and smiled down into the bright brown eyes. "You got cold by yourself with no ma, and come to sleep with old Karl, didn't you?"

Already at ease with this big simple man, Sarah stroked the ears of the pup as it peeked out from its hammock in Karl's shirt.

"I'm peeling," the man said, and gestured to a pile of carefully skinned potatoes on the sink sideboard.

"You oughtn't to be standing on your feet." Sarah got him a

bowl for the leavings and settled him at the table. "There's a lot needs doing. The morning stage from Buffalo Meadows is due in today. Mac and Noisy run the folks on down to Reno."

"Good slop pickings," Karl observed. "Ought to have a hog." And with less furor than the coyote pup had caused, Sarah assimilated Karl into life at the stage stop.

As Noisy steadied the horses and Imogene helped the passengers aboard, Mac glanced back into the shadowed interior of the bar. Karl, wearing a pair of overalls that Van Fleet had left, shuffled after Sarah, carrying a tray heaped with dirty dishes. Moss Face trotted close at his heels. "Looks like you've got yourself a couple of strays," Mac commented.

Imogene followed his gaze. "Mr. Saunders can stay until his feet heal."

"Maybe you ought to hire him on," Mac urged. "Big fellow. Might make you a good hand."

Imogene watched Karl, a quiet ambling man, following in Sarah's wake, seemingly content to help with the house chores and talk to the puppy. "He can stay as long as he likes," she said.

32

"HO, HO, HO!" THERE WAS A CRASH AND A GUST OF WIND, AND THE doorway of the Round Hole Inn framed the imposing figure of David Tolstonadge. He was laughing; an icy wind blew his long hair forward, mingling it with his beard. Gaily wrapped packages filled his arms, and there was a red bow pasted to his forehead.

Sarah, sitting by the hearth, tatting a lace collar for Imogene, threw her work down and ran to him. David dumped the packages on the nearest table and picked up his sister, swinging her feet off the ground and hugging her. "Merry Christmas!" he bellowed, and she cried and clung to his neck and laughed.

"You've been so long!" she said over and over.

"I'm a railroad typhoon. Responsibilities. Besides, I had to find you first." He rolled his eyes and tickled her until she screamed and broke away, out of breath. Then she was back in his arms, kissing him and pulling his beard. David growled an rubbed his bushy beard against her neck, eliciting a wonderful squeal.

"Stop it!" Sarah shrieked.

A heavy hand descended on David's shoulder and a dark furry form darted at his legs, growling and nipping at his trouser cuffs.

"It's okay, Karl," Sarah said quickly. "He's my brother, David."

Karl nodded and scooped up Moss Face. The little coyote had grown by leaps and bounds since spring and was a foot and a half high at the shoulder, but he still pounced and fell over himself with the graceless charm of a puppy.

As Karl departed through the kitchen door, David let his breath out in a whoop. "Who was that? He had a coyote! I wish I could see that dog up close."

Sarah laughed, dancing as if she were a girl again. "That's Karl, he hired on with us. He lives in the tackroom in the barn. Sometimes he does the dishes."

"Doesn't say much, does he?"

"He and I talk. He's not one for strangers." Sarah led her brother over by the fire and sat him down. "You're so good to look at, David."

He ran his hand over his head. "I'm almost bald," he groaned. "Too tall—my hair rubs off on the head of the bed."

Sarah pulled the long, light-colored fringe of hair forward over his shoulders. "What's gone on the top is made up for below the collar. It's long as an Indian's. With your hat on, you look like a storybook cowboy."

David caught her hand and smoothed his hair back. "Here come the boys."

"Brrrr." Noisy hurried in out of the cold, followed by Mac. He blew out through his moustache like a whale surfacing for air. "Close that pneumonia hole!" he bellowed. "You born in a barn?" Mac slammed the door with a satisfying crack.

Mac moved to the fire and stood with his back to it, rubbing his rear end. "The only man fool enough to go out in this cold without being paid's your brother here. Ross'll have an empty haul north."

"The railroad'll put you two out to pasture before too many years are up," David said. "Your business is dying off. You're too slow."

Mac snorted so hard he had to shake his head to clear his ears. "It'll be a cold day in hell when those engineers of yours take on the Smoke Creek."

"Where's Imogene?" Sarah put in. "She met the coach, didn't she?"

"Out getting a Christmas tree." Mac hit Noisy with his hat and laughed uproariously, and the stage driver looked sheepish.

Dragging David by the hand, Sarah grabbed a heavy scarf from the back of the chair and ran outside. Noisy roared, "Close the door! It's colder'n a well-digger's hind pockets out there!" and David closed it.

Clouds ran before a biting wind. The desert was colorless under the hard metal sky. The wind had scoured a curtain of dust off the alkali flat and held it against the ragged skirts of the Fox Range. Snow dusted the peaks, coloring them the same gray as the sky. The regular *chunk-chunk* of Karl chopping wood came to them from behind the house, and the smell of woodsmoke gusted under the porch overhang. The mudwagon, without its team, was parked in the lee of the stable. Sarah pulled her shawl tight around her shoulders. "Where's the tree?" she asked of no one in particular.

"There's Imogene, at any rate." David pointed up the hill behind the stop. Imogene was making her way down through the sage, a spiny branched skeleton of bitterbrush, nearly as tall as she, held over her shoulder. She caught sight of them and waved her arm in a wide arc above her head.

Huddled in the doorway away from the cutting wind, Sarah waited while David, covering the ground quickly with long, loping strides, met Imogene and shouldered her burden for her.

They reached the porch and he swung it down, balancing it on its stump. Blackish limbs thrust out asymmetrically. It gave off a tart, acrid odor that smelled of the outdoors. Sarah hugged herself and waited for Imogene to explain.

"This," Imogene said, "is a Christmas tree."

Sarah's face fell. "Noisy forgot."

David turned the snarled bush from side to side. "Put an angel on the top, and who will know the difference?"

Noisy had become suddenly busy poking the fire when they came in bearing the Christmas bush. "Noisy's getting old," Mac said, his voice heavy with sorrow. "It's good he's knocking off come spring. Mind's going. He'd be forgetting the routes, next thing you know, and dribbling folks all over the desert."

The bush was enthroned on an overturned washtub in the corner away from the fire. It would be decorated on Christmas Eve.

After supper, David excused himself to "see a man about a horse." Just after he let himself out, Karl, chuckling to himself, waved Sarah over to the window. Wondering what the excitement was about, Mac, then Noisy, then Imogene joined them. When David closed himself into the privacy of the outhouse, there were six pairs of eyes watching him. He was about to get his wish concerning Karl's coyote dog.

Moss Face had followed David at a distance, slinking from bush to bush, keeping to the shadows. As soon as the door closed, he crouched down low behind a hump of earth and waited. Sarah laughed excitedly and Karl winked at her. "Oh, you two! You never tire of this," Imogene reproved, but she was covering a smile with her hand. Soon the half moon swung out and David emerged into the cold blue evening light. Moss Face flattened his ears and wiggled his hindquarters in preparation. With a bound he was upon David, a happy growl deep in his throat, worrying David's trouser cuff.

To the immense delight of his audience, David reacted to the onslaught of his shadowy attacker with a great leap in the air and a heartfelt bellow of fear. He was halfway to the house before he heard the laughter.

The night stage from Fort Bidwell arrived after dark, carrying six passengers, one complaining loudly of backache and permanent internal damage from the jostling he had received. He was a slender, white-faced man with a neat goatee, dressed in the confining broadcloth and tight clothes of the Eastern cities. The harsh, windswept desert had shaken him, and he hid his fear with bluster. The others were too cold and tired to do anything but push close to the fire, sip Sarah's strong, hot coffee, and sniff at the savory smells coming from the kitchen.

David sat back from the bar, playing a quiet game of poker—matchsticks were the only stakes Imogene tolerated—with Noisy and Ross, the driver of the Bishop stage. Karl had come in from the tackroom-bedroom he'd fixed up for himself on the leeward side of the barn. He was near the end of the bar on one of the two stools where he could see through the open door into the kitchen. Occasionally he'd lean over the marred wood of the counter and call to Sarah in a stage whisper, "Missus, how you doing? I can wash up in a minute and lend a hand." Moss Face had curled himself into a neat circle that just fit within the four legs of Karl's stool.

Lamps burned along the walls and on the white cloths of the tables that the woman had pushed together to form one board for the evening meal; the room hummed with conversation. Imogene emerged from the darkness of the stairwell and stopped a moment to enjoy the scene, so warm against the bleak desert beyond the windows. Just then Sarah came out of the kitchen, her face flushed with cooking, carrying a platter of seaming venison ringed with small potatoes. Karl was quick to take it from her and carry it to the table.

The food was hot and good and the company cheerful with the season. The talk was of home and of times past. Even the man from the East forgot himself and, after being assured the northern Paiutes were not on the warpath, relaxed and joined in the lighthearted talk around the table. Afterwards, the company spread out to checkers, cards, and quiet conversations by the fire.

Around nine o'clock, Ross and his swamper left to bed down in the barn, the female guests retired, and the little Easterner excused himself for the evening. As he let himself out the front door to visit the outhouse, a stealthy four-legged shape slipped out after him. Karl nudged Sarah's chair with his foot and nodded toward the door. She looked up just in time to see Moss Face's long feathery tail disappearing into the night. Grinning at each other, they rose as one and went to the window. Imogene rolled her eyes heavenward and groaned. David joined Sarah and Karl, then Mac came, and Noisy. Soon the two remaining guests, unable to resist the sly glances and mysterious chortlings, came to swell the ranks.

Unaware that he had an audience, the man looked over his shoulder and peered into the darkness, starting at every small night sound. A coyote howled from a distant hill and he quickened his pace, trotting through the sage until he reached the safety of the outhouse.

"A coyote'd be more scared of him than he is of it," Mac snorted.

"He's got a coyote stalking him now, Mac," Sarah reminded him. She giggled and pressed her face near the glass, cupping her hands around her eyes to block the reflections.

The outhouse door swung closed and, true to form, Moss Face glided over the mound of dirt to the side and hunkered down. Mac and Noisy nudged each other, and the two strangers, unable to make heads or tails of the spectacle they were witnessing, craned their necks to see out the window.

A few minutes passed, the outhouse door opened, a widening ribbon of black cracking the weathered wood, and the New Yorker emerged from the darkness, still buttoning the fly of his trousers.

"You avert your eyes, Sare," David whispered.

Sarah blushed but kept her face pressed against the glass, her eyes on the tuft of fur, spiky and inky black in the moonlight, where Moss Face crouched.

The coyote waited until his victim was several yards from the outhouse. Then, low to the ground, as quick and silent as the cloud shadows, he darted from his hiding place. Growling at the last instant, he threw himself on the man's feet with a puppy's delight, sniffing and snapping at the hem of the trouser leg.

The result was spectacular. First the little New Yorker screamed and threw both arms straight in the air like a man held at gunpoint. In a moment he recovered himself and attempted to run. Doggedly, Moss Face hung on, wagging his rear end and pulling in the opposite direction. Tripped up more by his own fear than by the ministrations of the coyote puppy, the man fell to his hands and knees. Encouraged by the success of his game, Moss Face let go of the trouser leg and ran around in front of his chosen playmate to jump at him and bark.

Inside, the six onlookers howled. David laughed so hard his eyes were wet, and Sarah bounced and murmured "Shh, shh," between fits of the giggles.

Terrified by the eye-level view of his assailant, the New Yorker screamed again and scrambled to his feet. Moss Face danced back and raised one paw, his all-purpose and only trick. Fumbling in his coat pocket, the Easterner pulled out a lady's handgun and fired. Moss Face scampered several feet away, turned, lay on the ground and rolled belly upward to prove his innocent intentions.

Sarah pounded on the glass, crying, "Mister, no!"

Karl shoved Mac and David aside to get to the door.

The frightened man fired again and the little coyote was still.

Karl threw open the door so hard that one of the wooden panels broke as it struck the wall. He was upon the little man before the fellow had recovered from the fright his own gunshots had given him. Karl snatched him up as though he were a toy, one fist knotted in his shirtfront, the other twisted through his belt, and held him off the ground. Sarah, her face as white as the face of the moon, pushed past her brother and grabbed the gun from the New Yorker's hand. She threw it down and ran to the coyote pup.

Karl lowered the whimpering man as Imogene retrieved the weapon and dropped it down the one-holer. There was a dull smack as the gun hit the sewage.

"My pistol!" gasped the little man. "That's an expensive piece!"

Slowly, Karl lifted him again. When the Easterner's face was level with his own, he said, "I'm stuffing you down after it," and began walking his human bundle back into the outhouse.

"Put him down," Imogene said sharply.

"Yeah, put him down, you don't know where he's been," Mac added.

Karl hesitated for a moment, the trembling man clutched in his fists, deciding in his unhurried way whether to please Imogene or himself.

"Put him down, Karl."

He looked at her, as tall and dark as he, her eyes commanding, and gently he sat the man down.

"Karl," Sarah called from the shadows where she knelt, "come here. He's licking me. He's not dead."

Somewhat recovered from his terror, the Easterner began to splutter in a vain attempt to recover his dignity. "I ought . . . I ought . . ." he flustered at David.

"You ought to shut up before I shove you down the hole myself," David warned.

Mac watched the man stomping back to the house, his sense of injury stiffening his spine. "Can't say as I blame him entirely," Mac said. "The girls ought to mark that dog of theirs so's folks know he's a pet."

Moss Face had suffered only a crease along his jaw. His scratch was cleaned and he lay by the fire near Karl. Sarah and Imogene had stayed up later than usual to visit with David. Sarah, perched on a footstool with her back to the fire, read him the latest letter from home.

" 'Your Pa's no better'—Pa's taken to coughing since the accident at the mine," Sarah explained. "Where was I . . . 'and Walter has gone down into the mine—Sam couldn't afford to keep him on anymore. This fall, Sam got a disease in amongst that dairy herd. Those milk cows come out in blisters all over their underhooves and teats. It got so bad Sam had to put them down and burn the lot. Couldn't even be saved for beef. He and a few of the men got together a pile of dead trees and such and burnt the poor things. When a wind came up, the fire took part of the house, but that old stone barn stood fine.

" 'Matthew's growing like a weed and Lizbeth's almost grown up. She's going to be the prettiest of all my girls. Gracie's young man's gone out West.' Mam wrote that Gracie'd got a beau," Sarah interjected. "That was the first I'd heard it was more'n a flirtation. I thought Gracie was too sweet on Sam to pay attention to the boys."

"Sare!" David sounded slightly shocked.

"Well, it's so." Sarah ran her finger down the lines and continued, " 'Gracie's young man will send for her as soon as he's settled. Give David my love.' "

She handed David the letter, and the two of them sat quietly for a while, watching the fire and thinking of home.

Karl was asleep in his chair, his head back, his wide mouth agape, snoring gently. Moss Face lay between his feet, resting his chin on his paws.

Imogene had moved away from the circle of light, leaving brother and sister alone, and busied herself at a table near a window that looked out over the alkali flats to the south. By the steady light of a kerosene lamp, she glued the fragments of a china bowl together. She raised her eyes from the painstaking task and rubbed them. Far to the northeast, along the road to Deep Hole, a plume of silver smudged the roadway. There was no wind and the dust hung undisturbed for miles in the cold, dry air, catching the light of the moon.

"Riders coming," she remarked. "Maybe a freightwagon."

"It's late," David said. "People come in this time of night?"

"Sometimes. A wagon will break down or a horse throw a shoe."

She watched the cloud creep along the white track. It moved faster than a laden wagon and threw up too much dust for the plodding hooves of draft animals on a windless night.

"It doesn't appear to be a wagon," she said after a while.

It was nearly midnight when the night visitors rode into the compound: twelve men in the uniform of the United States Cavalry and, riding handcuffed between the two columns of six, a prisoner. All were death's-head gray with dust and moonlight. The leader of the troop called a halt, and with a creaking of saddle leather the soldiers reined in. One of the horses reared and turned for the spring. There was a brief flurry of hooves and curses before its rider had whipped it into line.

Imogene, wrapped in a thick woolen shawl, stepped out onto the porch to greet them, Karl and David behind her. The captain barked orders to dismount and the soldiers slid gratefully to the ground, only the man in manacles remaining mounted. Imogene saw his face clearly and stopped breathing. She shrank back into the shadow of the porch and laid her hand on Karl's arm. "See to them for me, would you? I'll be inside. That man"—she pointed to the prisoner—"needn't come inside. He can be put in the icehouse." Her voice was so low that Karl had to lean close, like a fellow conspirator, to hear. "The icehouse is warmer than the barn this time of year, and he can be locked in. See that he's given blankets." With that, she went back into the house.

The soldiers were glad of the warmth and welcome. Imogene and Sarah brought out cold venison, bread, and a pitcher of hot coffee. An enlisted man was dispatched to the icehouse with a plate for the prisoner. After they'd eaten, Imogene sent Sarah to the kitchen for a fresh pot of coffee, and as soon as the door swung shut behind the younger woman, she asked who the prisoner was.

"Man named Fox. Danny Fox," the captain replied. He was a ruddy-faced man with a ginger mustache waxed into splendid handlebars. His voice was deep and rich. "Deserter. Up near Fort Roop, there in the Honey Lake Valley just west of here. Some years back, before I was stationed there, he and four others were on patrol. Fox deserted during his watch, and the other four were killed in their sleep. Massacred. We think it was some of Chief Winnemucca's people. We found Fox in New Orleans."

"Dan Fox?" Imogene said half to herself. "Did somebody recognize him?"

"Indirectly. The widow of one of the men who was killed went back to New Orleans after it happened. Guess she fell on bad times. She was . . . well, she'd . . ."

"Go on," Imogene insisted.

"Well, she's a widow woman without any means, which don't excuse it, but she'd taken to the street. She all but admitted her dealings with Fox were of a . . . *professional* nature. Ferguson. That was it—Cora Ferguson." He snapped his fingers. "She was going through his pockets—he was out drunk—and took his wallet. There was papers in it saying he was this Danny Fox. She'd remembered the name and the description Fort Roop had put out after her husband was killed—said it was burned into her brain, was how she put it. Darned if she didn't tie him up with a black stocking and go to the police. They turned Fox over to us."

"What will happen to him?"

"Court-martial. It's been a while, like I say, and there's nobody at Fort Roop much remembers him; most never even saw him. Fox had been at the post less'n a week when he deserted, and I guess he kept to himself."

"The aay-ledged Fox," one of the soldiers interjected and the others laughed.

"Alleged?" Imogene repeated.

"When Fox was brought in, the officer in charge said they'd got his wallet from the whore—the widow," the captain corrected himself, "and asked was he Dan Fox. He swore to Christ he was, then turned around and swore to Christ he wasn't as soon as they clapped him in jail for deserting. They kept him there in New Orleans for a while, but nobody came forward to identify him as being anybody else."

"What will happen to him?" Imogene asked again.

"Firing squad," another soldier answered.

"That's enough, Jack," the captain said quietly. "He'll be tried, ma'am."

Long after everyone had bedded down for the night, Imogene lay staring into the darkness. Finally she heaved an exasperated sigh and sat up. Dark hair, shot with gray, tumbled around her shoulders, and she caught it back away from her face and stuffed it down the neck of her nightgown. Beside her, Sarah still slept soundly.

The head of the bed was pushed against the outside wall under the room's one window; she pulled aside the curtains. The night was perfectly still and cold, and her breath fogged the glass in an instant.

Sliding her feet into slippers, she pulled on her wrapper. Soundlessly she padded through the bar area and let herself out the front door. Across the coach road, beyond the pond, the icehouse stood stolid and dark. Railroad ties mortared together with sod and iron spikes formed a blunt, rectangular building. Tufts of grass grew out of the roof like the eyebrows of an old man. Half of the building was below ground; ice was stored there in summer, and goods that couldn't endure freezing were kept safe below the frost in winter.

Imogene crossed the packed dirt of the yard and skirted the spring. Shrunken to a silver disk the size of a dime, the moon was sinking toward the horizon. Its light fell on Imogene, picking out the white streaks at her temples and leaching the color from her face and robe. Immobile as a statue, she stood in the cold, staring at the black, square window of the icehouse. There was a stirring inside; the prisoner was awake. A face appeared in the window, a pale mask in the darkness of the icehouse. Shadows marked the sunken cheeks and hollow eyes of a haggard, frightened man. He gasped and let out a little groan of fear as his eyes lit on the apparition, and he shrank back into the shadow.

Unmoving, Imogene watched.

"You real?" he called at last, in a high voice.

She said nothing.

"Oh God, oh God," he moaned. Too frightened not to look, he returned to the window. "Get away from me!" he whispered, thrusting his face forward as far as the small opening would permit. "Get away, banshee."

"I'm not a ghost, Mr. Aiken."

Openmouthed, he stared at her, recognition dawning slowly. "Imogene Grelznik."

"Imogene Grelznik."

"Oh, thank God!" he laughed a little hysterically. "Imogene Grelznik." He laughed again and put an arm out through the window. There wasn't enough space for his arm and his face, and he quickly withdrew it. "Christ, am I glad to see you. Imogene Grelznik. It's me, Darrel Aiken, you know me. They were going to have me killed. I ain't no Dan Fox or anybody else. Jesus Christ, they'd've had me shot. Them boys let me know pretty clear what kind of trial I'd be getting. Everybody what knew Fox is dead or mustered out. Jesus Christ!" he said again. "Im-o-gene Grelznik."

There was a long pause and the laughter drained from his face. "You're going to tell them who I am, ain't you?"

"How did you come to have Dan Fox's wallet?"

"I found it. Swear to Christ."

Imogene turned and started to walk away.

"Wait! We were playing poker, I was losing bad. I put a knockout in his drink, and when he went under, I took his wallet."

Imogene stopped and looked back.

"You're going to tell them who I am, ain't you?" he pleaded, his breath clouding the frosty air. "They're set on killing me."

She turned from him and hurried back to the house.

"You gotta tell them!" The cry followed her.

From high in the foothills behind the house, screened from sight by the twisted arms of the bitterbrush, Imogene watched Round Hole come to life. Men and horses looked like toy figures below. Trails of smoke from the chimneys streaked the sky a shade just darker than the dawn. Tiny figures, erect in military blue, poured out of the house, and horses, spouting steam like teakettles, were brought from the stable and saddled. Two men broke away from the group and went to the icehouse at a trot.

Imogene tensed, her shoulders hunched and her hands clasped tight in front of her. The soldiers emerged from behind the blocklike building in a few minutes, marching their prisoner between them. He was agitated, talking and moving his hands animatedly. One of the men in blue called out, and a third soldier, the captain, came to join them. There was a long exchange, then the captain reentered the house. Moments later, Sarah Mary emerged, and the two of them began calling Imogene's name. All that carried up the hill was sound without definition. At length they gave up and the captain shouted an order to his men.

There was a brief struggle as the prisoner refused to mount. Pulling free, he tried to run. The soldiers subdued him with blows and forced him into the saddle. Again, the captain issued a command. The horsemen formed two columns, one on either side of the chained man, and, like pall bearers escorting a coffin, they rode out toward Standish, Susanville, and Fort Roop.

A wild wracking sob tore from Imogene and she pounded her fists against the frozen ground. "God, forgive me!" she cried.

"WHERE IN THE HELL IS MAC AND NOISY?" A GNARLED, BEARDED man called down from the seat of the mudwagon. Several of his front teeth were missing, and the gap made a neat channel for spitting tobacco juice. He aimed a black stream cleanly over his swamper's knees on the side away from Imogene.

"No Reno stage yet," Imogene replied; she'd come down from the porch to greet the coach. "They must have broken down somewhere along the line." It was a clear, cold January day, and Imogene had to shade her eyes against the glare of the winter sun.

As she spoke, the door of the coach opened and a young man stinking of hair oil and rum jumped down. The ground stopped him cold and he nearly fell. Instinctively, Imogene's hand shot out to steady him, but his bumbling entrance embarrassed him and he waved her away impatiently.

"That stage is over two hours late," he snapped, pulling out a cheap, showy watch and fob. "Two hours late coming in from Reno, and I'll know the reason why."

Ross spat again. "Dizable & Denning's latest. Maydley, meet Miss Grelznik. She runs Round Hole."

"Mr. Maydley and I have met," Imogene said dryly. "Mr. Maydley used to carry my packages for me." Ross inhaled some tobacco juice, and he was submitted to a thorough pounding by Imogene before he'd recovered.

"I'm an inspector now," Harland retorted. "I inspect all the stops. Make sure they're up to snuff." The January wind made his nose run. He sniffed and pinched it. His acne-scarred cheeks were a dull purple with cold.

"If he ain't here, he ain't here," Ross reasoned, ignoring the new inspector. "Let's cover these brutes and get in out of the wind."

Harland hurried indoors.

In the kitchen, Sarah heard the door bang and called out, "How many for lunch, Imogene?"

Harland stopped at the sound of her voice and followed it. The kitchen door was propped open with a stone. Inside, Sarah bent over the table, pounding a lump of dough. Strands of blond hair escaped their pins, falling in tendrils over her temples, a rosy glow flushed her cheeks, and the warm, homey smell of baking bread filled the kitchen. Harland leaned in the doorway, assumed a rakish air, and waited to be noticed. After a few moments, when his piercing stare failed to rouse her, he cleared his throat.

She looked up and started at seeing him so near. For a moment she stared at him without recognition. He took it as a compliment, smoothing back his oiled hair and running his palms down his waistcoat.

"Harland Maydley, inspector for Dizable & Denning," he said, and waited for the significance of his announcement to come home to her.

"Oh. The boy at the Wells Fargo office." She looked around the kitchen and, finding no new exits, fastened her eyes on the dough in front of her.

"I'm an inspector now. Dizable & Denning. I'm the one checks the stops, sees that things are running smooth. We just came down from Fort Bidwell way."

"Um." Sarah fumbled with the dough.

"I'd say this place is looking pretty good." He rolled his eye around the kitchen in a proprietary manner. "Just the three of you running the place?"

Sarah nodded.

"Your mister coming in for dinner and catching you talking to another man got you in a fluster?"

"No . . . I don't know . . . ." Sarah murmured.

"Your husband, he keep you running?"

Sarah favored him with a blank look. "You mean Karl? Karl's not my husband, he's the hired man. Karl Saunders."

"Just the three of you? No Mr. Ebbitt?" A crimped smile hardened Harland's face. Sarah realized what she had done, and her hand flew to her mouth. The flour on her fingers left two white marks, like cat's whiskers, on her cheeks.

"Sarah, has Karl come in?" Imogene called from the other room.

"Excuse me." Sarah scurried past Harland. Imogene was tying her white bar apron over her dress. "He ain't . . ." Sarah stammered, "He isn't . . . hasn't come in. He wasn't feeling well and went out to the barn to lie down. He said his stomach's been hurting him."

"What has you in such a fluster?" Imogene looked past her to Harland Maydley, who was just emerging from the kitchen. "Pay no attention to him, Sarah," she whispered, then went on in a normal voice, "Wednesday's coach might have brought in a touch of something. I feel a little under the weather myself. Why don't you go check on him? I doubt he's even built himself a fire. Try and get him to come inside." Sarah waited a moment. "All right," Imogene sighed. "Tell him Moss Face can sleep with him upstairs."

By sundown the Reno stage still had not arrived. Ross and Leroy, the swamper, not sorry to be by a crackling fireplace with good whiskey to drink, had unharnessed the team and stabled them for the night. Karl insisted on staying in the tackroom, so Sarah built a fire in the little woodstove and laid in a pile of wood.

After supper, Imogene brought him a plate of hot food, and a bowl of pan scrapings for Moss Face. She declined any supper for herself; the smell, she said, made her feel faint. Her color was bad and her broad face was covered with a sheen of sweat. Sarah urged her to go to bed, and as soon as the supper things had been cleared away, she succumbed to the younger woman's entreaties and let herself be led off to bed.

Her long, narrow feet were white against the floorboards and her arms angled out sharply from her wide shoulders as she stood in her shift before the washstand. Sarah hovered by, the towel over her arm. "You oughtn't to be washing. It's winter and you're coming down with something," she warned.

Imogene laved her face and neck. "You've even heated the water. What harm can come to me, with you looking after me?"

"I'm serious, Imogene."

"So am I." A wave of dizziness overcame her and she leaned forward, braced against the stand, her head hanging over the basin. Water, dripping from her nose and chin, steamed in the cold room.

Sarah took her around the waist, nudging her head under Imogene's arm, and said, "You're clean enough." Imogene let Sarah take her to bed. The younger woman tucked her in and patted her face and hands dry.

"You'll be all right?" Imogene asked.

"I should. There's only three. No freighters or anything. And Ross and Leroy are going to sleep out in the barn. In January." Sarah grimaced.

"Those men live moment to moment. They were paid the first of the month, and everyone but Mac is broke already. And Noisy, but he's saving up for his ranch."

"They're never too broke to drink."

"Maybe it keeps them warm." Imogene lay back and closed her eyes.

"Maybe. What were you and Mr. Maydley arguing about? I heard you in the hall when I was cleaning up."

Imogene snorted. "He expected to sleep and eat here for nothing as a representative of Dizable & Denning."

"You said no?"

"I said no."

Sarah smiled and tucked the hand she'd been holding under the blankets. "You're not scared of anybody."

"I am, but I just never let them know."

"I'm scared for Mac and Noisy."

"Don't be. They probably broke down and stopped somewhere for the night."

Sarah kissed her and blew out the lamp. "I'm going to leave the door open so some heat gets in. If you need anything, call me, okay?"

"I will. Good night, Florence Nightingale. Don't be afraid to wake me if you need to."

Sarah looked in on the men. They were clustered near the fire; Ross had brought a bottle of whiskey from the bar, and he and the swamper sat sprawled, their feet to the fire, drinking and talking quietly. Harland seemed to be the only one on whom the whiskey had an effect. He lounged against the mantel, his eyes wet with heat and bourbon and his legs spread wide to counteract his instability. Ross saw Sarah and waved a hand. Harland fixed her with a knowing look and swung out his hip, affecting a devil-may-care stance. The effect was spoiled when Ross let loose with a stream of tobacco juice aimed into the fire, and Harland had to dodge to save his trousers.

"We're doing fine," Ross assured her. "We can wait on ourselves. You go on about your business, Mrs. Ebbitt."

"Thank you, Ross. Good night." Sarah ducked out of sight and he and Leroy laughed good-naturedly at her shy disappearance. Harland joined in, too late and too loud.

The dishes were done and preparations made for the morning meal. Sarah dusted the last of the crumbs from the table and hung her dishrag over a chairback to dry. The scraping of chairs announced that the men were turning in for the night. She listened until the outer door closed behind Ross and Leroy and she heard the shambling tread of Harland Maydley making his way unsteadily up the stairs, then she slipped into the main room to blow out the lamps and check the fire.

There was a sound on the stair behind her, and she turned. Harland Maydley stood in the doorway, swaying slightly. He'd taken off his jacket and vest and greeted her in his shirtsleeves.

"You're up late all by yourself. Maybe waiting for somebody?"

"I was just going to bed, Mr. Maydley." She started for the hall door, but he moved to stop her.

"Since we're up, there's no sense going to bed without having a drink and some talk. No harm in talking, is there?" he wheedled.

"No, Mr. Maydley."

He stepped to the bar and poured the last of a bottle into two glasses. "We can't talk here so good. Let's get comfortable where it's warm." Reluctantly, Sarah crossed to the fireplace and perched on the edge of a chair. Harland seemed to enjoy her discomfiture. "Boo!" he said, and laughed when she jumped. "Don't sit so far away. I can't hardly see you. That ain't very good business, making a customer feel he ain't welcome."

"I have to go now." Sarah rose hurriedly but he caught her arm.

"What's your hurry? You ain't even finished your drink." He picked up the untouched whiskey he'd brought for her, and held it out.

"I don't drink," she managed.

He pulled her face close to his. "There's a lot you don't, I'm finding out. Like you don't have no Mr. Ebbitt, do you? Or leastways not here, you don't. You ain't no blushing schoolgirl, neither. Ebbitt must've taken care of that before he let you get away. Or Weldrick. You got nothing to hide from me, I'm just one of the boys. You got a taste for it? All alone in bed nights? Or does Karl do more'n water the horses?" He spoke in a rapid monotone, his voice low and his breath laden with whiskey. Sarah tried to pull away but he held her fast, his fingers digging into the soft flesh of her arm. "How about a kiss?"

Before she could react, he toppled her into his lap with a jerk and covered her small mouth with a wet kiss. Sarah cried, the sound choking deep in her throat, and tried to twist her face away. Grunting, Harland clamped his mouth viciously over hers, his tongue probing between her lips, prying at her clenched teeth. He held her on her back across his knees, one arm twisted behind her back. Her legs dangling over the arm of the chair, not touching the floor. With surprising strength, Sarah wrenched her face free of his, but before she could cry out he slammed his hand over her mouth and pushed her to the floor, her buttocks between his feet, her legs flung out in front of her. He pulled her head back against his crotch and wrapped his legs over her arms, pinioning them to the chair. "Got a little fight in you, don't you?" Panting from his exertions, he bent his face over hers and, watching her eyes, slowly slid a hand down and over her breast, kneading through the fabric of her dress. Sarah shrank against the chair.

"You like that," he whispered. The sparse hairs that sprouted through the acne glistened in the light. "You like that." Half a dozen buttons popped off her shirtwaist and clattered across the floor as he shoved his hand down inside her chemise and grabbed at her. "Oh my God," he groaned. He wasn't looking at her anymore, and Sarah thrashed with all her might, her heels drumming on the wood, muted cries sounding in her throat. She flailed her imprisoned arms and tried to bite the hand he held over her mouth. The violence made Harland's eyes shine and he tightened his hold until the flesh showed white where his fingers dug into her cheeks. A flash of pale skin caught his attention; she had kicked her skirt up over her knees. He ripped his hand free of her bodice and pulled the petticoats up above her waist. Bending double, his chest pressed down on her face, he tore away her pantalets and screwed his fingers into the wiry blond hair between her thighs, his eyes wide, devouring her naked belly and legs. With a cry that was almost of pain, he loosed her mouth to fumble in the warm thatch where her legs came together.

Freed, Sarah screamed, a short, high-pitched stab of sound. It was cut off almost immediately as Harland's palm smashed down on her mouth again.

"Shut up, you bitch," he whispered hoarsely. "You're loving it. You're loving it." He wasn't talking to her but whispering for his own ears. He swung free of the chair. Her arms fell helpless at her sides, the feeling gone from lack of blood. Harland slung her to the floor. He smashed his doubled fist into her temple and she crumpled, senseless.

Pawing like a dog after a gopher, he clawed her skirts aside and unbuckled his belt. Too impatient to unfasten all the buttons on his trousers, he pulled them down half-buttoned. His penis popped out and bobbed in the light of the fire. Grabbing one of Sarah's breasts in each hand, he supported the whole of his weight on her narrow chest and lifted himself, stabbing ineffectively between her legs. Muttering his impatience, he grabbed his penis to guide himself into her.

At that moment, Imogene appeared in the doorway. Maydley looked up, and it was as if her face had turned him to stone. Trapped in his hand, his penis withered, its tip disappearing into folds of skin and finally withdrawing completely behind his circled thumb and forefinger.

Imogene set the candle down. Her face was pale and set. Only her eyes were alive, but the gray had turned dark and they bored into him with a hatred that turned his bones to water. Harland tried to back away, to pull his pants up, but the trousers were jammed down around his thighs as tightly as ropes.

In two strides she crossed the room. She snatched a piece of firewood out of the woodbox. Swinging the wood from side to side like a scythe, she beat him. Harland shrieked and threw his hands up over his face. Grim, implacable, the blows rained down: crack, and his left arm hung useless; wood on bone, and a cut opened from eyebrow to chin. He fell and crawled across the floor on his belly, his naked pelvis scraping against the boards as he retreated. Imogene struck again and again, his legs, his back, his feet. The fabric of his trousers ripped, and his breeches fell down around his ankles. On hands and knees he made the door and crawled across the porch, bellowing with fear and rage. Imogene hurled the log after him, striking him a glancing blow on the head.

"Next time I see you I shall kill you," she said softly.

He managed to get to his feet and pull his pants up around his hips. He was crying and his face streamed blood. Holding his pants with his good arm, he shuffled out into the yard. Once out of reach, he turned to shout, "There ain't no Mr. Ebbitt." He spat out two of his teeth with the words. "I'll see you lose this place. By God, I will!" He started crying again and stumbled into the dark.

The commotion brought Karl in from the barn. He was bent over, clutching his side, but there was an ax handle ready in his right hand. "Trouble, miss?" he called.

"It's over, Karl. Get back to bed." She could hear him shuffling back to the barn and saying something to Ross.

Imogene went inside and bolted the door. Sarah had come to her senses and was sitting huddled by the fire, her swollen face held between her palms.

Imogene went quickly to Sarah and hugged her as they both began to cry.

The fire burned down to nothing and still they sat curled against each other, Imogene's wrapper pulled around them both.

"Imogene?" Sarah broke the long silence.

"What, dear?"

"Would you give me a bath?"

"Of course."

The clothes Sarah had been wearing, down to her petticoats and stockings, were burned to heat water for the bath. It was so hot that it reddened her skin, but still she complained it wasn't hot enough and Imogene added more until it slopped over the rim of the tub and darkened the floor. Imogene scrubbed her from head to toe with rough lye soap. As the callused palms and coarse soap scratched away the touch of Maydley's hands, Sarah felt the stain he had left inside, the knot of shame, begin to loosen its hold.

At last, naked and dry and glowing, she stood before the fire. "Feeling better?" Imogene's tender smile hid a word of hurt. Helplessness lay like a stone on her chest. Dark marks were forming on the perfect white skin of Sarah's breasts, fingermarks where Maydley had clutched at her. Imogene reached out and touched the bruises gently.

"Davie used to say it was your fight if the other fellow looked worse than you," Sarah said, and smiled crookedly into the older woman's eyes. "Hold me, Imogene. Please hold me." Her voice broke and Imogene cradled her like a child.

The stars were beginning to set, piercing a sky more blue than black, a desert sky, magnified by the dry air and scoured clean by high winds. Sarah's hair, red-gold in the light of the fire, spread over the two women like fine lace.

Imogene eased her arm to settle Sarah more comfortably on her shoulder. The younger woman sighed, nestling closer, loving the warmth and smell of Imogene. "Will we have to leave here? He—" She couldn't bring herself to say Harland Maydley's name. "He will tell that man at Wells Fargo—Ralph Jensen—that there's no Mr. Ebbitt."

Imogene held her tighter. The thought of leaving the Smoke Creek Desert and the new life that had begun for them was intolerable. A sudden thought banished the coldness that was welling up inside her. "We'll sign the lease over to Karl," she said promptly.

Sarah propped herself up on one elbow and looked down at her old teacher. She traced the outline of Imogene's wide mouth with a finger-tip. Her face was soft with love for her longtime friend. "Why are you so smart?"

"Because I'm not pretty—that's what my father used to tell me."

"You never talk about your parents. Why?"

"They weren't happy people. My father was a sickly man, the runt of the family. All his younger brothers were great, robust fellows over six feet tall. It bothered him all his life and he took it out on my mother. When I was almost grown—I must have been just eighteen that summer—Father was drunk and he hit my mother. I knocked him out with just my fists. He left that night and we never heard of him again. Mother never forgave me. She watched for him every day until she died."

"I'm so sorry." Sarah smoothed the hair from Imogene's cheek. "You're still warm; the fever's not quite left you."

Imogene caught her hand and kissed the palm. "I've never felt better. Not in all the years of my life. No one need be sorry for me."

The Reno stage rolled in just past one o'clock the next afternoon. Noisy had gotten so drunk celebrating his last run that he'd fallen out of a saloon in Reno, broken his shoulder, and couldn't drive. They'd had to hold the stage until his replacement arrived from Virginia City. The new driver, Liam, a lean and uncommunicative Irishman, seemed sullen and taciturn compared with noisy Dave. Karl was too sick to stand, and stayed in the tackroom.

As soon as the team had been changed, Harland crept painfully from the shadowy recesses of the barn where he'd hidden himself. His clothes were covered with straw and manure, his jacket and vest were missing, and his face was streaked with dried blood. One arm stuck out at an odd angle and he walked with difficulty. He crawled into the mudwagon and insisted that they leave immediately. Liam, new to the job, succumbed to his threats, though Mac cursed and fumed at cutting the rest period short and railed at Sarah to tell him "what in hell's going on." Sick, Imogene had kept to her room and Sarah refused to tell Mac anything. She was afraid he would kill Maydley. And she was terribly ashamed.

BY THAT EVENING, KARL WAS WORSE. HE HAD CURLED HIMSELF INTO a ball, trying to ease the hurt in his stomach, and the women feared it was appendicitis.

Imogene was cooking supper when Sarah ran in from the barn. Karl was dying. The two of them sat with him, bathing his face with cool cloths and easing him with kind words and gentle hands. Just after midnight the big, quiet man passed away. His body grew limp and the pain left his face. Outside, the moss-faced coyote began to howl. Kneeling by the bed, Sarah wept. Imogene went on holding the hired man's hand between her own. She felt old and tired, too tired to comfort, too tired to move.

Sarah recovered first, dried her face on her apron, and blew her nose. Then, with great care, as though afraid of waking him, she rolled Karl onto his back and straightened his limbs. His skin was still warm, still alive with blood, still damp from his sweat. For a moment Sarah held her breath, as if waiting for him to speak to her.

"There's so much dying, Imogene. We've seen so much dying. Somehow I thought Karl would just be worn away over the centuries, carved by the wind and the sand until he was as smooth and hard as the pyramids at the lake. Who'd have thought Karl would die?"

Imogene rubbed her face. Her eyes felt grainy, full of sand. "His appendix must have ruptured. There was nothing we could do. Nothing." She started to rise from the dead man's cot, but her legs were too heavy to lift and she sat for a while longer, staring past Sarah into the darkness beyond the window.

Moss Face howled again and was answered by the coyotes in the hills. The hair on the back of Imogene's neck stirred and Sarah shivered, though the room was warm. "He knows Karl's dead," she whispered.

"Don't be silly, you're scaring yourself," Imogene snapped, but she knew it was true and shook herself to be rid of the fear and loneliness. "Break up the fire," she said abruptly. "I'll open the windows. It will be better if it's cold in here."

Sarah hurried to comply, glad of something to do. "Will he—will Karl—keep till morning?"

An icy wind blew over the still and snuffed out the candle. Revived by the sudden gust, the fire in the stove flared to life again, and as suddenly died. "Karl will be fine," Imogene replied. Sarah drew strength from her nearness, and for several minutes they stood quietly in the darkened room, each saying their good-byes to Karl Saunders.

Supper had dried up to nothing. Both women were too tired and numb to sleep, and sat at the kitchen table hunched over plates of cold food. Outside, desolate howling rent the night. Sarah had tried to coax the coyote indoors but he had run from her like a wild thing. In the hall the pendulum clock pounded the dull minutes toward dawn.

"We should eat," Sarah said without enthusiasm.

"We should get some sleep," Imogene replied, but made no move to rise.

Another cry broke the night stillness, and Sarah shoved her coffee aside. "We'll have to leave Round Hole now, won't we, Imogene?" The older woman was silent for so long that Sarah spoke again: "Imogene? We will have to go, won't we? Without Karl to take over the lease for us?"

The schoolteacher's shoulders sagged and she pressed her palms to her eyes as though she were blind. "I can't think about it now. I can't think at all.

"Do you love me?" Imogene asked softly.

"You know I do," came the reply.

"We'll stay. We'll keep the stop. I'll think of something. Let's try to get some sleep now."

Morning brought no answers. At sunup they bundled into their coats and scarves to see to Karl's remains. A kernel of anger lay hard in Sarah's chest. "We're going to have to leave the stop," she said, knowing the words would hurt. "Maydley will tell Mr. Jensen. You know he will. We may as well start packing our things now. We're going to have to leave on the next stage." Imogene said nothing. She pressed her lips into a thin line and jerked mittens on over her gloves. Sarah felt mean and little. "Well, this isn't the first time I've been chased from my home."

Imogene looked at her sharply. "Are you sorry, Sarah?"

The hurt in her old friend's face took the bitterness out of Sarah. Gently she said, "No, Imogene, I'm not sorry. It's been a long time coming and it's right. I no longer believe in a God that rations out love only where the neighbors see fit."

Imogene nodded shortly.

A wind had risen with the sun and blew steadily from the northwest. Moss Face was standing guard before the tackroom door. Sarah scratched his ears as they slipped past him and inside.

Karl's room was as spare as a monk's cell. Against the wall, opposite the narrow cot where Karl's body lay, was a nail keg containing the entirety of the hired man's estate: a jackknife, a silver chain with a silver nugget, a faded photograph of a middle-aged woman, and, tucked in a tobacco tin, every penny they had paid him in wages since the day he arrived.

Sarah looked at the shrouded figure of Karl Saunders. "Somehow I expected to find that he was all right this morning, not to see him just like we left him." She started for the bed to turn back the cover from his face, but changed her mind.

"We haven't the lumber for a coffin," Imogene said. "We'll have to bury him in a shroud."

"I read somewhere that they sew sailors into sails before they bury them at sea," Sarah replied. "Could we do that for Karl? A horse blanket—a sheet is so thin it wouldn't keep out the damp." Her eyes strayed to the feet of her friend, thrust out from under the cover, so human and vulnerable in their mended stockings.

"Karl's too tall for a horse blanket," Imogene said kindly. "We would have to sew four of them together."

"We couldn't spare four."

There was a long silence while the cold seeped through their clothes and the coyote whined at the door.

"The best blanket in the house," Sarah declared finally. "The one the bishop's wife gave me." It was of fine wool and brightly colored. Sarah felt good for the small sacrifice.

Moss Face squeezed in as she opened the tackroom door, and was across the room like a shot. He stopped short of Karl's bed as though someone had jerked an invisible leash. A low moan built in his chest until it broke free in a howl. Imogene reached for him, soothing words forming on her lips, but he growled and darted under the bed. Imogene murmured and coaxed, but though he whined and thumped the floor with his tail, he wouldn't come out.

Sarah watched from the door, the wind whipping her skirts into the room. A gust caught up a handful of ashes from the stove and scattered them over Karl. "Let's go on with it," Imogene said as she stood up. "Moss Face is all right where he is, I guess." While Imogene fetched the long needles and strong waxed thread from the harness-repair kit, Sarah ran to the house for the blanket. When she returned they spread it on the floor beside the dead man's bed so they could lower the body down onto it.

Tentatively, Sarah pulled the cover back. Karl was gone; only the pale, lifeless husk remained. She looked at the bloodless face, the stiff shoulders, and knew with a rush of relief that she could bury him.

The moment they laid hands on Karl's corpse, the coyote went wild. Snarling, he exploded from under the cot like a wolverine defending its whelp. His usually soft brown eyes were narrowed, and hackles ridged his back. Crouching by Karl's body, Moss Face bared his teeth in silent warning. The women retreated to the far side of the room. Immediately Moss Face sat down, the hair along his spine settled, and he looked up at them sheepishly, the picture of canine remorse.

"Look at him," Sarah marveled.

The coyote crept toward them on knees and elbows. In the middle of the blanket he laid his chin on his paws and wagged his tail apologetically. Sarah started forward but the older woman stopped her. "We'd better give him a wide berth for a few days," she said. "He is pretty upset."

"We've got to get him out of here. We can't just leave Karl."

Sarah lowered her voice and glanced furtively around the room. "Mam says till you've been buried and last rites said, the spirit wanders. It can do people harm."

"You don't believe that, do you?"

"Moss Face feels it," Sarah insisted.

"If you don't stop, I'll be feeling it." Imogene resisted the urge to look over her shoulder. "Still, it isn't suitable to leave Karl any longer. Take the far corner of the blanket, I'll get this one. At the count of three we'll wrap Moss Face in it. I'll lock him in the house until he settles down." Their stealth put the coyote on the alert, but they were too quick for him. They folded him in the heavy wool and Imogene scooped him up. Inside the bundle, Moss Face fought, but the blanket was thick and Imogene held him tight.

Karl was so tall they had to lay him on the blanket corner to corner and fold it into a triangle like an apple turnover. The lack of dignity disturbed Imogene, but Sarah knew the big taciturn man would have enjoyed the joke.

The sewing finished, Sarah brought the wheelbarrow from the shed and they loaded the body onto it. The grave was to be on the shoulder of the hill behind the house, and they trundled their sad cargo up through the sage. Tools were fetched and Sarah was sent back to the house, out of the cold.

Imogene broke through the frozen ground with a pick. When the crust lay like paving stones by the side of the grave, she took up the shovel and began to dig. It was slow going in the rocky soil. Once, Imogene's spade struck a stone the size of a man's head. "Alas, poor Yorick," she said, and smiled a little as she threw the rock into the sage. Two hours later the grave was four feet deep and just over six feet long.

Sarah came up the hill with hot tea and stayed on to keep Imogene company and to avoid being alone. In the house, by herself, she kept hearing things. Looking down over the weathered buildings and gray alkali flats to the blue of the Fox Range beyond, Sarah sensed the emptiness of leaving and pulled her coat closer around her throat. "I've gotten so used to it here, I even like the alkali water. I don't smell the rotten-egg smell anymore."

Imogene stopped working and leaned on her shovel for a moment, the sweat shining on her brow and upper lip. "I love it here. It's a hard land, but it's clean. Clean of people."

"You haven't much use for people once they've turned twelve, have you?"

Imogene laughed. "Not much. I do love the children, they are so full of what people could be. But they almost never make it. The humanity is shamed or beaten out of most of them before they have turned twenty. They plod down the same narrow track their parents did, and never see the sky."

"We have got to go back," Sarah said softly. "We have to, now that Karl's gone. Back in among the people. Out here, we made the rules." A sad howl echoed up the hillside, adding finality to Sarah's words.

Imogene plied her shovel in silence.

After another hour the grave was dug. The two of them dragged the body, shrouded in its blue-striped envelope, to the edge of the hole. They tried to lower it gently, but it got away from them, and the remains of Karl Saunders tumbled the last few feet. In the pocket of her coat, Imogene carried the Bible. As she read the words over him, the wind snatched them from her lips. Sarah hoped that if they were blown to where Karl could hear them, they brought him comfort.

Working with both shovel and pick, they filled in the grave and, stone by stone, made a small cairn to keep the animals from digging it up. Imogene promised to build a cross.

Finally all that remained was to clear away the few personal effects Karl had left behind, the work of half an hour. "I guess we'll be packing our own things next," Sarah said, and Imogene crumpled as though she had struck her.

Sarah ran to her, clung to her, patting her back and shoulders. Imogene burst out in fresh cries, the dry sounds of a person unaccustomed to tears. "Please, Imogene! Please!" Sarah rubbed her neck and held her, kissed the rough cheeks.

"I'm going to lose you," Imogene cried. "I cannot bear it. We'll leave this desert and I'll lose you."

"My love, my love," Sarah murmured. "No. Never. Don't cry. It'll be the same. Just you and me. I promise. People won't make any difference. I promise they won't."

Even as she said it, Sarah knew it wasn't true and Imogene only sobbed harder, her face buried in her hands.

"Imogene!" Sarah cried frantically. "Please, stop it! Listen to me, Imogene!" Sarah tried to pull the schoolteacher's hands from her face. "We'll stay. Here on the Smoke Creek. I've got an idea. We can stay, honest to God. Damn you! Listen." Sarah swore fervently and tugged at Imogene's wrists. Imogene quieted a little. "We won't tell anyone Karl's dead," she went on hurriedly. "We'll sign the lease for him like we did for Sam last time. We'll pretend he's not dead, that he's still here."

Imogene shook her head, but she wasn't crying. "We can do it," Sarah pressed. "Noisy's quit the run and Mac would never let on. The other people that come through here are mostly strangers going someplace else, they'd never know a thing. Jensen never comes, and after the licking you gave Maydley, I bet he wouldn't dare. If somebody asked, we could say Karl had gone here or there and wouldn't be back for a few days, Karl didn't have any people, so there would be nobody to tell."

A momentary light showed in Imogene's eyes, but it faded quickly. "It wouldn't work, Sarah. Word would get back that there was no man here. Freighters would talk. Even Mac. Mac is as transparent as glass. You know he couldn't hide a thing." A bleak emptiness settled over Imogene's mind and, sad-faced and silent, she succumbed to it.

"No!" Sarah grabbed her by the shoulders and shook her. "I won't give up, not yet. We've got to try." She took Imogene in her arms and the big woman hid her face in Sarah's soft hair. Sarah hugged her close. "We won't give up Round Hole without a fight! 'One holy hell of a fight,' as David says."

They tore down the stones that marked Karl's grave and put his belongings back where he'd kept them. Imogene wrote a note to Ralph Jensen. She didn't apologize for deceiving him the first time, she simply stated that she and Sarah would give up without a fuss if he would agree to lease the Round Hole stop to Karl Saunders and, if Karl agreed, let them stay on. She asked that he send the lease out with the next stage. She would see it was returned to him with Mr. Saunders's signature.

They posted the letter with the next wagon through, and waited. The reply came back with unexpected alacrity. A freighter, bound for Oregon with a load of cheesecloth, brought it to them late Saturday afternoon. It read: *The hell you will. I'll be out on the Wednesday stage to see Saunders sign it his own damn self.—R. J. Jensen.*

THE NEXT DAY, SARAH WATCHED THE MUDWAGON FROM THE WINDOW
of the tackroom as, tiny and toylike in the distance, it wound its
way down from Sand Pass. It was Sunday, four days since Harland
Maydley had left Round Hole with more threats than teeth in his
mouth, three days before Ralph Jensen was due.

"You'd better get to the loft now," Sarah said without turning
from the window.

"You'll tell Mac?"

"I'll tell him."

The door between the tackroom and the barn swung shut. Sarah
pulled her thoughts from the oncoming coach and went back to
sweeping the floor. As the coach arrived at the inn yard, she finished
and emptied the dustpan into the barrel stove. The smell of burning
hair made her eyes water, and she sank down on Karl's cot, dabbing
at them with her dresstail.

"Sarah, coach is in!" came the call from inside the barn. She
ignored it and hid her face in her hands.

Mac hollered for Imogene, then for Karl. There was no reply.
He lowered himself gently from the high seat of the coach and
stomped the life back into his legs and feet. Liam, looking like a
man of ice, his chapped face colorless and his lips blue with the
cold, steadied the team. Steam rose from the horses' hides and

puffed from their nostrils. The sky was low and leaden overhead. Hobbling and stiff, Mac opened the coach door. "Watch that first step," he cautioned. "The ground's froze and liable to jar your teeth out."

The coach was full. Groaning, the men helped one another with the women and the baggage. A slender, handsome woman and her two pert teenage daughters, traveling with their elder brother, were handed down last and stood in a tired, unhappy cluster, small and out of place in the desert landscape.

Helpless under the distraught glances of the women, Mac looked around the deserted yard. "Gals are usually out to meet the coach. Miss Grelznik, at any rate. Miss Grelznik!" he called. "Coach's in." Smoke curled placidly from the chimney and the stovepipe behind the house; chickens, daring out of their coop in the bitter air, pecked the ground in a desultory fashion. But there were no faces at the windows nor Imogene's usual call of "Company!" to warn Sarah.

"Karl!" There was no answering shout. "What in the hell . . ." Mac muttered. "Begging your pardon, ladies. Go on inside, the gals must be tied up some damn place. Looks like they got a fire lit, anyway. Just make yourself at home." Relieved to get his unaccustomed duties over with, he hurried back to the company of the livestock.

In the dining room a fire burned high, holding winter at bay beyond the windows. A homey smell of onions and roasting meat permeated the air, mingling with the mellow smell of old wood and old whiskey. Cold enough to risk impropriety, the misses pulled their chairs close to the wide hearth and lifted their petticoats to toast their feet on the grate. Their mother hovered near, keeping a watchful eye on their modesty and on itinerant sparks. She had ventured a few hellos, but no one had come.

In the relative warmth of the stable, Mac rubbed down the horses and covered them with heavy blankets. A rustling just louder than a mouse caught his ear and he looked up over the horse's broad back.

"Mac," Sarah whispered. She was as pale as a wraith, her face the same dull pewter as the square of sky that filled the open door at her back. She wore neither hat nor coat.

"Where've you two been hiding? I've a coach full—" Mac's voice trailed off, then he said, "What's happened, Sarah?"

She opened and closed her mouth several times without produc-

ing any sound. Her eyes were distracted and her hand shook as she
pushed back a loose strand of hair. A horse kicked in its stall. She
jumped as though she'd been pinched, and sucked in her breath
sharply.

"Sarah?" Mac walked around the horse's rump, the currycomb
in his hand.

"Imogene is dead." Sarah moved her hands before her, the little
unfinished gestures of a crippled bird.

"Oh Jesus." Mac looked at her, then at the floor. "Jesus Christ."
He set the currycomb blindly on the partition between the stalls,
missing it by half a foot, and it clattered to the floor. Sarah came
to take his hand, warming the maimed, gnarled fist between her
small hands. "How did it happen?" His voice was thick. He looked
for a place to spit, but didn't.

"Two days ago—she was feeling poorly Sunday, she hurt
here"—Sarah pressed her hand to the side of her abdomen—"so
bad she couldn't stand up straight. The next day, Monday, she . . ."
Sarah's throat closed, choking off the words.

"No need now." Mac patted her shoulder clumsily.

"No, I want to tell it. Monday it was read bad, sometimes she
didn't know who we were." Sarah spoke in the monotone of a
schoolgirl reciting a lesson she's committed to memory. "Monday,
late, she died." Turning her face to Mac's shoulder, Sarah cried,
then abruptly stopped.

"We—K-Karl and me—buried her. We—had to take a pick to
the ground to break it." She cried again and Mac stood miserably
by patting her arm.

"Karl was under the weather too. Is he up and around?" Mac
asked.

Sarah stared at him dumbly, then stammered, "Up and around.
Yes. He is. Up and around," she repeated. Then she cried, "Oh
God!" and fell again to sobbing. In time she stopped and raised her
eyes. "Do you want to see the grave?"

Mac nodded and she led him from the gloom of the stable. After
the close, animal-warned air, the west wind cut like a knife, brittle
and clean and so cold it burned to breathe. Holding tightly to his
hand, Sarah went across the yard and around behind the house.
Fifty yards away, in a small clearing in the sage, a broken rubble of
clods bristling with sparse brown grass was heaped in a mound. At

one end, a rough cross of two-by-fours had been driven into the earth. There was no name on it.

Moss Face was curled up near the unpainted cross, his nose buried under his tail. He whined as they approached, and Sarah gathered him in her arms and hugged him close. He'd grown long and rangy, a faded red bandanna was tied around his neck, proclaiming his domesticity.

Mac pulled his hat off, his hands red and white with the cold. Sarah stood at his side, looking past the grave to the dark Fox Range. A narrow wedge of blue showed above the mountains. Pale rays of a cold sun shone through the break in the clouds, firing the snow on the peaks.

After a time of silence, Mac dug his knuckles into his eyes and spat carefully downwind. "Where's Saunders?"

Sarah jumped. "Karl? Karl has gone to Fish Springs for a wagon part."

He stared at her incredulously. "Now is a hell of a time to be going for wagon parts," he barked. "Why that goddamn, blockheaded, numbskulled, knucklebrained son of a bitch. If he had half the sense he was born with—"

Sarah started to cry, wailing loud and frightened like a child, and like a child, she clung to his arm. "Please don't. Please."

Subdued to a grumble, Mac walked with her to the house. Sarah's nose was strawberry-colored with crying and the cold, and her teeth chattered. Mac took her to the warmth and privacy of the kitchen, where she recovered herself somewhat, the necessity of seeing to the guests making her dry her eyes and stiffen her back. When he left, she was tied into her apron and tending to a savory venison stew.

Mac let himself out by the back door to avoid the clutch of people warming themselves with fire and whiskey in the main room. His grizzled head bent against the wind, his collar turned up around his ears, he walked to the barn.

Gaps between the boards, widened each summer as moisture was sucked from the already parched wood, moaned as the wind blew over them. Hard white light filtered through, draining color until the straw, the worn wood, the horse blankets on the wall, the leather harnesses, the coils of rope, the cans lining the crossbeams— all the contents of the barn—looked dull and lifeless. Mac, too, looked bleached with time and life, his shoulders stooped under his sixty-odd years; his sparse, wiry hair was almost white, and the fur-rows that seamed his face made him look less gnomish than simply tired. He slumped down on a half-filled nail keg and the sharp, tearing sounds of grief, sobs robbed of tears from years of being strong, grated from him.

In the murky half-light of the loft above, a shape shifted and the faded red plaid of Karl's shirt rose from the bales, the battered felt hat pulled low. For a moment, sympathetic gray eyes looked down on the grieving old man, then soundlessly ducked down behind the barrier of hay.

Sarah managed to show the guests to their rooms and get dinner on the table; then, exhausted to the point where she was shaking, she excused herself to pick at her own dinner in the comfort of her kitchen.

Mac joined her after supper. He knocked timidly. "Sarah, it's Mac."

"Come in, Mac." She lifted her eyes from the congealed mess of stew on her plate and managed a weak smile. He sat down heavily opposite her, and for a while neither spoke.

The sounds of feet on the stairs, as the guests said their good nights and carried their candles up to bed, roused Mac from his thoughts.

"You go on back with Liam. I'll stay on till Jensen gets a new boy."

Sarah stared, openmouthed. "Mac! I can't leave Imogene." Confusion clouded her face, and tears welled up in her eyes.

"Jensen was going to put you out anyway. I was to tell you. Soon as he found somebody else. He'd always pretty much known Mr. Ebbitt never showed, but there weren't no complaints and he was satisfied to leave things well enough alone. But your friend Harland Maydley make a stink. Said he'd go over Ralph's head if he had to. Since the lease was signed by two women, it ain't legal."

"Karl could take over, couldn't he? Sign a new lease or something?"

"And you'd stay on?" Mac gave her a long knowing look, and she bridled a little.

"It's not that, Mac."

"I wouldn't be pointing the finger if it was. A woman could do a hell of a lot worse'n Karl. He don't say much but he ain't stupid. Some fellas don't say much and you figure they're just duller than a hoe, and when they do speak up, sure enough, they ain't much sharper. But when Karl talks, he's not just beating his gums."

"It's not that."

"Not much company for you out here; there'd be folks your own age in town. Women."

"I'll stay. You'll be here sometimes."

Mac shook his head. "I don't know. I'm too old for swamping, been too old for fifteen years. This'll be my last winter. I don't mind telling you, Miss Grelznik's going's took the heart out of it." Sarah reached out for his hand and held it. " 'Course, I'd be more'n happy to stay on here if you need me," he added.

"No, don't stay," she said, a bit too quickly, and Mac looked both hurt and relieved.

The house was still, the fires burned down to embers. Mac sat alone in front of the hearth, the only one besides Sarah who was still awake.

Sarah had gone to bed and, warm under the wool, swathed in a heavy flannel nightdress, she lay staring at the ceiling. No shadows mottled the darkness, and even the square of the window was scarcely lighter than the wall. Restless, she threw off the covers and drew on her robe. With her face pressed against the glass, she looked out over the harsh lines of the Smoke Creek Desert. Under the overcast the stage was as black as ink, the outline of the privy barely discernible.

A long, eerie howl made her shiver. There was a moment of silence, deeper for having been so recently rent, then another cry. Sarah pressed her plans over her ears. Another quavering call went up into the night, this time close to the house. Snatching up her shawl from the bedpost, Sarah lit a kerosene lamp and tiptoed through the house and out the back door into the winter night. Pellets of snow stung her face and neck. She pulled the shawl over her head and squinted into the blackness. The howling came again and she shoved her fist into her mouth to choke off her own crying. Steadfastly she made her way out through the gate and to the clearing in the brush.

Moss Face perched on the freshly turned clods of the grave, his narrow face pointed at the blind sky.

"Moss Face," Sarah called, stopping near the fence about fifty feet from the mound of dirt. "Come here." The dog stopped his lament, looked at her, and whimpered. Pressing his chin down between his forepaws, he crept toward her on his belly. Sarah wouldn't go any closer to the grave; she crouched down and stepped on the tail of her nightgown, wrapping the loose flannel over her cold toes. "Come here, little fella," she coaxed, and the dog whined.

Wind gusted past the lamp chimney, making it throw an uncertain, dancing light. Just beyond its glow, a pale face appeared out of the darkness.

"Karl!" Sarah screamed, and lurched up, but the hem of her gown pulled her to her knees and the lamp fell from her hand. Its bowl shattered, and flames ran like liquid over the ground, whipping with a life of their own. "Karl! No!" Sarah covered her face and screamed again, stumbling back from the grave.

Strong hands caught her and held her. "It's me. Don't be afraid. I'm not a ghost. It's me." Sarah cringed and clung to the rough wool of the coat, burying her face in Karl's vest. The fire winked out, the kerosene consumed. "You go back to bed, Sarah. I came out to get Moss Face."

"Oh Lord, what have we gotten ourselves into?" Sarah cried.

"Hush! Do you want me to walk you to the house?"

"No. I'll be all right." Sarah's voice was a bare thread of sound, almost lost in the wind.

"You're sure?"

"I'm sure. Don't come near the house. Kiss me." They held each other for a moment, then Sarah said, "I'm going to hate sleeping alone again. Lord, but I'm going to hate it!" She turned and ran, without a backward look.

It was impossible to read the expression in the dark eyes that watched the young woman, hidden as they were by the night and the battered hat brim. The lanky figure slumped and muttered, "Lazarus Saunders, risen from the grave to help two ladies in distress."

A blunt-fingered hand touched the hair under the hat brim delicately, like fingers probing a raw wound. The hair was cropped short, a ragged cut done in a hurry with Sarah's sewing scissors. "The schoolteacher died of unnatural causes."

The wide shoulders almost filled the faded plaid shirt, and the dirt-encrusted workboots were only slightly too large.

Moss Face whined, calling attention to himself.

"Can't have you howling at the moon on a moonless night. It

will be warmer in the barn." A long arm scooped the coyote off the grave, and Moss Face nuzzled into the familiar smells of his master's coat.

Ralph Jensen arrived on Wednesday's stage, as promised. He was out of the coach as soon as the wheels stopped turning, and he marched into the house, leaving the other passenger to fend for himself.

"Mrs. Ebbitt!" He shouted, and Sarah appeared in the kitchen doorway.

"What is it?" The suddenness of the summons had frightened her. When Sarah recognized Jensen, all the color drained from her face. She looked as though she would faint and reached out and touched the bar to steady herself. "Mr. Jensen," she managed. The words croaked out of a dry throat.

Ralph Jensen, his jowls permanently purpled by years of high living and his nose rubbed to a like hue by the weather, glowered down at her. Sarah waited, her hands clasped at her waist.

"You don't bother meeting the coach?" he said after a baleful survey of her small person.

"Imogene always . . ." she began, and then said, "I will."

Her gentle demeanor and the black of her mourning band unsettled Jensen. He exhaled with a bellow's wheeze. "Lease is no good," he said flatly. He pulled a much-folded piece of paper out of his pocket. "It's not legal."

Sarah glanced past him. "Where's Mac?"

"I gave him the sack."

Sarah looked at him with blank-faced reproach.

"He was getting too old. Drinking."

"It was because of Imogene, then. Mac never drank too much before."

"He knew there wasn't any Mr. Ebbitt. He ought to've told me."

Sarah said nothing.

"He turned in his resignation for spring anyway. I just accepted it early, is all." He closed the subject with a jerk of his chin. "He said something about your hired man taking over the lease. I'm not adverse to that, long as he's sober and'll keep the place up. I haven't got men lining up for this place. Not in the middle of winter."

Sarah eyed the new lease as Jensen pulled it from his coat pocket. She reached out for it, but Jensen held it back and she let her hand fall to her side. "Could you leave it?" she ventured. "I'll have Karl sign it and we'll send it to you."

"I came on purpose to see him sign it himself. I don't mind saying, Mrs. Ebbitt, you don't have much credit with me on this score."

Sarah took a deep breath to calm herself. "Karl's outside," she said. "I'll get my coat." And without offering him a seat or any refreshment, Sarah ducked back into the kitchen, checked the bread she was baking, and put on the jacket Imogene used to wear when hunting.

When she came out, Jensen was bent down behind the bar.

"You'll find everything clean and in order, Mr. Jensen. Cleaner than we found it."

Caught off guard, he banged his head on the counter as he straightened. He groped a moment for something to say, gave up, and was rude: "Let's get on with it."

Sarah hurried by him and led the way across the yard toward the small meadow. She paused a moment by the coach. "Liam," she said in a shy voice, "will you tell the men they can go inside? There's a fire lit and the food's almost ready."

"Yes, ma'am," he responded.

In the crystal air the mountains shimmered close and unreal, the detail vivid and the colors rich, running the gamut from deep purple to white. Moss Face bounded out from under the porch to run ahead of Sarah and Ralph Jensen, leaping over the stiffened grass and darting at the heels of unimpressed horses.

Past the icehouse, halfway to the alkali flats, stood the windmill. On top of the platform, the bulky figure of Karl Saunders could be seen, his coat buttoned close and a battered felt hat pulled so low his ears were bent out under the brim. He labored in heavy gloves, his fingers thick and clumsy, hammering at the rusted bolts that held a damaged blade in place. A new one, silver-bright in the cold sunlight, glinted against one of the wooden uprights.

Sarah called up to him. "Karl? Mr. Jensen's here with the lease. Says there's no trouble." She laid a hand on her throat, trying to still the quaver in her voice.

There was a clatter, loud in the still afternoon, as Karl fumbled and dropped the hammer onto the wooden platform where he knelt. With an odd, nervous gesture he put his hands to his head, as though pushing in invisible hairpins. Just as his fingers came into contact with the rough-cropped hair, Sarah cleared her throat loudly. "Karl!" she said distinctly. "Karl, we need your signature, he says he's got to witness."

The gloved hands fell suddenly, self-consciously, to the hammer and chisel.

"I ain't coming down," came the muffled reply as Karl went on working.

Sarah looked at Ralph Jensen and smiled apologetically. "Karl's from New England," she explained. "Karl, can you drop a rope or something? I'll send it up." She turned to Jensen. "Is that all right? Can I send it up and have Karl sign it?"

"Oh hell, yes. By all means, send the damn thing up." He frisked himself for a cigar, found one, bit the end off, and spat it disgustedly at his feet. "Don't forget to send the son of a bitch a pen," he muttered under his breath.

"Need a pen," Karl called.

"For Christ's sake." Ralph Jensen stalked off a couple of paces and back again. Sarah ran to the house for pen and ink while Karl battled with the weathered bolts. Jensen, completely ignored, booted Moss Face in the rump.

Sarah sent the ink and pen up in a little pail tied on to the rope, and a moment later it returned with the signed lease. Ralph Jensen checked it perfunctorily. "Pleasure doing business with you, Saunders." He spat a bit of tobacco off his tongue and strode back toward the house.

Sarah served the men lunch as the clanking of Karl's tools on the metal windmill sounded in the distance. She served a second meal an hour and fifteen minutes later, when the coach down from Fort Bidwell arrived. Liam and Ross traded passengers, except for Jensen, who was returning to Reno.

Sarah stood on the porch as the coaches loaded passengers and switched luggage from one rack to another, enduring the crush of strangers for Mr. Jensen's benefit. Karl was nowhere to be seen; he'd finished with the windmill shortly before Ross rolled in, but hadn't come into the house.

"You're staying on?" Jensen asked her.

"Yes."

"With Saunders?" His lip curled in a knowing leer.

Sarah looked up the hill toward the broken earth of the new-made grave and didn't reply.

36

THE REST OF THE WINTER PASSED UNEVENTFULLY. SARAH MET THE incoming coaches as Imogene had done in the past. She'd watch them coming over the desert, and just before the wheels stopped turning she'd take a deep breath, pat her lips with the tips of her fingers, and say to herself, "They're people just like me."

Karl worked hard, and when there were no guests, he spent his evenings in by the fire and his nights with Sarah; when there were guests, he kept to himself in the tackroom.

The only physical difference in the stop was an old clothesline running up the pole where the meat was stored. A bit of red calico, faded nearer to pink, was tied on for a flag. After a coach had discharged its passengers, sometimes Sarah would raise the flag. On those days Karl did not show, and she tended the customers alone. Liam once questioned Karl about it. "It lets me know if I have any creditors aboard," Karl had answered with a slow smile. Liam had asked, too, about the woman, Imogene, whom he had never met, but neither Sarah nor Karl could be brought to speak of her.

Karl scratched his shoulders against the beam, unconsciously aping the movement of the horse in a stall next to him. Liam and his swamper, a quiet young Mexican whom Liam called Beaner, curried the tired horses and rubbed them down. Karl sat on a bale of hay against the wall, watching them work. His arms were folded and his long legs stretched out in front of him. The sleeves of his shirt were rolled halfway to the elbow, and his long underwear was pushed up to expose hard, stringy forearms baked leather-brown.

The masculine, horse-smelling tranquility of the shed was chased away by the sudden intrusion of sunlight and fresh air. Sarah threw open the wide door and ran in, flushed and breathless. "Karl, there's been a letter from Mam!" She waved several sheets of paper until they cracked. "Sam's dead and Matthew's coming home. Listen." She sat down beside him on the hay and spread the sheets on her knees, oblivious to the uncomfortable glances of Liam and the swamper. The two men mumbled quick excuses and left Karl alone with her as she began to read.

" 'Dear Sarah, there isn't a way to come up on this slowly, so I'll just put it as best I can. Sam passed away the day before yesterday. He'd had a lump on his neck big as a goose egg and it seemed to suck the life right out. Sam was a little man when he died, I could've lifted him in my two arms.' " Sarah stopped and pressed her palms against the page. "I never loved Sam. I wish I had now." There were tears glimmering in her eyes and she took a deep uneven breath to steady herself. Karl held out his hand and Sarah laid hers in it for a moment. "I'm okay. I'll go on. 'He was buried in the churchyard. It was a nice funeral, too, and took the last of the money Sam had—he owed from trying to get the farm back on its feet. The land will be auctioned off Saturday next.

" 'Gracie's young man sent for her finally and she's gone out West. All I got is Lizbeth home now, and Walter and little Mattie. Maybe you'll see Gracie. Is Oregon anywhere near Reno?' " Sarah smiled. "Mam's got no notion how big the West is." She went back to the letter. "There's some about Pa; his cough's no better and I guess some worse, from what she doesn't say. Here's the part: 'I think Mattie should come out to be with you. You're his Ma. He's a good boy and I'd want to keep him by me but things aren't like when your Pa was well. Mattie will be better off to come West. Lizbeth looks to be marrying soon and I'm feeling my age more. I've saved some money and the church managed a little and I've bought the ticket. I'll put him on the train as soon as I can get things settled here—maybe three weeks.' " When Sarah looked up from the page, her eyes were shining even in the dim light of the shed. "Matthew's going to be here. My son." Cool tears of joy ran down her face.

No girl ever prepared for the coming of her lover with more care than that with which Sarah readied the house—the entire stop—for the coming of her son. Every day she tied her hair back in a clean rag and, with her sleeves rolled up and a wooden scrub bucket in hand, cleaned and polished. She rearranged Imogene's old room half a dozen times and moved the schoolteacher's clothes out of the closet and drawers. It was the first time they'd been disturbed since Imogene stopped needing them. Sarah consigned some to the mending heap to alter for herself, and some to the ragbag. One of Imogene's summer skirts became curtains to replace the sun-bleached drapes. Sarah mixed whitewash and repaired and painted the chicken coop; she trimmed back the withered limbs of another group of doomed saplings, and watered the cottonwood posts around the spring. The fenceposts, with the perversity of nature, had begun to sprout, and a living fence circled the water.

Karl, Liam, and Beaner, and freighters on their regular runs through Round Hole, watched the whirlwind activity with bemused tolerance. To ease her load, Karl took over the cooking, withstanding the gibes of the men with quiet good humor.

One afternoon a week before the boy was expected, Karl found Sarah crying. She was alone in the barn, sitting on the floor in the loose hay, the gold of the afternoon sun striping her skirts. As he came in she looked up with red, swollen eyes, her cheeks streaked with tears.

He sat down beside her and waited.

"I'm afraid he won't know me. Of course he can't know me. I'm afraid he won't like me."

"There are the letters you've written him," Karl said. "I don't know how many hundred."

"I'm afraid I won't know him."

"You will."

"Do you want him to come?"

"Very much. Like Mac used to say, 'You can't run this country without kids.' "

"I want to be a good mother. I'm so afraid I won't be, that he'd be better off with Mam or Gracie or anybody."

"You're a wonderful mother, Sarah."

"Wolf died."

Each Wednesday and Sunday in the last two weeks of the month, Sarah went to the gate to meet the stage. On an afternoon in July her wait was ended. Her son arrived on the first coach she hadn't met. The mudwagon rolled in on a cloud of dust, and before it had settled, Liam yelled, "We got him, Mrs. Ebbitt."

Sarah ran out from the shade of the porch, then stopped before she reached the coach door, her hands flying to her hair and smoothing her dress. "Karl . . ." she called, looking suddenly young and frightened.

"I'm here." Karl walked across the packed earth from the stable. Calm and reassuring, he took his place beside her.

Sarah touched her hair and dress once again and, with a last look at Karl, opened the door of the coach. A very small boy, not yet six years old, with dark hair and light blue eyes, sat alone inside, looking smaller and more alone for the empty seats around him.

"Not much of a haul for sixty-odd miles overland, is it?" Liam asked. "Business is falling off, railroad'll have it all by 1890. Have it all. Beaner!" The wiry, mustachioed Mexican beside him looked up without rancor, recognizing the title as his own. "You swamper or ain't you?"

Beaner jumped gracefully to the ground, though he'd been riding for hours, and started talking to the horses in a soothing Spanish murmur.

Unconscious of the men around her, Sarah held tight to the door for support and gazed on her only child. He was slender and pale and perfectly formed. There was little childish softness to his solemn face, and his young body was firm and well defined. Margaret had dressed him in short pants and a jacket of black broadcloth. Both were rumpled and dirty from the long journey. Beside him on the seat, a large bundle of letters tied up with twine served as an armrest.

"Matthew," Sarah whispered, her hand out in a gentle unfinished gesture.

"I'm to ask for Mrs. Ebbitt," the child said, and pulled the lapel of his jacket forward to show Sarah the note pinned there. "Gramma T. said to give this to Mrs. Ebbitt." At the mention of his grandmother the little boy started to sniffle.

Liam grunted. "Boy's right as rain for umpteen hours. Show him a petticoat and he goes watery at the knees." Karl nodded absently, his attention fixed on the odd little drama.

Sarah leaned into the coach to unpin the note, her hands trembling as she lay her fingers on the curve of the child's cheek for an instant before grappling with the pin. She brought it out into the light where she could read it:

> Sarah, this is Matthew. I've done the best I knew how and he's a good boy. I saved all the letters you wrote him but I never read any to him. I felt I was doing wrong to read them, as Sam told Mattie you were dead and Sam would've been against it. Things turning out as they did I don't know that I did right but it's done. I sent the letters with Mattie.
>
> Love, Mam

Sarah read the note again and handed it wordlessly to Karl.

The sober little face stared at her expectantly from behind the stack of letters, years of her heart drawn into lines on paper—her relationship with her son, sealed and tied up with string. She put out her hand and he took it politely.

"I'm Mrs. Ebbitt," she said.

"After Papa died, Gramma T. said Mrs. Ebbitt was my mother and that's why she had the same name as me." Matthew eyed her suspiciously.

"God bless Mam," Sarah said.

"Papa said my mother was dead."

"Come on out now, we'll talk later," Sarah said. He clutched his packet of letters as she lifted him down from the coach. "You're quite a big boy." She held him a moment longer, then released him. "You hungry?" He nodded. "Let's see about getting you something to eat."

Karl followed them with his eyes, the woman and the child, walking slightly apart, neither of them talking.

"For an old bachelor you're quite a family man," Liam teased.

"It's beginning to look that way, isn't it?"

Sarah tucked the covers around Matthew's chin. Supper was over and the sun was setting. He squirmed from under them; the evening was too hot for covers. Sarah reached for them again, nervously, but stopped herself and folded her hands in her lap. A mosquito whined somewhere in the room.

"Can we talk now?" Matthew asked.

"We can talk now."

"Papa said my mother was dead." It was a challenge.

"She's not. I'm not. I had to go away when you were a baby. But I didn't die."

"Why did you go away?"

"I was—I was very sick," Sarah said slowly.

"And Papa thought you died."

"Maybe he did."

"Papa died."

"I know, honey." Sarah's voice broke and she smiled tenderly at the small face on the pillow. Her hand strayed to smooth an errant lock from his temple. "Do you miss him a lot?"

"Sometimes. I live with Gramma T. I miss Gramma and Aunt Gracie and Lizbeth."

"I do too. Gramma T. is my mam, my mother."

"She's Aunt Gracie's mother." Suspicion clouded his eyes.

"And Aunt Lizbeth's and Walter's and mine. We're all brothers and sisters."

He thought that over for a while. "You're my mother."

"That's right."

"You were never at our house."

Sarah looked through swimming eyes and bit her underlip until her teeth made a white crescent in the ruddy flesh. "I wrote you." It was difficult to speak around the lump in her throat. "I wrote you a little every day because I missed you so much I was afraid I would go crazy. Imogene was afraid."

"Who's Imogene?"

"A friend. She died." The tears spilled over her lashes and down the side of her nose. "Once a week I sent you the letters. Every week since I—since I got sick and had to go away. Your grandma saved the letters for you so you would know me and know I loved you. Love you."

She was quiet for a long time, crying.

"Mrs. Ebbitt, you can read me from the letters if you want to," he said at last.

Sarah smiled and touched his hair. "I'd like that."

She read him two letters, the first two she had sent. One was in

Imogene's bold hand and Imogene's straightforward sentences. The other was in such a shaky, spidery hand that she stumbled in the reading. Matthew listened, quiet and solemn-eyed.

Finished, she smoothed the dark fringe from his forehead. "I'm your mother, Matthew. I love you very much. Good night." She kissed him lightly, resting her cheek against his.

"Good night, Mrs. Ebbitt."

Sarah closed the door to his room and stayed leaning against it, the strength drained out of her. Through the wood she could hear the smothered weeping of a homesick child.

Karl was by a window, the sash thrown open to let in the night breeze. He wore reading spectacles and was poring over an old book of sonnets by the light of a lamp. Sarah heaved a sigh and dropped into the chair opposite. He closed the book and took off his glasses.

Sarah smiled. "I read him the first two letters I wrote, and I told him I'd written every day. Then he said, 'Good night, Mrs. Ebbitt.' "

"It will take a while."

"I know. I want to hug him. I feel like I could just crush him into me. His little face is so dear."

Karl levered himself out of his chair. "Driving the wagon stiffens me up," he groaned. They walked to the porch and stood together, watching the moon rise over the mountains. Floating on the horizon, it seemed to take up most of the sky.

Sarah threaded her arm through Karl's and rested her head on his shoulder. He started to pull away. "Liam and Beaner are playing cards upstairs," Sarah said. "They won't be down again tonight."

He let her stay. "You're shaking." He put his hand over hers. "Anyone would think you had gone up against a bobcat, not a little boy."

Sarah laughed and pressed his hand to her heart. "My heart's jumping like a rabbit's. Feel."

He pulled her to him, kissing her upturned face, her forehead, her nose, her parted lips. Her breath escaped in a sigh and he held her close.

"I want you with me tonight," Sarah said.

"I want to stay, but we have guests. No eyes for a hundred miles, remember. Dizable & Denning could cancel the lease on moral grounds if they wanted to—the widow Ebbitt living in sin with the hired man."

"Damn them!" Sarah muttered.

"Who?"

"Everybody."

He kissed Sarah again, and suddenly it was Karl who was trembling. He held her away from him. "I'd best go to the barn before I forget I'm a gentleman." Sarah put out her hand but he was already down the steps.

37

SUMMER BLEW BY, HOT, DRY, AND WINDY. EVERY DAY THE WIND CAME up around noon and blew until sundown. Matthew was used to the humidity of Pennsylvania summers, and his nose and lips dried until they cracked and bled.

Two of Sarah's chickens vanished one night in July. A talon and a handful of bloody feathers were discovered behind the sacks of barley in the barn several days later. Circumstances hinted at the possible guilt of Moss Face, but by tacit consent the hints were ignored.

On an evening in August when there were no customers at the stop and Karl and Sarah were playing cribbage on the porch, Matthew amusing himself with a wad of paper and the dog, a herd of deer came to drink at the spring. Entranced, the three of them stopped to watch. Mule deer, their great long ears turning to catch any sound of danger, their small heads held high and still, gathered around the watering trough below the spring and drank. Moss Face crept forward on his belly, a low hunting growl reverberating in his chest, but Karl sealed his muzzle with one hand and held him prisoner.

For a long time the deer drank and grazed; the light went from the sky, and the first stars of evening appeared over the mountains before they started away. Moving in twos and threes they headed down across the meadow, bunched their muscled haunches, and flew effortlessly over the fence. There was no sound, no thudding of hooves, as the animals came to earth and trotted off into the purple shadow of the sage.

The cards lay forgotten, and with a quiet good night, Karl and Sarah put the boy to bed and slipped off, hand in hand, to share the magic.

Business was good, there was money saved, and at the end of summer Karl made the trip to Standish to buy cattle and a saddle horse. Fifteen head—a humble beginning, he said, but a beginning. Karl had never herded cattle and had to hire two cowhands to bring them back to Round Hole. For so few head there was grazing nearby, but when the herd grew, as Karl and Sarah hoped, they would have to range for miles. It would take a hundred acres of the Smoke Creek Desert to support one cow.

In September the nights grew colder, and though it often reached eighty degrees during the day, there was usually frost on the meadow in the morning, and the air was crisp and buoyant. Karl and Sarah shared the task of giving Matthew lessons in the evenings from Imogene's books.

Matthew missed his aunts and his grandmother but accepted his new life with a natural resiliency and formed a fast friendship with Moss Face. Sarah forbade Matthew to sleep with him on general principles, but late one night when she couldn't sleep, she got up and went to the kitchen to get something to eat. She found that Matthew had deserted the warmth of his bed and lay curled up on the kitchen floor with his dog. Sarah carried him back to bed, and thereafter Moss Face slept with the boy.

Sarah poured coffee into a thick white mug, the aroma filling the warm kitchen. "Sun's coming up," Karl observed. Red fingers probed over the eastern horizon and squares of rosy light appeared on the wall behind the table as dawn reached Round Hole. Matthew made shadow rabbits with his fingers and tried to persuade Moss Face to bark at them. Ignoring his young master, the coyote retreated under the table, leery of being banished from the kitchen. Sarah poured another mug half-full and filled it the rest of the way with milk and a tablespoon of sugar for her son.

"How many, Matt?" Karl asked.

"Twelve," came the reply.

"He won't eat twelve, Karl. Make him six." Sarah got out of the way as Karl spooned batter onto the griddle. "Was it too cold in the tackroom?"

"Not too cold. I built a fire, and with the extra blankets I'm warm enough."

"If it gets too cold—"

"Sarah, I can eat twelve." Tired of shadows that couldn't elicit a bar, Matthew concerned himself with breakfast.

"Can you count to twelve by twos?" Sarah said to divert him.

As he was laboring past six, the sound of hoofbeats distracted them. A lone rider on a mud-caked draft horse trotted up the road from the direction of Pyramid Lake. Frost glittered on the ground, and the clopping of shod hooves on the frozen earth rang loud. The rider was bundled in the heavy woolen overcoat and cloth cap of a farmer, and his mount was better suited to pulling a plow than bearing a horseman.

"Better put on some more bacon, Sarah. I'll go bring the poor sod in out of the cold." Karl handed her the spatula and took his jacket from the hook outside the door.

"We'll bring the poor sod out of the cold," Matthew echoed and, aping Karl's movements, he too got down his coat.

"Watch yourself," Sarah warned mildly. "There'll be no 'poor sod' in front of our guest."

Griddle cakes were on the stove and more were in the oven, keeping warm when they returned. The newcomer introduced himself as Loony Wells, late from Virginia, Oregon-bound. Mr. Wells was overweight but hard-muscled, with a tired, weathered face. He, his wife, and two daughters had pulled their wagon off the road to camp by Pyramid Lake. He'd rolled the wagon over a sinkhole and mud had claimed it up to the axles. During the night the mud had frozen iron-hard.

After breakfast, Karl harnessed his team and two horses belonging to Wells Fargo, and headed back toward the lake with Mr. Wells.

By the time the breakfast dishes were washed and the chickens fed, the day began to warm up. Sarah went humming about her morning chores; she carried herself with a firm step and matronly calmness. Since she had come to the desert, Sarah's delicate good looks had roughened a little, though she was meticulous about wearing her bonnet. Her face had fleshed out and her back and arms had grown stronger. Four hands were left to do the work of six, and the chores around the house and yard had fallen to her.

The sun gathered strength as it climbed, burning mist off the pond. Matthew perched on the railing around the spring, watching a pair of mallards resting on their southward journey. Sunlight caught the boy's hair and clear skin. He was as agile as a monkey. Sarah watched him playing along the rail, his mind on the bright water birds, and pressed her hand over her heart, smiling.

"Matthew," she called, "come help me with the upstairs laundry."

"It's not Tuesday, Sarah." The ducks took flight, running first across the water, leaving momentary tracks on the glassy surface.

"It's Tuesday. All day."

Lost in the face of logic, Matthew jumped from the railing and ran before her into the house, bounding up the stairs two by two. Together they pulled the sheets from the cots and wrestled the bedding out of the windows to air.

It was early afternoon before the wash was done and ready to be hung out to dry. A long rope was strung taut between two T-shaped uprights planted in the backyard. Sarah draped a sheet over the line, holding clothespins in her mouth. In the distance a plume of dust announced the day's first freightwagon. The desert would dry the sheets long before the driver had any desire for bed. She finished hanging the wash and automatically scanned the yard for Matthew. He'd been quiet too long. He was settled by a corner of the stable, fashioning an intricate harness for his dog out of scraps of leather. She left him to his task and went indoors to start supper preparations.

Through the kitchen window she watched the wagon grow larger and finally take shape within its cocoon of dust. Over the months she'd come to recognize most of the teams and wagons that traveled the route through Round Hole. This was a new one: six horses, the lead team a mottled pair of browns, the others colorless with alkali. The wagon was loaded with wooden crates, BERTH-FARMINGTON FARM EQUIPMENT stenciled on the sides in black. The load was heavy, and the tired animals strained in the harness. As she watched, the wind changed and the dust blew out behind the freighter. All the horses threw up their heads at once, their ears suddenly forward, nostrils wide. The scent of water imbued them with new life, and the wagon came on at an accelerated pace.

Three hundred yards from the barn, the horses broke into an uneven trot. In an instant the driver was on his feet, the lines curled through his hands, leaning back on the reins and shouting. Sarah dropped her paring knife and ran outdoors, a half-peeled potato clutched in her hand.

Matthew had left the stable and was playing down by the spring, the soft blue of his shirt barely visible above the weeds. Oblivious to everything, he poked twigs into the ground, making tepees for his growing encampment of Paiutes.

"Whoa, Goddamn you, whoa!" The driver's voice rasped over the jangle of harness and the pounding hooves. The equipment was not made to race, and pinched the horses to bleeding. Already mad with thirst, the tearing of the furnishings drove them to frenzy, and dragging the overloaded wagon behind them, the wood groaning as if it would break, they turned for the spring.

Pale under sun-browned skin, the young man pulled on the lines with all his strength, attempting to turn the runaways. Boxes shook loose and several fell, bouncing end over end until the slats broke and machine parts scattered over the road.

"Matthew!" Sarah screamed. The dark head popped above the grass, followed immediately by the pointed hairy face of his constant companion. Matthew saw the onrushing horses and froze. The driver had fallen to one knee in front of the seat, the leads wrapped around his hands. He held on with dogged fury, fighting the six horses. Foam flecked the animals' hides, the lather churning the dust to mud on their flanks, and flew from them like dirty snow.

"Matthew, run!" Sarah cried, and sprinted across the yard toward the spring, on a collision course with the oncoming horses. Quick as a cat, the boy scrambled under the railing and lit out for the barn, Moss Face close on his heels.

"Get back!" the driver yelled at Sarah as the horses cut between her and her son. In an impotent rage she hurled the potato. It struck the near horse above the eye, but the beast took no notice. Sarah fell back as the horses plunged through the railing she and Imogene had built. Two-by-fours splintered under the impact as the lead team, driven by the smell of water and the team behind, plunged into the spring. They were dragged down, thrashing in the traces, the water whipped white by lashing hooves. The screams of the animals mingled with the desperate cries of the driver as he tried to pull the four remaining horses to a stop. Thirst, the momentum of

the overloaded wagon, and the pull of the animals already floundering in the spring combined to drag the next two horses over the
bank. Wild-eyed, they lashed out with their hooves against the draw
of the bottomless spring. The panicked blows fell on their fellows,
and the water reddened with blood. Lost, the last horses fell to their
knees and were pulled in. The wagon followed, the rear wheels
gouging the grass from the bank. Buoyed up by trapped air, the
wagon floated for a moment, poised on the roiling water, then the
right rear corner started down. The driver struggled to his feet,
untangled the leads from his hands, and threw himself as far from
the sinking freighter as he could.

Sarah caught sight of Matthew, staring round-eyed from a safe
perch on the paddock fence. "Rope!" she cried. He understood
immediately and hit the ground running.

Pulled under by its own weight, the freighter looked as though
the dark water were sucking it down. Within a minute it was sub-
merged, but for the seat and the front wheels upended to the sky.
Frantic, the horses fought its weight.

A rope draped around his neck like an ox yoke, Matthew ran to
his mother's side. She stood as near the edge of the spring as she
dared, her eyes riveted on the floundering man. "Good boy," she
said. Lifting the coils from his neck, she wound one end of the rope
a half-dozen times around one of the posts that had taken root and
sprouted. "Here!" She handed the short end to her son. "Hold
tight, don't let it unwind!" So saying, she tossed the coil into the
spring. The driver caught hold and began pulling himself to safety.
As he grabbed at the reeds, a slashing hoof struck his temple and
shoulder a glancing blow, and Sarah saw his hands relax on the
life line.

The water curled in on itself like a wounded snake, and the
wagon was gone from sight. Dark, silent shapes under the water,
four horses struggled. Only the heads of the lead team, mouths
squared with terror, breath coming in high-pitched screams, remained above the surface. Then they, too, were silenced and a vor-
tex formed as the water was drawn down after them. The rope went
slack and Sarah saw that the driver was sliding back into it.

She looped the rope once and slipped it over her head and down
to girdle her waist. "Hold tight, Matthew, Momma's going in." She
scrambled down the treacherous bank into the water, and shoved
herself from the safety of the reeds to grab the drowning man by

the hair. Together they went under. As the water was closing around her, Matthew cried, "Hold him, Momma! Hold him!"

With all her strength she kicked against her sodden skirts, kicked her tiny booted feet against the depths of the spring, her fingers twined in the young man's hair. Her head broke clear of the water for an instant. His face shining, confident, and yet afraid, Matthew held his post by the cottonwood, gripping the rope with all his might. Sarah pulled herself and her burden toward that shining face. The reeds were around her and the bank against her shoulder, but still she held on to the rope, unable to pull herself free of the spring. The freight driver was clasped to her breast like a lover. She gasped for breath.

"Momma!" Matthew called.

"Don't let go, honey!" Sarah said when she could find air. "Hold on tight." The man in her arms was coming around. He threw his head back and fought to free himself. "Stop it!" she begged. Her fingers slipped on the rope, burning, and her chin slid below the water. He clawed, trying to drag himself out of the water over her. Desperate, she sunk her teeth into his shoulder. He roared with the sudden pain, and the panic cleared from his eyes.

"It's okay, we're safe," Sarah reassured him. "Keep holding tight, hon," she called up to the child. The man in her arms looked at her with unfocused eyes, blood tricking in a grisly wash from his temple. He was young, not yet twenty, with straight, tow-colored hair and pale blue eyes.

Tight in each other's arms, hanging on to a rope held secure by a little boy, they regarded each other.

"I can't pull us out," Sarah apologized.

"I can boost you out, I think." He grabbed the rope and, circling her waist with his free arm, lifted her partway out of the water. She crawled the rest of the way up the bank and turned to extend a hand to him. With her help he managed to pull free and they collapsed, gasping, in the grass.

"Coby Burns," he managed, and coughed.

"Sarah Ebbitt. Pleased to meet you."

"Can I let go the rope?" asked a small voice.

Sarah held her arms wide and Matthew ran from his post to tumble into them. "What a fellow you are. I love you so." She kissed him until he laughed and squirmed. "You called me Momma."

"Momma," he said, suddenly shy.

"Coby Burns, this is my son, Matthew Ebbitt."

Matthew shook hands with the older boy. "I'm sorry about your wagon, mister." They looked at the spring; it was as smooth as glass, reflecting the deep blue of the sky. On the far side, a line of bubbles disturbed the surface, bursting into brown rings of mud-stained foam with a barely perceptible popping sound.

Coby Burns watched the water for a moment. "I sold everything my mother left me and went into debt to buy that outfit. I must be in the hole fifteen hundred dollars."

"In the Round Hole," Matthew amended.

Coby's face crumpled and he looked as though he would cry. But he laughed, laughed until his fair skin turned beet red and his eyes disappeared behind his cheeks. It was infectious and Sarah began to giggle, then to laugh, until she was holding her sides and rolling on the grass.

When they'd laughed away their fear and their relief, they wiped their eyes and stared soberly at the dark spring. Somewhere under the dark water, sinking into fathomless mud, were a loaded wagon and a team of horses.

Karl came back in late afternoon. On the seat beside him rode a girl of sixteen or seventeen, her clear, wide-set blue eyes and creamy complexion rescuing her simple farmer's face from plainness. Following in a canvas-topped Conestoga, gray with dried mud, were Lonny Wells, his wife—an older, no-nonsense version of the girl with Karl—and a ten-year-old girl, berry-brown, with a narrow, clever little face. All looked hot and tired and extremely dirty, Karl and Lonny most of all. Their clothes were caked so thickly with mud that the original colors were indistinguishable. Karl pulled up just off the road and waved the Conestoga in behind.

Two freightwagons were already parked in the yard, their teams unharnessed to graze for the night. Sarah came out onto the porch carrying a wooden spoon, a stained apron covering most of her dress. The sun was low and she shaded her eyes with her arm. The girl riding beside Karl was chatting animatedly, occasionally letting her hand rest on his arm. Karl seemed to be enjoying the attention and laughed often. Untying her apron, Sarah pulled it hurriedly over her head and tossed it back inside. She glanced at her reflection in the windowpane. Her dunking in the spring had done little for her hair; strands were pulled from the double crown of braids and hung limply over her temples. Halfheartedly she tried to tuck them back into their pins, then gave up and went to greet the wagons.

Karl jumped to the ground and the mud fell from his clothes like shards of broken pottery. Gallantly he extended his hand to the girl. With a simper she took it and leaped heavily to the ground.

"I shouldn't jump after sitting so long," Karl was saying as Sarah walked up to them. "The joints get stiff."

"You're getting old," Sarah said sweetly, and proceeded to introduce herself before he had the chance to do so.

Drawn by the creaking of harness and the stamping of horses, Matthew bounded out from whatever gully or bush he'd been playing in. He paused for an instant by the Wellses' wagon, caught by a scramble of pigtails and petticoats as Lonny lifted his youngest daughter from the high seat, but even the prospect of another child to play with couldn't slow him for long when there were adventures to be related, and he ran to be in on the telling of the day's doings.

Karl scooped the boy up and set him on his shoulders. Before his feet cleared the ground, Matthew began an enthusiastic though incoherent narrative of Coby Burns, the Round Hole spring, and six horses gone. At length the story was sorted out with Sarah's assistance, and Karl went inside to meet Mr. Burns.

Coby, wearing his own shirt and a pair of Karl's trousers rolled at the cuffs, rose from his seat by the fire to shake hands. The young man was of average height, slender, with wide, well-muscled shoulders and strong, bowed legs. Dry, his hair was almost white and his brows and lashes invisible. The two were immediately at ease with each other, and while Sarah started supper they talked. Coby was from Elko, Nevada. He'd moved there with his mother and father when he was nine, following the silver rush. When he was twelve, his father had died. Alone with his mother, Coby had worked wherever a boy could get a day's employment to keep them fed and housed. His mother, terrified of being alone after his father's death, refused to let him look for work too far from Elko, but within five years he'd managed to buy his mother a small house in town. She had died a year later. Coby had sold the house to buy a freightwagon, and had borrowed money against the wagon to buy the team. To get the horses cheap, he'd bought them green, figuring to break them to harness himself. The farm equipment that he was taking to Susanville was his first commission.

Karl had been listening, elbows on knees, intent on the boy's story. He leaned back and ran his hand through his hair, the white at the temples feathering out like wings. "Maybe we could save some of it, drop a line down and see if we couldn't pull the wagon up, or at least some of the cargo."

The drivers of the two freightwagons and Lonny Wells and his family had gathered around to hear the tale. The eldest Wells girl, her eyes full of Karl, piped up, "Mr. Saunders is very good at pulling things out of places."

"Seen and not heard, Lucy," her mother admonished.

"He got us out of a mudhole deeper'n anything," Lucy finished quickly.

One of the drivers took his pipe from his mouth. "Be that as it may"—he winked, and Karl colored slightly—"if you think you're pulling this man's wagon out of Round Hole, you've got another think coming. I heard tell Van Fleet tried plumbing that thing one afternoon. Rope went down from here to Timbuktu, hit nothing. I guess he tied another rope on to that, and a chunk of iron on it. It got sucked into that mud so's two men couldn't haul it out. Had to cut the rope and let it go. Weight of the wagon's buried those horses deep in mud by now."

Coby cleared his throat and pinched the end of his nose hard to cover his feelings. Sarah caught Karl's eye and motioned toward the kitchen. Quietly the two of them left.

Later, while Sarah set the table for supper, Karl spoke with Coby alone. They leaned on the porch railing and gazed out over the desert. In the sage, touched orange by the setting sun, the black figures of Karl and Sarah's small herd were scattered. Heads down to graze, they looked more like stones than like living cattle. The day was already cool, the thin air of the high desert not retaining the sun's warmth.

"Have you ever worked with cattle?" Karl asked.

"I worked a couple of ranches east of here, near Elko, before Mom died. Roundup, branding—when they needed extra hands."

Karl watched the young man covertly—a wide, unlined forehead; almost-white hair falling to his eyebrows; a slender, powerful frame, muscular and clean-limbed. As honest a face as a Minnesota farm boy. "You can hire on with Mrs. Ebbitt and me," Karl offered. "You'll not make your fortune here, but there's not a better place for saving your wages." Coby laughed, and Karl went on, "We could use another hand, a man who has worked with livestock. What

I know, I'm learning from books as I go along. And you would be free to leave as soon as you'd saved enough to get you on your feet again—no hard feelings."

The alkali flat to the south was dyed red, the sharp peaks above it deep purple against a silvery sky. Coby breathed deep of the tangy evening air. "I grew up in eastern Nevada. 'The back of beyond,' Mom always called it. I don't mind empty spaces." He put out his hand and Karl took it. "Thanks, Mr. Saunders."

"Two dollars a day and room and board is the best we can do for you."

"I've worked for less."

"Your room is the hayloft in the barn, though you are welcome to sleep upstairs in the house anytime there are free beds, and there usually are. But a person needs a place of his own sometimes."

Coby nodded. "The loft will be fine."

"I'll tell Sarah; she'll be pleased." They shook hands again and Karl left Coby on the porch, enjoying the last lavender and gold of sunset.

At supper, Lucy Wells seated herself next to Karl, a table's length away from the uncompromising eye of her mother. Throughout the meal she made eyes at him and took every opportunity to embellish the tale of her rescue. Mrs. Wells shot meaningful glances at her husband, but Lonny was a mild and doting father and did nothing to check his daughter. Sarah, constantly up to serve, watched the proceedings with a jaundiced eye. Karl was enjoying the young lady's attentions in an awkward but flattered way.

The dishes were done and Sarah sat in a quiet corner, the lamp turned up, reading *The Old Curiosity Shop*. Inside the cover, Mr. Utterback had written: *Imogene—not his best, but haunting nonetheless.* Sarah ran her fingertip over Imogene's name and her eyes unfocused for a moment, looking beyond the walls of the room. Her reverie was disturbed by the staccato click of heels on the bare floor.

"Mrs. Ebbitt?"

Sarah closed the book. "Miss Wells. Won't you sit down?" The girl plopped comfortably into the chair next to hers as the invitation was voiced. She was pleasant-faced and young, and Sarah smiled at her despite the irritations at dinner.

Lucy sighed deeply and rested her cheek on her hand. "He's so alone!" She smiled sadly at Karl's angular form as he leaned on the mantel, deep in conversation with Coby. He tipped his head back and laughed at something Coby said. "And so unhappy. Just listen." Her voice was fraught with secret understanding.

Sarah studied the lanky form, the broad face and flat cheeks bronzed by sun and firelight, the fine lines around the eyes made deep by the desert climate. "Karl seems happy enough to me," she replied.

"I know. To most people." Lucy shook her head knowingly, and Sarah hid a smile.

Karl, unaware that he was the object of so much speculation, said good night all around, stopping to take his leave of Sarah and Lucy on his way out.

"Take an armload of kindling with you," Sarah said. "It's going to be cold tonight."

"I have enough to last. I told Coby to take one of the beds upstairs for tonight; we can get him set up in the barn tomorrow. Sleep well, Sarah, you've done a good day's work today. I think Coby will be a good man to have with us." His eyes rested on hers for a moment, and Lucy fluffed in her chair until he turned to her. "Good night, Miss Wells." He bowed, a handsome Old World bow. Sarah pursed her lips and looked at him from under lowered brows, but he didn't repent, even to a wink, and left Lucy Wells in a twitter.

Sarah was the only one who saw the girl slip out after him, and she went back to her book.

Later, Mrs. Wells, deeming it past bedtime, came looking for her daughter. "I believe she stepped out for . . . air," Sarah said dryly.

Mrs. Wells rolled her eyes heavenward and clucked her tongue. "For Lud's sake. Is she bothering Mr. Saunders? That vixen'll send me early to my grave. See these gray hairs? That one give them to me, every one. She gets passions like other girls get headaches, and every one of them's a matter of life and death. Not six weeks ago she saw a flyer about a traveling lady preacher and took it as a sign from God. Drove us crazy for a week, reading tracts to us morning, noon, and night."

Lucy had followed Karl to the barn and waited outside the tack-room, gathering her courage. A candle burned behind the curtain and she could hear him laying a fire in the stove. Resolutely she rapped on the door. "I've come," she said when Karl opened it.

"So I see." They stared at each other.

She looked past him into the dimly lit room. It was clean and bare, his few belongings arranged on top of a battered leather trunk in a far corner: a faded photograph of a middle-aged woman standing beside a short pillar with a vase filled with flowers on it; a wallet of cracked leather folded beside the picture; a silver chain with a nugget of silver. Several changes of clothes hung from pegs on the far side of the room, and there was a bookcase under the single window, filled with books brought in from the house. The floor and walls were whitewashed and scrubbed spotless. Lucy rubbed her upper arms. "It's cold," she hinted.

"You'd better go back to the house."

"Can't I come in?"

"No."

Stumped, she paused. Clearly this was not the scene she had envisioned. She stepped close to him and, catching up his hand, folded it to her breast. "I know you aren't happy," she whispered. "I understand. I've understood you from the moment I saw you."

Karl tried gently to extricate himself from her grasp. "You are a very nice young lady—" he began.

"You refused to go in swimming with Pa, though it must've been a hundred, so you could be with me. You did!"

"I can't swim," Karl said patiently. "I visited with your mother and sister as well."

She dismissed that with a toss of her head. Karl held her away from him and looked into her face. "Lucy," he said kindly, "you're a lovely girl—a young woman—and I hope you are grown-up enough to forgive me for my behavior toward you; it wasn't all that it should have been. You tickled the vanity of an old fool, is all. You are very young and there are things you won't understand for many years. I'm very happy here, happy with things the way they are. Go on back to the house."

"Her." Lucy got right to the point.

"Yes. Sarah."

"I don't believe you! If it were true, you'd marry her."

"Lucy!" A stern voice sounded in the darkness.

"It's Ma," the girl said breathlessly. "I have to go." Quickly she pecked a chaste kiss on Karl's cheek and turned to run to the house.

Mrs. Wells emerged into the glow of Karl's single candle. "I thought I'd find you bothering Mr. Saunders." She took her daughter firmly in hand. "I'm sorry about all this, Mr. Saunders. Last week it was a lieutenant in the cavalry. And all she ever saw of him was his picture in the newspaper. It doesn't take much when you've cotton between your ears instead of brains." She gave Lucy a shake. "I've had about enough of you for one day." Still lecturing, Mrs. Wells marched her eldest back to the house.

In the morning Lucy would not come down to breakfast, but pleaded illness. "She's faking so she can stay and make eyes at Mr. Saunders," the second Wells daughter declared.

"That's enough out of you, miss," her mother chided, but it was plain she was of the same opinion. Only Mr. Wells entertained any real anxiety over Lucy's health. By the end of breakfast, Lucy had still not made an appearance and her mother was beginning to fume. Twice she'd started up the stairs to roust her daughter out, and twice Mr. Wells had insisted she give the girl more time.

The freighters were long gone, Coby and a sheepish-looking Karl had excused themselves to start the day's work, and Sarah was brushing the crumbs from the tablecloth, when Mrs. Wells growled, "That's it," and rose abruptly from the table. "I've no time for this."

"Mother, maybe she's really sick." Mr. Wells reached out to stop his wife, and she shot him a withering glance.

"This nonsense is as much your doing as hers, Lonny Wells. You let her get away with it. If I'd had my way, we'd be halfway to Fort Bidwell by now."

"There's going to be a scene," Mr. Wells moaned, "and she'll make herself sick if she's not already. My little Lucy's a strong-willed girl."

"So's your *big* Lucy," his wife snapped.

Sarah looked up from her work. She hesitated for a moment, then spoke. "If it wouldn't be interfering, I could talk to her," she ventured. "I think I could help."

"Fine by me." Mrs. Wells sat down to finish her coffee.

Lucy was not in bed. She knelt by a window in her dressing gown, resting her elbows on the sill, watching two tiny figures on horseback out in the sage. Sarah slipped through the curtain without being heard, and sat down on the girl's unmade bed. "Hello, Lucy, can we talk?"

Within half an hour, Miss Wells was dressed and downstairs, putting her overnight things in the wagon.

Coby and Karl rode in as the Wellses said their good-byes to Sarah. They dismounted to wish them well in Oregon and see them on their way. Lucy laid her hand on Karl's arm and looked deep into his eyes. "Mrs. Ebbitt is very good," she said, "and you are very brave." With a good and brave smile, she let her father hand her into the wagon.

Mrs. Wells poked her head back through the canvas as the Conestoga rolled out of Round Hole. "What brought you around so sudden?" she demanded.

Lucy leaned close to her mother, making sure her little sister wouldn't overhear. "Oh, Momma," she whispered, "Mrs. Ebbitt told me poor Mr. Saunders was born less than a man—you know, from the waist *down*. Not like other men at all. She stays there with him so he won't be alone. Isn't that sad? She's so good!"

Karl and Sarah stood together, watching the Wellses' wagon roll off toward Oregon. "What got her out of bed?" Karl asked.

Sarah linked her arm through his and smiled. "I told her you weren't man enough for the two of us."

Karl laughed but said, "Be careful, Sarah."

℘ 38

MATTHEW TURNED SIX AND GREW AN INCH. HE RANGED THROUGH the sage for a mile in every direction, the coyote at his heels, and ate like there was no tomorrow. Sarah seemed to grow along with her son. As he bloomed in the high desert air, she stood straighter and laughed more often, and her skin took on a warm tone.

Matthew continued to call her Momma, and the delight never palled for her. Often when he would call from another room she would pause before she answered, waiting to hear him shout "Momma!" again. Every night, Sarah read him some of the letters she'd sent him during the long years they'd been apart. Now when she cried over them, the little boy would twine his arms around her neck and pet her cheek until she was comforted.

Coby settled into life at the stop without a hitch, quiet and reserved, with a low-key sense of humor. Sarah, the child, and Karl all provided a sense of home, and he was content to stay.

Karl didn't seem to age at all; the white streaks at his temples might have been a little wider or the crow's-feet at the corners of his eyes a little deeper. Some evenings, when Sarah was busy with her mending and Coby was whittling or playing solitaire by the fire, Karl gave Matthew his lessons, the two of them poring over the books brought from Reno. Karl would sit with his eyeglasses perched on his nose, the boy with his lips moving in painful concentration as they unraveled the mysteries of the alphabet together.

Matthew had an agile mind and learned quickly. His imagination was active, and with Coby, who was almost a boy himself, he would sit spellbound by the hour while Sarah read aloud from *A Tale of Two Cities, Oliver Twist,* and, by spring, *The Three Musketeers.* Matthew was so open and affectionate, so fearless in his play and cheerful about his chores, that it was a matter of concern when in late spring he grew cranky and sullen.

Sarah dumped the envelope of seeds into her palm and knelt by the neat rows she'd spent the morning hoeing. She'd shoveled manure and chopped straw for the garden and dug it under with a spade, but the desert earth turned up a pale, unpromising dusty brown. She pinched up a few seeds and was sprinkling them carefully along the furrow when her elbow was jostled and she spilled the lot.

"Matthew, that's the third time you've bumped me. Stay back, you're spoiling the garden." He moved away a foot or so to crouch like an infant gargoyle on a row she'd already planted. "You're on my lettuce. All the way back. Over there." She pointed outside the garden fence. "If you want to watch, you can sit on that barrel. If you want to help, you're going to have to go to the shed and get another trowel out of the toolbox like I told you."

The boy watched her with round accusing eyes, his mouth pressed shut.

The anger went out of her for a moment and she dropped her hands in her lap. "What's the matter with you lately, Mattie? Are you sick? Do you hurt anywhere?" She pulled off a glove and lay her hand on his brow. "You feel all right." Matthew said nothing; his usually expressive face was still and the skin around his eyes dark and drawn. "You're going to bed early tonight," Sarah declared. "You're so sleepy there's circles under your eyes."

"No."

"Yes," she insisted. "There'll be no more about it."

He didn't argue but retreated to the barrel at a snail's pace, scuffing his feet over her neatly turned rows. He sat there, immobile, while she finished the carrots and began on the onions. Moss Face trotted out from under the house to whine and bark for him to come down and play, but when Matthew would only hold him too tight and pet him, he ran off again.

The sun was low in the sky and the afternoon had lost its warmth when Sarah took off her gardening gloves and smock and shook the dirt from her dress. "Half done. I'll finish tomorrow. Coby and Karl ought to be getting in. We don't own that many cows. Besides, it'll be dark soon. Looks like we've company coming, too." She squinted into the slanting light. "Freighters. The front one looks to be Jerome Jannis, doesn't it?"

Matthew's sharp eyes fixed on the distance. "It's Mr. Jannis."

"Then that must be Charley behind, eating dust. You'd almost think those two were yoked together." She gathered up her tools. "Hon, would you run these over to the shed and put them away for me? I'd best get supper on the stove."

An obstinate look came into his eyes and he wouldn't look at her. Pushing his hands deep in his trouser pockets, he poked the toe of his shoe at an unfortunate beetle crawling by.

Sarah took a deep breath and blew it out through her nose. "Never mind. It'll be faster to do it myself." She dumped the trowel and gloves into her smock and gathered up the corners. Matthew ran after he as she hurried to the shed, and hovered by the door, anxious not to lose sight of her. "What's got into you?" she said as she stumbled over him on her way out. He tagged behind her as she crossed the yard, following so close that he trod on her heels. With an exasperated sigh, she turned on him.

"Go on. Go play with Moss Face, air yourself off. The way you've been behaving lately, I can do without your help in the kitchen tonight." Again the accusing look. "Go on now, you're moping around. Run around some, maybe you'll sleep better." Still he hung about, never out of reach of her skirttail. She looked about for something to occupy him for a while.

"There." She pointed to the eastern road. Karl and Coby rode half a mile out, coming into the stop from the opposite direction as the freightwagons. Shadows crossed the valley, black fingers reaching over the road and touching the mountains to the east.

"Run and meet Karl and Coby," Sarah said to her son. "If you ask Karl nice, I bet he'll give you a ride in."

Matthew looked down the road. "It'll be dark." There was just the beginning of a whine in his voice, and it firmed Sarah's resolution.

"Not if you run. Scoot!" She swatted his behind and he took off as if all the devils in hell were after him, calling, "Karl! Coby! Karl!" at the top of his lungs before he had run as far as the gate.

The riders and the freightwagons arrived at the stop within minutes of each other, and Karl and Coby helped with the unhitching.

Jerome and Charley had started driving mule and rig over the desert early in the year, and now made a regular run. Round Hole had seen them several times a month since February. Both were in their forties, redfaced, round headed, and thick through the neck and shoulders. Jerome did most of the talking for the two of them; Charley seemed to be happy with the role of straight man and audience. They were immensely strong: one night, on a bet, the two of them had lifted an eight-year-old mule and its rider. They'd turned as blackfaced as storm clouds, and their necks had grown even thicker and redder, but they'd done it.

Matthew hung around the men, getting in the way, until Coby lifted him up onto the boxes in the back of one of the wagons, where he wouldn't get stepped on. When they started to the house without him, he cried out so frantically that Karl swatted his behind. "Don't scream like that, Matthew. Not unless you are really hurt. It's like the little boy who cried 'Wolf.' Remember that story? I will always come at a run when you scream, so will your mother and Coby."

The younger man nodded. "If you're not in trouble when I get there, you will be when I leave." Coby smacked his fist into his palm, but there was no malice in it and it helped take the sting out of Karl's lecture.

Sarah served the after-dinner coffee on the porch. It was a brisk spring night, the air fresh and sweet with the smell of sage, and the sky close with stars. Coby was indoors at the bar, writing a letter to his creditor in Elko. Karl, Jerome, and Charley sat with their chairs tilted back against the side of the house, their ankles propped on the porch rail, all in like postures. The wagoners smoked pipes, the bowls glowing orange when they drew on the tobacco.

Sarah handed the coffee cups to Karl and he passed them to the other men before she sat down on the top step and folded her hands around her own mug.

"Do you want me to get your shawl?" Karl offered.

"No thanks, Karl. I'm fine."

Jerome winked at the exchange. "You'll spoil 'er," he warned.

He struck a match on the sole of his partner's boot and grinned. Screwing up his face, one eye completely closed, he sucked the flame into the pipe. The light showed Matthew hunched, small in the corner, almost under Charley's chair. He was hugging his knees, listening to the talk. The pointed snout of the coyote protruded from behind him, his neckerchief red in the sudden light.

Sarah's eye caught her son's. "Isn't it time somebody was doing his chores?"

Matthew curled down smaller and busied himself with rescuing the dog's tail: Moss Face had swished it precariously near the spot where Charley's chair leg was bound to come crashing down eventually.

"Matthew," Sarah said in her high-priority tone. "Get those plates scraped. It'll only take you a minute, and Moss Face would probably appreciate the leavings. Go on now, honey."

"I want to stay," Matthew said in a voice meant to be too low to be heard.

"Go on now."

With agonizing slowness, the child uncurled himself and crawled under the propped-up legs of the men. He crept all the way out, flat on his belly, and lay still, gazing out through the bars into the stars-pricked darkness.

"Matthew, I'm going to get mad in half a minute if you don't get a move on." Sarah rapped the wood with her knuckles.

"Mrs. Ebbitt," Matthew muttered peevishly under his breath.

It was not so low it didn't reach Karl's ears, poised as he was above the boy. His chair slammed down and he planted one foot on either side of the prone child. "That does it." He lifted Matthew and strode into the house.

Sarah maintained her seat on the steps, but winced every time the crack of Karl's hand on her son's bare bottom sounded through the open door. Several minutes later, Karl reemerged.

"Did you send him to bed?" she asked.

"No. He's scraping plates."

Sarah met and held Karl's eyes for a moment until, conscious of the wagoners' attention, she went on to talk of other things.

Later, Karl helped Sarah with the dishes, a habit he maintained despite the ribbing he got. His sleeves rolled up, he scrubbed the bottom of a cast-iron kettle while Sarah dried the crockery and put it away. They had been worrying the subject of Matthew's sullenness all through the clean-up.

"Where is he?" Karl asked. "Is he still sulking over his spanking?"

Sarah hung a cup on one of the nails over the kitchen counter. "I imagine he's probably out with Jerome and Charley. Whenever they're through here lately, he can't leave them alone. He loves listening to the men. He's getting to be quite a little man himself. Did you ever notice him copying you? The way you walk? Sometimes he'll walk beside you all straight and long-stepping, just like you do."

Karl laughed, pleased. "He'd better not pattern himself on me."

"Why not? You turned out to be a fine man."

Karl answered her with a wry smile.

"Speaking of you, tomorrow's the coach from Bishop. Ross'll be driving, so you better plan to be somewhere else."

"I'm tired of leaving you when the old-timers come through."

"I know. I'm okay here. We've got Coby now, and he's a worker."

"I'll go over to Fish Springs Ranch. I've been meaning to look at a couple of bulls that Ernie Fex has, anyway. I've learned a lot about cattle from Coby and from the books we ordered. I think I know what to look for. I'd like to try to improve our herd. What do you think?"

"It never cost anything to look." Finished drying, she draped her dishcloth through the oven-door handle. "Do you think he's coming down with something? He's a good boy. I don't know what's eating at him. I've tried to talk to him but he clams up. Two nights this week he woke me, crying—nightmares about the most awful things. Graves opening and the dead bodies coming out. Fever'll sometimes bring on bad dreams, but he never felt warm or anything."

"I guess we'll just have to wait and see if he outgrows it." Karl heaved the kettle onto the still-warm stove and swabbed it out with a towel so it wouldn't rust. "I'd better be getting to bed. Good night."

Sarah took his hand and laid it against her cheek. The scarred palm was rough and familiar. "Tell Jerome and Charley good night for me. Their beds are made up and there are candles on the bar. And will you send Matthew in? It's past time he was in bed."

The porch was bathed in the clear, ghostly glow of a desert moon, just risen, hanging flat and white over the mountains.

"Ooooooooo . . ." A high round sound, eerie in the night. "They claw their way up through the dirt first. Their fingers all cloudy-like from digging. See, they wasn't buried proper and their chief, he wouldn't let the medicine man do his mumbo-jumbo over the grave. And so late at night they come pushing up out of the dirt and look for the folks that let them be buried like that without them death rites."

Jerome sat back in his chair and winked broadly at Charley. Matthew, his eyes seeming to take up all of his face, perched in Karl's chair, leaning forward.

"What do they do?" Matthew looked nervously into the darkness beyond the porch railing and scrunched unobtrusively closer to Jerome. "When they catch them, I mean."

Jerome feigned indifference. "Catch who?"

"The people," Matthew said urgently, "the people that buried them wrong."

"Oh." Jerome sucked at his pipe. It was dead. He knocked it on the railing and scraped the bowl with his pocket knife. "That's the thing, see." He leaned forward until his face was on a level with the child's. "They get kind of barmy, being dead and buried like that, and they don't know who it is has done the actual burying, so when they come looking, it don't matter who they find. And by this time they don't see any too good. They're pretty much moldy and falling part. They go sniffing around outside houses looking for just anybody."

"I hear they like little boys best," Charley put in.

"That's so, I heard that," Jerome agreed.

By this time, Matthew was crowded so near Jerome he was almost falling off his own chair. "How about people that aren't Indians?" He glanced fearfully across the black hole of the spring toward the double grave hidden in the high grass.

Jerome saw where he was looking. He sat back, propping his chair against the wall again, and nudged Charley. "White men are even meaner than Indians. Take them two fellas I hear is buried out by the spring. I'm surprised they ain't dug their way out already, seeing's they had no proper rites said."

"Look now." Charley leaned forward and peered into the dark, pretending to see something. "Look—"

"That will do, Charley." Karl spoke from the doorway. "You go inside, Matthew. Your mother's in the kitchen. I'll be in in a minute."

Relieved from his awful enthrallment, Matthew sped through the darkened room to his mother.

Karl pulled a chair around and sat down straddling it, his arms crossed on the back. "Have you been telling Matthew ghost stories for a while now?"

"Ooooeee!" Charley laughed. "His eyes get big as a calf's when Jerome spins one."

"I'm going to have to ask you not to tell him any more."

"Come on, Karl," Jerome said, "all kids like ghost stories. It don't hurt nothing."

"Don't tell him any more." Karl said firmly. "Don't tell that boy anything that isn't true. He likes being with you. He looks up to you. You tell him those stories and he believes them. He's just a boy, there's no call to lie to him. He's been having nightmares. Talk of something else."

"Hell, Karl, you're going to let that gal raise up a sissy. Teasing'll make a man out of him," Jerome protested.

"I've never known fear to make a man out of anyone. I've seen it make grown men cry like babies. Don't lie to the boy." Karl wished them good night and went inside.

Jerome hawked and spat expertly over the rail. "Jesus! We were just having a little fun with the kid."

"I, for one, am going to do as he asked," Charley said. "Karl's a funny bugger if he gets a hair up his ass over some damn thing or other. Fellow used to drive the stage through here told me he stuffed a greenhorn down the one-holder for kicking his dog."

Jerome grunted. "Must've had more meat on him then; he's tall, but there ain't nothing to him."

"Wiry," Charley said sagely.

Karl found Sarah and Matthew waiting for him in the kitchen. Matthew was whitefaced and silent, safe on his mother's lap.

"What is it, Karl?"

"Jerome has been telling him ghost stories." He sat down across from them. "Come here, Matthew." Reluctantly the little boy left his mother and came around the end of the table. Karl lifted him onto his bony lap, straddling his knees.

"You mad at me, Karl?" Matthew asked.

"Why would I be mad at you?"

"Because I been scared. Scared of the dark and to be by myself and go in the shed and stuff."

"No, I'm not mad at you. Everybody gets scared. It's nothing to be ashamed of. I get scared sometimes, and that was one of the scariest stories I've heard in a long time. Is that why you wouldn't tell your mother and me what was wrong? You thought we'd be mad?"

"I was afraid you'd be ashamed of me because I was afraid to go into dark places . . . like a baby."

"We'll never be ashamed of you for being afraid, Matthew. Those stories Jerome and Charley told you aren't true. Not any of them. Once people are dead, they never come back—maybe because they don't want to, maybe it's nicer where they are. I don't know. But they don't ever come back. Those two boys buried out by the spring had a proper burial. Your mother read the service from the Bible over their graves. Both of them were good boys—like Coby. Would Coby ever hurt you?"

"No."

"Neither would these boys. I don't know what else those two told you, but I'm willing to bet there's not a grain of truth in it."

"There's the ghost of a man drowned in the outhouse that'd pull you down into the hole by your . . ." He looked at his mother; at six he was well aware of the social restrictions. ". . . you know."

"I know," Karl said. "Beau Van Fleet dug that outhouse two months before your mother leased this place. Nobody has ever died there."

"People tortured to death by Chief Winnemucca cry at night and look for people to torture."

"Not true. I doubt Chief Winnemucca ever tortured anybody to death anyway."

"That's all," Matthew said.

"That's enough." Karl stood him on the floor between his knees. "Are you still scared?"

"Only a little left-over scared."

"Can you go wash up and go to bed?"

"I think so."

"Ask your mother for a candle. If anybody ever tells you anything that scares you again, come and tell your mother or me, and we will tell you if it's true or not. If not, there's nothing to be afraid of. All right?" The child nodded. "Now kiss your mother good night and get ready for bed. We'll look in on you in a few minutes."

Sarah hugged Matthew tight and kissed him. "Good night, honey. Take this candle, it's already lit. We'll be in in a minute." When he'd gone, she turned, smiling, to Karl. He looked back, strong and square-shouldered, his eyes warm with love for Sarah and her son. "Karl, I think you've slept in the tackroom long enough. Come in tonight. Every night."

He reached for her hand. "Are you sure? People will talk. And not about me, but about you. The gossip could do us harm."

"I don't care. I want to be with you in the sight of everybody. Let people talk. I'm tired of hiding and sneaking in our own home."

Karl spent the night in the main house with Sarah. In the morning the two of them stoically faced down the curious looks and half-heard jokes of the freighters. That afternoon, Karl's things were moved into the master bedroom with Sarah's.

Matthew asked why. "To keep a closer eye on you," his mother told him.

All Colby had to say was, "It's about time. I've been wanting to move into the tackroom for a while now."

Dizable & Denning couldn't have cared less; for the first time in years the Round Hole Stop was showing a profit.

IT WAS MID-JULY, AND AT SIX O'CLOCK THE SUN WAS STILL HIGH. ALL the windows were propped wide and the door blocked open to catch the breeze. Despite the heat, Karl had on one of the heavy flannel shirts he always wore, the edges of his long underwear peeking out at the neck and wrists. He wiped the bar and tossed the rag over a deer antler fastened to the wall. Round Hole Stop was full; the Reno coach had pulled in at four-thirty with seven passengers, miners bound for a rumor of gold northeast of Bishop.

Liam and Beaner sat slurping coffee with several of the young prospectors; sweat poured down their temples as they swilled the hot liquid. Keeping a low profile, Matthew built a wigwam out of kindling behind one of the tables near the fireplace. Flies buzzed in lazy circles and the company was dull with heat and day's end.

Beaner swirled the last of his coffee around, polished it off in a gulp, and set the cup carefully back in the wet ring on the tabletop. "Liam," he said, "I got a new lim'rick."

The driver looked up from contemplating the toe of his boot, and Beaner winked a round black eye.

Liam nudged the young man across the table, a hard-faced miner of twenty-five, from the silver mines in Virginia City. "Watch this," he grunted, and jerked his chin toward Karl. Liam's face creased slightly but the smile didn't quite break through.

"Hey, Karl," Beaner called across the room, his dark eyes twinkling. "I got one for you."

"Never mind, Beaner," Karl said amiably.

"There was a young whore from Peru . . ." Beaner began, undaunted.

Karl turned several shades of red and, muttering some half-heard excuse, left the bar for the kitchen. The swamper pounded his thigh and laughed uproariously. "Isn't that the damnedest thing? You can always get a rise out of Karl. I've seen him up to his ears in cowshit, castrating calves, but when somebody'd say something raw he'd color up like an old maid."

"It ain't like he don't know what it is. He's got it pretty friendly. I hear he's been bedding Mrs. Ebbit damn near since the schoolteacher died," one of the freighters put in. "You got promoted to the tackroom, hey Coby?"

"That's right," the young man said shortly, and stood to stretch.

The swamper winked at him. "Maybe when Karl moves on, you'll get promoted—inside." The others laughed.

"Watch yourself, Beaner," Coby warned as he left the room.

"He won't hear her made light of," Liam explained. "And rightly so. You were getting out of hand there. Mrs. Ebbitt's a lady, give or take a little, and oughtn't to be jawed over by the likes of you." The driver kicked Beaner's chair and snapped his mouth shut again.

"She's a widow woman, ain't she?" a middle-aged, potbellied miner asked. "Why don't he just marry her? She's a good little gal— better'n most—cooks a meal that's purely fit to eat."

"Maybe he's too damn tight to take a day off," a freighter suggested, and even Liam laughed.

"Maybe," Liam returned. "I've never known him to take a day off. Place looks a hell of a lot better than when Van Fleet had it. Food's sure a damn sight better; Van's missus couldn't boil guts for a hungry bear, from what old McMurphy told me."

Quietly, Matthew slipped from the bar unnoticed.

The spring was now completely enclosed by a fence built of heavy timbers. It had been Coby's first job. Matthew skirted it and ran through the coarse grass, leaping over the creek that ran through the meadow from the spring. He found Coby mending fence down past the paddock near the southwestern corner of the pasture, and climbed up to sit on top of the post nearest him. He patted his knees and Moss Face leaped up into his lap. For a moment the boy and the dog teetered, but Matthew recovered his balance, the coyote in his arms.

"Every time you climb the wires like that, it makes more work for Karl and me." Coby picked up a strand of barbed wire that had been stomped down by one of the horses, and nailed it back in place.

Before Matthew could respond, Karl came up. "Your Momma and I thought we'd take a ride up above the place. It's a nice evening and there's time before dark. Do you want to come with us, Matthew?"

Matthew deserted Coby without a backward glance.

The sun was on the horizon, flattened to a red oval. The sky was deepening to evening in the east and glowed a clear, translucent yellow in the west. Sarah and Karl rode up the hill single file, Karl in front. He sat stiff in the saddle, his spine rigid and his elbows out at the sides, more like a graduate of a riding academy for young ladies than one of the slouching Nevada cowboys. Sarah rode astride, her petticoats tucked under her, her hand resting on the pommel. Occasionally she'd lean forward to pat the neck of the little bay and murmur words of encouragement. She rode easily now, unafraid. Matthew rode behind, holding to her waist.

Up the hill behind Round Hole, a bluff of sandstone and rock pushed out through the sage, forming a shelf several feet wide that ran halfway around under the brown of the hill. It was just high enough to make a natural bench. Karl tethered his horse to a bush and helped Sarah to dismount. Matthew had already squirmed and slid his way over the round rump of the little mare.

Below, the desert spread out. The sunset touched the dead soil of the alkali flat to a living hue, and the mountains beyond were a dark, regal purple. Karl and Sarah sat several feet apart on the sandstone ledge and looked down over their home. Cattle dotted the landscape in small, isolated groups, with an occasional stray. A thin ribbon of smoke rose from the kitchen chimney. Those cottonwood posts that had sprouted around the spring continued to thrive, waving lacy green-black leaves over the water. Down by the icehouse, the windmill was utterly still. Several horses grazed in the meadow, and the hollow cracking of Coby's hammer echoed up the hill. He was working on a bench near the barn door, his tow-colored head a small orange dot, dyed by the setting sun.

"The air is so clear you can see a hundred miles," Sarah said. "In Pennsylvania, the world was smaller."

"I'm used to the space," Karl replied. "I like it."

Matthew scrambled down the slope behind, a miniature avalanche announcing his arrival. He settled himself comfortably between them and began pitching pebbles at Moss Face. The coyote leaped and snapped at them a few times before he tired of the game and wandered off. Long shadows were creeping across the desert floor from the west; soon Round Hole would be in shade.

"What's 'bedding' somebody mean?" Matthew asked suddenly, and Sarah started, her hands grating noisily on the sandstone. She looked over his head at Karl.

"Little pitchers have big ears," Karl said.

"You always say that," Matthew complained. "I'm not a little pitcher. What does it mean? 'Bedding' somebody?"

"Where did you hear it?" Karl asked gently.

"I was making mineshafts in the kindling—I put it all back in the woodbox," he added quickly. "That man drives for Standard Feed said you were bedding Momma. He said he wondered why you wouldn't marry her, because she cooked good."

Karl rubbed the palms of his hands on his thighs. "People like to hear themselves talk."

Sarah looked across the wide valley, her eyes on the first stars of evening. The shadows had coalesced over the desert, and the valley floor was a dark pool between mountain peaks. She had kept herself out of the conversation.

"What does it mean?" the boy persisted.

"It's two people living together without the blessing of God," Karl said softly.

"Without the permission of the law, Karl. God doesn't enter into it," Sarah retorted.

Matthew, startled into silence by the fierce declaration, sat meekly staring at his shoe tips. When he found his tongue he said, "Why won't you marry Momma?"

Karl spoke slowly, choosing his words with care. "I never thought to ask your mother if she'd marry me, Matthew. It never seemed to be a dream possible for the two of us. I would be proud if she would be my wife. That would make you my son, too. What do you think of that?"

"It'd be okay, I guess. Would I have to call you Pa?"

"No, Sam Ebbitt was your pa." Karl looked over the boy's head at Sarah. "Now I'm afraid if I asked she would say no."

She smiled, tucking back a wisp of hair. "Ask."

A week later, in the early hours before sunup, Karl and Coby harnessed the team.

"We'll be back late tomorrow," Karl said as he checked the horses' hooves one by one. "There are no stages due, and Sarah has made a big stew and bread. You should be able to feed yourself and any freighters that happen in. I expect Jerome and Charley might be through—and maybe the fellow that hauls for Stamphli's out of Elko."

"I was cook on a ranch one winter," Coby said.

"You are full of surprises. You shouldn't have any trouble, then."

"I don't expect any." Coby slapped the rump of one of the horses affectionately.

"How long until you can buy your own team and wagon?"

"A while. I'm in no hurry." He combed his hair back with his fingers and stood quiet, his eyes fixed on the dark bulk of the Fox Mountains. There was just a fingernail of a moon, already growing wan with the coming day. "I like it here. The place kind of grows on you. I've never been much for noise, even of my own making."

"Ready?" Sarah called from the porch.

"We are set here," Karl returned.

"Matthew, get your things," Sarah said as she went back inside.

The sun was just visible above the mountains when the wagon rolled out to the southwest, and the shadows of the horses' heads preceded them on the road. Moss Face ran alongside until Coby caught him and carried him back.

The trip was uneventful. They stopped at a spring on the west shore of Pyramid Lake to water the horses. Toward the southern end of the lake, about seven miles from where the Truckee River flowed in, they left Pyramid for the road into Reno. Stopping only twice more, in midday to eat and once more to rest the horses and stretch their legs, they reached Reno before dark.

Karl booked two rooms at the Riverside Hotel, Reno's grandest, one room for Sarah and Matthew, the other for himself. He seemed nervous and distracted. He wore his hat even indoors, the brim pulled low over his eyes. They took dinner in their rooms and visited no one. Sarah wanted to walk down the river past Bishop Whitaker's School, but Karl wouldn't accompany her and she didn't go without him.

At nine o'clock the next morning, Sarah and Karl, with Matthew between them, holding his mother's hand, walked from the hotel to the courthouse. Sarah wore her finest dress, a sage-green gabardine suit with a fitted jacket that flared gracefully over her hips, and a cream blouse that tied at the throat in a soft bow. Karl's clothes were worn and common, but as clean as soap and water could make them, and freshly pressed.

From beneath a glossy cap of hair, parted exactly in the center and combed wet so it was plastered to his skull, Matthew glowered at the world. He had been squeezed into the somber black traveling suit his grandmother sent him west in. It was far too small and pinched under the arms.

They stopped at the foot of the courthouse steps and gazed up at the intimidating structure. The heavy doors swung open and the dark, polished wood flashed as two men, stiff and proper in black broadcloth suits and rigid collars, came down the steps. Karl and Sarah drew back respectfully to let them pass.

"Reno's become such a city," Sarah whispered. Matthew, knowing only Calliope, Pennsylvania, and Round Hole, goggled at everything.

"Sarah?" Karl smiled, his gray eyes warm. "Shall we?" He gestured toward the open doors.

She hesitated, the color deserting her cheeks. Several dark-suited men passed, going up the steps and closing the doors behind them. "Maybe we'd better not." She was suddenly afraid and rested both hands on her son's shoulders to stop them from shaking.

"I love you, Sarah. I want to be with you always, in the sight of God and man."

Sarah nodded shortly, her lips pressed in a determined line, and took his arm.

The foyer was dark and cold, with high vaulted ceilings of burnished oak collecting gloom over floors of the same dark hue. The heels of Sarah's shoes clicked and echoed. They hurried to the less imposing offices beyond. In a drafty little room smelling of stale cigars, Sarah Ebbitt and Karl Saunders were married.

The justice of the peace was dry and papery, with the look of a man who has spent his life indoors. He fumbled a pair of spectacles from his vest pocket and read the ceremony without inflection, tired already, though it was not yet ten o'clock. An old clerk, hard of hearing and nearly blind, was the witness and he mumbled and chuckled to himself all during the vows.

Sarah had taken off the jade ring Imogene had given her, and handed it to Matthew to hold. Karl slipped it back on her hand as the justice said, "With this ring . . ."

The justice pronounced them man and wife and closed the book with a sigh. For a moment he blinked at them from behind his spectacles. "You may kiss the bride," he remembered.

"Oh, no, I couldn't!" Sarah protested and looked at the justice, the clerk, and back to Karl. He looked as uncertain as she.

"Kiss her," cackled the old clerk imperiously.

Karl tilted her chin and studied the lines of her face as though reading a long sweet story. Then he kissed her gently and the old clerk smacked his lips with satisfaction. Karl pulled Sarah's arm through his, and held his hand out for Matthew. "Son?"

The three of them left as unobtrusively as they had come, quiet and plain in their simple dress, but as they passed, people turned to look after them and smile.

"Can we go to the Broken Promise? Or the Bishop's Girls?" Matthew asked as they reached the hotel, repeating names he'd heard his mother and Karl mention.

"No, honey, we've got to be heading back as soon as we get our things together. Next time," Sarah promised.

"There won't be a next time," Matthew grumbled.

Their hotel rooms were across the hall from each other, Sarah and Matthew's overlooking the Truckee, and Karl's facing east, toward the mountains. In the hall, Karl knelt beside Matthew. "I'd like to be alone with your mother for a few minutes. Do you think you could find something to do in your room for a while?" Matthew agreed to try, and Karl ruffled his hair. "Good boy."

The door closed, and husband and wife looked at one another. "We did it," Karl said, and expelled his breath in a long sigh.

"Yes." Sarah laughed shakily and sat on the edge of the bed to unpin her hat.

"I have something for you." He pulled a chair up near the bed where he could sit facing her. "Something I memorized from one of the books your old-maid schoolteacher had. It's my wedding gift to you." He took her hands and began:

"When in disgrace with fortune and men's eyes
I all alone beweep my outcast state,
And trouble deaf heaven with my bootless cries,
And look upon myself and curse my fate,
Wishing me like to one more rich in hope,
Featur'd like him, like him with friends possess'd,
Desiring this man's art, and that man's scope,
With what I most enjoy contented least—
Yet in these thoughts myself almost despising,
Haply I think on thee, and then my state,
Like to the lark at break of day arising
From sullen earth, sing hymns at Heaven's gate,
For thy sweet love remembered such wealth brings,
That then I scorn to change my state with kings."

Sarah leaned over and kissed him. She was crying, and his eyes were moist. "I have nothing for you," she said.

"You are everything to me, Sarah."

ᘡ 40

THE DAY AFTER THEY CAME HOME TO ROUND HOLE, MATTHEW RAN
three-quarters of a mile to meet the Reno coach so he could be the
first with the news to Liam and Beaner. "Karl and Momma got
married," he puffed as Liam hauled him aboard by one arm.

"It's about damn time," the taciturn old driver replied, but he
was pleased and paid his respects with his hat in his hand when
they arrived at Round Hole.

The weeks passed and Sarah grew as quick to answer to "Mrs.
Saunders" as she had been to "Mrs. Ebbitt." Karl was slower, and
suffered the good-natured teasing of the old customers when he
referred to his wife as Mrs. Ebbitt.

The weather turned cold in late September, and life moved
indoors. Sarah or Karl would leave the guests after supper and
find a quiet corner where they could teach Matthew his lessons.
Sometimes they held hands or sat close, but Karl still absented
himself from the stop on nights when Sarah raised the calico
flag.

The Saunderses saved enough money over the winter so that the
following spring they were able to buy a bull. They hoped to have
a healthier crop of calves the following year. Coby's pay was raised
to two dollars and a quarter a day. He took better than half a week
off, and rode to Elko to pay his debts. When he returned, a free

man, with some money left over, he settled back into the tackroom and showed no inclination to move on.

Several more of Sarah's hens disappeared and she reinforced the wire fence around the coop. There were no more raids for a while; then, early in November, Matthew forgot to latch the gate behind him after gathering eggs for supper and in the morning three hens were gone. One was Sarah's best layer.

Karl and Coby had gone to Standish to buy hay and firewood for the winter. Sarah, enjoying the solitude, whistled breathily to herself as she checked the roost one more time, peering into the gloomy recesses of each box and poking her arm in to feel behind the messes of straw nesting. Her missing hens were nowhere to be found, but she inadvertently discovered an egg so old it broke when she touched it and the smell drove her out into the open. The sharp November air cleared her lungs of rotten-egg smell. Wrapping her arms in her apron for warmth, she took a last look around the henyard. Her flock, small and brown-and-white-speckled, scratched complacently. Corn kernels from the morning still littered the ground near the fence. Two snow-white feathers blew by her feet, catching her eye. She picked one up and turned it over in her fingers; the end was mangled and there was rust-colored matting near the tip. She let the wind take it, left the chicken coop, and hurried across the yard. Under the porch steps, out of sight from a distance, were more feathers—half a handful. Sarah knelt by the steps and stuck her head under the porch. Shadowy and indistinct, something crouched behind the feathers.

"Moss Face," she called, "come here, fella." Slowly the shadow crept forward, hunched down, his chin low over his paws. Sarah reached in, ducking her shoulder under the porch floor. Moss Face stopped, his brown eyes bright in the dimness. Small white feathers were stuck to the fur around his jaws. "Come on now, come here, boy, attaboy," she cajoled. The coyote crept forward another few feet and she grabbed at his neckerchief. "Gotcha!" she cried as she dragged him out into the light. All around his mouth the fur was spiky with dried blood. Holding on to his collar, Sarah smacked him. "Bad dog!" He growled and bared his teeth. "Don't you growl at me! And don't you go killing my chickens!" She spanked him hard. Writhing in her grasp, rubbery lips pulled back in a snarl, Moss Face twisted to bite. His teeth grazed her wrist, barely breaking the skin, but it scared her and she let him loose. He was around the corner of the house and out of sight before she recovered herself.

"It's Moss Face been killing the chickens," she told Karl that night as she brushed out her hair. He sat on a chair beside the bed, his heavy workboots neatly side by side under the window, sewing a button on one of his shirts.

"I thought it might be," he replied. "I guess no one wanted to know it for sure. Did you catch him in the henhouse?"

"No. Almost, though. He was under the house, too full to do anything but sleep. I got him to come out. He had feathers and blood all around his mouth." She pulled back her sleeve. "I spanked him and he turned and bit me. I think he's going back to being wild."

"Maybe. I remember Mac said he might. I guess we'll have to get rid of him."

Her hand flew to her cheek as though he'd slapped her. "That's Matthew's dog!"

"He's killing chickens. Today he bit you."

"We can't kill him." She brushed her hair vigorously for a hundred strokes. Adjusting the lamp, Karl squared up his spectacles and pulled the thread around and around the button before tying it off. With the light so close, his face showed the years, the lines chiseled through the flat cheeks and fanning out over the high cheekbones.

"We can't kill him," Sarah said again.

"We can't keep him, if he's killing chickens."

Sarah put the brush down and tied her long hair back at the nape of her neck with a faded blue ribbon. "Couldn't we take him somewhere and leave him? Let him go wild again?"

Karl thought for a moment. "We could do that. I'll do it tomorrow. Coby and I planned to ride south of here, toward Tohakum Peak. I think the cattle may be ranging too far; I'm afraid to let them get too near the Paiutes or we'll lose them." He smiled. "I don't want them eaten before they're paid for."

Sarah came to kneel between his knees. She still slept in the old flannel gowns Imogene had given her when she'd left Pennsylvania with nothing but the dress on her back. The fabric was yellowed with age, the hem frayed. She put her arms around Karl's waist and rested her head on his chest. "Oughtn't you be getting ready for bed?" she asked. "I laid out your nightshirt."

He let her bound hair slip through his hand, long and silken. "Mrs. Saunders," he said, and smiled.

"Mrs. Saunders." Sarah turned her face up to be kissed. "You need a haircut," she commented. "Put it off much longer and we'll have to get out the hairpins."

He touched her lips softly with the tips of his fingers. "Sarah, do you ever miss Imogene?" he asked.

She was quiet a long time, and when she replied her voice was warm with remembering. "A little. I miss the small things mostly, I think. Pushing in hairpins before any big jobs—things like that."

"Sometimes I miss her too."

In the morning he was ready to go before sunrise, before Matthew was awake. Moss Face had not been in his usual place in the boy's room, but under the porch, and he was uncharacteristically suspicious when Karl called him. He would only crawl into the light and whine, but wouldn't come close enough to be touched. Finally, Sarah came out in her nightgown and slippers. She put a piece of venison left over from supper on the ground, and when Moss Face came out to eat it, Karl grabbed him. They fashioned a leash out of twine, the coyote's neckerchief serving as a collar. He slipped out of it twice, but the third time they tied it as tight as they dared, and he couldn't wriggle free. Karl swung into the saddle and started out, but Moss Face would not follow; he braced his feet and fought the lead until, afraid he would be choked, Karl bundled him into a gunnysack, taking him out of Round Hole the way he had come in.

He leaned down from the saddle to kiss his wife. "Tell Coby I've gone out early to lose Moss Face. He can meet up with me at the bluff just south of Sand Pass."

"I'll send your lunch with him. It slipped my mind till just now." Sarah folded her shawl more closely around her, and held the neck of her nightgown shut. A lantern burned on the ground at her feet; in its uneven light, her breath steamed.

"You'd better get inside."

She nodded and picked up the lantern. "What shall I tell Matthew? First thing he'll look for is that dog." She laid her hand on the warm bundle by her husband's knee. Moss Face stirred inside, whimpering, and Karl's horse shied and sidestepped.

"Easy." Karl gentled the old gelding with a touch. "Tell him the truth, Sarah." A ribbon of light appeared around the porch door as it was opened a crack. "It looks like he's up. Do you want me to tell him?"

She glanced over her shoulder. "No. You go. Quick, before he comes out. You'll be at Sand Pass—south side—around noon?"

"That's right—don't forget my lunch." He touched her hair lightly and turned the horse's head to the southwest. Behind him the night sky was just beginning to lighten, stars paling into the day. The air was cold and still in the windless calm before sunrise. Karl turned his collar up around his ears and, looping the reins around the saddlehorn, shoved his hands in his coat pockets.

Where the desert began its ascent to Sand Pass, the road started winding, snaking up through the sage to a notch in the rounded mountains west of the stage stop. Over the pass, Karl turned his horse from the road and struck out through the sage, the eight-thousand-foot peak of Tohakum Mountain on his left and the ragged brown Pah Rah Range on his right. Moss Face lay quiet in his burlap prison. Occasionally he would shift or whine, and Karl would reassure him with soft words.

The sun was well above the horizon when Karl approached the pyramids at the north end of the lake. There was still no wind, but he rode with his coat buttoned high. The lake glittered a hard deep blue, the dark cobalt blue of the sea. He swung free of the saddle and threw the reins over the horse's head. It began cropping the sparse dry weeds with a tearing sound. Karl lifted the gunnysack from the saddlehorn and crouched to untie the mouth of the bag. Both his knees cracked. "I'm getting to be quite an old lady," he said, "creaking like her rocker. Come on, Moss Face, you're home."

On wobbly legs, the coyote ventured halfway out, the sack draped over him like a cassock, and looked around. He closed his eyes and pointed his nose at the sky, his nostrils quivering as he took in his new surroundings.

"There's water here, and even such a hearth-dog as you should be able to find enough to eat." Karl stroked the rough fur, then untied the neckerchief and put it in his coat pocket. "Come all the way out. I want my sack back." He upended the bag, poured the rest of Moss Face out, and scratched him behind the ears. "Good-bye, old fella, you'll be fine." He looped the sack over the saddlehorn, gathered up the reins, and, digging his heels into the horse, started off at a stiff trot.

Moss Face sat where Karl had dumped him, looking around

with the confused air of a sleepwalker awakened in a strange bed. As Karl rode past the first hillock, Moss Face shook himself vigorously and started out after him.

Karl turned for a last look and saw him. "Go on!" he yelled. "Git!" Moss Face stopped and sat down, but as soon as Karl rode on, he trotted along behind the same as before. Karl dismounted and picked up a handful of rocks. "Go on!" he shouted. Moss Face sat down to wait him out. Karl threw a rock at him. It landed short and the coyote nosed it curiously. "Scat." Karl threw another, closer this time. Moss Face tried to catch it in his mouth. The third rock struck him in the shoulder and he stopped cold to stare at Karl. "Go on! I mean it." Karl threw another rock, striking Moss Face in the side.

The coyote retreated a few feet, then turned back. The next stone struck him hard in the face, and Moss Face turned and ran. Karl threw rocks as long as the dog was in sight.

"Damn," he said when the dog ran out of view, and let the rest of the rocks fall from his fist. "Karl Saunders just lost a good dog."

The men got in late, after sundown; both were tired and cold to the bone. Coby's face was chapped raw from the wind. Sarah turned down their offers to help with dinner, and the four of them dined simply on bread and beans. The milk was still warm from the cow and there wasn't much of it. Karl and Coby cut theirs with coffee so Matthew could have the rest. He asked them if they'd seen his dog. He wasn't really worried, he said, Moss Face had gone off before for a day, and once he was gone overnight.

Karl shot Sarah a hard look and she avoided his eye. "Sarah, tell—" he started.

She shushed him, and the conversation was strained for the rest of dinner. Coby excused himself early and retreated to the tackroom.

By the time Sarah finished up her chores and came to bed, Karl was a formless lump under the bedclothes. The sheets were cold and Karl's back was warm, but she didn't snuggle close. She was afraid he was still mad at her. For a few minutes Sarah tossed and turned, hoping to wake him. "I'm being childish," she thought, and let herself drift off to sleep.

The frantic sound of chickens clucking and beating their wings woke them both several hours after midnight. Without lighting the lamp Karl pulled trousers and a wool shirt over his long night shirt and yanked on his workboots. Sarah sat up in bed. "What is it?" The violent cackling subsided, then burst forth in a fresh wave.

"Sounds like something is after the chickens."

"Bobcat?"

"Maybe."

She struggled out of the tangle of bedclothes, pulled on her shoes, and slipped Imogene's hunting coat over her nightgown. Karl led the way through the darkened house, stopping to take the Henry Repeater from its place in the corner behind the bar. Sarah took the lantern from its hook by the door and together they crossed the yard.

The night was cold and still, with no moon. Luminous, the Milky Way streaked across the southern sky, and overhead the Big Dipper poured out its mysteries. Starlight picked out the Fox Range and the ghostly silver of the alkali flats. There was no noise except the shushing sound of something softly scraping the earth. Sarah held the lantern high. Half a dozen maimed and dying chickens littered the henyard. Feathers and drops of blood, black in the wavering light, were scattered everywhere. Two of the hens flipped pathetically on the frozen ground.

Suddenly a brown shape streaked from under the coop and squirmed through a loose place dug under the wire. Karl pulled the Henry to his shoulder, fired, and the coyote dropped. Sarah ran over and set the lantern by the dead animal. "It's Moss Face." She reached out to stroke the coarse fur, but drew back without touching him. "He's dead."

"I thought it might be him, it was too bold for a wild coyote. You see where he wormed his way under the fence?"

"Karl?" The call came from across the spring.

"Go back to bed, Coby. Coyote in the chicken coop. We got him."

The chickens were quiet but for the two in the yard that were still thrashing. "He couldn't have eaten six chickens," Sarah said. "He must have killed them just for the fun of it." She looked down at the inert form. "Poor little fellow, he did good for so long." Imogene's coat fell forward, and Sarah held it back so it wouldn't touch the dead coyote. Blood trickled from the ragged neck fur and dripped onto the ground, bright glossy drops that rested like bugle beads on the frost. "We've got to bury him," she said firmly.

"Sarah, the ground is rock-hard, we'd have to go at it with a pickax. Let's worry about it in the morning."

"We can't leave him here—Matthew might see him."

"We'll cover him with sacking. Coby or I can take him out and dump him in the ravine behind the hill tomorrow."

"No. Matthew might see you doing it."

"He has to know sometime, Sarah."

"He does not." She rocked back on her heels and looked at him defiantly. "And don't you go telling him."

"I don't think we ought to lie to the boy."

"It's not lying!" Sarah said heatedly. "It's just not telling him something there's no need in his knowing, something that's just hurtful."

"What is it, if it isn't lying? What are you going to tell him? He'll look for Moss Face and wait and hope every day. If you don't tell him, I will."

"He's my son," Sarah declared. "If you had a child of your own, maybe you'd know. Matthew's my son, and don't you dare say a word to him about this."

He turned and left her.

Sarah lit her way to the shed. Behind one of the wagons, on the back wall, half a dozen burlap sacks were hung on a nail. Taking three of the sacks, she made her way back out to the chicken coop and Moss Face. In the house, a light burned in the bedroom window and she could see Karl's shadow moving behind the curtains.

The sacking disguised the coyote, making him an impersonal bundle, and Sarah was able to pick him up. Cradling him in her arms, she started out through the sage, away from the house. Uneven ground, darkness, and the snagging arms of the brush made her weave a little, but she held onto the dog and trudged up the hill. Over the crest, half a mile from the stop, a ravine had been cut by the short, fierce floods that had washed down over the years. By starlight it yawned black and sinister. It was close to fifty feet deep and partially filled with a dense tangle of sage and deadwood.

A few feet from the lip of the gully, Sarah stopped, her breath streaming out in clouds. She dropped her burden over the gully's edge and watched it tumble into the black, choking arms below.

Karl was gone when she got back. She checked the kitchen and the bar and looked in on her sleeping son. The hall clock struck half past four. Sarah sat down on the edge of the bed and pulled off her coat. There was a dark smear of blood on the front. She dabbed at it, but it was dry.

For half an hour she sat in bed with the lamp burning, waiting, listening. It was nearly daybreak when she blew out the light and lay back.

In the morning, as she was clearing up the breakfast things, she saw Karl through the dining room window. He went to the barn, spoke briefly with Coby, then saddled up and rode out to the south. Coby came in shortly afterward. Karl had gone out hunting, he said. Sarah set Coby to work cleaning the weeds from around the ice-house and cutting lumber for the new shelves she planned to build there. Matthew wanted to go look for Moss Face, but Sarah forbade him, giving him chores to do in the kitchen. She was curt and he sulked most of the morning.

The Reno coach arrived around two o'clock and Sarah went to meet it. Bareheaded, ears crimson with the cold, his bright blue eyes gone milky, McMurphy stared owlishly down from the high seat. Mac was older, bent and more gnomish then ever. "Mac!" Sarah cried.

"Sarah?" He blinked several times. "Sarah!" He climbed stiffly down and she ran to hug him.

"Oh, Mac! It's been forever. Since Imogene . . . But come in. You're so cold, your hands are like ice. Why didn't you wear a hat?" Sarah forgot Liam, Beaner, and the passenger, to take Mac indoors. Both of Mac's eyes were streaked white with cataracts, and though he pretended to see as well as any man, he held firmly to Sarah's arm.

"Wait a damn minute!" The door of the mudwagon was thrown open and a dirty yellow dog bounded out, followed by the lanky form of David Tolstonadge. "Man's own sister ignoring him for a dried-up old man not worth his boot leather! There's a fine howdy-do!" David reeled and steadied himself with a hand on the wheel. "Congratulations, Mrs. Saunders!" he roared. "Why the hell didn't you invite me to the wedding? I'd've dropped the railroad and come, hell or high water. Where's Karl? Me and Mac been celebrating all night. On two counts—you getting married and Sam Ebbitt being sure as hell dead, unless you've gone Mormon on me."

Sarah left Mac to embrace her brother and tug his beard. "You've been so long," she cried. "Years and years. It's so big out here. It's always so far. I've missed you. It's been so long."

David growled, bearlike, as he always did, and burrowed his great reddish beard against her neck until she screamed.

"Leave Momma alone! Leave her alone, damn you!" Matthew's face was purple; he was on the top step, his little body tense with rage, shifting his feet, not sure what to do.

"Honey, honey." Sarah ran to him, laughing, concerned, and pleased. "It's okay. Momma's okay. Oh, honey, I'm okay." She held him, and his anger started turning to embarrassment under the smiles of the company. He struggled to get away.

"I'll be damned," David exclaimed. "My nephew, I'd lay money on it. Some kind of hell-raiser. Did you see that?" he asked no one in particular. "He was ready to tear into the whole lot of us." He whooped. "He's going to be hell on wheels, give him ten years."

Matthew still squirmed uncomfortably, but the look of a cloud about to burst had left his face; the big man was obviously pleased with him. David loped over and thrust out a hand. Matthew shook it warily, his little hand vanishing from sight in his uncle's. Letting out another whoop, David caught the boy under the arms, tossed him into the air, and smothered him in a bear hug. When he set him on the ground again, Matthew was shaken up but smiling a little.

"That's how maybe he sees that the ice is broke," Beaner said.

"Dave's got a way with kids," Liam grunted. "Move it, Beaner. Let's get these horses stabled."

"You two come in out of the cold as soon as you've done. I'll have coffee ready," Sarah called as Liam shook the reins. The horses were reluctant to drag the mudwagon even the few feet to the barn.

Liam watched Sarah lead Mac into the house. Manny darted up behind to weasel in the door with his master, and Matthew came last, still on his guard. "She ain't half so shy as she used to be," Liam said. "I remember when old Mac retired and I started this run, it was more than you could do to get two words out of her. She hid out most of the time folks was here, and just did the cooking."

Indoors, David told them he'd been sent up from Los Angeles to work on a new railroad spur being constructed ninety miles south of Reno. He'd taken a room over the Bucket of Blood in Virginia City. On his first day off he'd taken the train into Reno to get news of Sarah and Imogene. It was more than two years since he had seen them.

"I ran into Mac at the Silver Dollar," David said. "He told me Imogene was dead and Noisy'd heard you and Karl had gotten married. Sare, I ain't heard one word from you in two years, how come? Last you wrote, the kid had come. You made no mention of Imogene's dying—she was a hard-bitten old gal but we got on well enough—and where the hell's the groom?"

Sarah stood, her head bowed under the onslaught of questions. When David paused for breath, she handed him one of the cups of coffee she'd been holding while he paced and growled in front of the fire. "You haven't written, either," she reminded him.

"I don't write anybody, Sare, it's a different thing altogether."

"Karl's out hunting. If he's lucky, we'll have fresh venison for supper. If not, it's rabbit stew. Mac?" She held out coffee for the old man. McMurphy was more wizened than ever, scarcely taller than Sarah. Alcohol had reddened his nose and scratched a cross-hatching of broken veins on his cheeks. White stubble bristled along his jaws. When he reached for the coffee, he was slightly to the left. Sarah guided the cup into his hands. He cradled it in his palm, the stumps of his fingers curled around, steadying it with his other hand.

"Thanky, Sarah. I don't see like I used to. Catracks, the doc said. Hell, Uncle Suley had the same thing and the doc said it was stone-eye." Mac slurped his coffee noisily.

"It's hot," Sarah warned.

"Mac'll snap at anything that doesn't snap back," David said.

Sarah smiled at the old man, laying a hand on his shoulder. "It's good to look at you, Mac, it's been a long time. You too, David, much too long." There was a scuffling of boots outside and Sarah fell suddenly silent, her hand at her throat. The front door opened and, with a last stomp to clear the mud from his boots, Coby came in.

"Karl's coming," he said. "Saw him riding up the west road. Looks like we'll be having spuds for supper tonight, unless he's got something hid in his bag. Maybe I'll go out and try my luck before dark."

"I forgot the calico flag!" Sarah whispered. She ran to Matthew. He was curled down by the kindling box, listening to every word, his eyes full of his Uncle David's dog—half-asleep under Mac's chair—and the old man's mangled hand. "Honey," she said as she knelt beside him, "get your coat on and run and tell Karl who's here. Tell him your Uncle David and Mac are here. Don't forget— Uncle David and Mac. Scoot now." She spanked him lightly on the bottom.

"Maybe he's seen Moss Face," Matthew suggested as she helped him on with his coat.

Sarah stopped him long enough to kiss him. "Maybe."

"Tell him the drinks are on his brother-in-law," David called as the door closed behind the boy.

Sarah watched out the window after him, her face drawn around the mouth. The sky was a sullen gray and, as it neared four o'clock, the light was leaving the desert to an early winter dusk. It was the time of day when there are no shadows and the sky seems close to the earth. Sarah cupped her hands to the glass. Matthew, square in his heavy coat, ran across the yard. His mittens were tethered by a string behind his neck and flopped out of his sleeves like a second pair of hands. Just beyond the stable, Sarah could see Karl; he rode slumped in the saddle, the reins looped over the saddlehorn, his hands tucked in his armpits. In a minute he would ride out of sight behind the shed.

Suddenly he jerked his head up like a man awakened. Matthew ran behind the buildings and reappeared a moment later. Karl had seen him. He levered himself out of the saddle and dismounted to walk with the boy. They stopped, Matthew hopping from foot to foot and waving his arms, and Karl, hands on knees, nodding. Sarah smiled when Matthew put both wrists to his chin and waved his fingers in pantomime of David's beard. Karl pulled the game bag from behind the saddle and handed it to the child. They talked a bit longer, then Matthew ran back toward the house. Karl swung into the saddle and turned the horse back the way it had come. Sarah expelled the breath she had been holding during the little scene, and turned from the window, smiling.

A few minutes later, Matthew clattered through the front door, the game bag flapping over his shoulder. "Karl got two ducks, Momma. He's been to the lake and back."

"He'll be all in," Mac commented.

"Momma, he said to tell you—"

"Come on, honey," Sarah interrupted, "tell me in the kitchen. I must get the coffee."

"All he said to tell you was—"

"Come on now." She hurried him out of the room. In the hall, she helped him out of his coat and hung it on a handy peg. "What did Karl say to tell Momma?"

"We're not in the kitchen," Matthew said mischievously, and Sarah laughed.

"That's right."

While she poured the coffee, Matthew took two female mallards from the bag and laid them on the chopping block. "Karl said he was riding back out. He said, 'Tell your mother I may be gone all night, I'll be where I always am . . . and not to worry.' Where'd he go, Momma? It's almost nighttime."

"Maybe he went to hunt some more. I expect that's what he did. Maybe he saw a big old buck and didn't want to lose its trail."

"He hadn't see Moss Face."

Sarah set the coffee down on the table. "Oh, honey, I'm sorry."

"I looked everywhere for him."

Sarah brushed the dark hair from his face. "Come on, you can help me carry the coffee. Careful not to spill, it's hot." Beaner and Liam had come in from the stable and were warming themselves before the fire. David and Mac sat with their feet stretched to the blaze, David chatting amiably with the driver and the swamper, and Mac, a dreamy look in his dim eyes, a smile on his lips, looking every inch at home. Occasionally the old man dropped his arm down to rub Manny's ears with his finger stubs, and the dog thumped his tail against the floorboards.

"David, Mac, there's a cup left," Sarah said. "Can I heat either of you up?"

"No thanky, Sarah," Mac replied. "I'm still nursing this one."

"Better save it for your husband," David added. "It's colder than a witch's . . ." Liam laughed and David winked at him. ". . . toe out there," he finished.

"Karl's gone out hunting a big buck," Matthew volunteered.

"He has, has he?" David ruffled his nephew's hair. "Don't you think maybe it's a little late for tracking? Be dark in less than an hour."

"It's true. Ask Momma."

"Hush, honey," Sarah said. "Why don't you go see if Coby's ready for supper?"

"Supper won't be done for hours," Matthew complained.

"Go on now, your coat's in the hall."

Reluctantly, Matthew left the fire and the dog and the strange old man and his new uncle.

David unfolded from his chair as the boy let himself out the front door. "I've been sitting for two days, one way and another. Guess I'll stretch my legs while it's still light out. Give your husband a hand with his horse. I haven't seen Karl since that tinhorn shot his coyote dog."

"David, Karl has gone out again. I don't expect he'll be back until late." Sarah busied herself collecting the empty cups.

"That's a hell of a note. A man's got to take a day off once in a while. We aren't going to starve." David shrugged into a heavy leather coat lined with creamy fleece.

Sarah set the cups on a table. She put them down too hard, and a chip flew from the bottom of one. Her face was tight. "David, where are you going?"

"Going to fetch him home. Can't have the wedding party without the groom."

"He's already gone. Long gone. I don't know which way he went."

"I'll ask Coby. He was out messing around, he might've noticed. Coby, that's his name, right? The blond kid?"

"Yes. Coby. Please don't go, David. It's so cold . . ."

He laughed. "You're as bad as Mam ever was. You're hanging on to a thirty-dollar coat. It kept some sheep warm over a west Texas winter, it'll do me. Let me go, woman, or I'll never catch him on foot." His feigned roughness failed to bring a smile. "I'll be back in half an hour, Sare, even if I don't catch up with him," he said more gently, and before she could say another word, he was out the door.

She ran and jerked it open. "David!" He turned and waved as he loped across the yard, his dog at his heels, toward the pump where Coby was finishing washing up. Slowly, Sarah closed the door and leaned her forehead against the frame.

"You okay, Sarah?" Liam called. "You want to sit a spell?"

She wiped her face and smiled weakly. "No thanks, Liam. I'd best get on with supper. It's too late for duck, but I'll rustle up something."

"You want company, Sarah?" Mac's gravel voice was as strong and sure as ever, and she smiled to hear it.

"I'd like that, Mac." And she went to take his arm.

The sun had long since set, and the sky was patched with stars where the wind had torn through the clouds. Twice, Coby had offered to go look for Sarah's brother, but she had insisted he stay by the fire.

At half past seven, Sarah served the dinner she'd kept warm on the back of the stove, and they sat down at the table without David. The biscuits had grown hard on the warming shelf, and the men sopped them around in their hash. Their chomping took the place of dinner conversation. Sarah was distracted and spoke little; even Mac failed to hold her attention. She started at every sound and ate almost nothing. Matthew had been fed earlier and now moped at the hearth, shoving his books about, pretending to study. Every few minutes he'd run to the door, insisting he'd heard Karl or horses or Moss Face scratching to be let in. Sarah gave up trying to get him to concentrate on his lessons; she didn't even bother to make him do his supper chores, but cleared the table and washed the dishes by herself.

At nine o'clock, Coby reached for his coat. "I'm going after him, Sarah. It's been too long now."

"No!" she snapped, and Coby looked at her sharply.

"What's eating you, Sarah? If David's hurt himself, your stewing won't do him no good. Let me go after him, I ain't afraid of the dark."

"No," she replied. "You are not to go after him, not if you want to work here. Take your coat off."

"I'll be going out to the tackroom," he said stiffly, and left, slamming the door behind him.

It was after ten when Matthew was put to bed. Being up so late made him peevish, and he whined to be allowed to stay up another hour and sulked and fussed until he knocked over his washwater and broke the pitcher. Sarah spanked him and put him to bed with a dirty face.

David returned just before midnight. He let himself in the front door without his customary banging. One of his eyes was blacked— a purple, puffy mark the size of a thumbprint near the bridge of his nose. Manny came in with him; his hackles were up and he stayed close on his master's heels. Liam and Beaner were at a game of checkers. Mac dozed by the fire and Sarah, her darning needles and yarn in her lap, picked through a bag of socks on the floor. She saw David first and rose to go to him, but his look stopped her before she was halfway across the room.

"What in hell happened to you?" Liam grunted.

David went to the bar, pulled an unopened bottle of rye whiskey from the shelf, and uncorked it. The glugging of the whiskey into the glass was loud in the quiet room. When the glass was full he turned and faced his sister. For a long minute he regarded her, his eyes unreadable, the line of his mouth hidden in the wild red beard. He jerked the glass high, slopping liquor over the floor. Sarah's hands flew to her face like frightened birds, and her fingers pecked nervously at her lip.

"To the bride." He sneered, threw back his head, drank the whiskey down, and hurled the glass the length of the long dining room. It sailed by Sarah's cheek to break into fragments on the stone of the chimney.

David grabbed another glass, slopped it full, made the same toast, drank it off, and sent it smashing into the fire. The rye was making his eyes water and flooding his face with color.

"Just a damn minute," Liam began as David reached for a third glass.

"Stay out of this," David growled. "You stay the hell out of this." He poured himself another, but turned his back on them and nursed it in silence.

"David . . ." Sarah took several tentative steps toward him.

"You stay the goddamn hell away from me!" he exploded. Sarah clamped her hand over her mouth and ran from the room. David tossed off the last of his drink and slammed his fist into the wall with a sudden violence.

"The son of a bitch, he is crazy," Beaner whispered.

"Leave him be," Mac said. "Davie's a mean drunk if you bother him. Leave him be and he won't hurt nobody. You go on now, turn in. I'll stay with him."

One-handed, David was pouring himself another whiskey. His right hand lay on the bar, already beginning to swell. Over the knuckles of his little and ring fingers, the flesh was rounded, smooth, discolored.

"Better let me take a look at that hand," Liam said.

"Stay the hell away."

"Go on," Mac urged. The driver and the swamper sidled past David and went upstairs.

Fully dressed, the covers pulled up around her chin, Sarah lay in bed, her eyes fixed on the door. In the hall, the pendulum clock

struck. For three hours she'd lain awake, listening to glass breaking
and furniture being overturned in the next room. Around one
o'clock there had been a terrific crash, as if a chair had been hurled
against the wall, and shortly afterwards her bedroom door was
opened a crack. It was Matthew, awake and afraid, coming to crawl
in with her.

She turned to look at the small face on the pillow next to hers.
"My son," she whispered, and kissed his cheek tenderly.

The familiar smack of the front door banging against the side of
the house made her start, and Matthew stirred in his sleep. Sarah
sang a lullaby softly. He didn't awaken and she lay back, listening,
but there was no more to hear.

Near four o'clock, as the moon was setting, Sarah fell asleep.
The sun was above the horizon and Matthew was gone from her
side when she awoke. She slipped on her shoes and hurried from
the room, her dress crumpled and her skirts askew.

Mac and Coby were cleaning the main room. The air was warm
with the smell of coffee. Matthew poked sticks into a growing fire
while Liam and Beaner slurped their coffee and threw out bits of
advice to Mac. Mac's sight was so weak he'd confined himself to
righting upended tables and chairs. There was a sizeable pile of
broken glass swept up near the hearth. Coby, broom in hand, had
worked his way down to the other end of the room. Sarah stopped
in the doorway.

Matthew caught sight of her. "Momma, Uncle David tore up
the room and broke all the glasses." He ran over from the fireplace
to take her hand. "Looky," he said, leading her to the far end of
the bar. There was a dent in the wall the size of a horse's hoof.
"Mr. McMurphy said Uncle David did that with his hand and broke
it all to hell."

"To pieces," she corrected him. "Don't swear, Matthew, I'll
give you a licking."

"Mr. McMurphy just said."

"Hush, honey. Why don't you go bring in some kindling from
the woodpile."

Coby looked up from his dustpan. "Looks like you better order
some glasses before Liam takes off. I don't think your brother
missed a one."

"Where is he?" Sarah asked.

"He took off around two, three o'clock this morning, Sarah,"

Mac replied. "Said he was going to walk as far as he could and sleep till the coach came."

"Was he okay?"

"His hand was mashed some. Swelled up three times its regular size. He was feeling no pain, but it's going to hurt like hell when he comes to this morning. He'll be all right. There's nothing on this desert going to mess with your brother, the mood he was in. Mean enough to bite a snake."

Sarah laid a hand on the old man's arm. "I'm glad you were here, Mac."

"What do you figure set him off like that?"

"Somebody get the door for me," Matthew called, banging on it with his foot. His arms were full of wood.

Sarah opened the door for her son and picked up the trail of kindling sticks he left across the floor. "I don't know, Mac. He used to get that way about Pa sometimes, when I was a girl."

The Fort Bidwell stage arrived shortly after noon. While Liam and Beaner traded gossip with Ross and Leroy, Mac wandered out across the road to lean on the paddock fence. His dim eyes were on the bright alkali flats and the blue shadows of the Fox Range beyond. A breeze came to him over the sage, and he quivered his nostrils like an old dog reading the news on the wind.

"Hello, Mac. Sarah told me you'd come."

Mac jerked, his half-blind eyes peering into the darkness of the barn. He took a sharp breath, and for a moment his eyes seemed to light up from inside. "Miss Grelznik . . ."

"It's Karl Saunders, Mac." Karl stepped partway into the light. His clothes were dust-streaked and the side of his face was scraped raw. He took Mac's hand. The stumped fingers and knobby thumb had browned and twisted over the years into the likeness of a gnarled old root.

"Karl . . ." the old man repeated, squinting into the light. "I thought . . ."

"Karl Saunders."

Mac shook his head. "You get old, your mind plays tricks on you. Good to see you, Karl. You get that deer you went after?"

"Never did, Mac."

"Missed a hell of a show here. I expect Sarah told you all about it."

"I haven't talked with Sarah."

"David find you?"

"He caught up with me a mile and a half from here. Those long legs of his really cover the ground."

"Something between you two set him off?"

"He didn't say anything to you?"

"No. Closemouthed as an old squaw."

"I don't know what it was, then."

Mac nodded to himself and chewed thoughtfully on a splinter he'd levered off the fence rail with a fingernail. Karl studied the seamed face; darker spots, burned black by years in the weather, dotted the old man's cheekbones like outsized freckles, snowy hair stood upright in the breeze. Karl smiled and dropped his hand gently on Mac's shoulder. "It's good to see you again, my old friend."

Mac shivered. "Your voice . . . somebody steppin' on my grave, I guess. Something's give me the willies this morning."

"Aayah!" Liam barked.

"Guess I'd better get a move on, or the coach'll leave without me." He spit over the rail, carefully downwind. Karl walked with him to the mudwagon and saw him off.

Karl didn't return to the house, though Sarah motioned to him from the window. Instead he shouldered an ax and set to work.

The dull fall of the ax, chopping out a regular rhythm, stopped. Karl dragged another log across the woodcutting rack, settled it snug with a kick, and the beat started again, hollow-sounding in the west wind. Sweat was running down the sides of his face, and his arms trembled. His coat was unbuttoned, his face raw with the cold. He'd been at it for several hours. He wiped the perspiration from his eyes, wincing as he brushed the salt sweat into the broken flesh on his cheekbone.

The kitchen window opened with a screech. "Karl," Sarah called. "You've been at that all afternoon and you were up all night. You're being silly. Stop before you chop yourself."

Karl grunted and swung the ax. It bit deep and he couldn't pull it free.

"Answer me!" Nothing. Sarah banged the window shut.

He rocked the ax back and forth, then planted his foot near the head and jerked. The handle pulled free of the head and Karl stumbled back into the small figure of Matthew Ebbitt. The boy stood square-shouldered, feet wide apart, ready to take on the world. Karl blinked at him, unseeing for a moment, then let the ax handle slide to the ground.

"Momma was crying," Matthew said accusingly. "Are you mad at her because she let Uncle David break the dishes?"

Karl pulled his kerchief from his hip pocket and mopped his face. "No, son, I'm not mad."

"Momma said you won't talk to her. She told me to come tell you she said you could tell me about Moss Face if you wanted to."

"Sarah said that? That I was to tell you about Moss Face?"

"That's what she said."

Karl leaned the ax against the wood stand and upended a chunk of wood to sit on. He folded the damp kerchief into a neat square and stared out across the desert so long that Matthew began to fidget. "Come here," Karl said at last, and his stepson came to stand between his knees. Karl pulled him up on his lap and wrapped his coat around him. "Last night I thought I heard something," he began, "out by the chicken coop. When I went out to see what it was, I saw Moss Face. He was with a pretty lady coyote. They ran out toward those mountains together." He pointed south to the blue Fox Range. "He grew up, Matthew, and had to go back to the wild to raise a family. Maybe we'll see him again, come spring. Or maybe we'll see puppies and they will be Moss Face all over again."

Matthew buried his face against Karl's shoulder, and Karl held him close.

❧ 41

MONTHS PASSED, A YEAR, THEN TWO. MATTHEW THRIVED AND GREW; on his tenth birthday he was five feet tall. "I'll be taller than Uncle David," he boasted. His Uncle had neither visited nor written since the night he'd gotten drunk and smashed every glass in the place. There was still a dent in the wall where he'd rammed his knuckles. Somebody had scratched DAVID TOLSTONADGE under it, and the date, with a pocket knife.

The stages ran less frequently, and even with the decreased service, there were fewer passengers on each mudwagon. David's predictions of railroad supremacy were fast coming true, but still no rails were being laid across the Smoke Creek or Black Rock Deserts. Freighters and, ever increasingly, cattle became the mainstay of the Saunderses' business. They had increased the size of their herd and now ran two hundred and fifty head of cattle on the rangeland.

Coby's responsibilities grew with the cattle ranching, and though he had enough money saved to buy a rig and a team, he stayed on as the Saunderses' foreman. Each spring he took the wagon into Standish and hired enough hands to help with the branding, and again in late summer, when the cattle were driven to the railroad to be sold.

Maturity settled on Sarah like a handsome cloak. Her features, soft and vaguely undefined throughout her early twenties, firmed

and took on substance. When she spoke, it was with the easy assur-
ance of a woman who knew her job and did it well. She had taken
on the task of raising pigs as well as chickens, and east of the barn,
downwind of the house, she had built a pigsty.

Early in the summer of 1885, Jerome Jannis rolled in from
Standish. His cannonball head was grizzled and his barrel chest
sloped off into a belly that pulled his shirttail out. For once his
partner, Charley, was not coming behind, eating his dust. He hollered "Halloo!" to Sarah as he drove in. She was kneeling beside
the pigpen, burlap sacking protecting her skirts and Karl's oversized
work gloves caricaturing her hands. She smiled, waved her hammer
by way of reply, and returned to her fence-mending. The board
nearest the ground had been rooted out from the post. As she
pounded new nails in, all of her brood stomped and squealed on
the other side of the fence, crowding each other to get near enough
to poke their snouts between the boards. They liked her.

"Where's everybody got to?" Jerome hollered. "Got Karl's winter wood here. Need a hand unloading it if I'm going to get to Fish
Springs today."

"Coby and Matthew are out with the cattle." Sarah stood and
shook out her skirts. "There." Beyond the spring, toward Reno,
two black dots, barely discernible as horsemen, rode in the direction
of the mountains. "Karl should be along directly. He's around here
somewhere. Karl!"

Karl came out from behind the shed, a blacksmith's leather
apron tied over his clothes. He'd grown even leaner and browner
over the years. "Hello, Jerome. We haven't seen you in a dog's
age." The men shook hands warmly. "Where's Charley? I hardly
recognized you all by yourself."

"Charley's got a bad tooth. His face was swoll up like a pump-
kin. That sawbones they got in Carson yanked it out for him, but
he was still sicker'n a calf when I left. I done the Susanville,
Standish, and back on my own."

Sarah made a hammock out of the gunnysack to carry her tools
back to the shed. "Let me put these away and I'll get you two
something to eat before you tackle that load."

After lunch the men sat in the shade on the porch, letting their
meal digest, the wagoner packing his pipe. The house was cool
inside, and a breeze came in through the open windows. Sarah
hummed as she cleared up the dishes. The window over the sink

faced east, the sun was directly overhead, and the shadows were small. The desert stretched, stark and clean, under a sky of perfect blue. In the distance two hawks circled on an updraft, tiny black specks over the northern curve of the hills. She watched them slide effortlessly toward the sun until they'd grown so small she could no longer see them.

Karl and Jerome came into sight around the corner of the house as she was starting on the flatwear. Jerome parked the wagon parallel to the fence, as close as he could get it. The back was piled high with cottonwood logs varying in length from eight to fifteen feet, the largest not much bigger around than a man's thigh. The longer ones stuck out over the tail of the wagon. Both men climbed atop the pile and, one at either end, began heaving the logs over the fence. Puffs of dust shot up as they bounced on the hard dry earth. Karl counted as they worked: "One, two, heave . . ." and the logs swung off the wagon, hitting the new pile in a battering rhythm. In the kitchen, Sarah sang a little song softly to herself, trying to fit the tune to the pounding of the falling trunks. When the wagon was less than half-full, Karl jumped to the ground and stood behind, hefting the logs out of the wagon bed, then over the fence. He'd stopped counting, and the rhythm slowed, grew irregular, and Sarah sang to her own beat.

It was hot, heavy work, and after a while Jerome stripped down to his undershirt and rolled the sleeves above the elbow. "Hold it a minute, let me get squared away here," he said, and sat down on the wagon seat to tuck the undershirt back around the belly.

Sweat streamed down Karl's temples but he didn't unbutton even his collar or take off the threadbare black woolen vest he always wore. He stood, hands on hips, looking out over the desert, catching his breath.

"Looks like the boys will be in sooner than I thought."

Jerome followed Karl's gaze. The two riders were still too far away to recognize. "The missus says Matthew's riding with Coby."

"That's right. We got him an old mare last time we were cattle buying. She's gentle as a pet—he climbs all over her and she just loves it. Coby is turning him into quite a horseman. He gave up on me."

"You got no style." Jerome grinned. "You ride like old Mrs. Pritchard, the circuit preacher's wife back in Ohio."

"I get there," Karl returned mildly.

"Well"—Jerome puffed out his cheeks and heaved himself to his feet—"let's get on with it."

The load shifted as he put his weight on it and one of the logs, several feet longer than the others, shot sideways. The butt caught Karl in the stomach. He grunted and doubled over, then slid down around the log to fall back against the wheel of the wagon.

"Jesus Christ! Karl! You all right?" Jerome ran down the logs, catlike for all his girth. Karl's eyes were glazed and wet, the color was fast draining from his face, and his head rolled drunkenly. "Sarah! Sarah!" Jerome shouted, and she looked up from her chores. "Get out here," he cried. "It's Karl." He jumped to the ground and knelt by the injured man. "Easy, fella," he said soothingly. "Easy now."

Sarah ran from the kitchen, the dishrag still clasped in her hand. She dropped to the ground beside Jerome. A gout of blood covered Karl's chin and stained the front of his shirt. His eyes were open but registered nothing. "Load shifted and a log shot out and caught him in the gut," Jerome said. "Poor bastard went down like a two-dollar whore."

Sarah touched the bloody jaw. "Did he hit his face when he fell?"

"No, ma'am. He vomited that up after. I was scared he was going to choke hisself to death, but he come out okay."

"Let's get him out flat," Sarah said, and Jerome took him in his arms, easing him down. Karl screamed and his eyes rolled back in his head until only the whites showed. Sarah pressed her palm to her mouth, her fingers spread wide and rigid like a starfish.

"Better move him before he comes to. He ain't going to feel it, at least," the wagoner suggested.

"The house."

Jerome worked his arms under Karl's shoulders and knees and lifted him awkwardly. "He's as long as a piece of string but don't weigh nothing."

Sarah walked ahead, opening doors. "Put him on the bed," she said when they had reached the bedroom. "Would you go for Coby? He's not far—you'd still get off in time to make Fish Springs before dark."

The driver looked hurt. "I'm staying till you don't need me. Fish Springs ain't going nowhere."

"Take Karl's saddle horse." Sarah closed the door behind him and returned to her husband's side.

"Sarah." He reached for her before he opened his eyes. "I hurt. Oh Lord, I hurt."

"I sent for Coby. We'll take you to Reno. Tonight. To the doctor there. You'll be all right, Karl. You'll be fine." Her fingers lightly touched his hair, his brow, his shoulders, as though she were reassuring herself that he was real.

"No doctors." He tried to sit but fell back with a groan and breathed shallowly for a minute, his lips white and pressed into a thin hard line. He closed his eyes and she clung to him, her face buried on his shoulder.

The pounding of hooves brought her head up. Coby and Matthew had ridden their horses into a lather. Matthew's mare was wheezing as if each breath would be her last. A minute later there was a timid knock on the bedroom door.

"Sarah?"

"Momma?"

"Come in, boys." They tiptoed in, covered with dust and reeking of horse sweat. Coby pulled off his hat; his forehead gleamed white above the hatband. Matthew took his off as well and, unconsciously aping Coby, held it before him in both hands.

"Jerome told us he took a log in the belly," Coby said.

Matthew inched nearer the bed, his eyes on the clay-colored face of his stepfather.

"He's throwing up blood, Coby. We've got to get him to Reno, there's a doctor there."

"No!" Karl said with such vehemence Matthew retreated behind his mother. "No doctor, Sarah. You know that." His voice sank to a whisper.

"I don't care, Karl. I only want you to be well again," she replied. "Shh. Rest now."

"Give me a drink of water."

"Coby." Sarah nodded toward the pitcher on the washstand. "There should be a glass on the next shelf." The young man poured out the water and handed it to her. Propping her husband's head on her arm, she pressed it to his lips and he drank. There was a grim choking sound and the water came foaming blood-red from his mouth and nose. Matthew ran from the room. "Coby, see to Matthew and wait for me in the front," Sarah said.

Coby and the boy were sitting on the bar stools, Matthew's elbows propped on the bar in the way of men. Jerome sat at a nearby table, drumming his fingers on the cloth and staring into space. All three looked up when Sarah entered.

"He won't go to the doctor," she said flatly.

"Of all the damn fool—" Jerome started.

"He has his reasons," she snapped. Then: "I'm sorry, Jerome, I'm sorry."

He waved the apology away. "I've already forgot it. I don't want to make things worse for you than they are already, Sarah. But I've lived on this desert a lot of years. That man of yours looks like death to me. If we don't get him to Reno, I don't think he's got the chance of a snowball in hell. He's broke up inside. A man don't cure himself of that."

"The ride would kill him."

"He'll die sure as hell here."

Sarah hid her eyes behind her hand. When she took it away, her mind was made up. "If he's no better by morning, we'll go."

"Suit yourself. I'm hitching up to go, then. You won't be needing me." Disapproval was in the set of his jaw and the hunch of his shoulders. He waited a minute for Sarah to change her mind, then said, "I'm going that way, I'd just as soon roll on into Reno." She said nothing. "Suit yourself," he said again, and stomped out.

"Help him with his hitching, Coby."

Sarah didn't leave the bedroom again that day. Coby cooked dinner for Matthew and himself. At ten he put the boy to bed and tapped on Sarah's door. "Sarah? It's Coby. How you doing in there?"

The door opened suddenly, taking him by surprise. There was the reek of sweat and blood and human excrement in the room. Sarah's lips were pale and the skin around her eyes was as dry and drawn as that of a woman twice her age. In her hands was a chamber pot. "Coby, get the wagon ready to leave as soon as it's light."

"I will, Sarah. We can go now if you like—soon as the moon's up."

"No, there's not enough light. The wagon could break a wheel— go off into the ditch. He can't be jostled around like that. He's bad, Coby." The tears started and she choked them back. "Here." She pushed the chamber pot at him. "I don't want to leave him."

"I understand. First thing in the morning. I'll bed down with

Matthew tonight so I'll be handy. You call if you need anything or just want somebody to talk to."

"Thanks, Coby, good night." Sarah turned the lamp down low and drew her chair nearer the bed.

The night was cool, the air soft and feeling of spring. Karl lay quiet, his eyes closed. A stale, fetid smell clung to his clothes, and the bedspread was scuffed with dirt. Careful not to jar him, Sarah worked his boots off and unbuttoned his collar and sleeves. A blanket was draped over the foot of the bed. She pulled it up, laying it loosely over him. When he was as comfortable as she could make him, she went to the window, propped it wide, and leaned out. The desert was utterly still under immobile, unblinking stars. Sarah breathed deeply, clearing her lungs. Impatiently she pulled the pins from her hair and combed out the plaits with her fingers, letting the clean night breeze play through it. A rustling, so slight it might have been a moth brushing against the shade, turned her from the night. "Karl? she whispered.

"I'm awake." He opened his eyes and smiled at her. Blood was crusted brown where his lips met, and around his nostrils. His words were more air than sound.

"Don't talk," Sarah said. "I just needed to know you were here."

"I'm here." He closed his eyes and let his head roll on the pillow, side to side, just a fraction of an inch. Around his eyes the flesh was blue and sunken. "God, I hurt, Sarah."

She stroked his forehead and hummed softly, a lullaby from her childhood.

"I'm hurt bad."

She crept onto the bed beside him, and though she was as gentle as she could be, he moaned when her weight made the mattress shift. She lay on her side, watching his profile, the rise and fall of his chest as he breathed. With an effort he moved his hand into both of hers.

The rooster crowed a premature dawn near three-thirty, and Sarah moved for the first time since she'd lain down at her husband's side. Her limbs were cramped and stiff. Slowly she crept from the bed. Already Coby was stirring, and a reassuring morning clatter sounded faintly from the direction of the kitchen.

Matthew and Coby had breakfasted. Sarah put a note on the

bar and weighted it down with a coffee tin: "Help yourself. Food's in the kitchen. Whiskey's under the bar. Leave money in the can."

While his mother and Coby loaded the wagon, Matthew hung anxiously about, underfoot, numbed by the sight of adults afraid. Finally, Sarah stopped long enough to notice him. "You're a good boy." She smiled for him and kissed his cheek. He was so tall she no longer knelt to embrace him. "Coby and I are going to bring Karl out to the wagon now. Could you run ahead and get all the doors for us?"

"I can carry."

"Just the doors'll be best for now."

As upright as a sentry, Matthew stood at the bedroom door while Sarah and Coby murmured together at the foot of the bed. Karl seemed unaware of them and didn't respond until Sarah spoke his name. His breathing was shallow and the muscles of his jaws were knotted against the pain.

Coby took one side of the blanket, clutching it near the injured man's shoulder and knee. Sarah did the same, and on a count of three they lifted him just clear of the bed and lowered the improvised hammock, with him in it, to the floor. They dragged him down the hall and out through the main room, Matthew scurrying ahead to pull rugs out of the way and see that the doors stayed wide. Coby had the wagon near the house, backed up to the steps.

They paused a moment on the porch to let Sarah rest, and Coby talked quietly with Matthew while she saw to Karl. He was barely conscious; the pain had dulled his eyes and shortened his breath. Beads of sweat studded his forehead and upper lip. Sarah pulled a towel from the waistband of her skirt and blotted his face. "Just a little more and we're done. Just a little more," she whispered. "Okay," she said to the hired man, and they took up the corners of the blanket again.

Matthew's mattress was on the wagon bed, with most of the house's pillows and blankets beside it. Sarah tucked the bedding snugly around Karl so he couldn't roll, slipped a pillow under his head, and settled herself beside him.

All morning they drove south and west, the sun warm on their backs and the shadows retreating before them. No one spoke much. Coby sat with his shoulders hunched, his blue eyes riveted to the rutted wagon road, conning the horses painstakingly around potholes and rocks. The boy sat quietly, sometimes facing forward, sometimes backward, his legs dangling over the bed, where he could see his mother. Sarah had moved; her back was to Coby and Matthew, and she was cradling her husband's head in her lap.

June touched the desert with a pale tinge of green, and the air was sweet with the scent of the bitterbrush in bloom. Along the roadside, on drab bushes of dusty green, fragile white poppies, the size of a woman's palm, blossomed, and the blue of lupine mixed with the gray of sage. There was no wind. It was so still that the whistle of a hawk's wings as it dove brought Sarah's eyes up. Karl heard it too, and together they watched it pull up on canted wings, a limp brown shape clutched in its talons. The bird circled just above the hilltops, fighting for altitude, the weight of its prey dragging it earthward. Then its wings trembled as it found an updraft, and it soared in solemn, majestic circles.

"I never dreamt I could fly," Sarah said. "Mam said everybody did. But I didn't."

"I still do." Karl smiled, the corners of the wide mouth turning up almost imperceptibly. "When I was a child, I could scarcely get off the ground. I'd skim along the streets of Philadelphia, just barely clearing the carriages by flapping my arms. Now I soar like that hawk and take off from a standing start." Sarah had to lean down to hear his words. It hurt him to talk, but she didn't try to quiet him.

"Sarah, you have been my life so long. I have had everything. Who would've thought I would have it all? Seeing the sunrise outside our bedroom window, your head on my shoulder. Nights, sitting quiet by the fire. Even a son. You made my life a miracle. The ministers—they said I would surely burn. Maybe. If I'd had your love only for a day, it would have been worth it. I don't want to die, Sarah, I want to live wit you."

"You won't die," Sarah said fiercely, and bent over to kiss him.

The team plodded on under the sun's trackless arc. Karl slept some during the heat of the day, with Sarah, ever watchful, above him. The bloodless face was made even more pallid by the desert dust, and twice he vomited blood. Though Sarah cleaned him as best she could, he had the black-lipped countenance of a nightmare. Fascinated and afraid, Matthew stole looks at him from the corners of his eyes.

Late in the afternoon of the next day they arrived in Reno. The doctor's office was on a quiet street, off Virginia, at the southern edge of town. It was a one-story wooden building, painted white, with a gravel drive curving from the street to a wide place in front of green double doors. Coby pulled the wagon to a stop. Before he could climb down, a nurse in a dove-gray dress, a white pinafore, and a short cape came out to meet them.

She introduced herself as Agatha Bonhurst. Agatha was a horse-faced though kind-eyed woman in her mid-thirties, with protruding teeth that she couldn't quite close her lips around. She gave Karl a cursory examination, peering under his eyelids and probing his abdomen with light deft fingers. Then, sucking her teeth thoughtfully, she walked to the side of the building. "Gunther," she called. There was a grunt, and a big blond man, speckled with dried mud and carrying a shovel, appeared around the corner.

"What can I do you for, Miss Bonhurst?"

"Can you leave off a minute and lend a hand?"

Karl was placed on a wood and canvas stretcher, and Coby and the big German carried him inside. Behind the double doors was a waiting room twice as long as it was wide, with two large windows having small panes and no curtains. Through an archway, across a narrow hall, was a small, clean, well-lit room with a single bed, a washstand, and a bare table. Under the nurse's guidance the men set the stretcher on the bed and withdrew the poles from their canvas envelopes. While Agatha went for the doctor, Sarah spoke with Colby and Matthew.

"Coby, I want you to send a telegram. The office is in the Wells Fargo, down Virginia Street—the street we came in on—a few doors down from the Silver Dollar."

"I saw it when we drove in."

"Good." She dug in her purse and drew out a black cloth wallet. "David said he was pretty much settled in Virginia City. Tell him he's got to come. This is the address he gave." She handed him a scrap of paper folded small, and dingy from the years in her pocketbook.

"That was some years ago, Sarah," Coby said dubiously. "I don't know . . ."

"Try." She turned to her son. "Honey, go with Coby to the Wells Fargo office. You'll see it, there's a big sign lettered on the side. While Coby's sending the telegram, you ask for Mr. Ralph Jensen."

"Mr. Ralph Jensen," Matthew repeated conscientiously.

"Tell him what happened, and that Coby will be going back out on tomorrow's stage to look after things. Do you have that?"

He nodded, and Coby held out his hand to him as he had since Matthew was six years old, but the boy was too grown-up to take it now.

As they left, a narrow-faced man with a shock of white hair came down the hallway. Deep lines in his face carved parentheses around a bristling anarchy of white mustache hairs. "Dr. White," he announced himself.

"Mrs. Saunders."

The doctor glanced into the room where Karl lay. "Your husband?"

"Yes."

"Come with me, I'll want to ask you a few things before I begin the examination." He was curt without being cold. Meekly she followed him into the sickroom, and while he peered into Karl's eyes and listened to his heart and breathing, she answered his questions about the accident. Karl lay uncomplaining under the doctor's hands, his gaze on Sarah.

Dr. White took off his jacket and folded it carefully over the foot of the bed. Karl's feet thrust out through the rails, his socks still stained from his day's labor. The doctor arranged his coat so it wouldn't come in contact with them. Nurse Bonhurst had returned and now stood near the door in the attitude of a watchful servant. "Agatha, light the lamps," Dr. White said crisply, "then take Mrs. Saunders into the waiting room."

"Let me stay," Sarah begged.

"I'm sorry, ma'am, I will have to remove your husband's clothing."

"No!" Sarah cried, then pressed her fingers to her lips. "Karl," she whispered, slipping quickly by the doctor to her husband's side, "I'll be outside if you need me. Right by the door." Karl laid his hand on her hair for a moment before she left him.

Within half an hour the boys were back. The wire had been sent. Sarah listened to their story in the hallway near the door to Karl's room. When they were finished, she sent Matthew outside to wait for Coby. "Take him out to supper," she said to the hired man. "Keep him out for a while. Get him some candy or take him to look at the trains. He's had a long day, poor little fellow." Coby refused the money she tried to give him, and patted her arm in awkward sympathy.

The waiting room was bare and clean. The windows overlooked the gravel drive and the quiet street beyond. Between them was a wooden bench with a low back. Sarah watched at the window until Coby and Matthew passed from sight around the corner. Across the street a neat row of houses, painted white and nestled among young trees, glowed warmly in the setting sun. Amber light spilled in the hospital windows, under overhanging eaves, turning Sarah's hair to auburn and touching her skin with color. For a long time she stood with her face to the glass, watching the feathery mare's tails over the Sierra turn from rose to gold. Finally the sun sank behind the mountains and the clouds took on a bruised purple hue. She turned from the window and sat on the end of the bench. Through the archway she could see the door to Karl's room. There was a ribbon of lamplight showing beneath it, and she could hear an occasional stealthy sound as the doctor moved about inside.

A man in the rough garb of a railroad worker came in, his left arm, useless, shoved into his shirtfront. He grunted politely at Sarah and waited for a few minutes by a small wooden desk with flowers on it set near the arch. When no one came, he pounded on the wall with his good arm. A moment later the nurse appeared with a clicking step and a peeved expression to lead him away. Sarah asked after Karl, but Nurse Bonhurst would only say she must wait for the doctor.

No one came to light the lamps, and Sarah sat in the dying light. The door to Karl's room opened, a sudden square of yellow, and the tall figure of the doctor emerged. Sarah bolted to her feet and waited, her hands clasped at her waist, her breath held in abeyance.

"Nurse Bonhurst," he called down the hall. With a rustle of starched skirts she was beside him. There followed a short whispered conference and he left, his footfalls retreating down the dark hall. A door slammed shut, then there was nothing.

Sarah started forward. "Miss?"

Agatha Bonhurst closed the door to Karl's room. "You'll be wanting some light in here, I expect." She reached into the pocket of her skirt and pulled out a box of matches the size of a first-grade primer. "Dr. White wants me to ask you a few questions."

"Can I see him?" Sarah's voice shook, and she pressed her fingertips to her lower lip.

"Not right now, dear, he's shut up in his office."

"Can I go to Karl?"

"Not for a bit. There." She lit the last lamp and came to take Sarah's elbow. In a soft Southern drawl she said, "Let's sit down, I been on my feet since six this morning."

Sarah let herself be led back to the bench. "Is Karl going to be all right?"

"You'll have to talk to Dr. White about that." Agatha seated herself next to Sarah and spread her skirts in a comfortable gesture. "For now we need to know if you've got folks—a father, a brother, an uncle, somebody who looks after you hereabouts. A friend of the family, even."

"I'm here with my son," Sarah replied, "and our hired man, Coby Burns."

"How old's your boy?"

"Ten. Ten and a half."

"There's no adult male you know here in town?"

"I've wired my brother in Virginia City." Sarah gave a sudden shake of her head. "Look," she said impatiently, "is Dr. White worried about money? I can pay." She pulled her purse onto her lap and undid the drawstrings.

Nurse Bonhurst laid a gentle hand on her arm. "Never mind that, dear, the doctor isn't concerned over pay. Will your brother be in soon?"

"I don't know." Sarah looked away, out the window. In the houses opposite, the lamps had been lit, and several stars shone in the western sky. "I haven't seen him in several years. We had a . . . falling out."

Agatha Bonhurst sat quietly for a moment, stretching her lips like a horse taking sugar from an outstretched palm, lost in thought. She sighed and patted Sarah's knee. "We'll just sit tight and wait a bit. I'll go tell Dr. White you've got a brother maybe coming. When did you telegraph?"

"Two hours ago . . . maybe closer to three. Can I see my husband now?"

The nurse straightened her skirt and squared her pinafore straps with a pert military gesture. "It's not more than an hour from Virginia City by train. We'll wait a while."

"I want to go in," Sarah said clearly.

"In a bit." Sarah had risen with her, and now Agatha pushed her gently back onto the bench. "I'll go talk to Dr. White," she said soothingly, and rustled out of the room.

Sarah waited, listening. Agatha's steps grew faint and died with the closing of a distant door. There was a newspaper on the far end of the bench. It was several days old, but Sarah leafed through it in a desultory fashion. The light was bad, and her eyes kept straying to Karl's room. At length she gave up and put the newspaper down to watch his door.

Twenty minutes later there was the sound of footsteps on the gravel. The doors opened and David stepped inside. He'd gone almost completely bald, and his beard, red-blond and as shaggy as ever, had grown nearly to his belt. Sarah let out a sharp little cry and ran to him, flinging herself into his arms, hiding her face in his chest.

"David, I was so afraid you wouldn't come." And for the first time that day, she gave herself up to tears.

His arms were stiff, not returning her embrace. "I'm here, Sarah," he said gruffly. "Though I'm damned if I know why."

"Please, David, don't." She pulled away and wiped her eyes on her sleeve. Dr. White came into the waiting room then, and Sarah quickly dried her cheeks with the back of her hand.

"Is this your brother?" he asked without preamble.

"Yes. David, this is Dr. White."

"Dave Tolstonadge." David extended a hand.

"Mr. Tolstonadge." The doctor shook hands with him. "I'd like to talk with you, if I may. If you'll excuse us, ma'am." He strode off, with David in his wake.

Bewildered, Sarah stood in the waiting room for a moment. "To hell with you all," she said, then crossed the hall with a light step, and slipped into the room where Karl lay.

The lamps had been extinguished but for one, and it was turned low. Soft shadows filled the corners and fell in misshapen squares over the floor. On the narrow bed, Karl lay still, a white sheet pulled up over his face.

"No, please . . ." Sarah fell to her knees and hid her face in her hands. A yawning hole gaped black in her mind, a hole that the shrouded figure had filled with warmth and light, and a sudden terrible fear that her reason was toppling clutched at her insides.

Muttering childhood prayers, unremembered for years, she rocked herself gently. "Karl," she whispered, "Imogene, lend me your strength, stay with me a little longer. I was never meant to live without you." Sarah squeezed her eyes shut and prayed and waited, but there was no reassuring presence, no healing touch in her mind. Her old friend was gone. Thoughts reeled like leaves in a whirlwind, and the black hole spread like a malignant shadow.

Then the image of the broad face, plain and strong in the sunlight after the first time they had made love, came to Sarah from the emptiness and she clung to it. With a will she remembered the shared dinners, the evening walks, washing up together in the kitchen. She held their love in her thoughts like a talisman, and the darkness receded a little. Breathing deeply, Sarah slowed her heart and stilled her mind. "I couldn't have borne it had I loved you less," she murmured and, after a moment, opened her eyes to look again on the corpse.

Rude, ungainly, the stockinged feet protruded from beneath the sheet, robbing death of any dignity. Sarah rose and made her way unsteadily to the bed. A moment's hesitation, then she folded back the cover from the face of her dearest friend, her lover. Loneliness welled up inside her, a dull ache that she knew instinctively would be with her each day of her life. She embraced the pain; without it she would be utterly alone. Silent tears streamed down her cheeks and dripped from her jaw. One spotted the sheet where her hand rested, as Sarah knelt to kiss the blood-blackened lips now empty with death.

"Get up, Sarah." David filled the doorway, his face twisted and angry.

She looked up.

"Get up!" he repeated.

Sarah rose, but didn't leave the bedside.

"Jesus Christ!" David exploded. "What the hell!" He took a couple of paces into the room. "Get the hell away from that bed!" he barked. "Jesus Christ, Sarah, what were you two playing at? The doctor asked me what was going on. What the hell was I supposed to say?"

Sarah fell back a step and threw up her hand as if afraid he would strike her. "David . . . Karl . . ."

"Imogene, goddamn you."

Sarah let out her pent-up breath in a long sigh. "Imogene." She looked back at the face on the pillow. "Of course—you knew. She said you'd recognized her."

"I knew it sure as hell wasn't Karl. When she got off her horse, I hit her and she went down like a sack of potatoes. Then I placed her." He looked a little shamefaced. "I thought it was a man when I swung."

"I know you did. She told me. She was sorry she hit you, after. She knew you wouldn't have fought back, knowing." Sarah smiled down at her beloved Imogene, her beloved Karl, her husband and her friend. The lined face was burnt brown, rough with the desert and the years, the cropped hair white at the temples. "She was the most just person I've known."

"You two been living as man and wife." David turned away. "I'm half sick, thinking of it." The dark look came back into his blue eyes and he balled his fists. The one he'd smashed against the wall in Round Hole wouldn't close completely. "Did you two kill Karl?" He was hoarse with emotion and kept his back to her. "Sneak up on him while he was sleeping? Club him to death? Did you cut the poor bastard's balls off and keep them, too?" Crossing the room he dragged Sarah from Imogene's side.

"Stop it, David!" She jerked free and slapped him across the face. "Karl died of a ruptured appendix, we think. We were going to lose the stop, so after we buried him, Imogene put on his clothes and I cut off her hair. She was near as big as he was and made enough like a man that we thought. . . . We never hurt anyone."

Softened by the light in his sister's eyes and the somber touch of death in the room, David quieted and moved closer to the bed. "Why did nobody else recognize her? Some of those drivers had seen her more times than I had—Karl Saunders, too."

"I met all the stages. If there was anybody she'd know, I ran a flag up the meat pole and she stayed hid out. After a while, all of the old-timers were pretty much gone, except for Ross, out of Fort Bidwell. The others had never known her as anybody but Karl."

A high laugh startled them both into silence. Harland Maydley stood just inside the door, fingering the telegram Coby had sent from the Wells Fargo office. Over his left eye, a red ragged scar attested to his vivid memory of Miss Grelznik. "A lot of folks'll be interested to hear that. Newspaper might even give me three dollars for a story like that." He smiled at Sarah in an unfriendly way.

David's arm shot out like a piston and nailed Harland Maydley to the wall. "If I ever hear about this from anybody," he growled, "I'm going to find you and break you into pieces so small they'll have to bury you in a cheesecloth. If the doctor tells his mother-in-law and she tells her dog and I hear, I'm going to come looking for you and there ain't no place to hide. You can't run far enough—I am the railroad. Are you understanding me?" He banged Harland's head on the doorframe to make his point. As he was about to impress him further, Coby and Matthew ran in from the waiting room.

His mad beard waving in the airless room, David looked as though he could snap Maydley's head off with his teeth. Harland's slicked black hair stood in a greasy fan against the white paint, and his chin was flecked with his own spittle. Sarah had retreated to the bedside, turning to Imogene, though her old friend was past helping her now and forever.

Eyes as round as saucers, Matthew looked to his mother. "Uncle David gone crazy again?" he whispered.

"Go back into the waiting room, honey," she said quickly. "Go on."

"Mr. Tolstonadge." Coby laid a firm hand on David's shoulder, though the man was a head taller than himself and broader of beam.

"Easy, Coby, we're all done here," David replied. He let Harland go, and smoothed the crushed coat front with a conciliatory gesture that nearly knocked Dizable & Denning's representative to his knees. "See this fellow to the door for me. I want to talk to Sarah a minute." He shoved Harland out, and Coby followed. David closed the door and turned a cold eye on his sister. "I'll give you train fare home. That's all I'm going to do, and a damn sight more'n you've got coming to you. You can move back in with Ma and Pa. Let them look after you and the boy."

"I'm not going back."

David laughed without humor. "You ain't living with me."

"I'll live alone."

"You can't run that stop by yourself."

"I expect not, but Imogene and I did pretty well for ourselves. I can sell the livestock."

"Who's going to look after you?"

"Damn you, David, nobody's going to look after me! I'm going to look after myself. I am not the frightened girl you left on the farm, I'm a woman now. Imogene did that for me. She took care of me when I was too weak and too foolish to take care of myself.

She carried me for years until she could teach me to stand on my own, and no one—not you, not anyone—can take that away from me."

David's reply was stemmed by the strength in his sister's voice and the stature her small frame assumed in Imogene's straight-backed, square-shouldered stance. He took a long look at the woman before him. "I'll be damned," he said softly.

Sarah nodded slightly, as if accepting tribute, and turned her back on him. Bending down, she kissed Imogene gently on the mouth. "Good-bye, my love. I will be fine."